STELIOS

Titles available in this series

Yannis
Anna
Giovanni
Joseph
Christabelle
Saffron
Manolis
Cathy
Nicola
Vasi
Alecos
John
Tassos
Ronnie
Maria
Sofia
Babbis
Stelios

Greek Translations

Anna
published by Livanis 2011

STELIOS

Beryl Darby

ISBN 978-0-9574532-8-9

Printed and bound by
CPI Group (UK) Ltd, Croydon, CR0 4YY

First published in the UK in 2016 by

JACH Publishing
92 Upper North Street, Brighton, East Sussex, England BN1 3FJ

website: www.beryldarby.co.uk

For Fayne who would have celebrated
his fiftieth birthday this year.

Family Tree

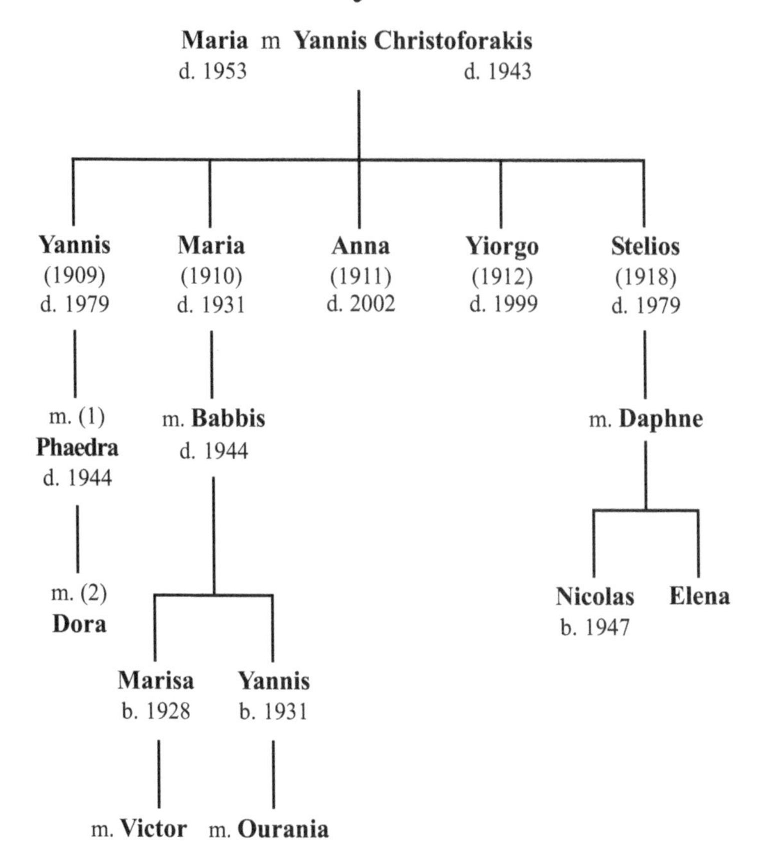

Maria m Yannis Christoforakis
d. 1953
d. 1943
Yannis
(1909)
d. 1979
Maria
(1910)
d. 1931
Anna
(1911)
d. 2002
Yiorgo
(1912)
d. 1999
Stelios
(1918)
d. 1979
m. (1)
Phaedra
d. 1944
m. Babbis
d. 1944
m. Daphne
m. (2)
Dora
Nicolas
b. 1947
Elena
Marisa
b. 1928
Yannis
b. 1931
m. Victor
m. Ourania

Author's Note

This is not meant to be a book about World War II. It is a fictional account of a young man and I hope his activities have a ring of authenticity about them.

My apologies to all those readers who are knowledgeable about WWII and particularly Greece for any mistakes I have made in the timing of the events that led to Greece becoming embroiled and subsequent events. I have hardly touched on the suffering of the people and their brave resistance.

The buildings and activities of Stelios and Tomas are a product of my imagination, as are all the principal characters. I have only mentioned the true names of any other people when relevant to specific events.

1929 – 1930

Stelios felt both miserable and resentful. Yannis had promised to return at Easter and there had been no sign of him.

'He may well have had to stay in Heraklion to catch up on his studies,' his mother tried to console Stelios. 'Due to your father's accident he had to stay with us far longer than he intended at Christmas.'

'He could have written,' said Stelios mutinously.

'He may well have done, and the letter is delayed somewhere. I'm sure we'll have news of him very soon. Your Uncle Yiorgo might bring a letter when he visits next.'

Stelios's one consolation was walking over to visit Babbis on his farm. He enjoyed talking to Babbis as he seemed to know where there was a bird's nest hidden in the trees or where a wild cat had given birth to a litter. As soon as he saw most of the work for the day was complete he would ask his father's permission to leave the fields.

Yiorgo finished filling a box with mouldy beans, tacked a piece of card across the top and looked out towards the sea. 'Pappa, Uncle Yiorgo is coming.'

Yannis looked up and shaded his eyes. 'I'd best go down to meet him. I'll come back up and help you load the cart.' Yannis limped away. Yiorgo arriving could well mean an extra consignment of brandy was arriving and he would be expected to store it until it could be taken out to the island along with the food that he sent regularly.

Yiorgo was feeling aggrieved. His father had promised to return to help him load the cart and there had been no sign of him. Taking the donkey by her leading rein he trudged back down the hill and into the yard. He was surprised to see his uncle and cousin standing there.

'What's wrong?' he asked.

As Andreas was about to answer Uncle Yiorgo shook his head. 'See to the donkey; then come inside.'

Hurriedly Yiorgo tethered the donkey and entered the living room. He stopped aghast. His mother was lying on her bed and his father and a priest were sitting at the table.

'Mamma? Is she dead?'

The priest shook his head. 'I had to deliver some rather bad news to all of you and it was a great shock to your mother.' Father Minos sincerely hoped the woman would not die from the shock he had given her and bring further grief to the family. 'I met your brother in Heraklion. He was very concerned as he had received a letter from the hospital. They wished to take further skin tests from him. He said he would return and let me know the results. Unfortunately I was out when he called and my housekeeper forgot to give me the message. It was by chance I met your cousin in Heraklion and he accompanied me to the hospital where I was proposing to say a prayer for those incurables who were being sent to Athens.' Father Minos swallowed. 'Sadly we saw your brother amongst them.'

Yiorgo looked from one to the other of his stricken family. 'You mean,' he licked his dry lips, 'Yannis is an incurable?'

'There is always hope,' said Father Minos. 'If he is receiving treatment in the hospital in Athens he could well recover.'

Yiorgo looked at the priest scathingly. 'Does Stelios know?'

His father shook his head. 'He went up to see Babbis. He's not back yet'

Yiorgo turned and left the room, calling back over his shoulder, 'I must see to the donkey.'

Babbis showed Stelios the nest of young field mice he had found in the corner of the barn and Stelios stood and stared at the small, naked, helpless creatures. 'They don't look a bit like mice,' he declared.

'They will in a few days. Their fur will grow and once their eyes are fully open they'll start to move around.'

'Where's their mother?'

'Probably out looking for food. She'll need to eat plenty as she will be feeding them.'

'Suppose a cat gets her? What will happen to the babies then?'

'They would die. They need their mother until they are large enough to fend for themselves.'

Stelios straightened up. If his father saw a mouse he usually hit it over the head and declared that it was vermin. He felt quite sad to think that his father could have killed the mother and destined her babies to an early death.

'Look,' he said as he gazed out to the bay. 'There's Uncle Yiorgo's boat. Maybe he has brought Yannis.' Stelios took to his heels, running over the uneven ground.

Babbis followed him more slowly and carefully. If their uncle was visiting Stelios's parents would be busy talking to him and it was possible that he would be able to spend an hour alone with Maria.

Stelios burst through the door and into the living room. 'Mamma, Maria, Babbis is here. Is Yannis with Uncle Yiorgo?'

No one answered him and he looked from one to the other. 'What's happened, Pappa?'

Yannis senior took hold of his son's hand. 'We've had some bad news. Yannis is ill.'

The colour drained from Stelios's face. 'Is he dead?' he asked. 'Is that why the priest is here?'

'No, but he is very ill. Father Minos came to break the news to us.'

'What's wrong with Yannis?'

'He's gone to the hospital in Athens.'

'What's wrong with him?' asked Stelios again.

'He has leprosy.'

Babbis had just reached the door of the living room and heard Yannis senior's words. Quietly he crept back across the kitchen and out of the door, before taking to his heels and running back up the hill to his home.

Stelios bit at his thumb. 'How has Yannis got leprosy?' he asked.

Yannis senior spoke angrily. 'What do you mean "how"? I don't know how you get leprosy.'

Stelios felt close to tears. 'I mean did he get it in Heraklion? He was alright when he left here.'

'He may not have been. We don't know.' He remembered the suppurating lump on Yannis's neck.

'So we all might have leprosy.'

'No, no.' Yannis senior shook his head, unwilling to consider such an awful catastrophe.

'Why not if Yannis had it whilst he was here?'

Father Minos placed a hand on the boy's shoulder. 'It doesn't seem to work like that. Just because you have lived in the same house doesn't always mean others are infected.'

'Even if you have slept in the same bed?'

Andreas held his breath. He had shared a bed with Yannis only a few weeks ago.

'Even if you have shared the same bed it does not mean you will have caught it. There have to be other reasons as well.'

'What reasons?'

'I don't know,' Father Minos had to admit. 'I am not a doctor.'

'What's happened to Mamma?'

'It was a great shock to her. She's lying down until she feels better.'

Stelios nodded. 'I'll go for a walk.' He hoped Babbis would

still be there and he could confide his fears in him, but there was no sign of the young man.

Yiorgo and Andreas, accompanied by Father Minos, finally left the house and walked back down to the quay. In the distance Stelios could be seen throwing stones as far as he could out into the sea and shaking his fist.

'I'll go,' said Father Minos and clambered over the slippery rocks. The string of obscenities coming from the boys lips surprised him. A boy of that age should not know such disgusting words.

'What good is that going to do?' he asked sternly.

'I hate them. Yannis hated them. They should all be dead.'

'Who do you hate?'

'The lepers. Their germs must have blown over and infected Yannis. They live out there on the island. Good thing too. No one wants them around.'

'Wouldn't you like your brother around even if he was sick?'

'That's different. He's my brother.' Stelios's lip quivered.

Father Minos sighed. 'They are all loved and missed by someone. You are fortunate to have another brother and sisters. Yannis has no one now.'

'I want him back. He will come back, won't he?' Stelios turned imploring eyes on the priest and the tears ran freely down his face.

'You must have faith that one day he will be cured and well enough to return to your family. Until then you have to be brave for the sake of your mother and father.'

Stelios looked at the priest and Father Minos could tell that much as the boy would like to believe his words he was not convinced. Stelios threw a last stone into the water and walked away. Father Minos returned to the quay and climbed aboard the boat, wishing he had been able to give the young boy more comfort.

'Before we leave could we sail over towards the island? Stelios has told me it is a leper colony.'

Stelios watched his uncle steer towards the island. Obviously the priest had not believed him when he said the lepers lived there.

Yiorgo steered his boat as close as he dared to the island whilst the priest scanned the high walls of the fortress and looked for any sign of life. Yiorgo was feeling guilty. Had Yannis contracted leprosy due to him taking him onto the island to move the smuggled goods that were hidden over there? If that was the case he might also have the disease. He would have to ask Elena to look at his body tonight for any tell-tale signs. Even if he was clean he would certainly not ask Andreas to help him move the contraband and risk infecting him.

Maria took charge of the house and looked after her mother, talking to her continually and being rewarded with a lop-sided smile. Maria looked pale and strained and Anna was concerned about her. Was she also ill?

'Maria, what's wrong? I know the news was a terrible shock to all of us, and you are working hard looking after Mamma, but you really do begin to look ill.'

Maria shrugged. She could not tell her sister that she longed to have a visit from Babbis, but also dreaded having to give him the news about Yannis. It was more than likely that once he knew he would never come near her again.

'Are you worried that you might be infected?' asked Anna. 'I've looked at myself, but I can't see my back. When we get undressed tonight would you look for me?'

'If you want.'

'I'll look at yours for you. I wonder if Yiorgo has looked at himself? I must ask him and tell him to look at Stelios also.'

'Suppose one of us is infected?'

Anna pursed her lips. She had not wanted to consider that possibility. 'Then we would have to go to the doctor in Aghios

Nikolaos and ask him to send us to the hospital.'

'I don't want to go to the hospital.' Maria's eyes filled with tears.

'Of course you don't,' replied Anna brusquely. 'No one ever wants to go to the hospital. I'm sure you have nothing to worry about, Maria.'

Anna took Yiorgo to one side when he returned from the fields. 'Have you examined your body, Yiorgo?'

'What for?'

'You know what for.' Anna looked at him sternly. 'If you want I'll look at you when you undress for bed tonight.'

'I'm too old now for you to look at my naked body.'

'I was only going to look at your back. Ask Stelios to look at you if you prefer and you look at him – all over, front and back.'

Yiorgo nodded. He had looked at his arms, legs and torso, but although he could feel nothing untoward on his back he was unable to look at it.

'What should I look for?' he asked.

'Patches of white or cracked skin or a little lump like Yannis had on his neck.' Anna sighed. 'If only that doctor had not meddled with it. He probably infected Yannis by using dirty instruments.'

Stelios lay on his mattress. Yiorgo had insisted that he stripped naked and allow him to examine him all over. It had been humiliating to expose himself to his brother's scrutiny, but he was relieved when Yiorgo had said he could not see any blemishes or discolouration on his skin.

How could Yannis have contracted leprosy? Could germs blow across the sea from the island? It was unlikely or they would all have the disease, along with the other villagers. Could Yannis have caught it from the old pottery they had collected together? Stelios shuddered. He certainly would not collect any more, he would not even go near the piles they had sorted and left to be examined at a later date.

Maria sat on the wall outside in the yard, pleased to have a short while to herself and be able to take advantage of the last of the sun. If Babbis did not visit her in the next week she would go up to his farm and ask why he no longer called on her. After the thorough examination Anna had given her body she was certain that she had no sign of the infection.

A shadow fell across her and she looked up to see Babbis standing there. Overjoyed she rose to her feet and stretched out her hands towards him. Babbis backed away.

'Please don't come any nearer, Maria. How is Yannis? Have you heard?

Maria flushed. 'He's in Athens, studying.'

Babbis shook his head. 'I heard the priest say that Yannis was ill. I haven't told anyone. Is there any way I can help?'

Dully Maria shook her head. She could not ask Babbis to take her in his arms and comfort her when he was not even prepared to come nearer than a few feet from her.

Babbis turned away and began to retrace his steps up the track to the hill. He turned and looked back at her when he reached the summit and Maria threw caution to the winds. She raced up the hill and looked around. There was no sign of him. She looked around, feeling both hurt and angry. Babbis must have seen her coming and hidden from her.

She heard a groan from behind a wall and climbed over carefully. Babbis was lying on the ground beating the earth with his fists.

Babbis stiffened as she touched his shoulder. 'Go away, Maria.'

'I cannot go away and leave you lying here if you're hurt.'

Babbis drew a shuddering breath. 'Are you sure you're not ill, Maria?'

Maria shook her head. 'I've examined myself all over. Anna has also looked at me. I haven't a mark on me. I wouldn't touch you if I thought I might infect you, Babbis.'

'How did Yannis become ill?'

'I don't know, but at least he's in the hospital being looked after.' A sob stopped her from saying anything more and the tears began to run down her face.

Babbis sat up and took her in his arms. 'I love you, Maria. I couldn't bear to think of you being ill with that awful disease and ending up disfigured and crippled.'

Maria sobbed all the more at his words and he stroked her hair, trying to calm her; then kissing her with a rising passion until he pushed her down on the grass and struggled to undo his belt.

Stelios was puzzled. Maria no longer lived in the farmhouse and would pay a fleeting visit to their mother whilst his father was working up in the fields. Anna had told him she was married now and her place was with Babbis. Since living with Babbis she had become fat and when he remarked upon it Yiorgo had laughed at him. 'Of course she is getting fat. She's having a baby.'

When Theora had married the church had been decked out with flowers, all the villagers had turned out to wish the bride and groom well and witness their vows, followed by an evening of eating and drinking. His mother had made cheese pies, enough for everyone, and the other villagers had also made vast dishes of food whilst the men brought barrels of wine. He wished he knew when Maria had been married. There had certainly been no village celebration or feasting for her.

Anna hurried into the living room as she heard the front door to the farmhouse close and her mother managing to give a slurred greeting to a visitor. She stopped and her face paled.

'I'll fetch Pappa,' she said as she saw he uncle, cousin and Father Minos standing there.

'There is no need,' Father Mino assured her. 'I'll walk up to the fields and see him.'

'You don't bring bad news?'

Father Minos shook his head. 'This is just a friendly visit as I was nearby.'

Anna felt limp with relief. 'I'll make some coffee.'

Andreas followed her into the kitchen and she turned to him immediately. 'Tell me the truth, Andreas. It has to be bad news if the priest has come.'

'No, Anna. Father Minos arrived at our house yesterday and was able to give us the address of the hospital where Yannis is receiving treatment but he has no news of Yannis.' Andreas took the jug from the shelf and went outside to the pump to fill it with water. 'How is your Mamma?' he asked when he returned.

'Much the same. I think her speech has improved. But maybe that is because I'm getting used to it.'

'And Maria?'

'Very happy. It won't be much longer now before her baby is born.'

'What about you, Anna?'

'I enjoy looking after Mamma and the house. Shall I prepare some rolls for you to take up to the fields?'

'I'm sure Pappa and Father Minos would appreciate that. How is Stelios?'

Anna shrugged. 'He's very quiet. He spends all his free time studying. He wants Pappa to send him to Aghios Nikolaos and let him try for a scholarship like Yannis.'

'I'm sure my parents will welcome him.' Andreas wrapped the rolls in a clean rag.

'Would you do something for me, Andreas?'

'Of course, if I can.'

'If I write a letter to Annita would you take it back for me?'

'That's no problem. I'm sure she would like to hear from you.'

'I just want to know how I have to help Maria when her time comes.'

'Won't the Widow be there?' asked Andreas with a frown. He knew childbirth could be quite a dangerous procedure and he was not sure that a young girl like his cousin should have the responsibility.

'She has promised to come, but she's becoming old and crippled. If she doesn't arrive in time I want to know I am doing the right thing.'

'I'm sure Maria will have no problems. I understand little Marisa was born quite easily, and Babbis's mother will be there.' Andreas tried to reassure Anna and crossed himself. 'Annita is going to Athens soon,' he said to change the subject.

'Athens?' Anna raised her eyebrows. 'What for?'

'She says she isn't happy living in Aghios Nikolaos now. There are too many memories of Yannis. Pappa has agreed she can go and the hospital will give her a good recommendation.'

Anna felt slightly envious. She would have liked the opportunity to become a fully trained nurse. She had talked for hours with the Widow, gleaning knowledge of healing herbs and the treatment of certain ailments, but she was certain she would have learnt a good deal more at a hospital.

'She's very brave to go so far away.'

Andreas nodded. He had an idea that his sister was only going to Athens in the hope that she would be able to nurse Yannis.

1931 - 1935

Stelios listened in growing disbelief as Father Minos described the conditions he had found on Spinalonga when he had visited the previous day. He looked at his cousin Andreas who had accompanied the priest on his journey as he nodded in confirmation of all Father Minos said. It was unbelievable that his brother was living on the island as an outcast.

His mother and Anna had sobbed uncontrollably at first and then demanded to be told yet again how Yannis had been taken there from the hospital, wanting a description of his house and how he lived.

His father had taken a bottle of brandy from the cupboard and poured a generous measure for himself and the priest. He held the bottle up to Yiorgo who shook his head. 'I need to get back to the fields. Thank you for visiting us, Father, and bringing us news.' He shook the priest's hand and left the house. He had heard enough and did not want to dwell on the life his brother was being forced to live.

Sipping at the glass slowly Father Minos answered the questions Anna and her father put to him carefully, but honestly, whilst Stelios sat in stony silence. The priest insisted that due to Yannis's hard work many of them now had a decent shelter they could call their home.

'They could do with so much more,' he sighed. 'The food

the government sends out to them is of the poorest quality; many do not have a decent mattress to sleep on or a blanket to cover themselves. Every so often a boatman will deliver sacks of old clothes and they fight and scrabble through to find something suitable to cover their bodies.'

'What else do they need?' asked Yannis senior, feeling guilty that he was one of the farmers who had always sent food that was destined for the rubbish heap.

'Everything you can think of.' Father Minos looked around the room. 'They need all the basic commodities that you have in your house and take for granted, along with building materials. If you could send some old pots and pans, blankets or clothes they would be grateful. Anything you could spare would be put to good use. An old torn sheet would make bandages for those who need them. They have no medication and no doctor to visit them so their disease is untreated and unchecked.'

Yannis senior rummaged in the cupboard again and placed a small cloth bag on the table, pushing it towards Father Minos. 'Take that and use it as best you can.'

Stelios rose abruptly and walked out of the house. It was unbelievable. His father was giving the priest money to buy goods for the lepers. Yannis's education had been paid for – and wasted – now his father was giving even more money to him. That money was rightfully his. It was to pay for his education when he gained a scholarship and went to Heraklion. The sooner his father allowed him to go to Aghios Nikolaos the better. He would not see that hated island every day and know that his brother was a prisoner over there.

Anna paced the floor, the small boy in her arms. She still cried hot and silent tears over him, wishing she had been able to save her sister's life. Once he was asleep she would place him on the bed beside her mother and be able to tackle the pile of washing that awaited her. Once that was done and placed outside to dry, provided little Yannis still slept, she would start the preparations for their evening meal.

Stelios complained bitterly when the baby woke in the night and disturbed him, but Yiorgo said nothing. He tried to help his sister a little by drawing the water from the well before he went up to the fields with his father, taking their mid-day snack with him. He insisted that Stelios washed the dishes each night whilst Anna prepared little Yannis for bed. Stelios had protested, saying that was not work for a man, but his father had pointed out that he had spent most of the day sitting with Father Theodorakis or with his head in a book, whereas Anna had been on her feet working since dawn. With a bad grace Stelios complied, wondering how much longer it would be before the child was returned to live with his father and grandmother.

Each day Anna would carry little Yannis down to the shore where she stood and waved her red scarf towards the island. Sometimes a figure could be seen waving back to her and she was convinced it was her brother. It meant he was still alive, although she refused to dwell on the appalling conditions that Father Minos had described to her. She had written to Andreas and asked if he could pass a message to Yannis to tell him of Maria's death, but did not know if her request had been possible. She hoped when Stelios left for Aghios Nikolaos in September her uncle would come to collect him accompanied by Andreas.

Stelios enjoyed living in Aghios Nikolaos, the town suited him far better than life on a farm in a small village. There were interesting shops where he could spend his time browsing after school, or buy tobacco without having to say it was for his father and receiving a suspicious look from the owner. The library where he could borrow books on any subject that interested him he found fascinating after the small selection that had been available from Father Theodorakis. He even had a bedroom of his own now Annita was living in Athens. He no longer had to put up with his brother's snoring or being woken by the two small children that Anna insisted lived with them now their grandmother had died and their father had found it impossible to care for them.

Grudgingly and sulkily he helped his uncle on his fishing boat when he could not think of a suitable excuse. He was thankful that he was not expected to take part in any of the night time fishing excursions that Yiorgo undertook, and whenever his uncle said he was visiting Plaka he would plead pressure of school work and the need to study for a scholarship to avoid returning to his family, even for a few hours.

His Aunt Elena would fuss over him, concerned that he was working too hard and puzzled at his reluctance to accompany his uncle on a visit to Plaka. 'I am going with Yiorgo next week. We could all go together. I'm sure your mother would be pleased to see you.'

Stelios shrugged. 'My exams are due soon. You can bring me back any news.'

However hard Elena tried to persuade her nephew he was adamant. He would see more than enough of his family when he had to return during the summer when he would be expected to help his father and Yiorgo on the farm. He did not relish the thought of spending all day up in the fields, but it was preferable to being on a rocking boat and smelling of fish. At least when the summer was over he would be going to Heraklion and he was certain that he would find life there even more enjoyable than he had in Aghios Nikolaos.

The summer holidays arrived all too quickly for Stelios and he had no excuse not to return to Plaka. He could not claim that his uncle needed his help as he had been deliberately slow at learning how to furl the sails, or steer in the direction his uncle indicated; even sorting the fish from the net into the incorrect buckets.

Yiorgo held his tongue. He did not like the boy as he had Yannis and would be relieved when he went home for the summer. It seemed that however patiently he tried to correct Stelios's mistakes the boy ignored his advice and continued to make the most elementary mistakes. Yiorgo hoped fervently that he was never out at sea with Stelios if there was an emergency as he had no faith that the boy would be able to assist him or even follow his instructions, thus putting them both in danger.

To Stelios's annoyance his uncle did not offer to take him to Plaka in his boat. 'The fish are in the other direction at the moment. They go with the current. It won't take you that long to walk.'

Elena was surprised her husband had refused to take her nephew to his home. Yiorgo shook his head. 'I know he works hard at school, but when it comes to giving me a hand he makes every excuse he can think of. He pretends not to understand, he's just lazy when it comes to physical work. The walk will do him good.'

Stelios looked out at Spinalonga. He could see people moving around and he turned away quickly. He had loved and idolised his older brother when he was a small boy and now he felt nothing but hatred. It was Yannis's fault that their mother was confined to a chair having lost the movement in one side of her body. He hated lepers, even if that meant he hated Yannis. His sister was dead and Anna was no more than a slave, his father crippled and Yiorgo began to look like a middle aged man due to working so hard. He hated all of them. His family was an embarrassment to him.

He could see movement on the island again and someone was waving. It must be Yannis. Stelios turned his back, a lump in his throat. Anna was standing there, the two children with her.

'Wave to Uncle Yannis,' she instructed and they both raised their hands and waved vigorously.

'You're sick,' commented Stelios as he walked past her.

Anna frowned. 'I'm taking the children up to see Babbis this afternoon. Do you want to come?'

'I've better things to do with my time,' Stelios threw back at her. 'It's about time Babbis faced up to his responsibilities and looked after his own brats.'

Anger seethed within Stelios. He would go up and confront Babbis now. He strode over the hill to where he could see Babbis digging vigorously, stopping every so often to mop his forehead.

'Hello, Stelios,' Babbis greeted him with a weary smile.

Stelios stood there glaring at him. 'When are you going to relieve my sister of your two children? It's time you faced up to your responsibilities like a man.'

Babbis looked both hurt and puzzled. 'I would love to have my children with me all the time, but it just isn't possible. If it were not for Anna being willing to take care of them they would have had to go to an orphanage.'

'Really,' sneered Stelios. 'I'm sure you would have found some way to look after them yourself. It's just too convenient for you, isn't it? My sister looks after them and you just call in during the evening for a meal and see them in church on a Sunday.'

'It would have been different if my mother hadn't died,' Babbis assured him. 'Anna has been a wonderful help and I love my children dearly.'

'A shame it was your mother that died then and not mine!'

'Stelios!' Babbis was truly shocked.

'Why don't you marry my sister if she is so invaluable to you? Make an honest woman of her before the village begin to believe they're her brats.'

Babbis felt his temper rising. 'Listen to me, Stelios. My arrangement with Anna is to look after my children, nothing more. Her reputation is not besmirched by her kind act. All the village know that my Maria died when she gave birth to little Yannis.'

'They'll conveniently forget that when it suits them. Has any suitor come forward for Anna's hand? No. They don't want two readymade children, whatever their parentage. You are blighting my sister's life due to your unwillingness to be responsible for them.'

Colour suffused Babbis's cheeks. 'I pay for their keep by working hard on my farm, which is more than can be said for you. When did you last do a decent day's manual work? You sat around in Aghios Nikolaos with your head in your books. I've no doubt it took brain power to gain a scholarship to Heraklion and I wish you well. I also wish you to leave my land now.'

Babbis took a step forwards, his fork in his hands. 'Go away. Go back to your books and your fancy life and stop trying to interfere in matters you know nothing about.'

'You are nothing but an uncouth lout. We all know why you had to marry Maria in the first place. My father would have done well to refuse you. If I were the head of the family I would throw your children out and not allow you to step over my threshold.'

'You are not the head of your family and never will be if I have anything to do with it. Now go away and leave me to get on with my work.' Babbis went back to his digging, ignoring Stelios's presence until the boy finally turned and walked back down the hill.

Babbis was hurt by Stelios's accusations and also concerned. Should he ask Anna to marry him? She could never take the place of Maria in his heart, but he was fond of her and would take her as a wife if it would be beneficial to his children.

Stelios packed his sack well in advance and declared his intention of returning to Aghios Nikolaos and catching the bus to Heraklion.

'It makes sense for me to go to Heraklion a week before the term starts. I have to find some suitable lodgings and it will also give me time to find my way around the town. It would be rather stupid not to be able to find my way to the High School and be late on my first day.'

No one tried to dissuade him from leaving Plaka, but his father was concerned about his lodgings. 'I suggest you go to the lodgings where Yannis lived. They may have a room available.'

'Yes, Pappa,' replied Stelios dutifully. He was not at all sure he wanted to go to those lodgings and possibly be given Yannis's bed to sleep in.

'I will give you the money to pay for them but be careful; it will be a considerable amount for a young man to be carrying around on his person.'

'You only have to give me enough to pay until Christmas. I will come back to Plaka then and provided the lodgings I have found are suitable for the remainder of my stay in Heraklion you can give me some more money to cover them until I return again at Easter. They do not need to have it paid in advance for two years. I might wish to move somewhere else and then that could cause a problem.'

Yannis senior could see the sense of his youngest son's argument and before Stelios left he gave him sufficient money for his lodgings, any books he needed, and some money to enable him to go out and enjoy himself.

'Don't waste it. I'm prepared to pay for your lodgings again at Easter and if you need any more books, but you'll not get any extra pocket money from me if you spend it all in a few weeks.'

'I promise I'll be sensible.' Unless the price of drinks and cigarettes was considerably more expensive in Heraklion than in Aghios Nikolaos he knew he had more than enough money to be able to enjoy himself as he pleased.

Stelios wandered up to Eleftherias Square from the bus station and asked directions to the High School of a shopkeeper. There might be someone there who could tell him where there was a room to rent. He had found the town of Aghios Nikolaos busy but it did not compare with Heraklion. There were shops selling the most unimaginable range of goods, bicycles, vans, lorries and even cars wove in and out of the pedestrians who wandered around and more than once he caused a driver to come to an abrupt halt as he walked heedlessly out into the road.

As he walked he looked in the windows for any sign that said there was a room to let, but he saw nothing. He found the High School easily enough along with the library; then walked down to the waterfront. All along were small tavernas and the quayside was crammed with fishing boats, their nets hung up to dry and buckets of fish being unloaded from some of those who had returned from their expedition later. He wrinkled his nose. He had had more than enough of fish when he lodged with his aunt and uncle. However suitable accommodation at a fisherman's might be he would certainly not want to stay there.

After two hours of fruitless wandering a feeling of panic began to overtake him. He had imagined there would be plenty of notices in windows to say there was a room available. What would happen if he was unable to find anywhere to sleep? He would have to spend the night in a doorway or lying on a piece of waste ground and hope he was not robbed. Finally he asked his way to Louisa's, where Yannis had lodged. He might have to stay there if nowhere else was available; he was also decidedly hungry.

He entered the taverna hesitantly, placed his sack by the table nearest to the door and walked up to the counter. An attractive young woman stood there and he guessed she was Louisa. He eyed her up and down; she looked healthy.

'May I have something to eat?' he asked.

Louisa nodded. 'I've some moussaka left from lunch time or I can cook you an omelette.'

The moussaka when it arrived, accompanied by a green salad and some thin slices of tomato was surprisingly good, but he found the little girl that ran backwards and forwards whilst he was eating an irritation. He would not stay anywhere where there were young children. When he paid his bill he decided he could at least ask the girl if she knew of any rooms available in the town.

'What did you have in mind?' asked Louisa. If he wanted a room and her services she could take Anna to a neighbour for an hour.

'Just a room for a couple of nights.'

Louisa shook her head. Students for the High School would be arriving within the week and she would rather have the room let for a term than just a few days. There was also something a little disconcerting about the young man. His face was vaguely familiar. 'Our rooms are taken. I suggest you go up to Eleftherias Square. There's a small hotel there that caters for people who are just passing through.'

Stelios was not sure if he was relieved or disappointed that he had not been offered a room. He certainly did not want to go to the hotel she mentioned. It would probably cost far more for a couple of nights than he could possibly afford to spend.

Shouldering his sack he walked back along the road and took a turning into a side road. He entered a small general store and enquired of the man in attendance if he knew of any lodgings.

The owner scratched his head. 'Well, there are plenty of the fishermen who would be grateful for a bit of extra.'

Stelios shook his head. 'I don't want to stay with a fisherman. I will be attending the High School and don't want to arrive each day smelling of fish.'

'So why don't you make enquiries at the High School? There's bound to be someone there preparing for the new term.'

Stelios felt annoyed with himself. Why hadn't he thought of going there? They might even have a list of suitable accommodation for their out of town students. 'Thank you. I'll go there now.'

He hoped desperately that he was not too late and would not find the building closed up for the day. He hurried back along the streets, hoping he remembered the way and would not get lost, finally pushing open the heavy door which yielded at his touch.

Breathlessly he walked up to a desk where a man sat surrounded by papers. The man did not wait for Stelios to speak or look up from his work. 'The new term commences next week.'

Stelios nodded. 'I know. That's why I'm here.'

'There's nowhere open. Come back next week if your name is on the list.'

'I was wondering if you had a list of accommodation for

students. I come from Aghios Nikolaos and have no relatives here that I can stay with.'

With a heavy sigh the man looked up at him. 'Are you a scholarship boy or a paying pupil?'

'Scholarship, but I have sufficient money to pay for lodgings. I want a bedroom that has a table and chair so I can work in there, some heat in the winter and a cooked meal each evening, oh, and no children.'

'Why don't you ask at some of the tavernas?'

'I have, but there don't seem to be any rooms available.'

'Ask me next week.'

'I really need to be settled somewhere by next week,' protested Stelios. 'I also need a bed for tonight.'

'And I need to have the students allocated to their respective classes and tutors by then. I don't have time to go running around looking for somewhere for you to stay.' Reluctantly the clerk handed Stelios a sheet of paper with a number of addresses and bent his head back down to the papers.

'Thank you very much, sir.' Stelios examined the addresses written there, but had no idea where any of them were located in the town. He was about to ask for directions when an elderly man approached the desk and the clerk stood up deferentially.

'Please, finish your business with the young man. I have only come to see if my list of students is ready.'

'I have finished dealing with this student. I'll have your list ready in a few more minutes and bring it through to you, sir.'

Stelios felt himself dismissed and walked out of the door. Once outside he studied the addresses carefully. He would have to ask at a barber's or local store and hope they would be able to help him.

He called into three barber's shops, tried a baker and two general stores, but each time he was greeted by a shake of the head. Feeling frustrated and also slightly anxious – he did not want to miss his chance of some respectable lodgings – he walked back towards Eleftherias Square, resigned to spending the night in the hotel.

Each time he reached a shop or taverna he asked if they could direct him to one of the address that was on the piece of paper and finally he had success.

'There's a taverna in the next road over that has rooms to let. You must have taken the wrong turning from the Square. Go back up and take the second on the left. About half way down go across the square and walk along to Gourdou. You can't miss it. That's the address you want.'

Thanking him and hoping he had been directed correctly Stelios hurried away. On reaching Eleftherias Square he stood to get his bearings, crossed into Gianari Street and could see the square the man had mentioned. He entered the taverna and looked for the owner. Behind the counter was a young man polishing glasses.

'Can I help you?'

'I was told you might have a room to let.'

'How long would you want it for?'

'This will be my first term at the High School. I am looking for lodgings and the list I was given had this taverna on the list.'

'I'm sorry. We're already booked up with students.'

Stelios's face fell. 'Would you know of anyone else who would be willing to take a student? Unfortunately I haven't any relatives here I can stay with. I need a bed for tonight and I could look for somewhere permanent tomorrow,' he added.

The young man nodded and put down the cloth he had been using. 'We can give you a room for a few days.'

Stelios smiled in relief. 'I'm terribly grateful.'

'What subjects are you studying at High School?'

'Mathematics.'

The youth nodded. 'I'm Vangelis. I'm taking History and Classical Greek.' He held out his hand to Stelios. 'Welcome to Heraklion. Where are you from?'

'Aghios Nikolaos.'

'I've not been there. Is it a big town?'

Stelios shrugged. 'A fair size. Nowhere near as big as Heraklion.'

'Do you want something to eat or shall I show you to your room?'

'I had a meal a short while ago, but I'd love to get rid of my sack.'

'I'll just give my father a shout.' Vangelis stood at the bottom of a flight of stairs and shouted loudly. 'Pappa, I'm taking a young man upstairs to one of the rooms. Can you come down to the taverna?'

A portly man appeared in a doorway and looked Stelios up and down. 'How long is he staying here?'

'Tonight, maybe tomorrow. He's a student at the High School and is looking for lodgings.'

'Ours are taken.'

'I know. I told him that, but he needs somewhere to stay until he's found a permanent lodging.'

Vangelis's father nodded. 'Has he tried your Uncle Christos? The last I heard he had a room available.' He went back inside and closed the door.

'Where's that?' asked Stelios eagerly.

'The next road over. I could take you there later.'

'I'd be terribly grateful. I don't know my way around and keep getting lost.'

Vangelis led the way up a flight of stairs. 'It isn't very big,' he apologised, 'but it's clean. Mamma makes sure of that.'

Stelios placed his sack on the floor and looked around. Despite the room not being very large there was a bed, table and chairs and a trunk.

'This is all I need,' he said. 'I won't unpack more than essentials as I have to move on.'

'Come and have a glass of wine. Pappa likes to have a rest in the afternoon when I'm at home. When he comes back down we can go round to see my uncle.'

Stelios moved into the taverna run by Vangelis's uncle the following day and unpacked his belongings. He now had four days before the start of the term at the High School. That would give him plenty of time to find his way around Heraklion, join the library and also make a visit to Knossos. Yannis had talked about Knossos and Stelios was curious to find out what his brother had found so fascinating about the site. He gave a deep sigh. He hated lepers, but he wished his brother was still on Crete and they could have spent their time together. In all probability, under Yannis's guidance, he would have concentrated on ancient history rather than mathematics.

He set out at a brisk walk, leaving the outskirts of Heraklion behind him and following the directions he had been given to the site. He covered the five kilometres in less than two hours and entered the small taverna opposite. He declined their offer of a meal, requesting just some bread, cheese and olives along with coffee and promising to return later.

Surreptitiously he placed the bread and cheese into his pocket. That would be sufficient for a mid-day snack and he knew he would be able to have a meal when he returned to the taverna where he was lodging.

Stelios walked up the short path and immediately found himself looking at low walls and buildings He decided he would go to the right and make his way gradually around the perimeter, investigating the inner buildings afterwards. He sat on the stone chair that had been declared the King's throne by Arthur Evans and admired the frescos on the walls, then moved into the other rooms that were described as the Queen's apartments.

The site was far larger than he had anticipated and he gazed in awe at the staircase that had been reconstructed, with replica shields hung above it. The larger than life fresco of the bull made him feel uncomfortable, but the giant pithoi that were still in situ in a chambered pit intrigued him. If they were used to store gold and jewels the inhabitants of the city must have been rich in the extreme.

As he walked he saw broken pottery lying around and was

tempted to pick up shards for closer scrutiny. Remembering that he thought they could carry disease he resisted touching them and restricted himself to bending down to examine them more closely.

Finding a tree that gave shade he sat down on the ground and pulled the bread and cheese from his pocket. He wished now he had visited Gournia, where Yannis had gone years earlier with his school teacher; it was only a few kilometres from Aghios Nikolaos. He ate thoughtfully, remembering Yannis had found a small gold axe in one of the cases at the museum. He must certainly visit there to see the finds from the site.

Stelios was enjoying his time at the High School and had no complaint about his lodgings with Vangelis's uncle. Most evenings, after his meal, he would meet up with some other members of his class and they would spend a convivial few hours in a local taverna, Vangelis joining them for a short while some evenings. They would play backgammon or cards, the winner having to buy the next bottle of wine. Stelios was completely happy with this arrangement and he managed to be the most frequent loser.

The young men discussed their aspirations and their families, but Stelios was reticent about his family.

'Have you got a girl back in Aghios Nikolaos?' asked Makkis.

Stelios shook his head. 'There's plenty of time to think about being betrothed when I've finished my education.'

'Don't you go to any of the locals?' asked Theo.

Stelios blushed. 'I'd rather wait until I'm betrothed.'

His companion hooted in derision and Stelios shook his head. 'I've heard of some of the horrible diseases you can catch from the girls you pay to visit. I'd rather stay healthy.'

'They're not all dirty.'

'How do you know? They might look clean on the outside, but you don't know if they've let someone with a disease use them,' replied Stelios.

'You don't know what you're missing,' sniggered Makkis. 'I went to one last week and she was really good.' He bent towards Theo and whispered in his ear.

'Really? I've not found one who would do that.'

'I'll give you her address. Tell her she was recommended by me and I might get an extra ten minutes the next time I use her.'

'If that's what she does you wouldn't last another ten minutes.'

Makkis grinned. 'I'd give it a good try.'

'Have you been to Louisa?' asked Theo. 'She charges by the hour so you can take your time.'

'I went once, but her prices are beyond me for regular use and she's only available during the day. In the evenings the taverna's open and her husband's there.'

'You know who he is, don't you?'

Makkis nodded. 'He's a teacher and was elected as a local government official. Maybe he could be persuaded to pass a law to say that their services have to be free.'

Stelios listened in disbelief. 'You mean the woman one of our local politicians is married to is a prostitute? Surely that can't be right.'

'It's right enough,' Theo assured him. 'Everyone knows Louisa Pavlakis and what she gets up to except her fool of a husband. I bet she puts some of the money she makes into the till and tells her husband the taverna has had a busy day.' Theo laughed at his own joke.

Stelios felt himself go cold. Yannis had lodged in her taverna along with his school teacher Yiorgo Pavlakis. Had the man married her and was it true that his wife was a prostitute? Was this where Yannis had contracted leprosy? She had looked clean and healthy when he had his meal there. He would certainly not have eaten on the premises if he had known she was a prostitute.

He shivered and pushed back his chair. 'I'm going home,' he announced. 'I'm not feeling too good. I hope I'm not going down with anything.'

'You're not going home,' Makkis shook his head. 'I wager you're going off to see if Louisa is free this evening. Tell us tomorrow what you think of her.'

Stelios shook his head. He would certainly not patronise Louisa's taverna and nor would he make use of any of the other prostitutes in the town.

He left the taverna with the cat calls and ribald comments of his companions ringing in his ears and walked miserably back to his lodging, feeling certain now that he knew where Yannis had contracted his disease.

The end of the term came all too quickly for Stelios. His tutor had commended him for his excellent results and agreed to recommend he be accepted into a science class.

'You should be well able to keep up with your mathematics studies and attend science classes at the same time,' smiled Mr Michelakis.

'Thank you, sir.' Stelios stammered his delighted thanks. 'My father will be proud of me.'

'So he should be. Enjoy you time at home and come back rested and refreshed ready for the new term.'

Stelios thought it extremely unlikely he would be rested and refreshed after the Christmas break. No doubt his father would expect him to help on the farm every day, regardless of the weather.

He decided he would visit the market and look to see what was on offer at the stalls. He would be expected to produce a present for each of his family as Yannis had done each Christmas. As Stelios passed the museum he realised he had still not set foot inside, despite intending to make a visit after his journey to Knossos. He would go inside and have a quick look at the items on display.

An elderly man sat dozing at the door and Stelios crept past him, unsure if he was supposed to pay an entry fee to the door keeper. He waited for his eyes to become accustomed to the dim lighting and began to study the cases. Again he felt a stirring of his long suppressed interest in pottery and spent far longer going from case to case than he had initially intended.

A man cleared his throat behind him and Stelios turned round.

'We are just about to close, sir. Why, Yannis, you've come back to us.' A broad smile spread across the man's face. 'Where have you been? We've missed you. Nothing has been touched since you went away.'

Stelios looked at the man in horror. He knew he resembled his older brother in looks, but he had not expected the museum curator to mistake him for Yannis. He shook his head.

'I'm sorry. You must have made a mistake. My name is not Yannis.'

'Oh,' the man still peered at him. 'You are very like him. Are you a relative? Would you have any news of him?'

Stelios shook his head. 'I have no relative of that name. I'm sorry, I cannot help you.' Swiftly Stelios made his way to the door and hurried off in the direction of the market. He would certainly not visit the museum again.

A gift for his father was easy; he always welcomed a pouch of tobacco. His mother was more difficult now she spent her time either in bed or in her chair. She was unable to sew or embroider as she had in the past and he finally settled on a shawl. He could think of nothing for Anna or Yiorgo and finally bought an apron for his sister and a belt for his brother, then buying the same again in smaller sizes for Marisa and little Yannis. He begrudged spending the money on Babbis's children, but knew he would be viewed with disfavour by everyone if he ignored them.

Stelios was relieved to be returning to Heraklion. He had not enjoyed the visit to his family. His father had expected him to be up at dawn and spend the day up in the fields working alongside

Yiorgo whatever the weather. He found the presence of the two children a nuisance, although they were polite to him and under Anna's instruction left him alone and did not ask him to pay them any attention. He finally walked back to Aghios Nikolaos, the money for his lodgings safely in his pocket.

He had made a point of describing the taverna where he lived to his parents and Anna in exaggerated terms, he was provided with an oil lamp and a stove in his room and the taverna was quiet and orderly. The customers never disturbed him. Of his prowess in mathematics he was rightly proud and declared that he would be just as proficient in science when he started the course upon his return to the High School.

Yannis senior had looked at his son with pride. 'What work do you plan to do when you have finished your studies?'

'Oh, I haven't decided yet. There's plenty of time. I'm going to try for a scholarship to the University next year. Once I have been accepted there I can begin to think about my future.'

Yannis senior thought about the little bag of drachmas that he kept hidden. There would be sufficient in there to pay for Stelios to spend two years at the University provided he did gain a scholarship.

As Aghios Nikolaos came into view Stelios had a feeling of relief. He would spend the night with his aunt and uncle and catch the bus to Heraklion the following morning. He had dreaded some accident happening to his father or Yiorgo that would have meant he had to stay in Plaka and help them for an indeterminate amount of time as Yannis had done.

Having spent a year in Heraklion Stelios felt totally at home; he enjoyed the mathematical work at the High School and the time he spent socializing with his friends, despite disapproving of their visits to the local prostitutes.

'Are you betrothed yet, Stelios?' asked Theo.

'I have no intention of getting married until I have finished my education and have a successful career,' replied Stelios firmly. 'There is no reason to think of getting betrothed before then.'

'Oh, I don't know,' Makkis said thoughtfully. 'I became betrothed at Easter and you'd be surprised what I'm allowed to do if we can snatch a few minutes alone.'

'Such as?' Theo raised his eyebrows.

'I can slip my hand inside her bodice and give her a squeeze. I actually had my hand up her skirt the other night. Luckily I heard her mother coming back.'

'She doesn't mind you taking liberties with her before you're married?' asked Stelios.

Makkis laughed. 'She pretends to be coy and shy, but I know by the way she sighs and smiles when I touch her that she enjoys it.'

'You be careful,' warned Theo. 'If her father catches you he'll thrash you.'

'I'm only touching. When I want more I go to one of the local girls.'

'When are you getting married?' asked Stelios.

'About two years time, I expect, when I've finished High School and have found some good steady work.'

'Suppose you change your mind?'

Makkis shrugged. 'It's not really an option. My parents agreed this match when she was born.'

'How old is she now?'

'Fourteen.'

Theo laughed. 'Not much in that bodice for you to get hold of yet then.'

'You'd be surprised. I'm longing to have a look.'

Stelios shuddered. He hoped his father had not made any such arrangement for him and thought about the village children. There were only two girls near enough in age to him to be considered and he disliked both of them, all the others were far too young.

'Wouldn't you like a look, Stelios?' asked Theo.

'I'll wait until I have my own girl.'

'If you don't get a bit of practice in you won't know what to do. I reckon we should take you out with us one night and educate you.'

'Even better,' said Makkis, 'why don't we see if we can arrange some time with Louisa? If we clubbed together we could probably have her for a couple of hours or so. Plenty of time for Stelios to get to know the ropes and for us to have some pleasure also.'

Stelios looked at his friends in horror. 'There is no way I am going near any one of the immoral girls in the town. I am quite happy to wait until I'm married.'

'You better be careful or you'll end up a monk.'

'Better to be a monk than to find I've caught some disgusting disease. Are we having another glass of wine or are you two intending to go off in pursuit of some willing young ladies?'

Makkis rose. 'I'm off. There's an address I sometimes call at on my way home. I'll see if she's available. Talking about Louisa doesn't help a man to keep control of himself.'

Theo laughed. 'I'll have another glass of wine. I can't afford more than that. I spent too much last week on a new girl.'

'Hope she was worth it.' Makkis raised his hand. 'See you both tomorrow.'

Andreas arrived at the Plaka farm with his father, hardly able to contain himself. He asked dutifully after his aunt, complimented Anna on being such a good mother to Babbis's children, confirmed that Annita was working in a hospital in Athens and that both his own parents were well.

'I have some very exciting news,' he announced.

'Yannis?' asked Anna immediately.

Andreas shook his head. 'I can tell you that he's well and working hard with some of the other islanders to rebuild the houses over on the island. Conditions have improved tremendously, and all thanks to Father Minos. A doctor visits once a week; sadly there is not a lot he can do for the sufferers except give them Chaulmoogra Oil capsules and reassure them their condition has not deteriorated since he saw them last.'

Anna smiled in relief. 'Did you manage to get a message to him about Maria?'

'I took it to him myself.'

'You took it?' Anna's eyes opened wide. 'You went over to the island again?'

'I went over with Father Minos and the doctor's regular boatman.' Andreas did not add that he had helped to hold down a young girl whilst Doctor Stavros amputated her arm with very little anaesthetic at his disposal. 'Father Minos has gained permission to go and live on the island.'

'Live there? Is he ill?'

'Not at all. He feels there should be a priest over there, to give them encouragement and also to hear their last confessions and officiate at their funerals. He has to find someone to take his place in his parish in Heraklion before the Bishop will consent.' Andreas's smile grew wider. 'Father Minos has suggested I take his place in Heraklion. If the Bishop agrees I will have my own parish.'

'Oh, Andreas, that's amazing. Your parents must be so proud of you.'

Stelios had avoided the parish where he knew Father Minos lived and worked. He was sure the priest would recognise him and had no desire to be asked how his family were faring. If he saw the man in the distance he would turn down a side road to avoid him.

He was surprised to see his cousin Andreas waiting for him outside the High School as he left for the day.

'Andreas! What's happened? Why are you here?'

Andreas smiled at him. 'There's nothing to be alarmed about. I wanted to tell you my news.'

Stelios swallowed. He did not want to be seen with the priest by his fellow students and questioned later. 'We can't talk here. Let's find a quiet taverna and have a glass of wine.'

'You could come back to my house,' offered Andreas.

'Your house?'

'I have taken over the parish from Father Minos.'

'What has happened to him?'

'I'll tell you when we are out of all this noise and congestion.'

Stelios opened the door of the next taverna they reached. He had called in to the establishment occasionally but never patronized it regularly and doubted if they would remember him. 'It should be quieter in here.' Stelios went up to the counter and ordered a bottle of wine. He had no idea how abstemious Andreas might be, but knew he would be able to consume the whole bottle without a problem.

He poured a glass for his cousin, offered him a cigarette which Andreas refused, and sat back expectantly. 'So what has happened to Father Minos that you have been able to have his parish?'

'Father Minos has gone to Spinalonga.'

Stelios gasped. 'He's an incurable?'

Andreas shook his head. 'Not at all. He has permission from the Bishop to live over there. Those sad, unfortunate people had no priest on the island. He is hoping that his presence will give them some comfort.'

'Live there? Live with them?' Stelios was incredulous.

'He saw it as a calling once he had visited. At first the Bishop refused, saying there was no one to take over the parish. Father Minos persuaded him that I would be the ideal candidate, so here I am.'

Stelios found the news hard to assimilate and drained his glass, pouring another immediately whilst Andreas took no more than a sip.

'I am incredibly fortunate to be given the opportunity of a parish of my own. I spent two weeks here with Father Minos as he showed me around and introduced me to his parishioners,' continued Andreas, but did not mention he had also visited the patients in the leper hospital along with the priest. 'I give thanks regularly for the day I bumped into him when I was up here looking for Yannis.'

Stelios glanced at him sourly. If Andreas had not met the priest they would not have known Yannis's fate and his mother would not have suffered a stroke when the news was given to her.

'I feel very guilty that I have not sought you out earlier, but I did not know the address of the taverna where you are lodging. I was also kept occupied by my new duties, of course. Whenever I thought I would have some free time something else demanded my attention. Today I was in this area and decided I would call at the High School.'

'How long had you been waiting for me?'

'No more than ten minutes. I knew the time that school finished and hoped you did not have a late class. Had you not appeared within the next few minutes I would have gone inside and enquired after you.'

Stelios drained his glass again, thankful that Andreas had not entered the school and asked. He would doubtlessly have said he was the priest who had taken over Father Minos's duties and explained the reason.

'It was good of you to think of me,' muttered Stelios. 'I wish you well.'

'I hope you will become a member of my church. Father Minos said he had not seen you at all.'

'I attend a church close to my lodging. I was introduced there by the taverna owner.' Stelios had no intention of visiting Andreas. Having avoided contact with Father Minos he certainly did not want to be associated with Andreas and it become known that he was his cousin.

'I am sure your priest would understand your change of allegiance.'

Stelios shook his head. 'He might, but the taverna owner might not. It could cause a problem.'

'If you explained that we are related.....'

'No,' interrupted Stelios. 'I am sure you have a full congregation and do not need me to increase their numbers.'

Andreas looked hurt and took another sip of his wine. 'You will always be welcome.'

Stelios nodded and drained his glass. 'I need to get back to my lodging. I have homework that has to be completed.' He added some wine to Andreas's glass and refilled his own, drinking it down quickly. 'I'm sure we will see each other around frequently.'

'I hope so,' smiled Andreas, trying to stifle his annoyance with the young man. He had not expected such a cool reaction, bordering on rejection of his relationship and friendship.

Mr Stephanakis sought out Mr Michelakis towards the end of the term.

'I have a problem with that young student, Stelios Christoforakis.'

Mr Michelakis raised his eyebrows. 'A problem? He is a model student, never late for class and his homework completed on time.'

'I have no complaint against him personally. It is his ability. He learns the chemical formulas and can recite any of them back to me, but he cannot apply them. If I write the formula for bronze he can tell me the metal immediately. The problem arises if I write the formulas for tin and copper and ask him to write the formula made by their combination. He cannot relate.' Mr Stephanakis shook his head. 'I don't think chemistry is a suitable subject for him to study.'

'Have you tried to explain the procedure to him?'

'On a number of occasions, but he seems unable to retain the information,' sighed the tutor.

'So what are you suggesting? I know he hopes to gain a scholarship to the University and he will need more than Mathematics to be accepted. Another subject is essential.'

Mr Stephanakis shrugged. 'I can only think that accountancy or book keeping would suit him better. Even if he was unable to go to University they would stand him in good stead for office work.'

'Are you planning to tell him you no longer want him in your class?'

Mr Stephanakis hesitated. 'It's only fair that he's told. He's wasting his time with me, but I wanted to speak to you first. Could you ask Mr Simonakis to tutor him next term?'

'What's wrong with you asking him?'

'You can explain the boy's flair for mathematics.' Mr Stephanakis smiled. 'If you talked to him and said Mr Simonakis had heard glowing reports of him and asked to be able to tutor him I feel sure he would be delighted.'

Mr Michelakis studied his colleague. 'So you actually want me to tell him he's no longer registered for a chemistry course?'

'If he knows he has a place in another class next term it will make leaving me easier for him. He might even be relieved. You know him better than I and would know how to explain the situation to him.'

Mr Michelakis sighed. 'I'll see what I can do.'

Stelios listened to Mr Michelakis mutinously. 'Are you telling me I'm stupid?' he asked finally.

'Not at all. You are a gifted mathematician, but you do not have a scientific brain. However hard you worked at the subject you would always struggle and probably never accomplish a pass in the exams. I have spoken to Mr Simonakis and he thinks book keeping would be more to your liking. If you found that enjoyable you could take a further course in accountancy. No doubt you would find both subjects were mastered easily by you resulting in good results.'

Slightly mollified Stelios nodded. 'Would I be able to attend University if I obtained good grades in those subjects?'

'Most certainly. A degree in mathematics would only qualify

you to teach, but if you also had a degree in accountancy you would have a number of other options open to you.'

Stelios gave an exaggerated sigh. 'Then I will have to follow your advice. Please thank Mr Simonakis and tell him I will be delighted to join his class next term.' Secretly he was relieved that he would no longer have to attend the science sessions. He had expected to make experiments, not spend all his time learning formulas and theories.

Stelios was surprised when he arrived in Aghios Nikolaos to hear that Annita had visited her family.

'She's getting married,' smiled Elena happily. 'She met a research scientist and he persuaded her to go and work for him as his assistant. He's been offered a scholarship in America and has asked her to go with him, as his wife, of course. She asked him if she could have time to consider his proposal and came here for a week. It was lovely to have her home.'

'I'm very pleased for her. I hope they will be happy,' answered Stelios. He wondered how her brother, Andreas, had accepted the news

'Annita is insisting we go to Athens for her wedding. Elias, the young man she is marrying, has an invalid mother. I'm beginning to feel really excited. We'll have to catch the bus to Heraklion and we can stay with Andreas then he will take the ferry over to the mainland with us and Annita will meet us there.'

'Do my family know?' asked Stelios.

Elena nodded. 'Her father took her to Spinalonga to say goodbye to Yannis and then over to Plaka.'

Stelios shuddered. He could not imagine why Annita should have decided she needed to say farewell to Yannis. He was the equivalent of a dead man.

'When are you going to Athens?' Stelios could imagine that he would be without a bed for the night on his return journey to Heraklion.

'Next month.' As if reading his thoughts Elena continued. 'We'll still be here when you come back from Plaka and when you come down in the summer you'll be welcome as always.'

Stelios nodded in relief. It was easier for him to walk from Plaka to Aghios Nikolaos than over the hills to Neapoli where he could have caught the bus.

Stelios related his change of subject news to his father. 'Mr Michelakis considers I am wasting my time studying science and it is not as interesting as I had hoped. He has assured me that I can still get a scholarship to University if I change my course to book keeping next term and also study accountancy.'

Yannis senior frowned. 'What's the difference?'

'Book keeping is entering numbers and making sure they total correctly. Accountancy is checking other people's business entries and ensuring they are accurate and have not been falsified. I will probably end up with a very lucrative job.'

Yannis senior nodded. Provided Stelios did not want to look into his little private book of transactions between himself, his cousin Yiorgo, and a couple of other men he did not mind which subjects his son chose to study.

Once again Stelios was expected to work on the farm alongside his father and brother, but at least this time it was not so wet or cold. He found the work mundane and could not understand the pleasure Yiorgo would express when they had fulfilled the quota of boxes for the island and still had time to tackle other jobs before returning to the farmhouse for the night. It was with a feeling of relief that he packed his sack and walked along the track leading to Elounda and on to Aghios Nikolaos.

He was welcomed back cordially by Christos and his wife, grateful to see that the oil lamp still sat on the table and a stove had been placed in his room ready for the winter months. He unpacked his sack and looked at his trousers and shirts. They were soiled from working on the farm and he would have to take them to the laundress before he could consider wearing them again

He had refused Anna's offer to wash them, preferring to return with dirty clothes rather than wet ones. Anna had thanked him for being so considerate to her as she had more than enough washing each day. Stelios had shrugged. He had not considered his sister; it was just more convenient for him.

He was pleased to have a bedroom to himself again and be back in Heraklion. Over a glass of wine with Vangelis and his Uncle Christos he answered their questions about his time away dishonestly. He assured them that his family were well and he had had a most enjoyable time, but found Aghios Nikolaos small by comparison to Heraklion. He made no mention of the farm at Plaka and was vague when asked about his brother and sister, giving the impression that Anna was married with a family and Yiorgo went out to work each day.

Telling them that Annita, his cousin, was going to be married in Athens and then travel to America turned the conversation away from him and he exaggerated wildly about the accomplishments of her future husband, claiming that he was an internationally famous chemist and America had been pleading with him for years to go there and impart his unique knowledge.

'And your cousin?' asked Vangelis. 'Is she also a chemist?'

'Very accomplished,' boasted Stelios, having no idea of Annita's ability. 'They work together.'

Christos frowned. 'It is unusual for a woman to be a chemist.'

'My cousin is an unusual young woman. She is a fully trained nurse. I understand that her future husband tutored her in chemistry and considers she is as knowledgeable as he is. I had hoped to emulate her by taking science, but it was not to be. Mr Michelakis says I am a gifted mathematician, but I don't understand the formulas for science and I certainly don't see the necessity for them.'

When Stelios met with Makkis and Theo he boasted again

about Annita's accomplishments and her forthcoming wedding. 'She is, of course, marrying into one of the best Athenian families. The marriage would not have been permitted otherwise.'

'Is that why you're not betrothed to anyone, Stelios? They cannot find an available girl from a good enough family?' Theo winked at Makkis.

However hard Makkis and Theo tried to encourage Stelios to visit a prostitute with them he refused until they both gave up trying to persuade him. They even discontinued talking about their experiences in front of him, sensing his disapproval.

Stelios found book keeping was easy and by the end of the term Mr Simonakis was certainly prepared to begin explaining the intricacies of accountancy and wished all his pupils were as able and industrious.

'Would it help if I stayed for a while during the Christmas holiday and you set me some work to complete?'

Mr Simonakis shook his head. 'You are certainly not behind in the class and there is no point in you being way ahead of the other boys. Just ensure that your numbers are always clearly written and you don't forget to write in the date and details of a transaction. Go back home and enjoy yourself.'

'Yes, sir,' replied Stelios obediently. The last thing he wanted to do was return to Plaka and work on the farm. He had hoped Mr Simonakis would give him a good excuse to stay in Heraklion.

His Aunt Elena could not stop talking about their visit to Athens. What a huge town, people everywhere and on top of the hill was the Parthenon that Yannis had talked about and shown them a picture of and now she had seen it with her own eyes. Elias was a very pleasant young man and his sisters lively and entertaining. His mother was charming and it was such a shame that she had been injured in a train crash many years earlier and unable to walk more than a few steps. Elias's uncle was a priest and Andreas had enjoyed talking to him, wishing he could have spent longer in the man's company than the two days he had stayed in Athens.

'You would never believe their apartment,' continued Elena. 'It is like a palace. The most beautiful furniture and ornaments, the like of which I have never seen before. They have a maid, and she does the cleaning and cooking. The little pastries we were served were excellent. I have never tasted better. I'm so pleased Elias did not come over here to Crete to meet us. What would he have thought of our fisherman's cottage? Now I've seen where he lives I would be so ashamed.'

Stelios listened politely, nodding his head. He was not interested in his aunt's repeated description of the time she had spent on mainland Greece. She had described their journey to Heraklion and the ferry over to Piraeus, along with the places Annita had taken them and the visits they had made to Elias's family in detail at least three times to him.

Elena suddenly looked sad. 'I do wish she had not gone to America. I'll never see her again now.'

Stelios shifted uncomfortably in his chair. He would have been delighted if he was going to America and knew he would never have to see any of his family again.

Stelios had disliked working on the farm previously, but now he hated it and was determined that he would not return to the drudgery in his next holiday from High School. The week before he was due to return to Heraklion he confronted his father.

'I'm sorry, Pappa, but I won't be able to return here for the Easter holiday.'

Yannis looked at his son in surprise. 'Why ever not? Where will you go?'

'I really feel I have to stay in Heraklion and concentrate on my studies. I have the scholarship exams after Easter and I need to ensure I gain a good pass.'

'Will the taverna where you lodge expect more money?'

'Well,' Stelios hesitated. 'I will obviously have to pay my board and lodge for the extra days I'm with them, but I will have saved the bus fare. It would be a help if you could give me my lodging allowance up until the summer.'

Yannis nodded understandingly. His son's education was far more important than a few days help on the farm and he still had plenty of money in the small leather bag he kept at the back of the cupboard.

Vangelis was delighted that Stelios was staying at his uncle's taverna over the Easter holiday. 'We always get together as a family for a meal after the church service. You'll be welcome to join us.'

'That's very kind of you. I'd be delighted, provided it was no trouble.'

'Of course it's no trouble. I'm sure Uncle Christos would prefer that you joined us otherwise he would have to cook you a separate meal and you would have to sit and eat it alone. That would be miserable.'

Stelios visited the library and returned to his lodging with books beneath his arm. He would only spend the minimum amount of time in the company of Vangelis and his family. He would not waste his time by participating in prolonged eating and drinking with their friends and relatives. To attend the church service was obligatory, but once he had eaten the Easter meal he planned to return to the taverna where he lodged and spend the remainder of the day in his room. He had selected books that explained how interest and percentages were calculated. Mr Simonakis had intimated that he would be explaining the procedure to them in the new term and Stelios was determined to be ahead of his fellows.

A week into the new term Stelios approached Mr Mikhaelis. 'Are you able to tell me when the examination will be for me to gain a scholarship to the University in Athens, please?'

'The beginning of May. You will have plenty of time to study for it.'

Stelios frowned. 'I understand all the mathematics, algebra, geometry and trigonometry you have taught us so far. Is it possible to move on to something more challenging after I have sat for the examination?'

Mr Mikhaelis looked at the eager young man and shook his head. 'When you are at the University you will be able to take Advanced Mathematics. I am not qualified to teach at that standard. I understand from Mr Simonakis that you are fully conversant with book keeping and accountancy. Maybe he can offer you something more to occupy your brain.'

'I have already spoken to him and he could only suggest that I read up on history or geography.'

Mr Mikhaelis smiled. 'That would be an excellent idea. It would give you a basic knowledge of how Greece has developed into the country it is today. We have been influenced by the geography of the terrain and also the many different countries and people who invaded and ruled us in the past. They all brought their own culture and customs which has had a bearing on our present political situation and the way we conduct our lives.'

'I am not very interested in politics,' demurred Stelios.

'I think you should try to cultivate an interest. You have an excellent mathematical brain and if you decided to enter the government you could well end up as Minister of Finance eventually.'

Stelios nodded slowly. 'I suppose that could be a possible career for me.' He had always avoided any political conversations with his friends, but the thought of becoming the Minister of Finance was certainly attractive.

Each week Stelios visited the post office, hoping he would have a letter from the University waiting for him. Anna had taken to writing to him once a fortnight. He did not bother to reply as her letter usually consisted of sheet of paper saying their mother was well, their father and Yiorgo were working hard and the children were thriving. On this occasion there were a number of pages and Stelios read them with a feeling of disgust and horror

How could Yannis be married? It was against the law for lepers to marry. They should be exterminated; then they would not be able to pass on their filthy disease. Greece would be free of lepers forever. He read Anna's description of asking their father for some chickens and how long it had taken her to catch them.

Stelios realised he was trembling with emotion and turned into the first taverna he saw and asked for a brandy. He drank it down quickly and asked for another.

The bar tender looked at him suspiciously. 'You should go easy on that stuff at your age.'

'I've had a shock,' answered Stelios, steadied himself against the bar and walked unsteadily out into the street. He felt sick and was unsure whether it was the result of the brandy or Anna's news.

When the summer holidays arrived Stelios had no excuse to prevent him returning to Plaka and he also needed to talk to his father. He had found the examination for the University scholarship easy and had been offered a place. He now had to ask his father for the money to enable him to travel to the mainland city and find lodgings there for a couple of years. Once he was established in Athens he would have a good excuse to only return to Crete during the summer recess.

He just hoped Anna would not want to continually tell him about Yannis being married. He had heard enough about weddings from his Aunt Elena and had a suspicion that she would tell him about their visit to Athens yet again during the evening that he stayed there.

Stelios was surprised. His aunt did not mention her daughter's wedding, but was full of plans for her and Yiorgo to go to America.

'America? Whatever for? Surely it would be easier for Annita to come back to Crete to see you.'

Elena smiled happily. 'She's having a baby. She can't possibly travel all the way back here. Yiorgo and I have discussed it and we have decided we will go over there and live.'

'Live in America?' Stelios was astounded.

Elena nodded. 'Andreas is settled in Heraklion and Yiorgo is not getting any younger. We'd like to be with Annita and see our first grandchild grow up.'

'Suppose you don't like living there?'

'Then we will come back.' Elena shrugged. 'We will close up the cottage so if we did decide to return we would have somewhere to live and Yiorgo can leave his boat chained up at the jetty.'

'When are you leaving?'

'In about three weeks.'

'Three weeks!' Stelios was horrified. He would have nowhere to stay when he returned to Aghios Nikolaos before catching the bus to Heraklion.

'I'm surprised Andreas hasn't told you.'

Stelios did not mention that he avoided Andreas. 'I've been too busy to socialise. I had to concentrate on my exams.'

'I understand you have done well and will be going to University in Athens.' Elena sighed. 'I wish Annita and Elias had stayed there. I'm sure you could have lodged with them.'

Stelios nodded, grateful that his cousin was not going to be in Athens. He was not going to stay anywhere with small children.

1936 – 1937

Yannis was proud of his youngest son's accomplishment, but annoyed that Stelios continually excused himself from work on the farm pleading a need to study.

'You have to understand, Pappa, I have to keep my brain working. I started reading history late in my course and I have only just progressed to politics. I need to be fully conversant when I go to University. Mr Michelakis has said that I will probably end up as Minister of Finance in the government.'

'A government minister?' Yannis could not believe his ears.

Stelios nodded firmly. 'Mr Michelakis has assured me that there will be a position for me. I would obviously have to start as a junior minister. I may even have to stay at University for some more training, but that won't be a problem, will it?'

'When will you be starting to do some work and earn some money? No doubt your lodging in Athens will cost more than those in Heraklion and there's the cost of the ferry.'

'You'll not regret it, Pappa. In a few years I will be earning more money than you have ever imagined and I will be able to pay you back,' promised Stelios rashly.

Yannis checked the amount of money he had hidden in the cupboard. He would be able to give Stelios a sizeable sum to take to Athens, but he was beginning to be concerned. With his cousin Yiorgo going to America he was not sure if he would be asked to store the contraband goods as often and that would mean less money coming in. The income from the farm and being paid for the food that was sent to Spinalonga, meant he was certainly not short of money, but he wanted to have a reasonable amount in hand to give to Anna as her dowry when he had finally found a suitor for her; Yiorgo would have the farm so he was provided for.

There was also Yannis to be considered. When he had floated over from Spinalonga in his bath tub he had assured his father that he had no need of money as he had his pension from the government. That money had enabled most of them to set up small businesses, but what would happen if that was discontinued?

Stelios insisted that he needed to leave Plaka two weeks before he was due to start at the University in Athens. 'I have to walk to Aghios Nikolaos, then catch a bus to Heraklion the following day. I am not sure how frequently the ferries run so I may have to spend a few days in the town. Once I arrive in Athens I have to find accommodation.'

'Where will you stay in Aghios Nikolaos now your aunt and uncle are no longer there?' asked his father.

'There's a lodging house where I can spend the night. If I was unable to get a bed there it would not hurt me to sleep out in the open for once.'

'Will you be able to stay in your old lodgings in Heraklion?'

Stelios shook his head. 'I'll go to Andreas. I'm sure he will be able to provide me with a mattress.'

Satisfied, Yannis added a little more money to the amount he handed to his son. 'Look after it. That will have to pay for everything you need until you return next summer.'

'Thank you, Pappa.' Stelios had hoped his father might have provided enough money to cover the cost of his two year stay in Athens at the University so he would not need to return to Plaka the following year.

Andreas forced a smile of welcome on his face when he opened his door and saw Stelios standing there. Stelios placed his sack in the hallway and looked around.

'You won't mind me staying with you for a few days, will you? I have to find out when I can catch a ferry to Piraeus and until then I need a roof over my head and somewhere to sleep.'

'Of course you can stay.' Andreas was relieved that Stelios had no plans to stay with him for longer than a few days. 'I'll show you here you can store your belongings and sleep.'

Andreas led the way down the passage and opened a door at the far end. Inside the small, white-washed room was a bed and a chair.

Stelios looked at the room in disgust. 'Is this it?'

Andreas shrugged. 'It is the same as my room, except that I have a chest to store my clothes. You don't really need anything more as you will only be here for a few days.'

'I would have expected you to have had more comfort now you are a priest in Heraklion,' observed Stelios.

'I have a comfortable room where I can work or sit and relax. I only use my bedroom to sleep in.' Andreas shrugged. 'Provided I am warm in the winter I ask for nothing more.'

'So am I able to use your comfortable room when I am not in bed and asleep?'

'Of course. Leave your sack there and I'll show you.'

Andreas opened a door further along the passage and Stelios walked into the Spartan room. There were two chairs, one each side of the fireplace and four at a small table that had a rag rug beneath it. Shelves on one side of the room held Andreas's books and another had three icons and a cross above a small desk. There was no way Stelios would have described it as a comfortable room. The sooner he found out the time of the ferries and left the better he would like it.

'There is a tap in the kitchen and I keep a small fire going in there to heat the water for washing. I'll have to ask my housekeeper if she has a piece of mirror glass I can borrow so you can see to shave.' Andreas looked at his cousin's smooth chin and wondered if he was mature enough to shave regularly.

'I'd hate to put you to any trouble. I can always go to the barber and have a shave. Where do you go for your meals?'

'My housekeeper cooks a meal for me four days each week. The other days I have a light meal that I prepare myself.'

'Why don't you ask your housekeeper to cook every day?'

'She is always willing to cook extra food if I have a visitor. When I am alone I have no need of large meals. Eating for the sake of eating is not good for anyone.'

'Suppose you're hungry?'

Andreas smiled. 'If that were so I could always have some more bread and cheese, but it hasn't happened as yet.'

'What do you plan to have for a meal tonight – or has your housekeeper already catered for you?'

'I have salad vegetables, cheese, olives and some bread. With a glass of wine it is more than enough. You will be welcome to share it with me.'

Stelios nodded. 'Thank you,' he managed to say. He was already hungry, but it was obvious that he was not going to be offered anything to eat until the early evening. 'I thought I would check the ferry timetable and then go for a walk around the town,' he said airily. 'Catch up with my old friends.'

'Of course. My door is never locked so you are welcome to come and go as you please. If I am not here I can usually be found in the church, unless I have been called to one of my parishioners,' smiled Andreas. 'Unfortunately that usually seems to happen just as I am sitting down to a meal or have gone to sleep for the night. I hope we can have an undisturbed evening and you can tell me about your family in Plaka.'

'There is not a lot to tell about them,' replied Stelios sulkily. 'There would certainly not be enough news to occupy an evening.'

'We'll see,' replied Andreas urbanely. 'I am going to the church now. I usually spend some of the afternoon over there. If any of my parishioners wish to talk to me they know where they can find me. I will leave you to your own devices and see you later.'

Stelios shuddered as Andreas hung a large wooden cross around his neck, picked up his Bible and left the room. Thank goodness he would not have to live with his cousin for the next two years. The life Andreas was living was certainly not for him.

Stelios sat at the table with Andreas, a plate of green leaves with a tomato to provide a splash of colour was in front of both of them. There was a loaf of fresh bread and a large slab of cheese on the table and Stelios was pleased he had called in at the taverna at the ferry terminal if this was all he was going to be offered to eat.

'I have bought my ferry ticket,' he announced. 'I leave the day after tomorrow. How long does it take to travel from Piraeus up to Athens?'

'About an hour if I remember correctly.'

'I should be there by early afternoon, then,' frowned Stelios. 'I hope I will have no trouble finding lodgings.'

'I will give you the address of Elias's family. I am sure they would welcome you and would probably be able to help you with accommodation.' Andreas rose and opened a drawer in the desk and took out a sheet of paper. He wrote down the name and address of the family in Athens and handed it to Stelios.

Stelios folded the paper and put it into his pocket. He had no intention of contacting the family.

'I will need a decent bedroom with a table where I can sit and write. I will want to have a stove in my room in the winter as I am not prepared to sit and freeze whilst I study. I also want hot water available each morning to wash and once a week there must be sufficient for me to take a bath.' Stelios still examined his body each week for any tell-tale blemish or mark that could indicate the onset of disease. 'I need a cooked meal every evening and expect my laundry to be done for me.'

Andreas raised his eyebrows. He was tempted to say that Stelios should have stayed at home where he knew Anna would have catered for his needs. 'I have no doubt you will find somewhere that will suit your requirements. What subjects are you planning to study at the University?' asked Andreas.

He had asked after the family at Plaka and Stelios had brushed his questions aside, saying both his parents were as well as could be expected, Yiorgo was working hard on the farm and Anna was running the house along with looking after her mother and her sister's children.

'Primarily Mathematics and Politics,' answered Stelios smugly. 'I have been told that I have a mathematical brain. My tutor at High School has assured me that when I have completed my studies I will have no problem entering the finance department of the government.'

Andreas nodded. 'You had no desire to go into history? I remember you enjoyed looking for pottery with Yannis and hearing his stories about the history of Crete.'

Stelios frowned. He never talked about Yannis. 'That was just a childish hobby,' he waved his hands airily. 'There are far more important subjects to study.'

'Subjects should not always be studied according to their importance. They should also be studied for pleasure.'

'I enjoy politics and mathematics,' replied Stelios sulkily. 'It takes a good brain to understand the complexities of finance and explain details to others.'

'I'm sure you're right, but I feel you should also have something else to turn your attention to as a form of relaxation.'

Stelios lifted his glass of wine. 'Are you suggesting I should spend hours reading the Bible?'

'Only if the Bible provides you with comfort and interest. There are many other books available at the libraries, history, politics, travelogues, biographies. I would suggest you look there and see if you can find something you would care to know more about.'

'Of course I will be visiting the library.'

'Whilst you are here you are also welcome to read any of my books, but please ensure you leave them with me.'

Stelios rose and looked at the books on the shelf. They all dealt with Theology. He shook his head. 'I don't think there is anything there that would appeal to me.'

Andreas smiled to himself. He had not expected Stelios to take him up on his offer. Andreas mopped his lips with a cloth from his pocket. 'When you have eaten sufficient I will clear the table and wash up the dishes.'

'Why don't you leave the dishes for your housekeeper?'

'There are occasions when that is necessary if I am called away. I try not to make a habit of taking advantage of her good nature and I prefer to come into a clean and tidy kitchen in the morning.'

Stelios poured himself another glass of wine and sat back in his chair. 'I have had plenty to eat, thank you, Andreas.'

He made no attempt to help his cousin take the plates into the kitchen area. By the time Andreas returned Stelios had poured himself yet another glass of wine and looked at the almost empty bottle ruefully.

'I presume you have some more in your cellar?'

'One bottle usually lasts me a few days. I am not opening another tonight as I feel certain you have had sufficient to drink for one evening.'

'How do you know if I have had sufficient?' Stelios rounded on him angrily.

'Then I will say I "consider" you have had sufficient. Any more tonight and you will be regretting it in the morning.'

'I'm going to bed,' announced Stelios angrily. 'Do you have a lamp I can take?'

'Certainly, but please ensure you put it out before you go to sleep. Oil is a precious commodity and should not be wasted. Sleep well.'

Stelios nodded curtly. There would have been no harm in Andreas opening another bottle of wine.

Stelios did not enjoy the ferry crossing to Piraeus. The sea was calm so the boat did not pitch and roll as his uncle's fishing boat often did in the slightest swell, but knowing he was miles from land made him uneasy and nervous. As the ferry negotiated the entrance into the harbour and moved slowly to the docking area he drew a breath of relief.

He had tied the mouth of his sack securely with string, leaving a loop that he kept slipped over his wrist. Most of the money his father had given him was in a pocket of the trousers that were packed in there amongst his other clothes and meagre possessions. He did not want to risk walking away and leaving the sack behind.

Despite the early hour of the morning the dock was a hive of activity. There was another ferry readying itself for departure and further along were much larger boats and queues of people waiting to board them. He wondered idly where they were going. He followed his fellow travellers towards the exit, stepping carefully over coils of rope and avoiding puddles of sea water.

There were three cars waiting at the side of the road and Stelios looked at them curiously. He had seen an occasional car in Aghios Nikolaos and there had been more in Heraklion. A couple went over to one and spoke to the driver. The man loaded their luggage into a compartment at the rear and they climbed inside.

A group of workmen stood on the side of the road, smoking and talking. They looked weary and Stelios thought they had probably been working during the night at the docks. Dubiously he joined them and nodded a greeting.

'I understand I can catch a bus up to Athens? Am I waiting in the right place?'

The man nearest to him nodded. 'Whereabouts do you want?'

'The centre I imagine.'

'It will take you as far as the terminal if that's any good.'

'How will I know when I'm there?'

The man gave Stelios a withering look. 'The driver and ticket collector will get off, If you're still sitting there they'll soon tell you to leave.'

'Is the terminus close to the University?' Stelios did not want to find he had travelled past his destination.

'It will be near enough for you.' The man spat the end of his cigarette onto the ground. 'You could take a taxi. There's one waiting.'

Stelios shook his head. 'I'm not in a rush.' He was not going to admit that he had never ridden in a car and was not sure if he would have enough money in his pocket to pay the fare. 'I understand the bus takes about an hour. I can always ask for directions from the terminal.'

The man lit another cigarette and turned away. He was tired and had no wish to enter into a prolonged conversation with the young man.

Stelios looked out of the grimy window of the bus as it travelled up the road towards the centre of Athens. Once the dock area had been left behind there was some open countryside for a while and then the outskirts of the city came into view and some of the passengers alighted. Stelios hesitated, there were a number of men still on the bus and he could not believe that such a poor looking area could be the centre of the city. The bus continued and entered an area that was far busier. Cars and lorries vied for space on the road along with donkeys and carts, whilst small houses jostled for space between the much larger buildings. Stelios craned his neck to get a better view of the Parthenon when it came into view, but within minutes the bus had turned a corner and he could no longer see it. The bus stopped again and only a few men were left sitting on the wooden seats, one man leaning against the window and snoring audibly.

Stelios felt a frisson of excitement. He was actually in Athens; the capital of Greece. This was where he would make a name for himself as the minister of finance and the city would become rich due to him. He was jolted from his daydream by the ticket collector calling out that they were at the terminus and Stelios realised that his fellow travellers had all left the bus.

He gathered his sack to him and muttered 'Sorry' as he stepped out onto the road and the driver locked the door behind him. Uncertain where he should go he turned back to ask for directions, but the driver and his companion were disappearing into a small wooden hut.

Stelios shrugged and placed his sack over his shoulder. He would go into the first taverna he saw; they were bound to be able to help him.

It took him some minutes before he found a sign above a window and pushed open the door. The interior had bare wooden tables and chairs, but looked clean and respectable. He nodded to the man behind the counter and took a seat.

'What do you want?' called the man, not making a move towards him.

Stelios rose, taking his sack with him, and approached the counter. 'Am I able to get something to eat, please?'

The man nodded. 'What do you want?'

Stelios wondered if the man was either deaf or stupid. 'Do you have some keftedes or moussaka?'

'What do you want?' the man repeated.

'Keftedes and salad, with a glass of wine, please.'

'Take a seat.'

Stelios sighed in relief. The man was neither deaf nor stupid. He just expected his customers to know what they wanted to eat when they arrived.

When his meal arrived Stelios ate hungrily. His last meal had been two evenings ago with Andreas. His cousin had left the house when he rose in the morning and there was no sign of the housekeeper or any food left out for him. When he reached the ferry terminal he had shown his ticket and boarded immediately, unsure how long he would have before it sailed. There was no food available on board and he had not risked visiting the taverna down at the port.

He went up to the counter to pay his bill. 'Thank you. I enjoyed that.' He did not add that the amount he was charged was double the amount he would have paid in Heraklion. If all the prices in Athens were more expensive he would have to be very careful with his money.

'Would you be able to help me?' he asked. 'Which way is the University from here?'

'Other side of the square. Take the main road, Stadhiou Street and walk down until you see the turn marked Korai Street. Go down there to the end and the University is across the road.'

Having thanked the man Stelios hurried away; he wanted to reach the University as soon as possible, hoping there would be someone available who could give him a list of suitable accommodation. He also needed to find somewhere to spend the night.

Stadhiou Street seemed to go on forever and Stelios was becoming worried that he had missed the turning. He was about to retrace his steps when he spied the name of Korai Street high up on a building. With a sigh of relief he crossed the road and hurried towards the large building he could see in front of him.

It took him some minutes to cross the road to reach the University as the traffic seemed unending. There were so many black cars with "taxi" written on the side. They all seemed to have an occupant along with the driver and he decided that it could not be very expensive to travel like that if so many people used them.

Taking advantage of a lull in the traffic he ran across the road and up the steps to the University, almost falling through the door as he pushed it open. He stood in the vestibule regaining his breath and looked for a suitable door on which to knock. Some had a man's name; others had "Admissions", "Information", "Registration" and finally he saw "Enquiries".

Stelios knocked tentatively. There was no reply and he tried the door cautiously. It opened at his touch and a man looked up.

'How can I help you?'

'I've just arrived from Crete. I'm due to start attending the University at the beginning of term and I was hoping you might have a list of lodgings available.'

The man passed a sheet of paper over to Stelios. 'I don't know if any of these places have been taken. Where are you staying at the moment?'

Stelios shrugged. 'Nowhere yet. I only arrived this afternoon. I was hoping you could help me.'

The man smiled benignly. 'I would suggest you go back to Plaka...'

'Plaka!' Stelios caught his breath.

'Yes, the Plaka area just below the Acropolis. There are a number of tavernas there that let rooms.'

'Oh!' Stelios felt foolish at assuming the man had told him to return to Crete. 'How do I get there?'

'It's not that far from here. Continue down the road from here until you come to Syntagma Square. Walk to the end of the square and cross over the road. You will then be in the Plaka district.'

Stelios entered the Plaka area, there was no motorised traffic in the narrow streets and he walked along, scanning the houses and small shops for one that advertised itself as a taverna. The first one he came to appeared full of men, drinking, smoking, playing backgammon, dice or card games. He hesitated in the doorway and then decided he would continue further down the road and see if he could find a quieter establishment.

He came to a small square which appeared to be residential and walked on down the narrow road, wondering if he had made a wise decision in ignoring the taverna he had looked in earlier. It was becoming late in the afternoon and he needed to find somewhere soon. He lowered his sack to the ground. The string from his sack had chaffed his wrist and he rubbed at it whilst he stood and looked at the buildings on both sides of the road. He lifted his sack onto his shoulder again and continued down the hill. There was nowhere that looked like a taverna and he wondered if the man at the University had told him correctly or just wanted to get rid of him.

Stelios entered a small shop that appeared to sell groceries and approached the man at the counter.

'I've been told there are tavernas in this area that have rooms to let. Are you able to direct me to them, please?'

'You need the square up the hill. There are plenty up there.'

'I thought they were private houses.'

'Some are; others are tavernas.'

Stelios made his way back up the hill, cursing himself for not investigating the buildings in the square during his walk down. He skirted the patch of grass that was surrounded by small bushes, looking at the windows until he saw a notice that said "TAVERNA – rooms to let" and pushed open the door thankfully.

It was hot and stuffy inside, but there were far less occupants. Four men were playing cards and an elderly couple were playing backgammon, three men sat at a table at the side deep in discussion. Feeling hopeful Stelios approached the counter.

'Would you have a room to let, please?'

'How long do you want it for?'

'I'm not sure, maybe two nights.'

'Money in advance.'

'I'd like to see the room first, please.'

The owner shrugged and called to a woman who was in the kitchen. She emerged, wiping her hands on her apron and looked at Stelios.

'Come with me.' She led the way through the kitchen and out of a side door that exited into a small courtyard. She opened a door on the far side and began to mount the stairs. By the time they reached the top of the flight she was puffing with the exertion and holding her chest. Three of the doors had a notice on them declaring they were occupied. She opened a fourth door and stood back for Stelios to enter.

It appeared clean, with just a mattress on the floor and a washstand in the corner that held a bowl and jug with a mirror above. A small oil lamp sat at the side along with a box of matches. It would do, he decided.

'How much?' he asked.

She seemed to consider his request. 'Six drachmas a night.'

'Does that include some hot water in the morning?'

'That's an extra drachma.'

Stelios sighed. At this rate the money his father had given him would not last around to the summer and he did not want to have to return to Crete and beg him for more.

'I'll take it,' he said reluctantly.

The woman took the notice from behind the door and hung it outside, declaring that room was also occupied and held out her hand. 'Money in advance.'

Stelios removed seven drachmas from his pocket and handed it to her.

'I thought you wanted two nights?'

'I'm looking for permanent accommodation tomorrow. If I find something suitable I will be leaving then.'

The woman frowned. If she had known he might only stay the one night she would have increased the price. 'Come down when you're ready. Meals are extra.'

Stelios nodded and waited until the woman had shut the door behind her before placing his sack on the floor. He sat down on the bed and began to study the list of accommodation that had been given him at the University. There were a number of addresses in Plaka and he wondered if it would be too late to call on any of them.

He untied the neck of his sack and rummaged inside until he found his trousers with the money in the pocket. He would take that out with him, rather than leave it in the sack in his room. He rolled the notes together firmly, placed them inside a sock and pushed them as far down in his trouser pocket as possible. He re-tied the mouth of the sack and left it lying beneath the blanket on the mattress. There was a small amount of cold water in the jug and Stelios wet his hands and rubbed them across his face, peering into the mirror, hoping he had removed the dust and dirt that had accumulated during the day.

Returning to the taverna he approached the owner again. 'I don't know this area and I was wondering if you could help me. I will be attending the University and have been given a list of people who let rooms. Can you direct me to any of these addresses, please?'

The man ran his finger down the list. 'That's Mr Radopolous over there.' He waved his hand towards the three men. 'You could ask him.'

'He won't mind me interrupting him?'

'How would I know?'

Stelios approached the men tentatively. 'Excuse me; I believe one of you is Mr Radopolous?'

A white haired man looked up at him. 'That's me. What can I do for you?'

'I'm looking for accommodation whilst I attend University. Your name is on the list they have given me.'

Mr Radopolous looked at his nearly full glass of wine and sighed. It would be foolish to refuse the opportunity to let their vacant room, but it would be equally foolish to leave his glass of wine. The young man looked a little dishevelled and weary, but spoke decently and was obviously intelligent to have gained a place at the University.

'Come and see me tomorrow morning. My house is only just down the road.'

'Thank you, sir.'

Stelios made for the door. He would find the man's address and if he was fortunate he would also be able to find the two other addresses in the vicinity that were on the list. When he did so one looked drab and dirty, the windows unwashed, the front door needed repainting and there were three children playing noisily outside. Mentally he crossed it off his list.

The second looked clean and well-tended and he knocked on the door. A man in his shirtsleeves answered him. Stelios repeated his request for accommodation and the man shook his head.

'You should have come last week. Our room is taken.'

Feeling despondent Stelios continued to walk through the narrow streets. He saw another taverna where a man was cooking octopus on an outside grill. The smell was permeating the air around and making Stelios feel hungry again. He decided to step inside and buy a meal there.

The octopus was succulent and Stelios mopped his plate with the bread and ordered a second glass of wine, suddenly heedless of the cost. Once he was established in some lodgings he could always make do with some bread and cheese and not go out to expensive tavernas. That way he would save money. He had been used to only having some bread as a mid-day snack, along with a tomato and onion or some olives when he had lived on the farm at Plaka.

As darkness fell he walked slowly along various small streets where oil lamps could be seen flickering in the windows until he finally reached the square and entered the taverna where he planned to spend the night. The same customers were there and had been joined by a few more who were eating from steaming bowls. Despite having eaten only a short while earlier the cooking smelled good and he wondered if he had been foolish to pay the price demanded for octopus.

He walked through the kitchen and up the stairs to his room, noting that it looked exactly as he had left it and no one appeared to have investigated the contents of his sack. He removed his boots, jacket and trousers, transferred the sock of money into his shirt pocket and lay down to sleep.

Stelios was awoken by a knock on the door and a girl entered carrying a jug of hot water. She nodded to him and placed the jug on the wash stand, returned to the doorway and came back with another jug of cold water, removing the one that was nearly empty.

As soon as she left Stelios checked the pocket in his shirt, breathing a sigh of relief when he felt the sock of money still in there. It was only just light and he continued to lie on the mattress, wondering what time would be suitable to call on Mr Radopolous. He did not want to drag the man out of bed, but he did not want another student to arrive before him and accept the room.

Taking advantage of the hot water he washed thoroughly and scraped his razor across his chin and down his throat removing the previous two days' growth of coarse hair. He transferred the sock of money to his trouser pocket, left his sack lying on his mattress as before and walked down to the taverna.

Once outside Stelios squinted up at the sun; it was later than he had realised. Due to the narrowness of the streets and the buildings being clustered together it took longer for the sunlight to penetrate than when you lived in the country and had nothing to obstruct the rays of the sun. He had not noticed this when he was in Heraklion, but the taverna where he had lived was in quite a wide street.

Everywhere seemed far busier than it had done the previous evening, and he found himself dodging carts as they drew up to unload their goods to a waiting shop keeper, or having to step out of the path of women carrying large baskets, a small child usually clutching at their skirt.

He found Mr Radopolous's address without difficulty and knocked on the door, waiting anxiously for the man to answer. He hoped he had arrived before the man went out for the day. The door opened wide enough to allow Mr Radopolous to look out. He looked puzzled as he eyed Stelios.

'Do I know you? Your face is familiar. Were you in my class last year?'

Stelios shook his head. 'I spoke to you last night, sir, about some lodgings whilst I'm at University. You said to come around today to see you.'

'What subjects are you taking?' Mr Radopolous did not want a boy staying who would be in his history class. He might be expected to help him with his homework.

'Mathematics, Book Keeping and Accountancy.'

'You'd best come in and speak to my wife.' Mr Radopolous opened the door wider.

'Thank you.' Stelios wiped his shoes assiduously on the doormat and followed the man through to the living room. He was relieved to see that it held more comfort than Andreas's. There was a cloth on the table and cushions on the chairs, china and glass ware sat on an open dresser and unlit oil lamps stood around. A plump woman sat in a chair shelling beans and she looked up as her husband ushered Stelios inside.

'This young man will be a student at the High School and he's asking if we have a room we could rent to him.'

She studied Stelios. He looked clean and presentable and Stelios was pleased he had scraped his razor over his chin that morning.

'Thranassis left at the end of last term. He has gone to Thessaloniki I understand so his room would be vacant.'

'May I see it?' asked Stelios. He did not want to find he was being allocated a room as sparse as he currently occupied or with just the minimum of necessities that his cousin Andreas seemed to find acceptable

'Before I walk up the stairs with you I need to know your requirements. No point in making the effort in vain.'

Stelios drew a breath. He thought his requirements were quite reasonable. 'I need a room with a bed, table and chair, a book shelf and a trunk to store my clothes. During the winter I would like to have a stove up there, and, of course, an oil lamp. I would also like a cooked meal each day and my washing done.'

'I don't do washing,' stated Tatiane positively. 'There's a laundry at the end of the road. You can take it to them. If you expect me to provide you with a meal each day it will be four drachmas extra each week. I don't do refunds if you don't turn up to eat it. The food will have been bought so you have to pay for it.'

'And a stove and lamp in my room during the winter?' asked Stelios anxiously.

'That will be an extra drachma. I don't expect you to pay for the weeks you are not here if you return to your family in the holidays, but if you want me to keep your room free you have to pay me a week in advance before you leave.'

'And the price of the room?' Stelios had been adding up the drachmas in his head, knowing he had plenty of money in his pocket at present, but did not want to find he had run out of funds before the end of the term.

'With the meals included it will be twenty one drachmas a week, with an increase of a drachma when you need the heat and light. No refunds if you stay out all night.' Tatiane regarded him sternly.

'I have no intention of staying out all night. I am at the University to work,' Stelios assured her.

'If you return late please come in quietly. We would not wish to be disturbed if we are asleep.'

Stelios nodded. 'I would make as little noise a possible.'

'Then I'll show you the room.' Tatiane shuffled her feet into her clogs and led the way up the stairs to a door. She pushed it open. 'Just be careful when you come out that you don't fall down the stairs.'

Stelios nodded and looked around the room. It was ideal. Two bookshelves were on one wall and opposite was a bed with two crocheted blankets neatly folded at the bottom. A rag rug was by the side to place your feet on when you first got up and there was another rug beneath the table that was below the window. In the corner was a wooden trunk that would be more than sufficient for his clothes.

'Is there somewhere I can wash each day and have a bath once a week?'

'You can use the scullery. There's a tin bath on the wall and you can heat the water on the fire that I keep alight in there.'

'I think it would suit me very well. I would like to take it immediately and bring my belongings later today if that is convenient for you.'

'Where are you staying at present?' Tatiane eyed him suspiciously. He certainly did not look as if he had slept in a doorway.

'At the taverna where I spoke to your husband last night.'

'Where have you come from?' asked Tatiane curiously.

'My family are in Aghios Nikolaos, Crete.'

'I would like the address of your father.'

'Is that necessary?'

Tatiane nodded. 'If you disappear back to Aghios Nikolaos and decide not to return I need to know. Also if you start to make excuses about paying me the rent I will approach your father.'

'I assure you that neither eventuality will occur. I think it would be better if I gave you my cousin's address; he is Father Andreas. He took over the parish from Father Minos in Heraklion and it would be far easier to contact him. I will certainly pay my rent until Christmas. I may decide not to return to Crete for the holiday. In that case I will then pay my rent until Easter.'

Tatiane smiled to herself. She had raised the price of the room by two drachmas and the meals by a drachma, also adding an extra drachma for heating and light during the winter. She would certainly be able to make some money from this young man who appeared willing to pay whatever she asked. She must remember to tell Abraham at the laundry that he should charge extra if her lodger wanted his shirts ironed.

'When may I move in?' asked Stelios eagerly.

Tatiane shrugged. 'Whenever it suits you. Just make sure you have the money to pay me when you arrive.'

'I certainly will,' promised Stelios. 'I should be back within the hour.'

Stelios returned to the taverna to collect his sack with a feeling of satisfaction. The lodgings were ideal for his needs and the family were obviously respectable.

Stelios counted out the money he had hidden in his sock. He had paid Tatiane five hundred drachmas to rent his room until Easter. It was a few drachmas short due to not having to pay for heating or an oil lamp until the weather was cooler. He had assured her he would pay the extra for each week he needed the facilities and Tatiane had not argued. He calculated he would need at least another four hundred drachmas to enable him to stay until the beginning of the summer holidays when he would be forced to return to Plaka and ask his father for a further sum of money to cover his expenses for the following year at University and explain that his lodgings were costing two drachmas each week more than his father estimated. It did not occur to him to ask how his father was able to hand over so much money to him each year.

He put money aside for his bus fare to Piraeus and his ferry ticket. Prudently he placed another fifty drachmas to one side, knowing that should be more than enough to cover his travelling expenses, but he added another fifty drachmas to cover any emergencies.

He was left with nine hundred and forty four drachmas in his pocket, giving him twenty drachmas a week to spend on cigarettes and entertainment as he pleased. He would certainly not pay for expensive books, but use the library, even if it meant spending a small sum to become a member. When he socialised he would insist that he paid for his own wine; that way he would not be expected to treat his companions. If he participated in a card game he would ensure that he lost no more than five drachmas in an evening.

Stelios spent the following week finding his way around Athens and the Plaka area intent on discovering the shortest route to the University. He was impressed by the Parthenon and spent time admiring the craftsmanship of the original builders. He wished Lord Elgin, the English nobleman, had not removed so many of the sculptures so he could have viewed it as it was intended to look when first completed. He had no hesitation in visiting the museum, knowing there would be no one in Athens who would mistake him for his brother. The black and red pottery on show was so different from the broken pieces he and Yannis had found that he felt decidedly curious, and made a mental note to visit the library and see if he could find a book that would give him the answer.

He climbed to the top of Mount Lycabbetos and was amazed at the size of the urban sprawl he could see spread out before him. He had thought he had explored the whole of the city, but now realised he had visited only the centre of Athens.

That evening over their meal he listed the places he had visited and asked Mr Radopolous if there were other areas of interest.

Mr Radopolous was in his element. 'All of Athens is of interest. Have you seen the Tower of the Winds?'

Stelios nodded. 'I walked past when I went up to the Parthenon.'

'You went up by the main road? You should have walked through the Agora and looked at the remains of the buildings that once stood there. It was the original market place for the city when the Romans were here. At that time you could buy anything you wanted from the market; spices, silk, jewellery; anything at all. The offices for the bankers, merchants and ship owners were situated there, along with an office for the inspectors who scrutinized that the measures for salt and oil were correct and if you wanted someone to speak on your behalf at court that was the place to find a lawyer. It would take most of a day for you to see everything and appreciate the amount of business that was carried on there.'

'I'll definitely go there tomorrow' promised Stelios.

'When you reach the end of the Stoa you will come out half way up the Acropolis. It is only a short walk up to the Parthenon, but if you have already been there you may prefer to go down the hill and up the other side. It is known as the Hill of Philopappos and his monument is on the summit. From there you can walk back down towards the town taking pathways and it is like walking through countryside. You will eventually reach the Pnyx and be able to walk back to the Agora. I have done the walk many times with students and it is most enjoyable.'

Stelios listened avidly, but hoped Mr Radopolous was not going to suggest he would accompany him. He had an idea that wherever there were the remains of a monument, however insignificant, he would receive a lecture on its history and construction.

'I'll certainly visit the places you have suggested, but I might leave the hill walks until it is a little cooler. It could be sensible to visit the library first and read up on the history so I know exactly what I am looking at.'

Mr Radopolous smiled in approval at the young man. Maybe he should have been studying history after all. They could have had some interesting and informative discussions.

1938

Mr and Mrs Radopolous had been quite happy for Stelios to stay with them over Christmas. They were both impressed by the young man; he was polite, no trouble at all, he never arrived home late or the worse for drink and spent much of his time in his room studying.

'We will go to church on Christmas morning,' announced Tatiane. 'We can have our meal during the afternoon. If you wanted to invite any of your friends to come around for a drink in the evening I'm sure my husband would not object on this occasion.'

'That's very kind of you,' Stelios assured her. 'I think my friends will all be with their own families at that time, but I can ask them.'

'I don't want to think of you spending all your time alone upstairs in your room studying. No doubt some of our friends and neighbours will call and we will invite them in. I'm sure they would enjoy meeting you.'

Stelios smiled and nodded. He had no desire to spend time making polite conversation to total strangers.

'It's such a shame you cannot go home and spend the holiday with your own family. I'm sure they will miss you.'

'They understand that having to travel so far at this time of the year is not always easy. I am not a good sailor and have a horror of being caught out at sea in a storm. I would far rather wait until the summer months to make the journey.'

Tatiane shuddered. 'It doesn't bear thinking about. I have never taken a boat trip, but there really isn't anywhere that I want to go.'

'You cannot imagine how cold it would be if it was raining and a strong wind blowing,' added Stelios.

'Like today,' sighed Tatiane. 'I was very wet and cold when I returned from the shops.'

'You should have asked me this morning to bring you in any shopping you needed. It would have been no trouble. I walk past the shops. It's most unpleasant out today, but at least I knew that once I was home I could get warm and dry.'

Tatiane smiled in appreciation of his words. He thought of their house as his home. He was just the kind of young man she would have loved to have had as a son.

'That's very thoughtful of you, Stelios.'

'I really mean it. Any time that the weather is bad I will happily go shopping for you. You will only have to give me your list.' If Tatiane expected him to do her shopping he could broach her regarding having a reduction in his rent.

Tatiane took Stelios at his word as the weather turned colder and he regretted his offer. Sometimes she only wanted a single item, at other times presented him with a long list, but always gave him the money before he left the house. He would place the items she had asked for on the table and leave the change beside it. Tatiane never checked the cost, simply placing the money into the pot where she kept her housekeeping money.

Tatiane had never offered him any form of remuneration for his efforts and Stelios decided to make a small experiment. He placed her change on the table, but deliberately left a five drachma note in his pocket. Tatiane did not appear to notice and Stelios went up to his room, his excuse ready if she challenged him at a later date.

It became a habit for Stelios to hold back a couple of drachmas when Tatiane gave him a list. He would keep the money in a separate pocket in his trousers and if she thought to ask him for the missing change he would pretend he had not realised and apologise. He looked upon the drachmas that he pocketed as due to him.

He still made his regular visits to the library, returning with books under his arm. Mr Radopolous smiled at him.

'Still studying hard, I see. What have you brought back this time?' He helped himself to a book that Stelios had placed in a pile on the chair whilst he removed his coat. 'The Acropolis.' He nodded. 'I'm pleased to see you have developed such a liking for history.'

'It's the measurements and construction that interests me. I often wish I had studied to become a draughtsman, rather than a mathematician.'

'No reason why you should not do a couple more years at the University and become proficient. Your knowledge of mathematics would be beneficial.' He sighed. 'Unfortunately we do not build like that anymore. You would be more likely to be asked to construct an office block or apartments than a temple.'

Stelios mulled over the words from Mr Radopolous. A further two years at University was attractive. He would not have to look for any work. He might speak to his father when he returned to Plaka in the summer and say he wished to continue with his education.

'We all have our regrets,' continued Mr Radopolous. 'I love history, but I often wish I had studied archaeology. When I see the artefacts in the museum I wish I could be accredited with the finds. Have you been to Knossos?'

Stelios nodded. 'It was very interesting.'

'Tell me about it,' begged Mr Radopolous. 'I have read descriptions and seen pictures, but I am never likely to have the opportunity to visit and see the site for myself.'

Stelios obliged, describing the extent of the site, the staircase with the shields, the plaster frescoes, and the chambers that were attributed to the king and queen. Almost an hour later Stelios sat back. He could remember nothing more that might be of interest to the teacher.

Mr Radopolous nodded his head in appreciation. 'I can certainly visualise the area now. I am thinking of arranging a visit to Delphi with my students after Easter. The Germans are excavating there and it could bring the history of the site to life for my pupils. Would you care to be included?'

Stelios hesitated. He was not sure how far away Delphi was from Athens. 'How long would we be gone?'

'Three days. We can travel to the nearest town by bus and stay in the taverna there for the night. That will give us a whole day to look at the site and the discoveries that have been made before we catch the bus back to Athens the following day. It would be during the holidays so you would not miss any schooling.'

'How much will it cost?' asked Stelios, conscious of the fact that the money he had left hidden in his sock had to last until he had visited his father in Plaka. Now the weather had improved Tatiane no longer asked him to go shopping on her behalf, although on two occasions he had taken a five drachma note from her pot when he thought she would not notice and bought himself a stock of cigarettes.

'No more than forty drachmas. The taverna, even including a meal, should not be more than ten drachmas, twelve at the most for a night.'

'I think I can manage that.'

Mr Radopolous beamed at him. 'I am sure you will enjoy the experience.'

Stelios found the students that accompanied him and Mr Radopolous were easy to talk with during the bus journey. They were excited; apart from visiting the Parthenon and other sites in Athens, this was the first time they had made an excursion into the countryside to see somewhere different.

They arrived at the small taverna early in the afternoon and Stelios looked at it in dismay.

'Will they have enough rooms for all of us?' he asked Mr Radopolous.

'We will all be in one big room. The other rooms have been taken by the archaeologists.'

'Is there nowhere else around here that we could stay?' Stelios did not relish having to share a room with six other young men and Mr Radopolous.

Mr Radopolous shrugged. 'It is only for a couple of nights.' He raised his voice. 'Follow me, boys and when we have deposited our luggage we will return down here for a drink. I will then tell you about the site and I will expect all of you to be able to describe any area I ask you about and also give me your impressions when we gather here tomorrow evening.'

Stelios hoped he was not included in that statement as he did not doubt that the other boys would know far more about Delphi than he, even after borrowing a book from the library a couple of weeks earlier. He listened carefully as Mr Radopolous gave an impromptu lecture on the original reason for building the site and the faith everyone had in the Delphic Oracle.

'Delphi was considered to be the Omphalos, the naval of the world, and there was a settlement here in Neolithic times. Delphi became the spiritual centre of the Greek world and as the reputation of the Oracle grew influential people from all across Greece would come here to consult the Pythia, asking questions about raising taxes to finance a war or would the war they were embroiled in have a successful outcome for the Athenians. The ordinary citizens would bring offerings and ask if a family member would be cured of an illness and young people who considered themselves in love would come and hope to be told they would soon be married to the partner of their choice. Even farmers would come and ask if their harvest would be fruitful that year, along with those women who were barren and desperately wished to have a child.'

Stelios listened sceptically. The reason people had visited and worshipped here was no different from going to church today. People always wanted something. He knew he was guilty of praying that he would be able to go to Aghios Nikolaos, then to Heraklion and gaining a scholarship. His current prayers were for good examination results so his father would not object to paying for him to return to the city and continue his studies.

Mr Radopolous led the way up the hill and through the gateway. There he stopped. 'We are now on the Sacred Way. Before us is the Temple of Apollo. Sadly much of the temple is in a ruinous state, but work is taking place to restore its previous grandeur. Due to the importance of Delphi gifts were brought to the city from various parts of Greece and each area built their own treasury in which to store them. We can see these, although little but their foundations remains.

In front of the remains of each building Mr Radopolous stood with the students around him and described in detail the date of the original construction and its purpose. Stelios was bored. He had expected to see buildings similar to the Parthenon or a restored palace as there was at Knossos. The low walls that delineated the buildings meant little to him and he wished he had not agreed to join their expedition. He wandered a short distance away, and inspected the stone foundations. They were no different from the ones he had looked at previously.

Stelios waited until Mr Radopolous finished talking and began to walk on again. 'Excuse me, sir, but would you object to me going off on my own and looking at the site? My historical knowledge is not good enough to understand all the information you are imparting, but I would enjoy viewing more of the architecture where it is still visible.'

Mr Radopolous looked concerned. 'It is a very large site. If you stray from the pathways you could very well become lost.'

'I will make sure that I keep to the paths and not wander up into the woods. I am sure I will be able to see you and know where to return.'

Without waiting to hear Mr Radopolous reply Stelios walked away rapidly. He would find a quiet spot and sit down and have a cigarette. He reached what appeared to be the end of the Sacred Way and a flight of steps rose up before him. His curiosity piqued he began to ascend, the foliage that pressed around him probably hiding him from the sight of Mr Radopolous and the students.

He was surprised and gratified to find that on reaching the top of the steps an amphitheatre lay before him. He sat on a block of marble and savoured his cigarette. It had been worth the climb; this was of far more interest to him. He admired the construction of the semi-circle of tiered stone seats. They would have given an unobstructed view of the stage area and ample knee room.

Rising to his feet he looked back the way he had come and was surprised to have a view of the sanctuary. If the trees and bushes were removed the whole of the site would be revealed from this vantage point. Slowly he climbed down to the floor of the theatre, counting the tiers of marble seats, until he reached the ground. From there it looked even larger than it had from above and he guessed that the remains of the small rooms he could see had been for the actors and musicians.

Taking a pathway between the buildings he could see that statues had once stood on a plinth and he wondered what had happened to them. Despite looking at the ground he could see no signs of debris that would indicate they had fallen and disintegrated over the years. The path began to wind upwards and he followed it, finally arriving at the stadium where the Pythian Games had been held. Once again he counted the marble seats. At a conservative estimate at least five thousand spectators could have been accommodated. Much as he admired the construction he could not imagine why the population would make the arduous climb and be interested to sit and watch men running from one end to the other until they were exhausted or wrestling each other to the ground.

There were a number of small paths leading further up the

hillside and Stelios disregarded Mr Radopolous's advice and began to push his way through the overhanging branches until he finally met an impenetrable barrier of foliage. Reluctantly he turned back. There was obviously nothing more to be seen further up the hill.

Stelios returned to the theatre and gazed again out across the extensive site. He noticed there were a group of men at the far side and wondered if they were another group of students. He watched them for some minutes, but was unable to discern their activities. He decided to return to the Sacred Way. It was unlikely that Mr Radopolous had finished explaining the history of the Temple of Apollo to the other boys and he would skirt around the temple and see what lay beyond on the far side.

He was disappointed once again to see there were only low walls marking out where buildings once stood and there was no clue to their original usage. He walked lower down and came upon the group of men he had seen earlier. Some of them were scraping over the top soil with trowels, whilst others were removing bushes and dumping them further away.

A young man looked up and smiled at him. 'Good morning. You have come to work?'

Stelios returned the greeting and shook his head. 'I am with a group of students visiting the site.'

'Please, more slowly.'

Stelios repeated his sentence and the man nodded. 'It is interesting. Yes?'

'Very, but I wish more of the buildings were intact.'

'Please, what is "intact"?'

Stelios realised the young man was one of the German archaeologists. 'Intact is complete.'

'Ah, yes; I understand. That would be good to find. We have made many other good finds, but they are not so big.'

'You speak very good Greek,' observed Stelios.

The man smiled with pleasure. 'I try. My father teaches me.

He is in charge of the work. I am Herman, his son.' A soil stained hand was extended to Stelios and he felt compelled to shake it.

'I am Stelios.'

'You are archaeologist?'

Stelios shook his head. 'No. I am interested, but I prefer architecture.'

'What work do you do?'

'I am at University.'

'To study architecture?'

'No, mathematics and politics.'

'Politics. That is interesting. I would like to know more about the Greek politics.' Herman rose to his feet. 'You can tell me.'

Stelios frowned. 'What do you wish to know?'

'How your government makes decisions; why you have a King as the head of your country. Does he make the laws?'

Stelios realised he did not really know the answers to Herman's questions. 'We have always had a King, but the government makes the laws,' he answered evasively.

'So you do not need a King? The government could make all the laws without him.'

'I suppose so.'

'So why do you not get rid of this King?'

Stelios shrugged. 'We have always had a King,' he repeated. 'I come from Crete so we have little to do with him.'

'France, also, always had a king until the revolution. Then they realise he was not necessary. We had Kaiser Wilhelm II until he abdicated in nineteen eighteen. Now we have Hitler and good men in our government. We do not need a king. Countries do not need a king. It is Hitler who has arranged for us to come here and make discoveries. What has your king done? Nothing.'

'I am more interested in mathematics and buildings than politics.' Stelios did not want to get into an involved political discussion with the vehement young man.

'Buildings? You will draw buildings so the workers know

what they have to build?'

'A draughtsman. No.' Stelios shook his head. 'I'm still at University and I haven't decided yet on a career. What about you?' He did not think it advisable to tell Herman that he planned to become the Minister of Finance. It would only lead to more political questions.

'I am a Captain in the army. I applied for leave so I could accompany my father and work on the site with him for a few weeks. You would like to see some of the artefacts we find?'

'Very much.'

Herman wiped his hands down his already dirty trousers and called something to his fellow workers. They looked at Stelios curiously, but made no comment. He led the way along a narrow path to where there was a tarpaulin covering the ground. He pulled back a corner and arrayed on boxes were pieces of pottery, some items were almost complete whereas others were fragmentary.

He pulled the tarpaulin further back still. Two statuettes came into view and Herman grinned knowingly at Stelios.

'You know their names?' he asked.

Stelios shook his head.

'We believe they are Cleobis and Briton, the twins who sacrificed themselves here to help their mother, Hera. Of course, until they have been studied by the experts we cannot know for sure. It could take many years. We have given them much work to do.'

'Will they eventually go to the museum in Athens?'

'For a while, maybe. We plan to build a museum here where all our best finds can be on display.'

Stelios leaned closer to get a better look. He might never have the opportunity to view them again. He felt his heart constrict. How Yannis would have loved to come here. He pushed the thought away. Yannis no longer existed.

'I will show you one more, then I must return to my work.' Carefully Herman pulled the tarpaulin back over the boxes and led the way to the far end. Lying on the ground and wrapped separately in a tarpaulin was a column. As Herman exposed one end Stelios could see marble figures of dancing girls.

'It is beautiful, yes?'

Stelios nodded. 'It certainly is magnificent.'

'It is the decorative element on the top of the column. We believe there may have been many more similar, but we have found only fragments. We hope they may be fixed together and then we will be able to see.' Herman replaced the tarpaulin carefully. 'My father found,' he announced proudly. 'What does your father do?'

Stelios swallowed. He could not admit that his father was only a farmer. 'He's a business man.'

'What kind of business?' asked Herman as they walked back down the hill together.

'He's responsible for sending goods to other parts of Crete.'

'What kind of goods?'

Stelios began to feel annoyed by the questions Herman was asking. 'Anything that is requested.'

'He has lorries to move these goods?'

'Of course, many of them,' lied Stelios.

'So you have good roads in Crete?'

Stelios thought of the cart tracks that were used by everyone. The only road he knew that had any sort of surface was the road from Aghios Nikolaos to Heraklion. 'Naturally, the roads from one town to another are excellent,' he answered.

'We also have good roads. Do you have the railway?'

'Not on Crete. There are too many mountains.'

'They can be moved or a tunnel made.' Herman dismissed the problem with a wave of his hand. 'If you had a man like Hitler in charge of your government you would have railways. Goods can be transported more quickly by rail than on the roads. It is more efficient. We believe in efficiency. We would remove the cripples and feeble minded to a place where they could be cared for properly and not continue to breed. We would also remove the criminal element of society that live along with the other useless and undesirable citizens like the gypsies and the Jews. They would be taken to specially constructed houses. The women would work as housekeepers and tend the vegetable gardens whilst the men would work on construction projects, the roads, railways, and bridges.'

Stelios nodded in agreement although he had no problem with the Jewish community in Athens and rarely came into contact with the gypsies who tended to frequent the Piraeus area.

'Where would you build these new houses to accommodate the people?'

Herman waved his hand airily. 'Away from the town. In the countryside. In a few years you would thank us for the improvements we had made.'

'I am sure we would.' Stelios was not at all sure why Crete would want a railway and did not think the Athenians would welcome the changes he proposed to their society. 'I think I ought to return to my group.' He was now beginning to feel uncomfortable in the presence of the man. 'They will be wondering what has become of me.'

Herman nodded. 'It has been a pleasure to meet you and talk with you.'

'Thank you for showing me the finds.' Stelios shook the earth stained hand again. 'I hope I will soon be able to visit these exhibits in the museum.'

'These and many more. I am sure Hitler will arrange for the excavation of all the other sites that you have neglected.' To Stelios surprise the young man raised his arm. 'Heil Hitler.'

Unsure of what his response should be, Stelios smiled and muttered, 'Yes, of course.'

Mr Radopolous was standing before the Bouleuterion, explaining to his students that this had been where the senate members met.

To Stelios the ruined building looked no different from any of the others. Mr Radopolous broke off from his lecture.

'Did you find anywhere of interest, Stelios?'

Stelios nodded. 'I did. When we take a break I'll tell you.'

Mr Radopolous squinted up at the sun. 'We could stop and have our lunch now. We still have a good part of the afternoon before us to see the remainder of the site.'

Stelios felt sceptical that they would be able to accomplish a tour of the whole site if Mr Radopolous insisted on stopping every few yards and giving a lecture.

'We can make ourselves comfortable over at the treasuries.' He led the way a short distance further back along the track and placed the bag he had been carrying on the wall. 'The taverna has packed us a snack and that should be sufficient until our evening meal. I trust you all still have some water?'

The boys ranged themselves along the wall and Mr Radopolous handed each one a cheese roll. 'Now, Stelios, tell us what you discovered.'

Stelios finished chewing the mouthful of roll and then stood up. 'I climbed the hill and visited the theatre there. It is very big and in a good state of preservation. I then walked up to the summit of the hill where the stadium is situated. The markers and the seats are still in place. From there you can view most of the site. After returning to the theatre I struck off to the side and came across a group who were excavating. I spoke to one of them. His father is the archaeologist in charge of the work. Herman showed me some recent important finds, two figurines and the adornment from the top of a column, along with fragments of pottery and marble.'

'How very exciting. Do you think if we went over to them they would be willing to show us?'

'I don't know, but I could certainly take you over to where they are working.'

'Boys, the choice is yours. When you have finished eating you can climb up the hill to the theatre and stadium or accompany

Stelios and myself to see if we are also able to view these finds.'

Stelios could see a look of relief on the faces of his companions and thought they would probably appreciate being able to go off alone and not be continually lectured by Mr Radopolous.

'You are not coming with us, sir?'

Mr Radopolous shook his head. 'I would very much like to see the theatre and stadium, but I know I cannot climb the hill as quickly as you young people. I will have to save that expedition for another day. Meet me here when you return.'

The students hurried away gratefully whilst Mr Radopolous accompanied Stelios to the far side of the Temple of Apollo. Although the tutor slowed his pace to look at the remains as they passed he did not insist on telling Stelios the history of the building a second time.

Herman greeted Stelios with a smile. 'You come back.'

'This is Mr Radopolous. He teaches history at the University and would be very interested to see the finds you showed me earlier.'

'My father is here now. You will have to ask him.' Herman called to a man in a guttural language that Stelios did not understand.

With a frown on his face the man came over and was introduced to them by his son. 'No one is supposed to view the finds until they have been transported back to Athens for cleaning.' He did not add that their most important and valuable finds would be taken to Germany.

Mr Radopolous's disappointment showed on his face. 'I may not have another opportunity. You could make far more spectacular finds in the future and then these would be stored away and not put on show. It would mean a great deal to me to be able to have a quick glimpse.'

Mr Steiner sighed. He would have to remind Herman that he was not to show casual visitors any of their recent finds. 'I can spare only a few minutes.'

Mr Radopolous nodded eagerly. 'I understand.'

Grudgingly Mr Steiner led the way to the tarpaulin covered boxes and pulled back a corner, exposing the two figurines Stelios had seen earlier.

'Cleobis and Briton; they cannot be described as beautiful, but they are certainly interesting. Whereabouts did you find them?'

Mr Steiner did not answer him. He did not want the man coming back during the night and making a search of his own. 'I believe my son also showed the korias.' He walked to the rear of the stack of boxes and pulled back a portion of the tarpaulin exposing the dancing girls.

Mr Radopolous sucked in his breath. 'Beautiful, quite beautiful. I am most envious that you had the opportunity to find them. They could have been lost to us forever had you not been excavating here. I appreciate that you allowed me to see them.'

Mr Steiner replaced the tarpaulin. 'I am not prepared to show you any more artefacts. We are busy working and do not have time to spend with visitors.'

'Of course. I feel very privileged. I wish my other students had accompanied us. I am sure they would have been most impressed. I appreciate your time.'

Mr Radopolous held out his hand, but the archaeologist did not take it; instead Mr Steiner lifted his arm and said 'Heil Hitler,' as Herman had said to Stelios as they parted.

Stelios and Mr Radopolous walked back towards their designated meeting place with the other students, a broad smile on the tutor's face. 'I am so pleased you met the archaeologist's son and I was able to have a quick look at their finds. I do hope they will be on show in the museum very soon. I would have liked to have spent far longer talking to the archaeologist, but he made it clear that he was too busy to talk at length.'

Stelios nodded dutifully. In retrospect he found the attitude of both father and son strange and unwelcoming. The visit had been something of a disappointment to him.

Stelios waited for his interview with the principal of the University. He already knew his results for mathematics, book keeping and accountancy were excellent, although he had done less well than he had expected with political history. All he wanted from the principal was a letter of recommendation to present to the government which would enable him to be offered a position in the establishment.

Mr Kartalapous looked at the eager young man who sat before him.

'I'm afraid your tutor in Heraklion neglected to tell you that you need experience. You have to make public speeches and convince your listeners that there is an advantage to them to have you in the government. They are not going to listen to a young man who has just left University. You need to have some experience of life. Go and teach in a High School for a few years, get your name known in the community.'

'I don't want to be a teacher,' replied Stelios sulkily.

'Your only other option is to spend two more years at University taking politics as your main subject. You obviously concentrated hard on your mathematical studies, but you only just managed a pass on the political questions you answered.'

'Two more years! Would I be able to get a scholarship?'

'You can apply, of course, but usually further scholarships or grants towards an educational course are only available for science or medical subjects and the student has to be quite outstanding to warrant the privilege.' Mr Kartalapous shook his head. 'Even if you completed another two year University course concentrating on politics it would still not guarantee you entry into the government. If you have no wish to teach you could become a book keeper or enter the bank and earn promotion. After that it would be up to you and how you presented yourself to the people. You need more than a degree in mathematics to make the government take notice of you.'

Stelios left the principal's office feeling sick with disappointment. He had been confident that the government would have welcomed him and had believed Mr Mikhaelis when he had told him he could become the Minister for Finance. Now all his dreams were shattered. Two years studying at University wasted if he was only qualified to become a teacher. He should have borrowed more books from the library and concentrated harder on the political lectures he had attended.

He sat on a seat in Syntagma Square and drew deeply on his cigarette. Becoming a book keeper for one of the import and export companies would certainly never bring him to the attention of the government. His only other option was to enter the world of banking. He ground his cigarette out with his heel. If he was to apply to a bank he ought to seek an interview with a manager immediately, before other graduate mathematicians had the same idea.

Stelios entered the banking hall, trying to exude confidence, although feeling intimidated by the quiet and studious air around him. He approached the first desk and waited until the man looked up from his papers.

'I would like to see the manager, please.'

'Have a word with the messenger. He'll know if the manager is expecting you.' The man bent his head back down to his paperwork and Stelios walked to the other side of the banking hall where a man stood before an upright wooden desk.

'I would like to see the manager, please.'

'Do you have an appointment, sir?' The messenger certainly did not recognise the young man as being an employee of any of the large businesses that used the bank.

'I didn't know I needed to make one.'

'It is customary to make an appointment in advance. The manager is busy.'

'I really do need to see him urgently.'

'May I ask the nature of your business, sir?'

Stelios swallowed. He could not tell the man he was looking for employment. 'It is confidential.'

'Your name, sir?'

'Mr Christoforakis.'

'Wait here, sir. I will speak to the manager and see if he is able to spare you a few minutes.'

The messenger shuffled off down the hall and disappeared. It seemed to Stelios that he was gone for an interminable amount of time and he wondered if he had been forgotten. Finally the man reappeared and beckoned to him.

'The manager has agreed to see you quickly, sir. Please follow me.'

His head held high, hoping he looked as if he was on important official business; Stelios followed him through an archway where the man knocked deferentially on a door before opening it and announcing him.

Stelios stood just inside the door and waited for the man at the desk to speak. His mouth felt dry and his tongue thick in his mouth.

'What can I do for you, Mr Christoforakis?'

'I have just finished University. I have excellent grades and I would like to apply for work in the banking sector.'

The manager nodded. 'The subjects you took?'

'Mathematics, book keeping and accountancy.'

'Is that all?'

'I also studied politics.'

'What about the stock market? Have you any knowledge of share dealing?'

'No, sir.'

'Investments?'

'No, sir.'

'International trade transactions?'

'No, sir.'

'So what makes you think you would be suitable as an employee of the bank? You need far more knowledge than you appear to have to be a competent cashier.'

'Can't I start as a trainee and work my way up?' asked Stelios desperately.

'My cashiers do not have the time to act as a tutor to you. I suggest you spend two more years at University studying the principles of banking. It is certainly not the same as book keeping. Provided you obtain good grades come and see me again then. You know your way out, don't you?'

Stelios flushed and clenched his fists. He felt he had been ignominiously dismissed. He certainly did not want to work in a bank if this derogatory attitude was prevalent. No doubt the manager would tell the other staff and they would all snigger and think it amusing.

His stomach churning with annoyance and frustration Stelios walked back to Syntagma Square. He smoked another cigarette to calm himself and tried to get his thoughts in order. He watched the people passing by, some strolling, others hurrying, the women with their shopping basket in their arm. A man arrived and set up his low stool and an array of polish and cloths hoping to attract the attention of any men who wanted their shoes or boots cleaned. A man in army uniform stopped and placed his foot on the stool and the man set to work vigorously until the boots shone.

As he walked away the shoe shiner grinned at Stelios. 'Comes every day for his boots to be cleaned.'

Stelios nodded, not really interested, as the man walked into a building across the road

Mr Radopolous asked if he planned to return to lodge with them at the end of the summer recess and Stelios looked at him warily.

'I'm not certain yet. If I do spend a further two years at the University I would obviously like to stay with you and your wife again.' Stelios did not mention that he had collected a letter from the University telling him that his application for a second scholarship had been rejected.

'We will be delighted to have you. What subjects are you planning to study?'

'I think a second course of politics would be useful to me. There is a tremendous amount more that I need to know before I will feel able to put myself forward for election.'

Mr Radopolous raised his eyebrows. Mr Kartalapous had spoken to him about the boy's ambition to become the Minister for Finance.

'You don't think that a few years work could stand you in better stead – give you more experience of life?'

Stelios's lip curled in disgust. 'I have no wish to become a teacher, standing all day in front of a class, most of the boys uninterested in the subject.'

'I have found it most rewarding. There is always at least one pupil who loves the subject and is anxious to learn as much as possible from me.'

Stelios pursed his lips. 'I will return to Aghios Nikolaos at the end of the week and speak to my father. I am sure he will agree that it would be to my advantage to study politics in more depth.'

Yannis listened to Stelios, pleased and proud that he had done so well in his final examinations.

'What do you plan to do now? Apply to become a teacher in Aghios Nikolaos?'

Stelios shook his head. 'I certainly do not want to be a teacher and nor do I want to spend the rest of my life in Aghios Nikolaos. I want to return to Athens University for two more years to study politics more thoroughly. I am certain to be given a government post then, probably the junior Minister of Finance to start with.'

'Two more years at University? Have you been offered another scholarship?'

Stelios shook his head. 'They don't give students a second one,'

Yannis frowned. 'That would mean paying tuition fees along with your lodgings.' He shook his head. 'I can't afford to give you that much money, Stelios. I have to think of Yiorgo and Anna, also the children and Yannis.'

Stelios felt the colour suffusing his face. 'Yiorgo is content on the farm and Anna has a home here. The children are not your responsibility and nor is Yannis. The government looks after him.'

Yannis senior shook his head. 'The farm is not paying as well as it used to do. If Marisa was still alive I would want to give some of my money to her. It's only fair that the children have a small share.'

'Babbis should provide for them.'

'He contributes to all their expenses, but he is struggling to manage his farm single handed. Yannis receives a small pension from the government now, but that does not cover his need for a new coat or boots.'

Furious Stelios stalked from the room. 'Yannis probably hasn't any feet to put boots on!' he called back over his shoulder and slammed the door.

Yannis senior sat where he was thinking deeply. He had given his son Yannis sufficient money for his stay in Heraklion whilst he attended the High School. It was not his son's fault that he had not been able to make use of his education. Stelios had already had twice as much money from him, due to his stay in Heraklion and then in Athens. It would not be fair to Anna and Yiorgo to give him any more. The boy should be out earning his keep.

The other worry that haunted him was his wife. There had been no marked deterioration in her condition; if anything it had improved, but if she suffered another stroke and became completely bedridden Anna would be unable to cope. A village woman would have to be paid to do the washing and keep the house clean whilst Anna nursed her mother and looked after the children. He needed to ensure he had sufficient money for that eventuality.

Stelios strode down to the shore and shook his fist at Spinalonga. If his brother was not incarcerated over there he would be out at work now and there would be money available for him to continue at University. Had his father helped his Uncle Yiorgo and Aunt Elena financially to enable them to travel to the United States? He felt resentful. Everyone but him seemed to have enough money to be able to do as they pleased.

He would certainly not stay in Plaka or Aghios Nikolaos. He still had some money in his pocket and he would ask his father for the ferry fare back to Athens.

Yannis senior regarded his son sadly. 'You have to realise, Stelios, that money has to be earned. It cannot always be given to you. I will pay your ferry fare back to Athens and give you seventy drachmas. That should be more than sufficient for you to stay somewhere whilst you look for work.' Yannis looked at Stelios sternly and continued. 'You will have to earn this money by working on the farm with Yiorgo and myself throughout the summer holidays. If that is not agreeable to you then it is best you return to Athens now, but all I will give you is sufficient for the ferry.'

Stelios had a longing to pack his sack and leave immediately, but common sense told him he would be foolish not to spend four weeks working out in the fields. At least it would be warm and dry at this time of the year.

'Very well,' he said stiffly. 'I will stay for the summer.'

The time dragged for Stelios. He disliked having to share a bedroom with Yiorgo again and was embarrassed when he was unable to comprehend whatever his mother tried to say to him. Anna, Yiorgo and his father, even the children, seemed to have no problem understanding her slurred and sometimes muddled speech. Babbis would join them for a meal each evening and Stelios would sit in sullen silence, whilst Babbis ignored him and concentrated on talking to Marisa and little Yannis. Anna could sense the tension within the family and hoped that Stelios would not decide to stay and work on the farm.

When she broached the subject with him his lip curled in disgust. 'I am certainly not staying here for the rest of my life.'

'So what will you do, Stelios?'

'I plan to return to Athens. I am sure to be able to find some suitable occupation there until I am accepted in the political world.'

In truth Stelios was worried. His father had refused to pay for him to attend University for a further two years and the bank had refused to employ him. He appeared to have only one option left – to approach some of the shipping companies based in Piraeus and see if one would give him work as a bookkeeper. That would mean he had to live down in the town and from what little he had seen of the area he did not think it an attractive proposition.

Refusing to be too despondent Stelios thanked his father grudgingly for the drachmas he gave him at the end of the four weeks. Yannis had added an extra ten drachmas, feeling that maybe he had been a little harsh in refusing to give him more money to take to Athens with him.

'Make sure you contact Andreas so he will know where you can be found if we should need you here,' Yannis reminded his son, 'and say goodbye to your mother properly.'

Stelios nodded. Now the time had finally arrived for him to return to Athens he was anxious to depart for Aghios Nikolaos as soon as possible.

He booked into the small taverna that let rooms and proclaimed grandly that it was a hotel before making his way to the bus station to find the time of the bus to Heraklion that would depart the following day. He had the depressing prospect of having to ask Andreas for a bed for the night, but he could not afford to spend any more money on lodgings.

Stelios took his seat on the crowded bus, placed his sack on the seat next to him to deter anyone from sitting next to him and waited impatiently for it to leave. The driver seemed in no particular hurry and was willing to wait for a young man who waved frantically at him as he ran across the waste ground.

'Thanks,' he said as he jumped aboard and looked for a vacant seat. He stopped beside Stelios. 'Would you mind moving your sack so I can sit here? I'm going all the way to Heraklion.'

Grudgingly Stelios placed his sack between his feet.

'That was fortunate for me that the bus was late in leaving. I would have been in a lot of trouble otherwise. I'm in the army and they're very particular about punctuality. What do you do?'

Stelios hesitated. Should he exaggerate wildly? 'I've just completed my University course.'

The youth looked at him admiringly. 'You must be clever. What subjects did you take?'

'Mathematics, book keeping, accountancy.'

'So what are you going to do now?'

'I have various options open to me. I just have to decide which would be the most profitable for me to accept.'

'I'm glad I chose the army. I could have stayed in Aghios Nikolaos and helped my father in his shop. He doesn't really need any help and would only have been able to pay me a bit of pocket money. Of course, I would have been living at home, but it would have taken me years to save up enough to get married. Being in the army I get a wage along with free living accommodation and my food. I'm Lucas.'

Stelios nodded, his interest suddenly increased. If you did not have to pay for lodgings and were also paid a wage whilst in the army he might investigate further.

'My name's Stelios. What do you do in the army?'

'I'm still being trained. I've done all the basics, of course, and now I'm learning Morse code. When I've mastered that I can go into the communications section.'

'What's Morse code?'

'Bit difficult for me to explain without having the equipment to demonstrate to you. You have a little machine and press a lever making long and short sounds. We call them dots and dashes. Each series is a letter and when you put them together they spell out words. You can send messages that way to other army units.'

'Why don't you just write them a letter?'

'It depends how urgently the message needs to be received. Sometimes the unit we need to contact is stationed miles away and it could take days for a messenger to get there, even with one of the motorised bikes. If we send it in Morse it only takes a few minutes.'

'Is it difficult to learn?'

Lucas shook his head. 'Not really. After a week or two you begin to be able to hear the difference between the lengths of the sounds.'

'Does everyone learn this code?'

'No, there are plenty of other jobs you can learn if you don't want to be an ordinary soldier. I thought about going into the supplies department, but that means being able to add up and keep records. I'm not that quick with adding up or doing sums. It would suit someone like you. I understand they are always looking for competent office workers. So many of the new recruits can hardly read and write, let alone add up.'

Stelios nodded slowly. This could be something for him to think about. 'How do you go about joining the army?'

'There's an office in Heraklion. I could show you where it is if you're interested. I'm sure they'd be only too eager to employ you.'

'I'm actually on my way to Athens.'

'There's bound to be an office there. If you registered in Heraklion they would send your details through to Athens; probably by letter, though, not Morse code.' Lucas grinned. 'I don't have to report back in until four this afternoon so I'll have a few hours free when we reach Heraklion. What do you say about having a quick meal together and then I can point out the office to you.'

'Suppose I registered here and then changed my mind later?'

'Then you wouldn't go to the office in Athens would you?' replied Lucas logically.

The remainder of the bus journey was spent with Lucas telling Stelios how he had spent his week's leave in Aghios Nikolaos, but that he had missed his army companions. He tried to draw Stelios out about his own family, but Stelios was reticent. He made no mention of the farm at Plaka and gave the impression that his sister was married with a family and his brother was still at school.

'You're lucky to have a brother and sister. I have a number of cousins, but it isn't the same. That's why I enjoy having so many friends at the army base.'

Stelios listened to Lucas's words. Lucas should be grateful that he did not have a family of whom he was ashamed.

On reaching the bus terminal Stelios insisted that he called at the ferry office and purchased his ticket for the following day before they went to a taverna. After a leisurely, but indifferent meal, Lucas picked up his sack.

'I ought to head off now. I have to go through Eleftherios Square and if you're going that way I can point out the office to you.'

Stelios nodded agreement. Now he was back in Heraklion he did not want to bump into Andreas and have to introduce him to Lucas. The sooner he was able to go about his own business the better.

Lucas shook Stelios's hand. 'If you do decide to go into the army and if I ever get sent to Athens I'll look out for you,' he promised.

'That would be extremely good of you,' replied Stelios. If by any stroke of bad luck Lucas did turn up in Athens he would pretend not to know him and insist the young man had made a mistake.

Stelios stood outside the army office and smoked a cigarette whilst Lucas walked off along the street, raising his hand at the corner. Finally Stelios decided he had nothing to lose by making enquiries and pushed open the door.

A man sitting at the desk greeted him with a smile. 'How may I help you?'

'I wondered if you could give me some details about joining the army.'

The smile became even wider. 'Certainly I can. What exactly did you wish to know?'

'Well,' Stelios hesitated, 'I've been told that the army needs office staff. I certainly don't want to be an ordinary soldier. I have good grades from University and I am looking for remunerative work that I would enjoy.'

'What other work have you applied for?'

'I'm waiting to hear from a bank, but I was not impressed when I visited. I don't think I would be happy working there.' Stelios was not prepared to admit that he had been told he had insufficient knowledge and qualifications. 'I have also applied to some of the shipping companies for employment in a book keeping capacity, but I do not want to live in Piraeus.'

The man raised his eyebrows. 'It would not be necessary to work in Piraeus. There are shipping companies in Heraklion.'

'I do not wish to live in Heraklion. After spending two years at the University in Athens I want to return to the city.'

'Do you have family over there?'

'I have no family now.' Stelios managed to make his voice sound sad and brushed his face, as if to wipe away a tear. 'I am only in Crete now as I had to attend the funeral of my last living relative. I have friends in Athens and I am sure that with their help I will be able to overcome my natural grief.'

'Of course,' the man nodded sympathetically. 'I will give you a form to complete with your details and have this sent through to our Athens office. If you call on them when you return to Athens I am sure they will be able to help you. The army is always in need of intelligent young men like you in their administrative offices.' He produced a form from a drawer in his desk and handed it to Stelios. 'There is a desk over there where you can sit. When you have finished bring it back to me.'

The words "administrative offices" stayed in Stelios's ears. That would mean he was in charge, and no doubt that would also mean he gained rapid promotion. He wondered how long it would take before he reached the rank of Major. Once he had accomplished that he would apply to become a member of the government and they would be unlikely to refuse him.

Stelios read the questions carefully. He obviously had to enter his name and date of birth. Where it asked for the name and address of his father or closest relative he wrote "deceased" and added "no family". In the space for his address he wrote the street where Mr Radopolous lived, but did not add that it was in the Plaka area and put "temporary" in brackets beside it. He listed his qualifications from University, tempted to include Science; then thought better of it. If the army decided to check up it would be discovered that he had only spent a term studying the subject.

He handed the form back to the man on the desk, pleased at its neat appearance. He waited whilst it was read, hoping he would not be asked for any more details about himself. The man tapped the form with his finger nail.

'This address that you say is temporary. How long do you plan to stay there?'

'That will depend. The man is a tutor at the University and I lodged with him and his wife for the whole of my two years whilst I was studying. If I was working locally I would ask him if I could stay there indefinitely, but I understand the army provides its own accommodation.'

'Would this gentleman be able to give you a reference if it was required?'

'A reference?'

'Would he be willing to state that you were honest, worked

hard and did not keep unsavoury company?'

'I am sure he would.'

'Very well. Sign there.' The paper was pushed back across the desk to Stelios and he signed his name with a flourish.

'I plan to return to Athens tomorrow.'

'Then give it a week and call in at the office there. Do you know where it is?'

'Syntagma Square, I believe.' Stelios hoped that the man who had his boots cleaned every day had entered the army office across the road from the shoe shiner.

'Off you go then, and good luck.'

Stelios looked at the man curiously before turning on his heel and walking out. Why would he need good luck? The army really could not afford to turn down a young man of his calibre.

Stelios walked up to Andreas's house and knocked on the door. There was no answer and he felt relieved as he pushed open the door and deposited his sack. He wanted to go up to the taverna where Vangelis lived and see if he was able to make contact with any of his old acquaintances. Had Andreas been at home he would doubtless have expected Stelios to stay and talk to him.

Vangelis was delighted to see him and suggested they went to one of the tavernas they had patronized as students. 'I'm sure we'll find Makkis there sooner or later.'

Stelios sat and sipped his wine slowly; listening to Vangelis telling him that having completed his Classical Greek course at the University in Thessaloniki he had accepted a position at the library there.

'It's a wonderful opportunity,' he enthused. 'They have agreed that I can continue to study history by attending the classes whenever I have a free day. It will take me a long time to complete the course, but I don't mind how long it takes.'

'I'm pleased for you,' replied Stelios and took another sip of his wine.

'Well, fancy seeing you here! May I join you?'

Makkis slipped into the seat next to Vangelis. 'So, tell me, Stelios, how did you get on studying in Athens?'

'I obtained a good pass.'

'So what are you planning now? Are you going to become a teacher?'

Stelios shook his head. He was not going to admit that he was unable to gain a scholarship and his father had refused to pay for him to have further tuition. 'I was offered a further scholarship for another two years, but I turned it down. There was nothing that particularly interested me,' he lied easily. 'I have been approached by the army with an offer too good to refuse. They need men like me and within a short while I will have earned promotion. This time next year I should be a Lieutenant.'

Vangelis looked surprised. He had never heard of the army approaching individuals.

Makkis shook his head. 'There's a lot of trouble in Europe at the moment. You never know when it could turn nasty. If we get involved and you're in the army you'll be expected to fight.'

Stelios pushed his chair back. 'I will be in administration, not a common soldier. Germany's annexation of Austria is of no concern to us. What about you? When are you getting married?'

'Not for a while yet,' grinned Makkis. 'I've been offered another science scholarship so I shall be spending another two years at the University.'

'Up in Thessaloniki?' asked Vangelis. 'Can we share a lodging again?'

Makkis nodded. 'We had some good times up there. I found a girl who for a couple of extra drachmas would do just about anything I asked. Have you got a girl in Athens, Stelios?'

Stelios was not prepared to admit that he had still not experienced a sexual relationship. 'The girls in Athens virtually fell over themselves to get my attention.'

'And do you take advantage of them?'

'Naturally.' Stelios felt his face flush as he told the lie and he could tell by the grins on the faces of his companions that they did not believe him. He felt resentful. Why should Makkis have been offered a second scholarship rather than him?

'So when are you returning to all these girls who can't wait to get their hands on you?'

'Tomorrow. I bought my ferry ticket as soon as the bus arrived here.'

'Are you staying with my uncle tonight?' asked Vangelis.

Stelios shook his head. 'I've been invited to stay elsewhere. I would be a fool to refuse.'

Makkis raised his eyebrows. 'Pity you won't be here tomorrow to tell us what you got up to.'

Stelios almost laughed. He would certainly not be getting up to anything whilst staying with his monkish cousin. 'You'll have to wait until the next time I'm in Heraklion.'

'Yes, well, I'm off to tell my father the good news about my scholarship. I only picked up the letter from the post office an hour ago.'

'I suppose I ought to go as well.' Vangelis picked up the almost empty bottle of wine and poured the remaining contents into Stelios's glass. 'I wish you well in the army and hope you receive the promotion you're expecting.'

Stelios watched his friends leave. He sat morosely over his wine and wondered how long he needed to wait before he would find Andreas back at his house.

Andreas opened the door and Stelios was struck by how weary his cousin looked. He was ushered in and placed his sack in the small bedroom where he had slept before. He hoped the accommodation provided by the army was more comfortable than this bare room.

'So how is your mother?' asked Andreas.

Stelios shrugged. 'Much the same.'

'And your father and the rest of the family?'

'Working hard. I felt obliged to stay and help for a few weeks.'

'What other plans did you have?'

'Oh, the army has asked me to take up an administrative position. It really was an opportunity too good to refuse. Even with a scholarship for another two year University course I did not feel I could accept any more money from my father. He begged me to do so, but I was adamant.'

'You are not concerned about entering the army in these unsettled times?'

'Of course not,' answered Stelios scornfully. 'I have ideas for a complete restructuring of the book keeping system. By the time I have completed the task we will have plenty of money to buy army equipment and be invincible regardless of whatever happens in Europe.'

'I do hope you are right.'

'Of course; I know what I am talking about.'

Andreas made no comment, but took a letter from his trouser pocket. 'I received a letter from my sister yesterday. She and Elias have a little girl and she has enclosed a photograph. I understand she has also written to Anna.'

Stelios gave the photograph a cursory glance and nodded. 'Anna did not mention it, so I can only assume it had not arrived in Plaka before I left.'

'Probably not.' Andreas replaced the letter in his pocket. 'You'll not forget to write to your parents once you are settled, will you? I know they will want to hear about your work. You can always send the letters to me and I will ensure they are passed on to them. I can ask a boatman to take them down and it is quicker than the regular postal system.'

Stelios nodded. 'Of course I will write. It may not be for some weeks as no doubt I will be extremely busy at first.'

'Naturally,' agreed Andreas. 'I hope you will not mind if we eat fairly soon. My housekeeper has left a meal and it will be sufficient for us to share. I then wish to have an early night. Sadly

I was called out last night to an elderly lady. I then had to visit the family again this morning to try to take them some comfort and this afternoon I was at the hospital. It is a shame that your arrival coincided with me having such a busy time.'

Stelios was not at all dismayed by being told that Andreas wished to retire early. It would save having to make conversation and he could easily trip himself up within the web of lies he had been telling people recently.

'I have my ferry ticket ready for tomorrow, so I will need to be up early. Going to bed soon after our meal will be beneficial.'

Stelios walked into the army office in Syntagma Square with a swagger. He approached the desk and rang a bell to alert someone that his attention was needed. A man looked through a glass panel in the door and looked away again. Stelios rang the bell again more vigorously and the man opened the door.

'Yes?'

'I believe you have been contacted by your Heraklion office and my papers sent through to you. I have applied for an administration position in the army.'

The man nodded and the door closed again. Stelios wondered if he was expected to ring the bell again or wait the man's convenience. Just as he was losing patience the door opened and the man returned bearing papers in his hand.

'Your name?'

'Stelios Christoforakis.'

The man leafed through the papers until he found the one that had Stelios's name. He read the details Stelios had supplied and nodded.

'There does not appear to be any reason to refuse you provided you pass the medical check.'

'Medical?' Stelios felt alarmed. What did they think was wrong with him?

'Routine. Every recruit is given a medical check. We don't want sick men in the army.'

'I am certainly not sick,' replied Stelios firmly.

'Good. In that case you won't be with the doctor very long. Come back tomorrow morning. He will be examining all the recent recruits then. Provided he is satisfied with the state of your health you'll join the others the following day for transport to the training centre.' The man collected the sheaf of papers and walked back through the glass panelled door.

Stelios walked back to the cheap taverna where he had booked a room for the night. He did not want to visit Mr Radopolous and ask for a room. No doubt the man would know that he had not entered his name for tuition starting in the autumn term. He would prefer the tutor did not know that his father had refused to pay for any further education and that he was now joining the army.

When he prepared for bed he undressed completely and examined his body closely. He had a small bruise on his arm where he had bumped it against the side of the ferry and two small moles beneath his right knee. They had been there as long as he could remember. As far as he could see there were no other blemishes on his body; his skin had a healthy tan down as far as his waist where he had worked without a shirt in the fields for his father.

As he walked back down to the army office the following morning he had a slightly sick feeling in the pit of his stomach. Would there be any way the doctor could tell that there was leprosy in the family although he had no signs of the disease at all. He stood in Syntagma Square and smoked a cigarette to calm his nerves before finally crossing the road and entering the building.

Three other young men were waiting, all looking apprehensive. They smiled nervously at Stelios as he entered and he nodded back to them, hoping he would be called first and able to leave.

'How long have you been waiting?' he asked.

The youth shrugged. 'Not that long. My friend Elias is in with the doctor at the moment and there was someone in there when we arrived. He seems to be pretty quick. I guess that's because we're all healthy.'

Stelios nodded again and turned his attention to the notices on the wall. There were a list of occupations open to recruits and they could apply for any course that interested them when they had completed their initial training. He ran his eye down them. He would be interested in learning how to drive one of the motorised vehicles, but he had no desire to understand how they worked by becoming an engineer. The only other advertisement that appealed to him was typewriting. That was intriguing. He might enquire about learning the skill.

One by one the young men were called into a side room and all but one emerged smiling happily.

'Why were you refused?' asked Stelios.

The young man pulled up his left sleeve and exposed a withered arm. Stelios automatically drew back from him.

'All I wanted to do was work as a book keeper. My arm would not have been a hindrance.' He pulled his sleeve back down and walked out of the door.

Stelios was the last to enter and he felt annoyed. Had he known he was going to have to wait in a queue he would have made sure he was the first arrival.

The doctor looked him up and down, checked his name and age and then told him to remove his shirt. Stelios submitted to the doctor's hard fingers tapping his chest and his back, he dutifully opened his mouth and allowed his teeth to be examined and was then told to sit down and remove his boots. The doctor wriggled his toes and stroked the sole of his foot making him squirm.

'Now drop your trousers and remove your underwear.'

'My underwear! Why do I need to take that off?'

'I cannot say I have given you a complete examination without seeing your whole body.'

Stelios looked at the doctor suspiciously. It was one thing undressing before his brother when he was a boy, but the doctor was a complete stranger to him and he was a man now.

Reluctantly he removed his belt and allowed his trousers

followed by his underwear to drop to the ground. The doctor regarded him impassively.

'Turn around, bend over and touch your toes.'

Shaking with trepidation Stelios complied, feeling the doctor running his fingers up his spine.

'Straighten up and turn around to face me. Spread your legs.' To Stelios's horror the doctor cupped his testicles in his hand. 'Cough,' he ordered.

Stelios tried, but it was no more than a clearing of his throat.

'I said "cough". Try again, nice and deep.'

This time Stelios was more able to reproduce a cough and the doctor seemed satisfied. 'Get dressed.'

Hurriedly Stelios replaced his underwear and trousers. He was sweating from his anxiety; he had been sure he was going to be molested. He pulled his shirt back over his head and rubbed his arm across his forehead, hoping the doctor had not noticed his fear and embarrassment.

'You appear to be fit enough. Report back here at eight tomorrow with your belongings. You'll be taken with the others to the training camp. Don't be late.'

'No, sir,' Stelios managed to utter and left the room with alacrity.

He walked back across Syntagma Square and lit a cigarette with trembling hands. At least the examination had taken place in private and not ignominiously in front of the other recruits.

Stelios was surprised when the bus he was travelling on along with the other recruits left the centre of Athens and made its way through the suburbs. Finally it drew up outside a closed iron gate where a soldier stood guard. The soldier opened the gate and the bus continued up a winding road until a collection of wooden huts came into view.

'Collect your belongings,' called the driver.

Stelios felt bemused as he picked up his sack and followed

the other young men off the bus. He had expected to be taken to an office. The bus drove back down the road leaving the men standing in an uncertain group.

'Recruits,' a loud voice shouted at them. 'Follow me.'

The men shambled along the path that led between the wooden huts until the soldier escorting them stopped at one and ushered the men inside. A line of camp beds stood on each side, dividing each one from the next was a low cupboard flanked by a taller one.

'Decide which will be your bed and place your sack on it.'

Stelios stepped forward. 'Excuse me. I think there must be some mistake. I was expecting to have a room to myself.'

'Were you now? You're in the army and you accept what you're given and be grateful. Place your sack on a bed.' The soldier raised his voice. 'Get in line and follow me to supplies to collect your kit.'

Stelios hesitated. 'You too,' the Lieutenant commanded and Stelios joined the end of the line.

They were walked briskly between the huts and over to a far larger building. 'Stop in front of each soldier and hold out your arms. You will be given a piece of your kit. When you have everything we will return to your hut and I will explain the procedure to you.'

Stelios followed his companions and a sturdy sack was placed on his outstretched arms along with a heavy coat. This was followed by two pairs of khaki trousers, three khaki shirts, two matching jackets, a pair of short trousers and a vest, puttees, belt, cap, tie, a pair of boots and a hard hat, until he felt his arms would break. Struggling to keep up with his companions and avoid dropping anything he was breathing heavily when they reached the hut.

Thankfully he dropped his load onto the bed.

'Hang your uniform and great coat in the long cupboard. Place your boots and puttees on the floor inside with your belt beside them. Your cap goes on that hook and your hard hat on the other. Your underwear, shorts and vest and any other personal possessions go into the small cupboard. Fold your sack when it is empty and place it beneath your boots. Make up your bed and stand beside it when you have done so.'

Stelios opened his mouth to protest and was met with a steely glare. 'Get on with it.'

Stelios complied and finally spread the two blankets over the thin mattress. The Lieutenant walked to each bed in turn, opening the cupboards and checking that everything was stowed away as he had instructed and the beds were neatly made. He stopped at Stelios's bed.

'Tuck the blankets beneath mattress.'

'I prefer to have my blankets loose.'

The Lieutenant glared at him. 'In the army you tuck your blankets beneath the mattress. That is an order. Is that clear?'

Sulkily Stelios tucked the blankets in. 'Happy now?'

The Lieutenant wheeled round. 'Any more remarks like that from you and you will be on an insubordination charge.' He strode over to the doorway. 'Listen to me. I only give instructions once. Remember the number on the door of your hut. Check you are at the correct one before you open the door and walk in, particularly at night. You will be woken at six each morning and will have twenty five minutes before you report to the exercise yard in your shorts and vest. An hour later you will return to your hut to wash and change into your uniform. Breakfast is at eight and is finished at nine. There is then an inspection of your hut to ensure that it is clean and tidy. Today you are able to have some free time to look around and familiarise yourself with the camp. A mid-day meal is served from twelve until two each day. You are to return here after your meal today and change into your uniform before being taken to the administration headquarters for your assignments and instructions. Everyone understand?'

Ten heads nodded and Stelios felt relieved. If they were being taken to the administration office this afternoon he would be able to explain that a mistake had been made and he should not be sharing a hut with nine other young men.

Stelios stood before the Major, feeling uncomfortable in the unaccustomed army uniform that he was wearing.

'Excuse me, sir, but I think there has been some mistake.'

The Major raised his eyebrows.

'I joined the army for administrative duties and I have been placed in a hut with nine other recruits.'

'You are expected to do your basic physical and munitions training the same as anyone else who joins the army. At the end of the six weeks you could be unsuitable and discharged. Provided you are up to the standard expected training will commence for administrative duties then.'

Stelios felt thoroughly depressed. 'I'm not sure the army is the right career for me. How do I go about getting released?'

'Released?' The Major tapped the paper that Stelios had completed and bore his signature. 'You signed on for two years. You have been here half a day; hardly sufficient time to decide whether the army should be your future career.'

'Two years!' Stelios gasped. 'I didn't know I had agreed to serve for that length of time. What would make me unsuitable and allow for my release?'

'That would be up to us to decide, not you. Now, you say you want to become part of the administration unit. What qualifications do you have that would make you suitable to be considered?'

'I attended Athens University and gained good passes in Mathematics, book keeping and accountancy. I also studied politics.'

The Captain wrote the details down. 'If we decided to offer you a position we would expect you to take an examination to prove your ability.'

'That would be no problem and I'm sure the University would confirm that I am more than proficient.'

'We prefer to conduct our own examinations. Do you have any inclination to learn any of the other skills we offer?'

Stelios hesitated. 'Typewriting interests me, and learning to drive.'

'Anything else?'

Stelios shook his head. 'Not at the moment.'

The Major studied the young man before him. 'I will give you some advice and it would be to your advantage to remember. Whenever you address an officer of higher rank than yourself you always say "sir". I allow the formality to be excused during a first interview, but not in the future. You will obey your Lieutenant without question at all times. Whilst wearing an army uniform you will be expected to be clean and smart. Failure to comply with these basic conditions will mean that you are put on a charge that at the very least means withdrawal of your privileges. Understand?'

'Yes. I mean yes, sir.'

The Captain nodded. 'That's better. You can leave now and return to your hut. The Lieutenant will be joining you shortly and giving you further necessary instructions. I will speak to you again at the end of six weeks.'

Stelios rose and walked away, his legs shaking. What had he done? Lucas had made life in the army sound enjoyable.

Stelios was thoroughly miserable. Each morning he was awoken by the loud banging on the hut door. The Lieutenant would enter and if he found anyone still in bed he would poke him with the stick he carried. It was a scramble between the men to use the unsavoury latrines that were outside and shared by two other huts before hurriedly changing into shorts and a vest and running up to the grass area that was used for the exercises.

At least a hundred men were there at a time and expected to work solidly at running or jumping on the spot, swinging their arms, bending in every direction and touching their toes. At the end of the hour Stelios felt breathless and exhausted and wished he did not have to scramble for his turn at the wash basins before changing into his uniform and take his place in the queue for a cup of coffee and a couple of slices of bread.

On leaving the mess hut they had to wait until the Lieutenant called the number of their hut and then form up before him whilst he inspected their uniform. Some men were sent to the hut to fetch a forgotten cap, neck tie or belt, whilst others were sent to clean their scuffed boots or put on their puttees.

Once the Lieutenant was satisfied that their uniforms were in order they were taken straight to the large, flat area where they would spend the next hours marching up and down, continually shouted at to keep in step with their neighbour before they were allowed a break for lunch.

After the meal Stelios would have liked nothing better than to be able to lie down and have a siesta, but again they were led away to learn how to erect a tent for shelter if they were out in the open. After that they were instructed in the correct way to pack their kit in the sturdy sack and reminded that they would have to carry it if they were out on manoeuvres, along with the tent and a blanket.

At the end of each day they were served a substantial meal and told they could have the remainder of the evening to themselves, but were expected to be in bed at ten when the lights must be extinguished. Some of the men would start a card game, whilst others chatted amongst themselves. Stelios would sit apart and try to concentrate on a book, but found it difficult with the continual noise and movement that went on around him.

The second week he found a little easier than the first. The mornings were still taken up with the physical exercises and drilling that he hated, but in the afternoon they were taken to another hut. Inside were rifles and revolvers. They were each given a revolver and shown how to clean and service it, practising removing it quickly from the holster that was given them to attach to their belt. Stelios had expected to be asked for the return of the firearm at the end of the session but was told they must now wear them as part of their uniform to become accustomed to the weight.

The following week rifles were handed to them and once again they had to learn how to break the weapon down, clean and reassemble it swiftly and correctly. Stelios was thoroughly bored. He had quickly learned how to reassemble the rifle and stood around waiting for his companions to complete the task. This was such a waste of his time. A rifle was allocated to each man and they were now expected to wear it slung on their back whilst they drilled and remove them to aim at an imaginary target when ordered.

Every man made basic mistakes. Some had not released the safety catch, other had not ensured it was on whilst they were carrying it.

The Lieutenant lectured them seriously. 'This is important. Before you place your rifle over your shoulder you must ensure the safety catch is deployed. Should you stumble when traversing rough ground the rifle could be discharged accidently and could well shoot whoever is following you. If you have to fire at an enemy you need to remember to remove the safety catch before pressing the trigger. An enemy will not give you a second chance. You will be a dead man.'

Stelios listened to him sceptically. Who were these enemies they were proposing to fire at? The guns were not even loaded.

More recruits had arrived at the camp and were being inducted into army life and Stelios realised that he had actually spent three weeks in the unpleasant conditions, his day continually regimented and organised. The physical exercises no longer left him aching from the exertion, but he found the marching incredibly boring and unnecessary.

The training with the guns had become more interesting when they were finally taken to a shooting range and given ammunition. He managed to hit the target once, all his other shots going wide.

The Lieutenant glared at him.

'Do you have something wrong with your eyes?'

'No, sir. I don't think so, sir.'

'Try again. You're right handed so close your left eye and concentrate on the target.'

Stelios still found it incredibly difficult to hit the target and at the end of the afternoon the Lieutenant called him to one side. 'I am arranging for you to have an eye test. If they confirm there is nothing wrong with your sight I shall assume you are deliberately missing. That will result in a charge against you.'

'It isn't deliberate, sir. I am trying, sir.'

'We'll find out.'

Cross with himself, Stelios ate his evening meal morosely. He had tried to hit the target and did not know why he had missed so consistently. The only consolation was that he would be attending the eye appointment whilst his companions were marching up and down.

'Read the letters on the board in front of you,' ordered the optician and Stelios obeyed.

Smaller letters were introduced and again Stelios read them easily. The optician made a note on his pad and looked at Stelios suspiciously. Was the man pretending to have a vision problem in the hope that he would be discharged? He took a torch and peered into Stelios eyes, moving back with a frown.

'Close your right eye and read those letters again.'

Stelios read them without a problem.

'Now close your left eye and read them.'

Stelios frowned. 'Are they the same letters?'

'Yes. What makes you think they are different?'

'They look, I don't know, fuzzy around the edges. I can't see them properly.'

The optician nodded and approached Stelios a second time with the torch, shining it directly into Stelios's right eye, lifting his eyelid, then pulling down the lower lid before finally moving back. 'Close both your eyes for a few minutes and then try again using just your right eye.'

Stelios had no more success the second time and felt both alarmed and puzzled. 'Why can't I read them?'

'You have myopia.'

'What's that? Where have I caught it?'

'You don't catch myopia. It is a condition you can be born with or develops. Your right eye does not focus properly, probably due to a short muscle in the eye. You need spectacles to correct it.'

'I've never had a problem in the past.'

'Have you ever tried to focus on anything with just your right eye? I doubt it, so the left eye has compensated for the defect. Using both eyes together in everyday life would not cause you any difficulty. Do you get headaches?'

'Sometimes.' Stelios took a shaky breath. Would his eye problem make him unfit to be in the army? He sincerely hoped it would be a good reason for them to discharge him.

The optician held up a lens before Stelios's right eye. 'Can you read the letters now?'

'They still look fuzzy.' A second lens was held up and Stelios realised he could see the letters far better.

'Do they look clearer?'

Stelios nodded. The second lens had made a good deal of difference.

'I'll write a prescription and get some spectacles made up for you,' continued the optician. 'Once you have them I'll have a look at your eyes again and see if they are correcting your sight sufficiently.'

The Lieutenant listened to Stelios when he explained that he had been diagnosed with myopia. He had already had a report from the optician.

'You will be excused target training until you have your spectacles. I shall expect to see an improvement in your performance then.'

'Yes, sir. Thank you, sir.'

'Whilst the other men continue with their armaments training you can spend the afternoon helping out in the catering department. They can always do with an extra hand.'

Stelios's heart sank. He had hoped the Lieutenant would say he was unable to shoot straight and therefore unsuitable for a position in the army. Now he was being sent to work in the kitchens.

For five days Stelios spent his afternoons scouring dirty pots or preparing vegetables for the evening meal. It was degrading menial work and he was relieved when he received a message to say he was to report to the optician as his glasses were ready.

Although Stelios was not sure he liked wearing the spectacles that he had been issued with he could not believe the difference they made. His right eye could see as perfectly as his left. He wished he had known about the problem earlier. When he had been studying for his examinations he seemed to have a perpetual headache and had assumed it was due to concentrating for hours at a time, often by the light of an oil lamp.

The first time he reported back to the shooting range he found that he was able to focus and hit the target four times out of every five shots fired from his revolver. Using a rifle was more difficult as he had to steady it with one hand whilst taking aim, but once he became used to the recoil his confidence increased and the Lieutenant finally declared he was as proficient as his fellow trainees.

At last there was only one more week of the hated physical exercises and drilling to endure. He had learnt how to erect his tent swiftly, pack his sack with the heaviest items at the bottom and carry it on his back along with his rifle and bandolier for most of a day. He had quite enjoyed the exercise where they had been taken to a wooded area with markers attached to the trees and told to aim at them with their revolvers.

He did not enjoy the second experience when they had to camp out in the area and were awoken in the middle of the night, told to take their rifles and shoot as if their lives depended upon it. There had been no time to put on his jacket and the bandolier and rifle strap cut into his shoulders as he sprinted across the rough ground with the others, only remembering at the last moment that he was not wearing his glasses. He hoped he would manage to satisfy the Lieutenant and not be asked to participate in the exercise another time.

At the end of their six weeks of arduous training each man was interviewed and Stelios once again asked to be transferred to the administrative department. The Lieutenant had spoken quietly to the Captain and Major and finally all three nodded their heads.

To Stelios's immense relief he was told that due to his defective eyesight he would not be suitable as a field soldier and would be sent for administrative training in Athens.

1939 – 1940

Stelios was feeling exceedingly pleased with himself. He had his own desk in the office he shared with other members of the administration staff. The first few weeks had been mundane, being shown the different forms that needed to be completed. Each training camp would send in the number of new recruits they had admitted and kitted out. A note of the clothing needed to replenish the stock was sent down to the stores and the items dispatched. The same had to be done for the armaments section. It was certainly not difficult.

Three afternoons each week he went to a separate room where he was instructed in the use of Morse code. At first he found it difficult as he struggled to hear the difference between dots and dashes. Once he saw the dots and dashes written down he had no problem translating them into words as he had made himself conversant with the letters they represented.

The other two afternoons he attended a typewriting course and was enjoying becoming more proficient, using the correct fingers for the keys and increasing his speed. When he was given a cover for the first time to place over the keyboard he looked at it in dismay. If he could not see the letters on the keys how would he know which one he should press? For the next two lessons he struggled, then realised that if he learnt the exact order of the letters he would be able to work out their position under the cover. Each night when he lay in bed he would repeat the order of the letters, along with the numerals and punctuation. Once he had mastered the sequence of the keys the lessons presented him without any difficulty

He no longer had to share a room with a number of other men, but had been placed in lodgings with five other men, each of them having their own small room. He received sufficient salary to enable him to buy his meals at a local taverna or the army canteen and enough money in his pocket to keep himself supplied with cigarettes and a little over to spend or save as he wished.

His immediate colleagues and the men he shared the lodgings with were more congenial than the recruits he had met whilst at the training camp. They would take a cigarette break together during the day, chatting amicably and often arranging to meet up during the evening and eating at the same taverna.

At first the men had talked about their families and Stelios had been reticent. Finally he was asked directly about his father's occupation and he spread his hands, a sad look on his face.

'I have no family unfortunately.'

The men had looked a little uncomfortable, but Tomas had asked for further details.

'I was an only child. My mother died when I was quite young and I spent time with my aunt and uncle. This enabled my father to work and save. He died just after I received my scholarship to the University, but fortunately had left enough money for me to be able to accept the place.'

'What about your aunt and uncle? Where are they?' persisted Tomas.

'Their daughter married and went to live in America. They decided to join her there now I was of an age to look after myself.'

'When we are given leave you'll have to come and meet my family. I'm sure they'll welcome you.'

'That's very kind,' replied Stelios without enthusiasm. 'Where do they live?'

'On the outskirts of Piraeus, away from the harbour. If one of us has passed our driving test by then they might let us borrow a bike and we could drive down there. That would be a laugh.'

Stelios smiled. He thought it very unlikely they would be allowed to use a motorised bike for their pleasure.

Stelios and Tomas formed a firm friendship, spending most evenings in each other's company, visiting church together on a Sunday morning followed by a walk. Stelios enjoyed imparting his knowledge of the Parthenon, its history and the surrounding area.

'How do you know so much about it?' asked Tomas. 'I've lived close by all my life and only visited a couple of times.'

'I lodged with a history teacher. I became interested in the building and structures that had been erected hundreds of years ago. Whenever I look at the Parthenon and the surrounding temples I never fail to be amazed at the mathematics that was involved in the construction. Each supporting pillar had exactly the same measurement and was tapered slightly at the top so they would look symmetrical. It must have been a magnificent sight when it was complete and painted in bright colours.'

'Painted?'

Stelios nodded. 'Bright red, blue and yellow. The paint has worn off over the years and an Englishman took away some of the carvings from the pediment and also a statue from the Erechtheion. It should never have been allowed to happen. It was robbery. No doubt the man would have liked to have taken away every stone and probably all our other monuments.'

'I'm exceedingly pleased that he did not. I particularly like the Tower of the Winds.'

'Why?' asked Stelios.

'Well, apart from it being beautiful it is not too large. You can see all the detail by walking around in a small circle. At the Parthenon you can only see a small section at a time. It's impossible to get a view of it as a whole building.'

'We'll go to the Hill of Philopappos next week. You have a magnificent view of the Parthenon and the outlying area of Athens from there. You can also tell me what you think of that monument.'

Stelios watched his colleagues carefully. He was far swifter at calculations than they were. His requisition orders were always completed well before theirs and he had never had them returned with a request for a recalculation. He felt it was definitely time for him to receive promotion.

He requested an appointment with the head of the department who also happened to be a Major. He entered the room and saluted smartly.

'Permission to speak, sir?'

The Major nodded, expecting a request for additional leave.

'I have been very happy working in the supplies department and enjoying the comradeship of my colleagues, but I would like to apply for a transfer and promotion, sir.'

The Major raised his eyebrows. 'Why do you think you warrant promotion?'

'I would like the experience of working in the financial department. I understand to have a position there I have to be at least a Second Lieutenant. At present I am only an Officer Designate, sir.'

'Apart from not having achieved the desired rank do you have any qualifications that would make me think the finance department could benefit from your work?'

'Yes, sir. I have a thorough knowledge of all aspects of mathematics, sir.'

'So do many other young soldiers. Put your request for promotion in writing and it will be placed before the Board when they next meet. Dismissed.'

'Yes, sir. Thank you, sir.' Stelios saluted and left the room. He knew the Major would want a report on his work and conduct and was confident that both would describe him as exemplary.

Stelios had mixed feeling when the Major sent for him three weeks later and said that his request for promotion had been granted, but his transfer to the finance department had been denied.

'An amount of time spent in the communications department could be beneficial to your knowledge of the overall organisation of the army. I understand you are a proficient typist and have also learnt Morse code?'

'Yes, sir. I'm also learning how to drive a motorcycle, sir.'

'You will move into the communications department next week and be responsible for typing some of the reports that come in. Two days each week you will relieve your companions and receive the messages sent in Morse. On occasions you may be asked to take a message to a unit. Whatever you are asked to deliver will be confidential and not to be read by yourself or any other person apart from the addressee. I suggest you study the map showing where the various units are positioned so you will know how to reach them if necessary. Dismissed.'

'Yes, sir. Thank you, sir.'

Stelios broke the news of his promotion and removal from the department to his colleagues and they appeared genuinely sorry that he was leaving them.

'Why did you ask to leave us?' asked Tomas as they stood clustered together in a corner of the room and smoking their cigarettes.

'It was nothing personal. I've enjoyed working with all of you. We'll still be at the same lodgings so we can still be friends and go out and about together.'

'So what's so attractive about communications?'

Stelios shrugged. 'I want promotion. If I am going to make the army my career I want to be a Major General at least, maybe even ending up as a General. I asked to go to the finance department as I knew I would have to be made a Second Lieutenant. The first step on the progress ladder; besides my mathematics are excellent and I know all about book keeping and accountancy. Hopefully it will only be a matter of time before I am moved there.'

Tomas laughed. 'Big mistake. They never place you in the most obvious job according to your ability. I wanted to learn to be a mechanic as I'm good with my hands and look where I am.'

'So why don't you ask for a move into communications? You're far better at Morse than I am.'

'I've decided I quite like it here and it isn't difficult work. If I trained as a mechanic I could be sent off anywhere to make repairs to the bikes or lorries. Working outside would be freezing cold in the winter and boiling hot in the summer.'

'I will be typing reports and recording the Morse code messages. I may be asked to take an urgent message to a unit using a bike.'

'I thought that was the job of the dispatch riders,' remarked Stathis.

Stelios shrugged. 'The Major only said I might be asked. I expect I would only be called upon if all the dispatch riders were already out.'

'Why don't they use a field telephone to communicate orders?'

'Something could be too confidential to be spoken of over a telephone. You never know who else might be listening.'

'Like who?' scoffed Stathis. 'I don't see why they employ dispatch drivers when they can speak over a telephone or use Morse code.'

'I suppose they could be out of range,' frowned Stelios. 'When I know the reason I'll tell you.'

'Why don't you ask if you can have this weekend off?' asked Tomas. 'I have Saturday and Sunday free and we could go down to visit my parents.'

'I'm on the rota to work.'

'I'll swap with you,' offered Andros.

Tomas turned to Stelios with a delighted smile. 'That would

be great. We could catch the bus to Piraeus and it would only be a short from there to my home.'

'What about getting back?'

'We can stay with them overnight, go to church in the morning and after lunch walk back to Piraeus. The buses run regularly for the workers.'

Stelios nodded. He did not particularly want to visit Tomas's family but he could not think of a suitable excuse.

Alighting from the bus they had taken as far as Piraeus Tomas led the way along the coastal path away from the port where activity was going on all around them and into the centre of the town.

'It's busier than Heraklion harbour,' admitted Stelios.

'We are a bigger country than Crete so we have need of more raw materials and food imports. The goods from here are transported to all corners of Greece, including our many islands. They collect olives and carob and bring those back to be processed here.'

Stelios nodded as if he was knowledgeable about such trade, but he had never given it a thought previously. 'Does your father work here?'

'No, he's a carpenter. He has his own workshop. What did you father do?'

Stelios hesitated. What had he said his father did for a living? 'He had a general store,' he said at last.

'So if you left the army you would be able to take it over?'

Stelios shook his head. 'It was sold when I took up my scholarship in Athens. I don't have any inheritance due to me.'

'Is that why you haven't found a girl you like – or are you already betrothed to one back in Crete?'

'I'm not promised to anyone, thank goodness.'

'What do you think of the girl in the laundry where we take our trousers to be sponged and pressed?'

Stelios shrugged. 'I've never taken much notice of her.'

'I'm going to speak to her father next week. I want to ask his permission to visit and get to know her better.'

Stelios stopped and looked at his friend in amazement. 'Are you serious? She works in a laundry.'

Tomas shrugged. 'What difference does that make? I could work for my father and become a carpenter. Of course, she may already be betrothed, but her big dark eyes have me enthralled.'

Olga and Nikos were delighted to see Tomas and greeted Stelios warmly. A friend of their son was welcome to stay the night and be treated as part of the family for a short while. Stelios had never been inside such a magnificent private house before. Tomas had shown him upstairs where the front bedrooms had balconies overlooking the street and the equally fine houses opposite. Stelios sat quietly sipping at a glass of wine and helping himself to olives or almonds as he fancied, whilst Tomas talked to his father.

'Are you happy staying in the supplies department?'

Tomas nodded. 'With the winter approaching it will be warmer there than working outside.'

'And you, Stelios? Do you work in the same department?'

'For one more week; then I move to the communications section.'

'Stelios is a Second Lieutenant now,' announced Tomas proudly.

Nikos raised his eyebrows. 'You should also be a Second Lieutenant by now Tomas. What is holding you back?'

Tomas gave a lazy grin. 'Probably my lack of ambition. Stelios wants to become a Colonel or even a Brigadier. I'm just happy plodding away and filling in forms.'

'Is that so, Stelios? You aim to become a Colonel?'

Stelios felt embarrassed. 'I'd like to think I was able to move up through the ranks. Whether I ever become a Colonel is another matter.'

'But you have made the first move in the right direction.'

Stelios nodded firmly. ‘I hope so. I really wanted to go into the finance department. After a few months I’ll apply for the transfer again.’

‘I wish you every success. You’re obviously an ambitious young man. You should follow his example Tomas. Why don’t you ask to move into the communications department?’

Tomas shook his head. ‘I’ll bide my time. I’m sure that if I ask to go to a particular department I’ll be sent somewhere else and get stuck there hating the work. I may not stay in the army anyway after the couple of years I signed on for. I’ll see what opportunities are around in the outside world.’

‘You know you can always join me in the business.’

Tomas shook his head. ‘I know I am good with my hands, but I don’t have the same meticulous eye for detail that you have, Pappa.’ Tomas turned to Stelios. ‘Feel free to wander around and have a look. Anything that is made from wood came from his workshop.’

Stelios looked at the ornate dresser that stood against the far wall. ‘Did you carve that, sir, or just make the framing?’

Nikos regarded the piece of furniture proudly. ‘I made it all. The basic structure and then I carved the pediment. It took a good deal of time, but it was worth it eventually.’

Stelios rose to take a closer look at the flowers and leaves. At each end of the pediment there was a figure of Poseidon, his trident reaching up to make the angle of the triangle.

‘That is quite amazing. No doubt you would have been asked to work on the Parthenon if you had been around in those days.’

Nikos shook his head. ‘I have never attempted to be a stone mason. At least if your chisel slips and you ruin a piece of wood you can usually start again. Imagine what a disaster it would be if you were putting the finishing touches to a capitol and you chopped off a leaf!’

Stelios smiled. ‘I can’t stop looking at it. I am trying to find a defect. Do you make furniture like this for all your customers?’

'Very few could afford such work. My carving is really a hobby. Occasionally I am asked to carve an angel on a crib. That will then be used time and again and then passed on to the children when they begin to have a family of their own. We still have the crib that I made for our two children. I hope one day it will be used again.'

Tomas rolled his eyes. 'You're worse than Mamma. She's always hinting to Daphne or me that we should think about getting married.'

'Who is Daphne?' asked Stelios. 'Are you betrothed to her?' Stelios remembered their earlier conversation when Tomas had mentioned his liking for the girl in the laundry.

'She's my sister,' grinned Tomas. 'You'll meet her this evening.'

Stelios found the shy, pretty girl attractive and on their return journey to Athens he asked Tomas about her.

'She's a seamstress. Pity she wasn't a boy. She's good with her hands and has inherited my father's eye for detail. She would have made an excellent carpenter.'

'Have your parents decided on a suitor for her?'

Tomas grinned. 'I think they're open to suggestions. Why? Are you interested?'

'I'd like to get to know her better.'

'So I imagine you'll be a frequent visitor to our house in the future.'

Stelios nodded. 'I've certainly not seen any girl around in Athens who has caught my eye.'

'Nor had I until I saw Miriam.'

'You really are serious about her?'

'Yes, despite her working in her father's laundry and being Jewish.'

'Jewish!'

'Yes. What difference does that make?'

'None at all to me. I'm thinking of what might happen in the future.'

'What do you mean?'

'Well,' Stelios hesitated, 'When I visited Delphi I met a German man who was excavating there. He asked me questions, mainly about Crete, but he claimed that Hitler was making the world a better place to live in.'

'I'm all for that.'

Stelios shook his head. 'The ideas were a little radical. He said that anyone with a marked disability would be taken to a special centre to be cared for.'

'Like a hospital, you mean?'

'He said special houses would be built for them, along with others where undesirable members of the community would be sent to live and work. He mentioned gypsies and Jews as undesirable.'

Tomas shrugged. 'Some of the gypsies are a perfect nuisance when they follow you around and beg, but there's no reason why the Jewish people shouldn't be left alone to get on with their lives.'

'From what I've heard the Jewish population of Germany and Austria are made to wear a yellow star so they can be recognised.'

'Why do they need to recognise them? Miriam and her family have lived in Greece for years. They're no different from us.'

'Maybe I misunderstood. If I hear anything more I'll let you know.'

Working in the communications department of the army meant that Stelios often knew far more about the events taking place across Europe before the ordinary Greek citizens. He knew Italy had made a pact with Germany, promising to support each other if either was threatened by war from other countries. The agreement had not stopped Italy from invading Albania and a large contingent of Greek troops had been amassed on the Albanian border as a deterrent to Mussolini advancing further. He hoped Greece would be able to avoid becoming embroiled in the situation.

In August he read that Russia and Germany had formed a non-aggression pact and he felt that was a reassuring move. His hopes were short lived. News that Germany had invaded Poland just nine days later and massacred many Poles, Jews and prisoners of war inflamed his concern for Tomas again, despite hearing that Britain had joined in the war to liberate the countries that had been occupied.

Tomas shrugged off his friend's worries. 'I know it is terrible for the people of those countries to be subjugated to such atrocities, but we are miles away. We have not promised to take sides with one or the other country or offer help to those who have been invaded. We are just sitting here minding our own business and keeping an eye on Turkey. We don't want the Turks back on our soil.'

Nothing Stelios said could make Tomas seriously concerned for his own and his family's safety.

'Now I'll tell you my news,' he said smiling happily. 'I've applied to become a Second Lieutenant and move into communications with you so that I get a pay increase. Miriam's father has agreed we can be married eventually. I was worried he would refuse me outright as I'm not Jewish. I've agreed to go to classes at the synagogue with him and learn about their faith. He's obviously hoping I will be converted.'

'And if that doesn't happen?'

'It won't. I'm not prepared to be circumcised. Miriam says she'll insist that she marries me anyway, provided I do not interfere with her religious convictions.'

'Why don't you try to convert her?' suggested Stelios.

'I might, once we're married.'

'How do your parents feel about you marrying a Jewish girl?'

Tomas shrugged. 'They're not happy. I took Miriam and her parents to visit them. I hired a taxi to go there and back and it cost me almost two months salary. Now they've met Miriam and her parents they agree they are very nice people. If they were of the Greek Orthodox religion there would be no problem at all.'

'So where will you get married? In the church or the synagogue?' asked Stelios.

'Nothing is arranged yet. I agreed, rather reluctantly, to wait at least a year. It's going to be difficult and I'm never alone with her. A chaste kiss on arrival and leaving is the most I'm allowed. How are you progressing with Daphne?'

'Slowly. I think she likes me.'

Tomas grinned. His sister had spent most of the weekend talking about the young man.

More disconcerting news arrived from Poland. Anyone who disobeyed an order from a German soldier was given the death penalty for disobedience. Stelios was accustomed to obeying orders given to him by his superiors during the day, but if he was about in the town in his own time he could not be commanded by an army official to undertake any task and if asked was free to refuse.

The news of the German advance and atrocities was published in the newspapers and discussed freely in the tavernas. Stelios listened, not disclosing that most of the facts were already known to him and sometimes the stories were exaggerated and others were not always reported in their full horror.

The women were particularly scandalized when they heard that children had been taken from their natural parents in Poland to be brought up in Germany and indoctrinated with the beliefs of Hitler.

'Why would they do such a thing?' asked Olga of Stelios when he visited their house to call on Daphne.

'I can only imagine that if children are taught from an early age that whatever Germany does is right they will believe it. They will grow up convinced that anyone who disobeys is deserving of death and agree that the atrocities we hear about are legitimate retribution.'

Olga shook her head. 'If anyone had tried to take either of my children away I would have refused to let them. Don't the Polish mothers care about their offspring?'

'I'm sure they care just as much as you,' Stelios spread his hands, 'but what can they do? If they resist they are shot and the children taken anyway. Better to stay alive and hope that one day you may be reunited.'

Olga regarded Stelios sceptically. 'Do you think the children will be returned?'

Stelios sighed. He suddenly felt overwhelmed with guilt. He had only written once to his family since his return to Athens and disowned them to his associates. How much grief and anguish had he caused his mother? It was too late now to make amends.

'I hope so,' he replied lamely.

Stelios's work in the communications department changed. He was promoted to a Lieutenant and no longer spent the days typing out documents that were no more than speculation on the moves Germany intended to make in Europe or their latest positions in the occupied countries. He now spent every day listening to Morse code and was expected to type out messages, usually from the units in Albania, as they arrived in the office and take them immediately upon completion to his commanding officer, the Major.

Stelios had a horror of being sent to the borders of Albania as a communications officer and decided the time had come to request a transfer into the finance department again.

The Major regarded him sternly. 'This is your second application for a department transfer. You appear to be dissatisfied wherever you are placed.'

'No, sir. I've been happy working in communications, but my first love is mathematics, sir. I miss working with numbers, sir.'

'You are not requesting this move in the false hope that you will receive promotion?'

'No, sir. I became a Lieutenant recently, sir. I don't expect to be promoted again for some time, sir.'

The Major scribbled Stelios's name on the pad before him. 'I'll have a word with finance when I next see someone around.

I don't hold out a lot of hope that they'll have a vacancy.'

'Thank you, sir.' Stelios left the Major feeling disheartened. He had hoped he would be granted an almost immediate position, making him safe from a transfer to an area where fighting was taking place.

'Are you sure this is correct?' asked the Major when Stelios handed him a short typewritten note saying that the "Elli" had been sunk at the island of Tinos.

'Quite certain, sir. The information was repeated to me a second time, sir.'

The Major pushed back his cap and read the news again. 'This is confidential until it has been verified by an independent report. It could be propaganda to stir up unrest.'

'Yes, sir. Understood, sir.'

'Contact the naval authorities and find out if they confirm the report is authentic.'

Stelios saluted and returned to his desk. It took him some time before he was able to make contact with the communications department in the naval office by the radio and when he finally received details of the sinking of the ship he was horrified. The "Elli" had been at anchor and most of the crew preparing to go ashore to participate in the service to commemorate the Icon of the Holy Virgin that had originally been found on the site.

'What about the crew?' he managed to ask.

'At present nine confirmed dead and twenty four wounded,' replied the disembodied voice. 'Fortunate not have been more casualties as the "Elsi" and "Esperos" were also at the harbour. The torpedo missed them.'

'Who fired it?'

'Not known at present.'

Stelios took the information through to the Major who read it swiftly. 'This is the work of the Devil. The navy will pass the information on to the media. That is not up to us, so no idle talk in the taverna. I must inform the Generals of the situation. This could change things dramatically.'

Without formally dismissing Stelios the Major left his office and Stelios hurried back to his desk. He wished he was able to attend the meeting to ascertain what action was going to be taken to avenge the sinking of the cruiser.

When the Major sent for Stelios three days later his heart sank, sure he was going to be transferred to the Albanian front. He saluted and waited until the Major looked up at him.

'You requested a transfer to the finance department – is that correct?'

'Yes, sir.'

'You can move there next week. Dismissed.'

'Yes, sir. Thank you, sir.'

Stelios was elated and also relieved. Finance for the army was dealt with in Athens. Dispatch riders would arrive with a request for money for a collection of outstanding bills that needed to be paid in the area where a battalion was stationed. The amounts were checked and a total sum withdrawn from the bank to cover the debts and taken back to the units by the dispatch rider the following week.

Stelios was enjoying working in the accounts department. It was good to be working with numbers again. His speed for addition and subtraction had not left him and he found he completed his duties easily. He began to look forward to a dispatch rider arriving and handing over a bulging case of papers. He would examine them diligently; putting aside those that he needed to pass through to the supplies department where replacement items of uniform, tents, ground sheets and blankets; guns and ammunition had to be accounted for separately, along with the petrol that was used by the motorised bikes and lorries.

He had separate account ledgers for the baker, butcher, general stores and pharmacy. Each bill had to be entered individually and the amounts totalled. He would then enter the final amounts into the master ledger, double check that the totals agreed and then send a chit for that amount to the bank.

When the messenger returned he would check the cash and then place the correct total on each pile of bills. He would wrap the bills around the notes, replace them into the case and lock it in the safe until the following week when the dispatch rider would return. The routine did not vary, some days more than one dispatch rider would arrive but due to Stelios's efficiency they were not delayed.

To his consternation one week he could not get his figures to agree. He had totalled the bills, entered each one into the ledger and sent the final figure to the bank. Now he had separated the money to pay the different accounts, added them together again and there was a five hundred drachmas discrepancy between his original total and the amount sent by the bank.

Stelios rechecked the amount of cash he had received and the amount he had allocated to each pile of bills. There were five hundred more drachmas from the bank than the total of the individual accounts. Despite checking his addition twice more he could not understand the reason. He placed the five hundred drachmas to one side. The bank cashier must have made an error and when it was discovered he would be requested to return the sum.

No message came from the bank and the problem continued to worry away at Stelios. He would lie in bed at night and think about it, finally deciding that he must check again that the figures in the individual ledgers agreed with the totals he had transferred to the main ledger.

At the end of a fruitless hour, when every entry and all the addition was correct he sat back perplexed. He removed his glasses and rubbed his eyes, leaning his head on his hand, but still looking down at the page in the ledger. Then he saw it. Where he was short sighted in his right eye it acted like a magnifying glass if he inspected anything closely. The badly written three in the total looked like an eight. He had misread it time and again and obviously the cashier had done the same.

Stelios pushed the ledger to one side. What was he going to do? He was not willing to admit that the error was his, but there were five hundred drachmas sitting in his drawer that he could not account for. If challenged he could say that he was looking for the discrepancy and if the bank sent a demand for the repayment of the sum he had it there to hand. Satisfied he turned his attention to that day's work.

Three weeks later the money was still sitting there. Stelios decided that no one had spotted the mistake and decided to experiment. When he added the final total together ready to send to the bank he again wrote a number three that could well be confused with an eight and waited to see what happened.

The messenger returned and handed the money to Stelios, waiting whilst he checked that the money was correct. Stelios looked up and nodded.

'To the drachma, as usual,' he declared.

Having distributed the money between the bills he slipped the extra fifty drachmas into his drawer. The five hundred was still sitting there and he decided that he would take it back to his lodging that night. If he was ever challenged now about the discrepancy he could show that the total of the bills and the entries in the main ledger agreed. No one could prove that he had received any extra cash and suspicion would automatically fall on the cashier.

Stelios hid the money in his kit bag. He had no intention of spending liberally so that Tomas and his other friends began to question the origins of his sudden wealth.

It became customary now for Stelios to write a number three so that it would look like a number eight unless you gave it a close inspection. He never tried to falsify any other number, sometimes increasing the bill by no more than a few drachmas, but he was often able to add fifty drachmas to his horded notes and occasionally adding five hundred.

Stelios was not the only person working in the government department that helped themselves whenever the opportunity arose. Before Tomas left the supplies department he had taken some extra blankets for his family and also for Miriam's and every man requisitioned an extra box of ammunition for their revolver and rifle. If they did not need them there were plenty of men who lived in the countryside who would welcome some additional bullets to shoot the wildlife and be willing to pay.

To the joy and pride of the Greek people their army had entered Albania, pushing back the Italian forces until they regained control of at least a quarter of the country. Stelios was relieved that he was not with them. The winter would be cruel to those who were living under canvas or marching through torrential rain and bitter winds. Stelios, along with the remainder of the population, was convinced that Mussolini would realise the futility of continuing to fight and his forces would retreat back to Italy now the winter had arrived. The British had joined the Greek air force in bombing raids hoping to dislodge Mussolini's forces from the area. Contrary to their expectations, the Italians had not withdrawn their troops, but asked Germany to join them.

Whilst waiting for the additional support, the Italians held the ground they had occupied and also sent a contingent over to Africa and were fighting the British for occupation of Somaliland. Stelios felt depressed. Greece was becoming surrounded by enemies. Only Turkey was not embroiled in the conflict, but he was sure that if they asked for Turkish help they would once again be relinquishing their country to a foreign ruler.

The German army continued to advance through Bulgaria and began a pincer movement to join up with the Italian forces who were still trying to dislodge the Greeks from Albania. Although the British sent a ground force to assist the Greek army they were hopelessly outnumbered. Finally Mussolini ordered the Greek government to allow his Italian troops to enter and occupy the country or face the consequences.

Prime Minister Metaxas was still hoping that Greece would be able to stay neutral and not be involved in the conflict and his reply was an immediate "no" that was broadcast to the nation. Most of the population of Greece approved his decision, but Stelios was seriously worried.

'If Germany is going to join forces with Italy and fight us on the border of Albania what chance do we have?'

'Our army will hold them off,' Tomas assured him, but Stelios shook his head.

'The men are fighting bravely, but we don't have the resources available. If they manage to break our lines of defence they'll not stop there. They'll continue into Greece and we will be occupied like the other European countries. We've heard of the reprisals against anyone who dares to oppose them. Metaxas refused them entry. No doubt they'll take their revenge on the government. Accuse them of treason against Hitler or some such nonsense.'

'You mean we are in danger?' For the first time Tomas looked alarmed.

'They're not likely to bother with us. We are just insignificant workers. We are not responsible for making political decisions.'

'So we don't have to worry.'

'I wouldn't say that. I think we are all in danger; an innocent word could be misconstrued. I begin to wish I had stayed in Crete and not joined the army.' Stelios sighed. 'This would have to happen just as I have been given the job I wanted.'

'Maybe I could resign and go back and work as a carpenter for my father. I'm sure you could come with me and he'd find you a job. You could keep his accounts for him,' suggested Tomas.

'I don't think the army would let us resign at the moment. We'll just have to wait and see what happens.'

Two weeks before Christmas Stelios and Tomas were both told they were entitled to two days leave. At Tomas's urging, Stelios agreed to go down to his friend's family and spend the time with them.

'We can catch the bus down when we finish on the twenty fourth. It will be dark, of course, when we walk to Piraeus, but I can get hold of a couple of torches. We can walk back to Piraeus on the twenty sixth and be back to work the following morning.'

'Won't your parents mind us just arriving? They may have other plans.'

Tomas shook his head. 'I'll send them a letter so they will expect us. We can join them for the midnight service; go to church the next morning and then spend the remainder of the day at home; besides, I'm sure Daphne would like to see you.' Tomas winked knowingly.

Stelios blushed. He was not averse to spending time with the attractive girl. He was envious of the men who discussed the merits of marriage or their latest encounter with a loose woman, and much as he would like to experience the pleasure they claimed to enjoy there was no way he was going to visit a prostitute. They were dirty.

'I'll need to buy a gift for them, and for Daphne,' he added. 'What are you buying Miriam?'

'I'm not. They don't celebrate Christmas.'

Stelios looked at his friend in annoyance. 'You're no help! What are you getting your parents?'

'My father's easy. A wood carving knife.'

'And your mother?'

'Bit more of a problem, but I saw some woollen stockings the other day. I'm sure she'd appreciate a couple of pairs to wear in the winter.'

'And Daphne?'

'I'll probably get her a pair of stockings as well.'

Stelios nodded. He could buy some tobacco for Nikos and a pair of gloves for Olga, but Daphne was another matter. He spent the evening thinking about his friend's sister and decided he would speak to Nikos and ask if he could be considered as her suitor. If he was not betrothed soon the other men would be looking askance at him and making lewd suggestions.

He counted out the money he had hidden in his kit bag and considered carefully. He had planned to buy a wireless so he could listen to the news each night and also a wrist watch so he no longer had to rely on the church bells telling him when it was time to rise or arrive at work. Finally he wanted to have enough money to buy a motorised bike. Provided Daphne had no objection to being betrothed to him having a bike would enable him to ride down to Piraeus to visit her. That would be beneficial, but if he was going to buy her a gift that announced they were betrothed he would have to spend some of the money on a traditional gold necklace.

Having made the decision to speak to Nikos, Stelios pocketed five hundred drachmas, having no idea how much a gold necklace would cost, and returned the remainder of his savings to his kit bag. He needed to make an arrangement with a jeweller so he could return the necklace and reclaim his money if he was rejected by the family. In that event he also needed another small gift that he could present to her. He was certainly not going to give her a gold necklace if she was not interested in eventually becoming his wife.

Tomas waited impatiently whilst Stelios locked the door to his room and pushed at it to ensure it was securely fastened.

'I don't know why you bother to lock it. These locks are so flimsy the door could be pushed open.'

'If I left it unlocked I wouldn't know if anyone had come in to borrow anything.' Stelios dropped the key into his pocket where it joined another smaller one that belonged to the cash box he had purchased.

'What would they want to borrow? We only have our army kit in there.'

'You might have, but I have my books. I would be very annoyed if anyone borrowed those and didn't return them,' replied Stelios. He was not going to admit that he had a locked cash box containing a quantity of drachmas hidden in the bottom of his kit bag. 'I doubt if you'd be very happy if you found someone had 'borrowed' your jacket or trousers whilst you were away and left torn and dirty ones in their place.'

Tomas looked slightly alarmed. 'Do you think anyone will?'

Stelios shook his head. 'It's very unlikely. If they wanted some new uniform they would just fill in a requisition slip and send it through to supplies.'

'Well if you are now satisfied that the fortress is secure we ought to get to the bus station. We don't want to miss the bus as there won't be another one tonight. Have you got everything?'

Stelios picked up his almost empty sack and nodded. He had checked and double checked that the gold necklace he had bought for Daphne was in the box and tied securely with a piece of string. To his delight it had cost him less than he had anticipated and he had been able to replace nearly three hundred drachmas back into his cash box. He had also purchased a small silver brooch with the traditional Greek 'eye' to ward off evil set in it. If her father refused him as her suitor he would give Daphne that as a present rather than the necklace and no one would be any the wiser.

As they approached the residential area of Piraeus there was a lamp in nearly every window where the occupants were having a late meal before preparing to go to church for the midnight service. Stelios yawned. He hoped he would not disgrace himself by falling asleep in the church. He had worked all day and now having walked from the bus stop at Piraeus harbour he would have been happy to have gone to bed.

Tomas opened the door to his house and his mother greeted

him excitedly. 'We hoped you would be here before we had to leave for church. I wouldn't want you to arrive at an empty house. I've saved some food for you both and you'll have time to eat before we have to go.'

Stelios shook hands with Nikos and Daphne and allowed Olga to clasp him to her and kiss him on both cheeks. 'I'm so pleased you were both able to get leave at the same time. You would have been welcome here, Stelios, even if Tomas had been unable to join us. I wouldn't like to think of you spending Christmas on your own without any family around you.'

'Thank you,' muttered Stelios, wishing Olga would release him so he could ask Nikos if he could speak to him privately for a few minutes.

'Come and sit down. Daphne, fetch the moussaka. I've been keeping it warm for the last hour.'

Stelios joined Tomas at the table and ate hungrily. He was obviously not going to have the opportunity to speak to Nikos yet.

The midnight church service over Stelios sidled over to Nikos and spoke to him quietly. 'Could I have a private word, sir?'

'Of course.' Nikos was fairly certain that Stelios was going to ask if he could marry Daphne. The young man was eminently respectable, had obtained promotion in the army and was a friend of Tomas, what more could he ask of a suitor?

'Tomas, walk your mother and Daphne safely home. We'll catch up with you in a few minutes.'

Tomas grinned. He had an idea that Daphne was going to be the subject of their discussion.

Stelios stammered and stuttered, blushing furiously, as he tried to ask Nikos if he would object to him becoming betrothed to his daughter.

Finally Nikos took pity on him. 'I understand you want to marry Daphne?'

'Yes, sir.' Stelios frowned. 'That is, of course, if she is not already promised to someone and is willing to consider me.'

'You'd have to ask her that yourself. I've not heard that her eye has alighted on anyone in particular. I'd not force her if she decided you were not for her, although I think she'd be a fool to refuse a nice young man like yourself.'

'Thank you, sir. Maybe I could escort her back from church tomorrow and broach the subject?'

Stelios sat through the Christmas morning service without listening to the words of the priest. He could see Daphne sitting on the other side of the aisle with her mother, looking demure and innocent. He wondered if her father had spoken to her.

He was unsure how he should go about asking Daphne and was worried that she might refuse him outright. That would be so embarrassing. He wished now that he had asked her father to speak to her on his behalf.

Stelios waited outside the church until Daphne and Olga finally emerged.

'I must speak to Maria and Yiannis,' announced Olga. 'You two walk on without me.'

Daphne smiled shyly up at Stelios. 'It was a very nice service, wasn't it?'

Stelios blushed. 'I'm afraid I was not paying a lot of attention. I had something else on my mind. I spoke to your father last night, Daphne. I asked if he would give permission for us to be betrothed, provided you had no objection, of course.'

A delighted smile lit up Daphne's face and she blushed more deeply than Stelios. 'I have no objection, Stelios.'

'Really?' Stelios could not believe that it had been so easy.

Daphne nodded. 'I liked you when you first visited us with Tomas. I have got to know you better during your subsequent visits and I think I could be happy married to you.'

Stelios let out his breath. 'I was so worried you would say no; that there was another young man that you preferred or you did not like me sufficiently to consider marriage.'

'I think you would make me a good husband, Stelios. Mamma and Pappa think highly of you and you are Tomas's best friend.'

'I have bought you a special present to celebrate our betrothal.'

'Suppose I had refused you? What would you have done with the present then?'

'I made an arrangement with the jeweller that I could return it to him if it was not acceptable.'

Daphne raised her eyebrows. Stelios was certainly practical when it came to financial matters.

Stelios slipped the slim gold chain over Daphne's head, whilst her parents and Tomas clapped.

'A toast,' declared Nikos, filling the wine glasses. 'A toast to the newly betrothed couple. Welcome to the family, Stelios.'

Olga kissed Stelios on both cheeks whilst Tomas hugged him and clapped him on the back. 'I've always wanted a brother. When are you two going to be married?'

Stelios was taken aback. 'I haven't really thought that far ahead yet. I need to make sure I have sufficient money saved to rent an apartment. I don't want Daphne living in a one room lodging like we do.'

Nikos nodded his approval. 'Maybe we could think about May, before the weather turns too hot.'

'I'll find out the cost of apartments in Athens. Provided I have enough saved by then and have found somewhere suitable for us to live May would be an excellent month.'

1941

Stelios purchased a wrist watch, but hesitated at the purchase of a wireless. He had decided that a motor cycle was impractical due to a shortage of petrol in the city although it would have enabled him to visit Daphne frequently and on the weekends that he was scheduled to work he could have lent it to Tomas to visit his family. If they had the same time off together they could both travel down without the need for the bus to Piraeus and the walk to Tomas's home, but without sufficient petrol being available it would be useless.

He continued to falsify the figures for the bank withdrawals whenever it was possible to do so. He was confident that if the discrepancy was ever detected he would be able to claim innocence. His ledgers agreed and the correct money had been sent to the various units. It had to be the fault of the bank cashier who had entered the total into his ledger incorrectly and pocketed the extra money.

During the evenings he would spend his time wandering around Athens looking for suitable accommodation and eventually found two rooms that he felt would be acceptable. There was a small room that could be used as their bedroom and the other was large enough for a dresser and a table and chairs. At the end of the hallway was a kitchen and toilet with a basin, both of which would be shared with the other two tenants on that floor. He hoped Daphne would find it acceptable after living in a house. He would assure her that it was only temporary and that within a year he would have found an apartment with their own kitchen and bathroom that they would not be expected to share.

Now he had become used to the idea of getting married he was quite looking forward to it. He just hoped that he would not find any ugly blemish on Daphne's body that would repulse him. He still examined his own body each week for any sign that he had contracted leprosy from his brother, but had found nothing.

He just wished the fighting on the Albanian front would come to an end and a peace agreement could be signed.

The whole of Greece had waited with bated breath for the outcome of the fighting on the Albanian border. The Germans had advanced through Bulgaria and Yugoslavia to meet up with the Italian forces. Despite having British forces sent from Libya to assist them the Greek forces had been driven back and by the twelfth of April they were in full retreat, allowing the Germans to enter northern Greece and terrorise the inhabitants. The German invaders pressed on, wiping out any resistance from the people, helping themselves to food supplies and anything else that took their fancy from the shops and local houses.

The progress of the German troops was remorseless and on the sixteenth of April the British began to evacuate their troops from Volos and Piraeus. On the twentieth of April the news arrived that Metsovo had surrendered and the following day it was the turn of Ioannina to capitulate. Finally on the twenty third of April Thessaloniki was taken and Lieutenant General Papagos resigned from his position as head of the armed forces. The Greek army that had been assembled at Piraeus began to crowd onto every available vessel to take them across the sea to Egypt.

Stelios wished he was back in the communications department so he would know exactly what was happening. During a break he climbed the stairs to where the communications rooms were situated. The men were gathered in small groups discussing the most recent events in hushed tones. Stelios walked across to Emmanuel who he had been friendly with when he worked there.

'What's the latest, Manu?'

'Lieutenant General Papagos has resigned.'

'I heard that,' nodded Stelios. 'Is there any further news?'

Emmanuel hesitated. 'I've heard that King George is being taken to Crete for safety.'

'What about the government?'

'I understand they'll go with him. Set up a government in exile I expect, although what they can do from there goodness knows.'

'It's just a mess,' sighed Stelios. 'Who are we supposed to take our orders from now?'

'Probably the Germans,' replied Emmanuel dourly. 'I'm thinking of handing in my uniform at the end of the week and taking my wife and children to Nafplio. We have family there.'

'Good idea,' agreed Stelios. If the Greek army was now going to be taken over and run by Germans his lucrative scheme would be at an end. 'If you hear any more let me know.'

Emmanuel nodded. He had more important things to think about than keeping Stelios abreast of the news and troop movements.

Stelios sought out Tomas. 'What are you going to do?'

Tomas shrugged. 'There's not much I can do. I doubt if I could fight off the German army single handed.'

'Remember what I said that young German told me about sending people away to be resettled and work for them? Shouldn't you warn Miriam and her family? If they were sent away you'd probably not know where they'd gone and never see her again.'

'We don't know if they'll enter Athens.'

'So why has King George fled to Crete? Why has Papagos resigned? They know full well that the Germans will enter Athens and when they do they'll be looking for the government ministers and then the army. When they've finished dealing with them they'll turn their attention to the sick and those they call undesirable.'

'Where would they go? The only movement by sea is reserved for troops.'

'Would your family be willing to look after them? If they were closer to Piraeus they could have the opportunity of boarding a ship for Egypt once all the troops have been ferried over.'

Tomas turned anguished eyes on his friend. 'I wouldn't want to take the chance that the ship she was on was bombed. They might be safer down with my parents. I'll speak to Abraham tonight and see if he will agree to leave the laundry.'

Abraham shook his head when Tomas suggested he closed the laundry and took his wife and daughter to Piraeus.

'I cannot do that. I have other relatives in Athens, my two aunts are old and my uncle lives miles away. I cannot turn my back on them, besides; the Germans will need to have their uniforms cleaned. It could be quite a profitable time for me.'

'Couldn't you send Naomi and Miriam?'

'And who would help me in the laundry? No, we are good law abiding citizens and we will stay here. I thank you for your concern, but we are in no danger.'

Nothing Tomas could say would persuade his future father in law to leave the city.

Stelios requested an interview with Major Colonomous and asked to be transferred back into the communications department.

'I thought you were happy to be in finance?'

'I am, but I'm sure I could be more useful in communications rather than adding up figures or running away to the safety of Egypt.'

Major Colonomous regarded Stelios gravely. 'You may consider that going to Egypt is a safe option, but the men will be joined with the Allied troops and expected to take their place alongside them and fight whenever necessary.'

Stelios swallowed. 'I appreciate they will be risking their lives, but I do not consider that I would be any use to them. When I did my initial training I was found to have defective eyesight. If I lost my glasses I would not be able to see well enough to shoot at a target.'

The Major frowned and Stelios persisted, ignoring protocol. 'You will need to be in contact with Egypt to know what the forces there are planning. You know I am proficient in Morse code. I could be more use to you here than sitting in Egypt. If the Germans do come into the city we need to let the Allied Army know so they can come to our assistance. Why don't you ask a small nucleus of men to stay in Athens? My friend, Tomas, would be willing to stay and I'm sure some of the other men would prefer to be here where they can keep an eye on their families, sir.'

A week later Stelios was informed that he was moving back to the communications department as the finance section was no longer viable. The banks did not have the requisite funds available to pay those who had supplied food to the army outposts. The Athenians were hoarding their money at home and even if the cash had been available there was no safe way of transporting it. Those who were owed money would have to save their bills and claim recompense at a later date.

Stelios found he was no longer given any reports to type. All his time was spent listening and interpreting the Morse code messages that were coming in from all over Greece. Disconcerting news arrived saying that the Germans had captured the bridges over the Corinth Canal, effectively cutting off supplies and troops from the rest of the mainland. Athens was alone, dependent upon the hurriedly recruited troops and police force to defend their city. Those who could afford to do so, rushed to the shops and bought rice, flour and lentils, but even these basic commodities were in short supply. To assist their invasion of Greece the German Luftwaffe methodically bombed any Greek ship they saw, either sinking them outright with all the crew or crippling them so they were forced to limp into the nearest friendly port capable of accepting them.

The Germans finally swept into Athens on the twenty seventh of April, their tanks, lorries and motor cycles progressing unhindered into the heart of the city, whilst the army was being hurriedly evacuated to Crete or Egypt leaving the citizens defenceless. The Greek flag was taken down from the Parthenon and the German flag, with the black swastika, was flown in its place.

Each German soldier was given a hundred marks each to purchase whatever they wanted from the Athenian shops. Most of them ignored the money in their pocket, simply entering a shop and removing any goods they wanted. Cameras, radios, boots, shoes, stockings and clothing were the items they preferred, but if none were available they would take anything else that sat on the shelves until the warehouses and shops were empty. They would then turn their attention to the leather workers and help themselves to a suitcase, pack it full of their booty and send it back to their families in Germany.

Raw materials, leather and metal were seized effectively closing down the factories and manufacturing premises. Construction was halted, leaving essential repairs to buildings incomplete due to the lack of both nails and cement.

The chemists' stores were emptied and the contents taken to supplement the German field hospitals' medical supplies before they turned their attention to the hospitals which they systematically stripped of medicines and equipment.

Every Greek citizen was ordered to take any vehicle they possessed to Syntagma Square, where they were parked along with trucks and buses; even a bicycle was included and had to be taken to a depot and handed over. All the fuel in the city was confiscated and on the coast the fishing boats were taken along with donkeys and carts. The University, schools, libraries and public buildings were closed, food shops placed notices in their windows to say there was no food available and left their doors open for the people to see the truth of the statement.

Those who had been in regular employment suddenly found they had no work to go to; the shop or factory was closed, there was no public transport available and drivers were not needed. Most of the populace cowered inside their homes, shocked into submission by the speed with which their lives had changed within the space of a few days.

The tavernas were closing steadily due to lack of customers and supplies unless they were willing to serve the Germans. If they were included on their "hospitality" list there was no shortage of wine or spirits. The Germans also wanted women to entertain their needs and many girls were forced to prostitute themselves in the establishments to ensure they were safe from the marauding soldiers who would discard them into the gutter when the group had satisfied itself.

Stelios was frightened. When he saw the red German flag with the black swastika he gritted his teeth and cursed the invaders beneath his breath. He wished now that he had gone to Egypt with the fighting men. He could have volunteered to work in the communications department over there and been in a place of safety. The Germans appeared merciless. He had seen three of them knock an elderly woman over and when her husband tried to assist her to her feet they had knocked him down also and begun to kick him. Stelios had promptly turned and retraced his steps. He would not be able to help either of them and certainly did not want the same treatment meted out to him.

'What do you think we should do?' asked Tomas.

'There's nothing we can do. We can't fight against them,' replied Stelios miserably.

'I know that! I meant should we go and see if our army office is open? Should we report for work? We don't want to be considered deserters.'

'That would be rather foolish, putting on our uniform and marching along the street telling the Germans we are part of the

Greek army. We'd probably be shot on sight.'

Tomas shook his head. 'I'm not suggesting we wear our uniform. If the main door is unlocked we could slip inside and see if the Major is around.'

'More likely to be a load of Germans.'

'If there are Germans in there they are likely to be talking. We'd know immediately they weren't Greek.'

'Do you think they would just leave the door unlocked and no one there on guard?'

Tomas shrugged. 'In that case we say we were looking for a friend who is missing and get out quickly.'

'You think they will believe that?' asked Stelios sceptically.

'Can you come up with a better idea?'

Stelios shook his head. He hoped they would find the door locked, although he had no idea how long he would be able to survive in Athens without his regular income from the army. His illicit savings would probably last him no longer than a year, even living frugally.

'You go out first, walk to the left slowly and I'll go out a short while after you and turn right. We'll meet as if by accident and then walk on together. If we're stopped we'll say we're looking for work and food.'

Tomas shook his head. 'I'm not telling them I'm looking for work. They'll probably send me off to work on building those accommodation blocks you spoke about.'

'I doubt if anyone will stop us, but we'll say we're teachers, looking for food and on our way to see if the school is open again if that makes you happier.'

'Why should we leave separately? We lodge in the same house.'

'Unless they already know the lodgings belong to the army and are watching the building it's as well for them not to know that there are a collection of young men here. We'd probably be accused of holding meetings.'

'Alright,' Tomas held up his hand to stop Stelios interrupting him. 'We'll leave separately and meet up. I just think you're being a bit paranoid.'

Stelios gave his friend a sour look. It was better to be paranoid and see danger lurking everywhere than wander around in blissful ignorance and be shot.

'Walk slowly, look into the shops as you go past,' ordered Stelios.

'What for?'

'If we're stopped and they've seen us looking into the shops it will lend credence to our story that we're looking for food. If we rush along the road they'll think we're in a hurry to meet someone,' explained Stelios patiently. 'When we get to the offices we'll stop and light a cigarette. Whilst we're doing that we can try the door and see if it's unlocked. If we're unable to get in we finish our cigarettes and just walk on.'

Stelios slouched along the road towards Syntagma Square, his hands in the pockets of his trousers and his head down. He did not want to draw attention to himself. His eyes continually darted left and right, noting that German soldiers could be seen on the rooftops and on every corner there was an armed German who would often stop someone for no obvious reason. He should have anticipated the presence of the troops in the centre of the town and taken to the back streets.

Stelios felt a hand on his shoulder and turned around, expecting to see a gun pointing at him.

'Where are you going?'

'To see if the school where I work is open.'

'That is unlikely. What work do you do?'

'I am a teacher.'

The uniformed German scrutinised him carefully. 'Your face is familiar. Where have I seen you before? Have you been brought before me for questioning?'

Stelios shook his head. 'I live locally. You may have seen me around, but I've not been arrested for any reason and questioned.'

Herman snapped his fingers. 'I remember you now. You are the student who came to Delphi when I was working there.'

Stelios looked surprised. 'Fancy remembering me.'

'I have an excellent memory for faces. You are the young man who was more interested in architecture than our finds. You brought your tutor over to us.'

'That's right. Are the excavations continuing?'

'I have no idea. I am a Major in the army now and I am expecting to gain further promotion,' Herman boasted.

'Yes, you look very smart in your uniform.' Stelios thought it wise to ingratiate himself with the German.

'I think we will adjourn to a local taverna. You people seem resentful that we are in Greece. When I have spoken with you I am sure you will understand why we are here.' Herman placed his hand under Stelios's elbow.

Stelios felt dubious that he would be persuaded to agree with the German but felt it unwise to refuse to have a drink with the man. He could see Tomas approaching along the road towards them and hoped his friend would walk past without acknowledging him.

Herman walked into a taverna and settled himself in a chair. He looked far older than when he was at Delphi and had an air of authority about him. He snapped his fingers at the man behind the bar who instantly brought over glasses and a bottle of wine. Stelios felt uncomfortable being in the taverna in the company of the German. At the same time he knew it could be to his advantage to find out whatever he could about the intentions of the invading army.

Herman raised his glass. 'To the success of our beloved Fuehrer.'

Stelios lifted his glass. He had no wish to drink a toast to Hitler. His reluctance was not lost on Herman.

'I understand that you feel resentful that we have invaded your country. It is your own fault for resisting us. Had you not refused to allow the Italian army to march through Greece there would have been no need to fight. We would have arrived peacefully and improved your lives.'

'How?' asked Stelios.

Herman emptied his glass and poured another for himself. He waved his hand airily. 'I told you before. Hitler plans to build special housing for all the infirm where they will be taken to be looked after. Those undesirables who are unwilling to work will be taken to areas where construction is taking place. They will be housed there and in return expected to work on the roads or railways. Those who work hard will be rewarded. They will become the overseers of the work force and receive many benefits.'

'Suppose they are too old to work?' Stelios took a cautious sip of his wine.

'They will be disposed of. Such people are a drain on the economy. They have outlived their usefulness and should not be expected to be looked after by their relatives or subsidised by the state.'

Stelios felt slightly sick. 'How would you dispose of these people?'

'Quite humanely,' smiled Herman. 'The same as we would remove the other unwanted populace. To succeed a country needs a pure race, preferably of Aryans as we will have eventually in Germany. The mixed breeding that has gone on is unacceptable to the Fuehrer. These countries must be cleansed.'

'So if I wanted to marry a German girl I would be forbidden to do so?'

'Very likely. Your ancestry would be scrutinized. Provided you had no Jewish antecedents and could prove you had Aryan blood your application might be considered suitable.'

'What is wrong with Jewish people?'

'A good deal. It would be easier if you asked what was right about them. They follow their foolish religion and insist on acting out meaningless ceremonies, having to be home before the light fails on certain days, refusing to eat certain foods that they consider are unclean.' Herman shook his head. 'We can do without people like that in the world. Do you know any Jews?'

Stelios took another sip of his wine and pretended to consider. 'I don't think so.' He felt guilty at disowning Miriam and her family.

'You must have seen many around.'

Stelios shrugged. 'Probably, but I have never taken any notice of them or had any dealings with them.'

'Then you will be wise to continue to avoid them.'

'I will take your advice,' agreed Stelios humbly.

'It would be beneficial for you to take my advice and also to think about our proposals for the future. When you realise they are not only inevitable but also for your own good it could be to your advantage to tell me.'

Herman rose and waved the half empty bottle of wine at the bar tender. 'Put that to one side until my colleagues come in for refreshment. I have to leave now and I will not detain you any longer, although you will find your school is closed, the same as the others in the area.'

'I am sure you are correct, but I feel I should check for myself. Thank you for the wine, Herman, I mean Major.'

'You may call me Herman when we meet together; we are friends. If I am in the company of my troops then I must be called Major as a mark of respect.'

'Of course. I understand.' Stelios was not at all sure that he wanted to consider Herman as a friend.

Herman saluted Stelios and then frowned as Stelios stood there unmoving.

'You are expected to return the salute.'

'I was not sure if I should as I am not a German.'

'It could save you from a beating if you are stopped by a German patrol.'

'Thank you. I'll remember. Heil Hitler,' muttered Stelios without enthusiasm.

'Don't forget to salute as you praise our Fuehrer.' Herman turned on his heel and walked out, leaving Stelios relieved and also worried.

Stelios returned to his lodgings by a circuitous route that took him over an hour. He saw German soldiers stopping people occasionally as they walked along, even women had their empty shopping baskets searched and the men made to turn out their trouser pockets. He was relieved to find Tomas was already at their lodgings when he finally arrived.

'Where have you been? That gave me a fright when I saw you talking to that German. I thought you had been arrested and then I saw you going into a taverna with him.'

Stelios sat down heavily on Tomas's bed. Now he was safely back at their lodgings he realised that he was trembling. 'Thank goodness you are here.'

'Why? What's happened?'

Stelios related his meeting with Herman. 'He told me it was our fault that they were in Athens; that we should have let the Italians march through. He mentioned again the plan that the man Hitler has to build special houses where some of the people will live and be made to work. He said if they were too old to work they would be disposed of.'

'Disposed of? What does he mean?'

'I think he meant killed.' Stelios shuddered.

Tomas looked at Stelios in horror. 'You mean that in about ten years time my father could be declared too old to work and be,' he hesitated, 'disposed of?'

Stelios nodded. 'And no doubt we could look forward to the same fate eventually, although he claims to be my friend.'

'There has to be a way to get rid of these maniacs from our country.' Tomas spoke grimly. 'We have to do something.'

Stelios shrugged. 'What can we do? Did you find anyone at the army office?'

'When you didn't arrive I decided to walk on and when I saw you with that German I thought it better to return here. I didn't want to lead him to the offices. There are Germans on patrol outside at the front so I don't think that is an option.'

Stelios wrinkled his brow. 'I'm sure there has to be another way in. We'll try again tomorrow and look around the back of the building.'

Stelios and Tomas repeated their movements of the previous day and when they met they continued to walk past the front of the army office and took the next side turning. Tomas squinted up at the shuttered windows.

'It looks completely empty,' he sighed.

'Let's try these doors at the back. One of them may be open.'

Whilst Tomas continually looked up and down the road to ensure that a German soldier did not appear and want to know their business Stelios tried the doors, finally finding one that yielded to his push. With a last look down the road they slipped inside and stood in the semi-darkness until their eyes became accustomed. Stelios pointed to the flight of stone stairs that led upwards and as quietly as possible they began to climb them, trying each door they passed to see if they were able to gain access to the army offices. After climbing three flights, their way was barred by a stout door with a padlock. Stelios shrugged.

'There's obviously no one around. We may as well go back down.'

Not treading so cautiously now they began to hurry back down the stairs and had reached the first floor when a door opened and a revolver was pointed at them. Automatically both men raised their hands and they were waved into a room.

They stood there fearfully, the gun still trained at them. Three men were seated at a table and they looked at the two young men suspiciously.

'Why have you broken into this building? What are you looking for?'

Stelios's mouth was dry as he replied. 'We were looking for a way in to the army office. We are employed in the communications department.'

'Search them,' ordered the man who appeared to be in charge.

Whilst one man kept them covered with the revolver another turned out the pockets of their trousers and jackets before patting them down to see if they were carrying any concealed weapons. Their belongings were placed on the table and it was obvious that they were carrying nothing threatening about their persons.

'You may put your hands down.'

Both men let their hands drop to their sides and Stelios was relieved to recognise Major Colonomous. He had never seen the man out of uniform and unshaven before.

'Where did you break in?'

'We just pushed the door at the bottom of the stairs and it was open.'

The man who was interrogating them turned to another. 'Did you not lock it behind you?'

'I didn't know I was last to arrive. I did not want to lock you out, sir.'

By way of an answer the man held up a large key. 'I would not have been locked out. Go down now and make sure it is locked and bolted.'

'Yes, sir.' The man scuttled away and the man once again turned his attention to Stelios and Tomas.

'Did you not know this building had been evacuated?'

'Yes, sir.'

'So what was the object of gaining entry? Were you looking for something to steal?'

'No, sir. We hoped there might be someone here who could tell us what we should do.'

'Which departments did you work in?'

'I was in the finance section and asked to return to communications.'

'And you?' he pointed to Tomas

'I worked in supplies before being moved to the communications department.'

Major Colonomous nodded. 'I can vouch that these men worked for me.'

'Take them in there.'

The man with the revolver waved it at them and Stelios and Tomas had no option but walk into the small side room. They heard the key being turned in the lock after them and gazed fearfully at each other.

Major Colonomous looked at his companions. 'They could be useful.'

General Michaelaous raised his eyebrows. 'In what way? Sarefis won't have any use for them.'

'We could do with some more men here. The man from the finance department requested to stay in Athens rather than go to Egypt. He was excellent at Morse and we could set him up with the others at the Argyrious firm. The other one was meticulous in his recording of the supplies in and out and was proving his worth in communications.'

General Michaelaous nodded. 'Very well, we'll give them the opportunity. We can always move them elsewhere at a later date.'

'What do you think they plan to do with us?' asked Stelios fearfully.

'Shoot us, probably,' replied Tomas morosely. 'There's no way we can escape from here.' He pointed to the small window that was situated high up in the wall. 'If I climbed on your shoulders I might be able to reach it.'

'Even if you could open it I doubt if you'd be able to squeeze through and you don't know what's outside. It could be a long drop to the ground. I'd rather be shot than end up smashed to pieces on the road below. At least Major Colonomous recognised us as employees.'

'So are we just going to stand here and do nothing until they decide what they will do with us? Why don't we try to smash the door open and demand to be released? We haven't done anything wrong. We didn't break in. The door was unlocked.'

Stelios shook his head. 'I think they'll just tell us to go away and not come back. If we start making a fuss they might decide it would be easier to shoot us. They could dump us outside and blame the Germans. No one would know any difference.'

'Surely someone would see them?'

'Not if they waited until it was dark. I'm all for being quiet and patient until they unlock that door and then try to talk our way out.'

Tomas shrugged. Was his friend's pragmatism due to the fact that he had no family who would care about him if he was no longer alive?

They walked up and down for a while before leaning against the wall, and then recommenced their pacing until they finally heard the key turn in the lock and they were ushered out. Two chairs had been placed before the table and they were ordered to sit.

'So you came here in the hope of receiving orders – is that so?'

'Yes, sir,' they answered in unison.

'I understand both of you are conversant with Morse code and the use of a radio?'

'Stelios is quicker than I am at Morse. I have not been in the department for very long. I worked in supplies before my move.'

'And you would like to continue this work?'

'Yes, sir,' they both answered again.

'As you know, most of our troops have been evacuated to Egypt. We need men here who can intercept messages from the Germans and send them on for translation. We also need to be able to report to Egypt on the situation in Athens; whether more soldiers arrive or if some are withdrawn. Would you be willing to undertake those duties?' asked Major Colonomous.

'I would,' answered Stelios quickly, trying not to smirk. He had suggested he undertook these duties and now they were being presented as if the Major had thought of them himself. Tomas nodded his assent vigorously.

'You realise that if you are discovered you will probably be shot?'

Stelios shrugged. 'We'll probably be shot eventually anyway,' he muttered.

'What do you mean by that statement?' barked the man who still held the revolver pointed at them.

Stelios shifted uncomfortably. 'May I speak freely, sir?'

The four men looked at each other and General Michaelaous nodded.

'Some years ago I met a German who was excavating at Delphi. We only had a brief conversation, but he claimed that Hitler would make Greece a far better country to live in. I was not comfortable with some of the ideas he proposed. He stopped me in the street yesterday and insisted I joined him for a drink in a taverna. He appears to think that because we met once before we are friends. He blamed the situation that Greece is in on ourselves; he said we should have allowed the Italians to march through. Then he talked about the other proposals Hitler had for this country along with the others he has occupied. Apparently he wants a pure race of people and those whom he considers 'undesirable' and do not fit his criteria will be sent away to work until they are too old. When that happens they will be "disposed of". I imagine he means they will be shot.'

'So who are these people who are undesirable?' asked Major Colonomous.

'He mentioned the gypsies and the Jews and anyone who had a mental defect.'

The men were listening intently to Stelios. 'So what else did this soldier tell you?'

Stelios licked his lips. 'I don't know how much of what he said is true. He may have been making it up to frighten me.'

'We would like you to tell us. We will then make up our own minds regarding the veracity of the statements.'

'He said those that were mentally sick or crippled would be taken away to a hospital where they would be cared for. The people he classed as undesirable would be sent to build the establishments until they were too old to be of any further use. He said they would be humanely disposed of so their family would not have to care for them and they would not be a drain on the state's economy.'

When he had finished the four men exchanged glances and the man finally laid his revolver on the table, although he kept his hand on it.

'Have you any plans to meet up with this man again?' asked General Michaelaous.

Stelios shook his head. 'I won't be searching him out.'

'If you do encounter him again encourage him to talk to you. Allow him to think that you agree with his ideas. Find out as much as you can about any proposals Hitler may have for the future and let us know. If we know what he plans in advance it may be possible to thwart him.'

'You mean, be a spy?'

'Not exactly. More an informer. Does he know you are in the army?'

'No, I told him I was a school teacher and on my way to see if my school was open when we met yesterday.' Stelios was not at all sure that he wanted to meet with Herman again. He would certainly not be wandering around Athens hoping to bump into him. It was quite possible that the German had been transferred somewhere else and Stelios would be able to report, quite honestly, that the man was no longer around.

The General turned his attention to Tomas. 'What did you tell him?'

'I saw my friend talking to the German, but I have never met him,' Tomas assured the men.

'Where are you living at the moment?'

'At the army accommodation. We both have a room there.'

'You will need to lodge elsewhere. The Germans are sure to

find out that the building was being used by the army and will raid it. You are not to come here again. Make your way to the bus terminal tomorrow. Go separately and be there at ten. Have your personal belongings with you. Leave your army uniform behind packed in your kit bag, but make sure you leave nothing that could identify you. Understood?'

'Yes, sir.'

'Am I able to contact my family to tell them I am safe and well?' asked Tomas.

'Provided that is all you tell them. No mention of where you are living or the work you are doing. Do not discuss your activities with anyone outside of this room. Security is ....'

The noise of someone banging on the door below stopped the General from speaking further and he held his finger to his lips. He signalled to Stelios and Tomas that they should go into the small room where they had been held earlier and they obeyed without question.

A splintering crash could be heard as the door gave way and feet pounded up the stairs. Three shots were heard in rapid succession, followed by another two. Stelios and Tomas looked at each other. The Germans had obviously found out that there was a meeting taking place in the building and shot the officers. It would be their turn next.

Within minutes the door opened and both men raised their hands expecting to see a German with a gun. Instead the Major stood there and beckoned them out.

'Get out now. Go separate ways.'

Stelios and Tomas were only too happy to comply with the order. Two of the men they had met with earlier were rapidly emptying the contents from the pockets and removing the uniforms of the five German soldiers who lay dead on the floor, whilst the General looked on.

As quickly and silently as possible Tomas and Stelios returned to the ground floor and the shattered door. Stelios peered outside cautiously, expecting to see more German soldiers, but the street was deserted. He gave a quick nod to Tomas and began to walk away rapidly.

Stelios looked at the revolver that had been issued to him the previous year when he did his initial training and decided he should take that with him rather than leave it behind to fall into enemy hands. Most of his money he placed inside his boots, although having done so they pinched his toes. Twenty drachmas he put in his pocket hoping he would find somewhere to buy a meal and some cigarettes once his meeting with the officer was over. He stuffed the revolver as far down inside his boot as possible and hoped he would not find walking too uncomfortable.

He packed his kit bag with his army clothes and folded the blankets neatly on his bed with his greatcoat beside them. At the last minute he placed his empty cash box inside his sack.

Avoiding the main thoroughfares he walked warily in the direction of the bus terminal. He waited for a car bearing the German swastika flag to pass by before he crossed the main road, desperately hoping he would not be stopped and questioned by any of the soldiers who were saluting the car. He could not claim he was on his way to work anywhere if he was carrying his sack. The only excuse he could think of was to say he was walking into the countryside to his parents' home.

The bus station was deserted of people when he arrived and he checked his wristwatch hoping he was not late and that Tomas had already left. He dared not stand around as if waiting for a bus, knowing full well that the petrol had been drained from the tanks and there was no public transport available. He stood in a doorway, his sack on the ground behind him and lit a cigarette, hoping not to draw attention to himself. He should have been getting married this month, not skulking in a doorway in fear of his life.

A man limping badly and leaning on a stick approached and Stelios shrank back. As the man drew level with him he stopped and bent over his stick.

'Your bus is in the third row,' he wheezed. 'Best hurry.'

Grabbing his sack Stelios walked as fast as he dared between the lines of buses. Did the man mean the third row up from the road or the third row in from the terminal building? Finally he spotted Tomas and relief washed over him.

Stelios dropped his sack at his feet. 'Do you think those men we met yesterday have been arrested for shooting those soldiers? If they have they're not likely to be meeting us here or anywhere else.'

'What shall we do? Go back to our lodging?'

Stelios ran his hand across his forehead. 'Give me a minute. I'm finding it difficult to think straight.'

His thoughts were in turmoil. Had he been asked he would have said he trusted the Major and the other elite army ranks, but having witnessed their ruthless behaviour the previous day he no longer felt so confident, but nor did he feel they had a choice. Once the Germans discovered they lived in army accommodation they would not be safe and he had no idea where else they could go. If they refused to do whatever was asked of them now or at a later date they could well meet the same fate as the Germans who had broken down the door of the army offices.

'Have you eaten anything?' asked Stelios finally.

'Not since yesterday evening.'

'Why don't we see if we can find a taverna open and have a meal?'

'Do you think we should leave here? Suppose the officer has just been delayed.'

Stelios gave a deep sigh. 'If he isn't here by the time I've smoked two cigarettes I'm going to find a taverna.' He sat down on his sack, realising just how much his feet were hurting. He would have to find a more satisfactory way to carry his money around.

Tomas sat down beside him and lit his own cigarette. 'Who told you to come here?'

'An old man with a stick.'

'Sounds like the same one who told me; seemed to appear out of nowhere. Did you see where he went after speaking to you?'

Stelios shook his head. 'I didn't look back. Where do you think they'll send us?'

'No idea, but I hope we'll be close enough to be able to meet up occasionally. I posted a letter to my parents on the way here. They may never receive it, of course.'

'What did you say?'

Tomas shrugged. 'Not much, more or less what I was told I could say. That we were both safe and well and would contact them when possible.'

'What about Miriam?'

'I slipped into the laundry and told her I was moving from the army accommodation. She wanted to know where I was going. I told her truthfully that I had no idea, but I was sure I would be sent somewhere suitable and would visit her whenever I could. If this officer doesn't show up I suppose we could walk to Piraeus and stay with my parents.'

Stelios shook his head. 'I'm sure we'd be stopped sooner or later. There are Germans everywhere. They seem to be leaving the ordinary people alone now, but one of them is sure to become curious about the sacks we are carrying.'

'Did you see anything of the other men?' asked Tomas.

'What other men?'

'The ones at our lodging. I knocked on Thranassis's door last night and again this morning, but there was no answer and there's been no sign of Emmanuel.'

'He said he was going to Nafplio. He has family there.'

Tomas pursed his lips. 'I'm not sure that's the direction I'd choose. Better to go up towards Thessaloniki.'

'It wouldn't be any safer up there. It's a shame we can't get over to Crete. I have friends in Heraklion who would help us.'

'Maybe that's where we'll be sent.'

Stelios shook his head. 'That wouldn't be very practical if

they want us to let them know what's happening here. How much longer are we going to wait?'

'You said you'd smoke two cigarettes and you've only had one.'

'That's because we were talking.' Stelios took another cigarette from his packet and looked at the few that were remaining. 'I hope I'll be able to buy some more soon.'

Tomas stopped his friend from lighting the cigarette. 'I saw some feet; under that bus over there,' he said quietly.

Stelios replaced the cigarette into the packet and looked in the direction that Tomas had pointed. He could not see any feet beneath the bus. He turned back to tell Tomas that he was mistaken and as he did so he realised that Major Colonomous was standing in front of them. Hurriedly both men scrambled to their feet.

The Major held out a slip of paper and both men leaned forwards to read it.

'This is your new address. Remember it. They are expecting you. Be ready to report for duty at eight tomorrow but do not leave your lodgings. I will arrive and give you further instructions then.' The Major tore the piece of paper into shreds and let them flutter to the ground.

Before Stelios was able to ask for any directions the Major walked swiftly away. He looked at Tomas and shrugged. 'Well, I suppose we might as well make our way to our new home. At least we'll be able to get rid of our sacks. I feel very conspicuous carrying this around.'

'Where is it? Any idea?'

'The other side of Lykabettus I believe.'

'Shall we walk together?'

Stelios hesitated. He would feel far safer being with Tomas than walking alone. 'I don't think we should. We were told to walk here separately. At least if one of us is stopped and questioned we won't know where the other is.'

Stelios was relieved when he saw the street name and looked

for the number on the apartment block where they had been directed. It was much quieter here than in the centre of the city with far fewer soldiers patrolling the streets. He entered the main door and a flight of stone steps led upwards. A door on the first floor was opened by a tiny elderly woman and she beckoned him inside.

'I believe you are to stay here along with your friend for a while.'

Stelios nodded. 'I hope my friend has remembered the address correctly or he could be wandering around forever.'

'I'm sure he will arrive soon. Your room is at the end of the passage. Go and make yourself at home whilst I continue to wait for your friend.'

Stelios walked along the hallway, the first door he opened was obviously the woman's bedroom and he closed it hastily, the next was a small lavatory with a basin and a tin bath propped up against the wall. Opposite was a kitchen and at the far end were two unoccupied rooms. He chose the larger one for himself and placed his sack on the floor. At last he could remove his boots; they had become most uncomfortable due to the money and revolver he had hidden in them.

Wriggling his toes in appreciation he unpacked his sack, placing his belongings into the empty chest and debated where it would be safest to hide his money. He finally decided that the cash box, wrapped in his sack and placed at the bottom of the chest was the only possible option. His revolver he placed beneath the mattress, pushing it as far towards the centre as possible and hoping it would not be too uncomfortable whilst he slept.

He was not sure if he should return to the living room or wait in his bedroom and was relieved when Tomas finally knocked on his door.

'I took a couple of wrong turns,' he admitted. 'At least there weren't any soldiers around and I asked a child where I could find the road.'

'You didn't tell her the address I hope.'

'I said I was a stranger in Athens and a friend had arranged to meet me on the corner.'

'Well if we find a group of Germans waiting for us when we go out we'll know why,' observed Stelios darkly.

'Why should she tell anyone I'd spoken to her?'

'It's as well not to trust anyone, not even a child.'

Tomas sighed. 'Just because the Germans have taken over the city and are patrolling the streets it does not mean that every Athenian citizen is happy with the situation and will co-operate with them. The Major would not have sent us to this address if the area wasn't safe.'

'Is anywhere safe now?' asked Stelios morosely. 'We ought to go and speak to the woman. I'd like to know if she is planning to feed us or if we have to go and look for a taverna.'

Despina greeted both men warmly. 'I hope you will be comfortable in your rooms. You are welcome to join me in here during the evenings if you wish. Occasionally I visit my sister, but I am used to being alone so you must not feel obliged.'

Stelios smiled. He felt it unlikely that he would want to spend his evening making polite conversation with the woman. He would prefer to read or spend his time playing a card game with Tomas.

'I wanted to ask you about food. Will you be providing it for us or are we expected to find a local taverna?'

Despina shook her head. 'There are three tavernas close by where you should be able to buy a meal. I can provide you with some rusks and coffee in the morning.'

'Are there soldiers around?' asked Tomas.

'Occasionally they march up or down the street, but I've not been bothered by them.'

Stelios nodded. 'In that case I suggest we go and have a look at these tavernas and see what they are offering.'

'You will need to be able to open my front door.' Despina delved into her apron pocket and handed each of them a key. 'It is safer these days to lock the door and I will not always be looking out of my window to watch for your arrival.'

The meal at the taverna they chose was adequate, but by the time Stelios rose in the morning he was grateful to see the plate of rusks and jug of coffee. Whilst they ate Despina stood by the window and finally she nodded.

'I believe we are about to have a visitor.'

Both men looked up at her in alarm.

'I will let him in and then retire to my bedroom to allow you to complete your business in private.'

Major Colonomous, who had given them instructions at the bus station the previous day, entered and accepted a cup of coffee before Despina disappeared and he sat down at the table with Stelios and Tomas.

'We have decided on a slight change of plan. You,' he pointed to Stelios, 'Are a book keeper for the Argyrious shipping firm. They have suffered great losses and you are doing your best to ascertain the final figure. There will be papers around that add credence to your story. You will be working with two other men as the messages coming in have to be continually recorded. You do not discuss anything you hear with them. Once you have decoded and typed out any information you have received you will take it to Major Kokliakous. No one else. He may ask you or one of your fellow workers to reply to a message. Any questions?'

'Yes, sir. Where is it situated?'

'Alkiviadrou Street, a couple of roads up from Liossion Street, down towards the railway station. It is the only business premises in the street that are open. You should have no trouble finding it.'

Stelios frowned. 'I understand that the Germans are often down at the railway station'.

'They are busy supervising the unloading of their supplies that arrive and trying to prevent the pilfering that is taking place. It is doubtful that they will take any notice of you. You will be in no more danger there than anywhere else in Athens.'

'Yes, sir.' Stelios felt snubbed. 'When am I expected to be there?'

'Tomorrow you will start at eleven and work until seven. You will be advised if your times are changed.'

The Major turned to Tomas. 'You will be working in the morgue.'

'The morgue!' Tomas was horrified.

'Don't worry. You'll not be asked to deal with any dead bodies. We are using it as a storage depot. It is a very quiet and safe place for you to carry out your activities. It is most unlikely anyone will come looking for you there. If they do, you are listing the names of the dead and any details you have about them so their relatives can be informed. Again you will have paper work that confirms your story.'

'Will anyone else be working with me?'

'A couple of other men. You will receive deliveries that will consist of both Greek and German military equipment and munitions. They have to be recorded and stored separately. You will be shown the system. If a consignment is requested to be sent out it is essential that you are able to find and pack the correct items swiftly. I understand you were very efficient when you worked in the supplies department. You will work from ten until six. That way you and Stelios do not leave or return to the house together, but there is no reason why you should not walk out together during the evenings. Both of you will still receive the same army pay as before. I have spoken to the bank and for the time being the money is available to pay you each week. The cost of your lodgings will have been deducted.'

'If we experience any problem is there a way of contacting you?' asked Stelios.

'No, but I'm sure I will be informed if attention is directed to either of you and the necessary action will be taken.'

Stelios did not like to ask what that action would be.

Stelios arrived at the shipping firm and was greeted by the manager. There was something familiar about the man, but Stelios could not place where he had seen him before. He was shown up winding stairs until they arrived at the top of the building.

'I am sure you noticed a number of doors leading off the passage ways. The whole building is like a rabbit warren. If you remember that you are working on the top floor and continue to climb the stairs you will eventually arrive in the right room.' The manager smiled at Stelios's puzzled look. 'When all the offices were in use we had a floor plan and department names on each door. The rooms and staircases all interconnect. They are now locked. I will give you a master key that you can use in an emergency.'

'Emergency?' Stelios raised his eyebrows.

'If we have uninvited visitors you will be able to make your way back to a ground floor exit whilst they are busy breaking down doors to empty rooms. In such an eventuality a bell will ring twice in your workplace. You will immediately place your Morse machine into its rectangular case and then into the drawstring bag. Put it into your pocket and take it with you back to your lodgings. One man will always stay here and be working on the figures and information that is provided. If we are supposed to be examining accounts it would look suspicious if there was no one here working.'

'Suppose I am stopped on my way back to my lodging?'

'We will hope that doesn't happen,' replied the manager grimly. He unlocked the door in front of them and two men raised their heads and looked at Stelios curiously.

'This is Stelios. I told you he would be joining you today.'

Stelios nodded to both men and one held out his hand. The other continued to listen to a message he was receiving and writing it on a pad of paper. Between them on the table was a radio into which their Morse equipment was plugged. On each table was a typewriter and on the floor was a stack of folders and a suitcase.

'Manos and Dimitris,' the manager waved his hand at each of them. 'If you have a problem they should be able to help you. Save you running up and down all those stairs to me! Now, I have told you what you have to do if the bell rings twice. Should it sound only once it will mean we have visitors, but it is just a general inspection; not a raid. Once again you will put your Morse equipment in the case, and then the drawstring bag. Place it in the cushion cover along with those of your companions. The cover is then pushed towards the back of the cupboard. You should have plenty of time to place the rubbish back in front of it and be seated back at your table with the shipping papers before they reach this floor. One of you will have unlocked the door and the other will have tuned the radio to the German propaganda station.'

'My job today,' said Manos holding up a large key. Stelios licked his dry lips. The manager made it all sound so easy.

'When you have received and typed out a Morse message you will take it through to the Major who is working in the adjoining room. He may give you a message to send back or require that you send the information on to other units. These will have to be transposed into Morse code. At the end of each day you will place your coding machine into the case and place it inside the cushion cover behind the rubbish. Here is the master key. In the event that you have to make use of it toss it into some bushes or down a drain once you are out of the building and leave the area as quickly as possible. We have plenty of spare keys.'

'What about the Major?'

'You don't need to be concerned about him. He also has a key. He will lock the adjoining door and remove all traces of his occupation if the bell rings once. At two rings he will evacuate the building in the same way as you. Any more questions?'

Stelios shook his head. In the corner there was a small stove where he would be able to make a cup of coffee and through a door that was ajar he could see a lavatory.

Messages arrived continually and whichever man was free would listen and transcribe the Morse into a readable message, type it out and then take it to the Major. The first time Stelios encountered him he was surprised to see he was the same man he had met in the army building when the Germans had been shot. He would have liked to ask if there had been any reprisals to the event, but did not think it was his place to question his superior officer.

It was galling to Stelios to be working on the radio communications rather than in the finance office. There was no opportunity here to increase his income. The price of the most basic commodities had increased drastically and Stelios found that he was charged two drachmas for a pack of five razor blades instead of the ten lepta they had cost previously. At that rate he would have to consider growing a beard.

Most evenings Stelios and Tomas spent the time either in one of the tavernas or conversing together in their rooms. Tomas told Stelios how he listed the items of equipment that arrived and then placed them in a box to be taken into the part of the morgue where the bodies were stored.

'What do they do with them then?' asked Stelios.

'Well,' Tomas lowered his voice, 'I understand they put the uniforms in a sack beneath the body; German one side of the room and Greek the other. I'm glad I'm not expected to do that. You'd be amazed at the number of revolvers and rifles we have stored down there. I think that when they feel the time is right they'll arm all of us and we'll be expected to fight.'

Stelios shuddered. 'I hope they won't include me. I was turned down as a fighting man due to my eye sight.'

'I have flat feet. All that drilling and marching was agony for me, but I can shoot straight.'

'Suppose the Germans pay you a visit and raid the place?'

'The boxes of clothes and boots that are beside my desk I claim to have come from recent corpses, along with any guns or ammunition. They'll no doubt confiscate any weapons they can see immediately, but I doubt they'll start searching dead bodies.' Tomas smiled complacently.

'I hope not, or you could be taking your place down in the morgue.'

'I think I'm safer down there working than at the top of a building like you. Suppose you didn't hear the warning bells?'

'I'm sure one of us would. Do you want to go out and see if we can get a glass of wine at that taverna we found?'

Tomas nodded. 'I'll meet you at the post office. It's close to Miriam and I thought I'd call in and just check that all is well with them. If I'm stopped I'll say I'm on my way to the post office to see if they'll be open tomorrow. I'll see you there in half an hour.'

Stelios found it irksome to be unable to walk into any taverna he wished, order a meal and drink as much as he wanted. The small taverna he and Tomas had discovered in a back street did not appear to be patronised by German soldiers. Stelios was convinced that the bottles had been stolen from the Germans and the taverna owner was buying them and the food he provided illicitly. The prices were ridiculously high for a plate of indifferent food and one glass of wine.

Each morning Stelios forced himself to walk slowly along the back streets that led to the shipping office, avoiding the area where goods were being unloaded from the trains that had arrived during the night. If he did encounter a German patrol he was more likely to be stopped and questioned if he appeared to be in a hurry, although so far they had ignored him. When Herman suddenly emerged from a doorway and stood in front of him he stopped abruptly.

'Heil Hitler,' he managed to say and raised his arm in the salute.

Herman nodded. 'I am pleased you have remembered how to greet an officer. Where are you going?'

'To work.'

'And what is this work you are engaged on? You said you were a school teacher, but the schools are now closed.'

'I've found a position as a book keeper.'

'Really?' Herman raised his eyebrows. 'How very fortunate. Maybe I will escort you there.'

'If you wish.'

Two armed soldiers approached and Herman waved them away. 'There is no problem here, I know this man,' he said in German. 'Lead the way, my friend, to the establishment where you say you are employed.'

Stelios did not like Herman referring to him as a friend. He remembered the General's earlier instructions to meet the man and find out anything that could be used against the occupying army. This was an ideal opportunity.

'I'm pleased you think of me as a friend. Not everyone is unhappy with your presence in our city.'

'So you have thought about our earlier conversations and decided that the aims our Fuehrer has for Europe will be beneficial?'

'Of course. To have the unfortunate imbeciles prevented from increasing in number and being a drain on society is an admirable idea, along with the other proposals you told me. Where would you build their accommodation?'

'In the countryside.'

'That could be difficult for their relatives to visit them.'

'If you had an imbecile as a relative would you want to visit them?'

Stelios gave an involuntary shudder. He would certainly not visit Yannis, although he was not mentally impaired unless the leprosy had attacked his brain. 'Certainly not,' he replied stoutly.

'We would then ensure the parents were prevented from bringing any more such undesirables into the world.'

'How would you do that?'

'We have doctors who are investigating how medical intervention can deal with the problem.'

'They must be very clever.'

'Of course they are clever. They are the most intelligent and highly skilled doctors in the world. When the world has been cleansed of unsuitable occupants you will appreciate the benefits we have brought to you.'

'Is it your job to talk to people and help us to understand how you will make our country a better place to live in?'

'It is every German's duty to convince the backward nations that our aims are in their best interest, but I work as an interpreter. It is useless to try to interrogate a man in a language he does not understand.'

'Naturally.' Stelios nodded. 'As usual you are correct. I appreciate you have taken the time to explain the situation to me.' Stelios stopped in front of the door to the shipping office. 'This is where I work.'

'Then I would be interested to enter with you.' Herman laid a hand on Stelios's arm. 'It is not that I disbelieve you, my friend, but it is always wise to ascertain the truth of a statement.'

'Certainly.' Stelios wished Herman would remove his hand; it was giving him shivers down his spine. He pushed the door open.

'Good morning, Mr Argyrious. My companion would like to ascertain that I really am working here. I'm sure you will confirm that for him.'

'Good morning, Stelios. Of course you work here.' Mr Argyrious turned to Herman. 'Is my word good enough or do you want to go to the accounts room?'

Herman's eyes swept around the sparsely furnished vestibule, taking in the two chairs and table opposite the large, solid, manager's desk. At one side stood a typewriter with a letter inserted in the carriage and an open folder sitting beside it.

'I would like to see it.'

'Very well. Please follow me.' Mr Argyrious eased himself up from his chair and began to limp across the room. Stelios suppressed a smile as realisation dawned on him. He now knew where he had seen the man before; he had given him the message at the bus station.

Stelios mounted the stairs behind Mr Argyrious with Herman behind him with a feeling of trepidation. He had not heard a bell ring.

Mr Argyrious proceeded slowly, resting every few steps and breathing heavily.

'What is behind these doors?' asked Herman.

'Empty rooms.' Mr Argyrious sighed. 'They were once offices where the employees arranged the import and export of goods and prepared the accounts. We no longer have that business so the rooms are closed up. I can get the keys if you want to see inside.' The manager continued to mount the stairs, wheezing and puffing. 'I do not often come up here. It is too far for me these days.'

'Why do your men work at the top of the building, then?'

'The light is considerably better as there are skylights in the roof.'

Upon reaching the room Mr Argyrious opened the door whilst Stelios held his breath. Manos and Dimitris had papers spread out before them and a pile of folders sat in readiness on Stelios's desk. The radio was broadcasting Nazi propaganda and Herman reached forward and turned it off.

'You're late,' growled Manos.

Stelios spread his hands. 'I'm sorry. I was held up.'

Herman walked around, inspecting the paperwork on each man's desk, picking up the folders at random and flicking through the pages of figures. He opened first the door to the lavatory and then the one that led to the Major's room only to find it bare and empty. He pulled open the cupboard door and was met with a quantity of broken chairs and empty boxes.

'Such slovenly inefficiency,' he muttered. 'That should all be thrown away.'

'I agree, but I am not capable of carrying it down the stairs.'

'Your book keepers could quite easily carry down one piece of rubbish each night when they leave.'

'But where would they put it? If it was left outside in the street

I would be in trouble for causing an obstruction to the pavement and littering. It is not in anyone's way there.'

To Stelios's relief Herman slammed the door shut and turned to face them. 'I suggest you men continue with your work. I can see myself out.'

Stelios slipped thankfully into his chair as he heard Herman clattering back down the stairs. He pulled a folder towards him and looked at the figures on the page before him. They seemed to jump around before his eyes and he took off his glasses and polished them on his trousers. Manos and Dimitris ignored him, their heads bent over papers, muttering to themselves as they added the columns of numbers.

Footsteps could be heard outside and Stelios hurriedly picked up his pencil, pretending to be concentrating on his work, whilst his heart was hammering in his chest.

'You can relax now, he's left.' Mr Argyrious stood in the doorway, perspiring from his hurried ascendency of the stairs. 'Well done.'

Dimitris pushed a folder to one side. 'You gave us plenty of time,' he smiled.

'You know how difficult it is for me to climb all the way up here.' Mr Argyrious winked. 'I knew he wouldn't take the chance of going ahead of us in case we hit him over the head.'

Stelios let out his breath in relief. 'I'm very sorry,' he apologised. 'I don't think he believed me when I said I was a book keeper and insisted he wanted to see where I was working.'

'Well, now he's seen for himself let's hope he leaves us in peace. What made him pick on you, Stelios?'

Stelios hesitated. How much should he tell the men he worked with? 'I happened to meet him years ago before the war. I then bumped into him in Athens and he remembered me. He just appeared before me this morning and I didn't think it wise to refuse to allow him to come here with me. He's a Major in the German army and works as an interpreter when people are interrogated.'

'You did the right thing,' said Mr Argyrious. 'Had you refused he would probably have arrived with some armed soldiers later and forced his way in. We would all have been interrogated then. Hopefully he will not feel the need to return.'

'Shall we retrieve our equipment?' asked Manos.

Mr Argyrious shook his head. 'Give it an hour or so.'

His encounter with Herman and the visit he had paid to their offices worried Stelios and he decided he should speak to Major Kokliakous

'May I speak to you, sir?'

The Major nodded.

'As you are aware we had a visit this morning from a German officer. He is the one that I know slightly. I had not seen him around for a number of weeks and did not even know if he was still in Athens. He accosted me on my way to work and I tried to find out more about the invaders' intentions as the General requested. I'm afraid I found out very little. He works as an interpreter when a Greek is interrogated. I asked him about the proposals he mentioned about caring for those who have problems whereby they are unable to work or live as ordinary members of society. He said they have doctors working on ways to prevent their parents having any more children that could be born imperfect.'

'Nothing more?'

'I'm afraid not, sir. Everything else he said was telling me how wonderful our country would be when they had cleansed it of undesirables. I pretended to be impressed and agree with him.'

Major Kokliakous nodded. 'Very well. Let me know if you see him again and glean any further information.'

'Yes, sir. Thank you, sir.'

In the following few weeks Stelios went to and from work by the most devious routes he could find, fearing that Herman would once again appear and demand to be taken to the shipping offices, but there was no sign of him. He knew that many of the men from Athens had joined up with resistance movements that were hiding out in the hills as Tomas would often announce that a consignment of boots had left that day or blankets were being collected ready to send out to the men when it became colder. Messages from the various army units that were either hiding out in the hills or had made their escape to Egypt came in regularly to Stelios; and he typed them out quickly before taking them in to the Major.

The consignments of equipment that were requested did not always reach their intended destination, although the drivers led their loaded donkeys along trails that had previously been used by sheep and goats. Despite taking these precautions there were occasions when they ran into a German patrol and had to abandon their bundles. The uniforms burnt, whilst blankets, tents and ammunition were taken by the Germans for their own use. Messages came through from the resistance workers in the mountains and foothills, often reporting that their planned ambush had been thwarted by finding the Germans had moved away from the area.

At the beginning of October Stelios typed a message that really disturbed him. Despite being in Morse code it stated quite clearly that the King had been taken to Egypt for safety as the Germans were preparing to invade Crete. Stelios read it through a second time after he had typed it out. He really must speak to the Major.

He placed the typewritten sheet on the table at the Major Kokliakous's elbow, took a step back and saluted smartly.

'Permission to speak, sir?'

Major Kokliakous looked up. 'What is it?' he asked irritably. 'I'm busy.'

'This message, sir. It says the Germans are planning to invade Crete, sir.'

'We know that. We have forces there and when they try to land in the harbours they will very soon find themselves outnumbered and defeated.'

'Yes, sir. I'm sure you're right, sir, but that is not what is concerning me.'

'You have family over there?'

'No, sir,' lied Stelios. 'I deciphered this message in a matter of minutes although it came through in Morse with the usual coding. I imagine the Germans have a similar system for monitoring communications and someone with knowledge of Morse and Greek would find it simple to read the contents, sir. That German who escorted me here the other month told me he was an interpreter.'

'We have German speakers who attempt to decipher their messages.'

Stelios frowned. 'You say "attempt", sir. If they are familiar with the German language they should have no problem.'

'Their communication systems are more complicated than ours. It can often take some days before the code they are using can be broken, if at all.'

'That's what I mean,' exclaimed Stelios. 'The code we use is too simple. A child could break it. You just remove the numbers and read the words from right to left.'

The Major looked up at him sharply and Stelios added "sir" quickly to the end of the sentence.

'What's your name?'

'Stelios, sir, Stelios Christoforakis.' Stelios was sure he was going to be reprimanded for insubordination.

'Well, Stelios Christoforakis, if you consider the code we use too simple maybe you would be able to devise something more difficult. Dismissed.'

'Yes, sir. Thank you, sir.'

For the following two weeks Stelios was a poor companion as he spent his evenings trying to work out a communications code that would be more difficult for the Germans to understand. Finally satisfied that he had devised a system he asked Tomas to help him,

'If I tap out a Morse code message to you will you write it down, please?'

'Why can't you just tell me the message? I know you've been very quiet for a while, but we're still speaking, aren't we?'

'Of course,' smiled Stelios. 'I just want you to help me with something I've been working on for Major Kokliakous.'

Tomas raised his eyebrows. 'I didn't realise you two were such good friends.'

'We're not. Are you ready?'

Stelios tapped the table with a spoon and Tomas copied down the message, his frown deepening as he did so.

'Now work out what I've said and read it back to me.' Stelios lit a cigarette and sat back waiting for Tomas's reply.

'Can you do it again? I think I've made some mistakes.'

Stelios complied and Tomas compared the two messages. 'I haven't the faintest idea what the message says,' Tomas said finally and Stelios smiled.

'Good. That was the answer I was hoping for. If you can't understand it then the Germans shouldn't be able to either.'

'That's all very well, but how are the people who need to receive it going to know what it says?'

'They will be told how to work it out and it can easily be changed if necessary.'

'What made you think of this?' asked Tomas curiously.

'I took a message to say that the King had been taken to Egypt and the Germans were planning to invade Crete. I spoke to the Major and told him how easy the code was to break. He was rather scathing and said that if the Germans invaded Crete the forces over there would prevent them from landing. Well, we know what has happened. They obviously knew we were expecting them to come by sea so they parachuted their troops in. Our men were in the wrong place and despite the Cretans putting up a desperate fight the allied forces were unable to reach them in time to avoid defeat.'

'So what difference would this make?'

'I think the Germans are intercepting every signal we send. That means they know exactly what we are doing or proposing to do. We don't have the same knowledge about them as they are using a more sophisticated code for their messages. We need to have a code that is superior to theirs.'

'Why didn't you work on trying to break their code?' asked Tomas.

'I don't speak German,' replied Stelios simply.

Stelios arrived a little earlier than usual at the shipping office and having greeted Manos and Dimitris knocked on Major Kokliakous's door.

He saluted and he held out a piece of typewritten paper to the Major who took it without a second glance. Stelios hesitated; then left the room. He felt sure the Major would send for him when he was unable to read the message.

It was no more than ten minutes before Major Kokliakous opened his door and demanded that Stelios should explain the strange message he had delivered.

'When did you receive this?' asked the Major.

'I didn't receive it, sir. I made it up. You asked if I could devise a more difficult code that could be used in our communications and I believe I have done so, sir.'

Major Kokliakous frowned. 'So what does this say?'

From his pocket Stelios took a folded sheet of paper. 'It is a verse from the Bible, sir. I have transposed the letters randomly and instead of using the vowels I have used numbers or symbols. Not always the same numbers. For example the letter "a" can be either of the numbers three or four used either alternately or the same number each time whatever the sender preferred. The letter "e" can be a question mark or apostrophe. For "i" you would use numbers five, six or seven, "o" would be eight or nine and "u" would be a comma or full stop. Letters that needed to be doubled would have x2 after the appropriate letter. Once the receiver knew the code he would be able to decide which vowel had been used so the word made sense. It would be easy to vary the combinations or change the numbers for other letters every few weeks. If the Germans broke the code they would find it was different the next time they tried to decipher it, sir.'

'Now I know this is not a genuine message I will look at it later when I have the time.'

'Yes, sir. Thank you, sir.' Stelios left the Major feeling dejected. He had expected to be praised for his ingenuity and industry.

The next time he had occasion to take a message through Major Kokliakous was not in his room and Stelios was in a quandary. Should he leave the message on the desk or take it back with him? If he left it and the office had an inspection would he have time to retrieve it before a German arrived? He stood there hesitantly. Then decided he would take it back with him and ask his companions' opinion.

'The Major isn't there?' said Manos in surprise. 'He was earlier.'

'I know. I spoke to him. What do you think I should do? Leave the message on his desk or wait until we know he's returned and take it to him then?'

'Better to wait. It's not wise to leave messages lying around. Your friend might decide to pay us another visit.'

'That German is certainly not my friend and I don't trust him. He's very plausible when he talks about the ideas he says come from Hitler that would benefit our country. I often wonder if he is watching me as I seem to see him around far too frequently, although he ignores me.'

'What ideas are they?' asked Dimitris as he poured a cup of weak coffee for himself. 'Do you want one?' he asked Stelios who nodded.

'He told me that Hitler proposes building large hospitals in the countryside to care for the sick and disabled. On the face of it that sounds good, but then he went on to say that people who have a child who is crippled in some way, either mentally or physically, would be prevented from having any more.'

'How would they do that?'

'He said the German doctors were working on medical ideas. He said that when people were no longer able to work they would be "disposed" of. I didn't like the way he said that. Maybe he meant they would also be sent to a building somewhere to be looked after,' added Stelios hopefully.

Dimitris pulled a face. 'I hope that by the time I'm too old to work I will have a wife and if she is unable to care for me I will have children nearby who will take on the task. I wouldn't want to be sent miles away so that I never saw my family.'

Stelios sipped at his coffee thoughtfully. He had no wish to see his family, but nor did he like to think of his mother being sent away somewhere to be cared for so she would never be able to see his father or her other children again.

The door to Major Kokliakos's room opened and Stelios placed his cup on his desk and picked up the message he had received.

'In here, Christoforakis.'

'Yes, sir.' He hurried into the Major's room and was surprised to see General Michaelaous sitting with him at the table.

'Sit,' ordered the Major and Stelios obediently sat down on a vacant chair in front of them. 'You will explain to the General the system of code that you have devised.'

'Yes, sir.' Stelios started hesitantly, then began to warm to his theme as he realised the General was listening to him intently. 'The letters and numbers can be transposed frequently to prevent the Germans becoming familiar with the system and understanding how the code works,' he finished finally.

'Could it be used with the Morse equipment?' asked General Michaelaous.

Stelios nodded vigorously. 'Yes, sir. You would use the Morse code for each letter or symbol and simply spell out the words. For example; if I said "hello" I would tap out "s, question mark, px2 9".' Stelios wrote it down on the paper, then frowned; 'I'm sure anyone would very soon realise that whenever there was a letter with "x2" it denoted a double letter, so it might be better not to use double letters in the spelling of a word. I will have to give that some further thought.'

'Very ingenious. It might need some refining, but it's definitely worth considering,' said Major Kokliakous.

'Thank you, sir.'

'Why did you choose a verse from the Bible?' asked General Michaelaous.

Stelios shrugged. 'I thought it would probably be a verse that everyone would know. I could just as easily have taken a sentence or paragraph from Plato or Aristotle. It was only for me to keep a record of the transposition and use it as an example. If the system of code was adopted any paragraph would suffice, provided everyone knew how the letters corresponded.'

'Do you speak German?' asked General Michaelaous.

'No, sir. I only speak Greek.'

The Major nodded. 'You may return to your desk. Dismissed.'

'Yes, sir. Thank you, sir.'

The General looked at his companion. 'The man is obviously intelligent. Should he be moved into the de-coding department?'

'He says he doesn't speak German. Do you think he'd be able to learn the language quickly?'

'I'll speak to Sarefis,' said General Michaelaous. 'It could be worth our while to send him for lessons.'

'I understand he has an acquaintance in the German army,' said the Major. 'Under the guise of asking for his help in mastering the language he could find out some useful information.'

'I think Sarefis could find him useful as a decoy. Sarefis has a list of high ranking Germans that he would like to track down and eliminate. We should give this young man the opportunity to prove himself.'

'Suppose we found out that he was working on their behalf?'

The General gave a thin-lipped smile. 'He has no relatives so if he gives Sarefis any cause for concern he would be – expendable.'

1942

General Michaelaous had sent for Stelios and congratulated him for devising the new code that was now being used to send messages; for every three genuine messages that were sent out another was sent in the old code and the German or Italian response to the incorrect information noted. Stelios had not boasted to his companions that he was responsible for the new code, and they were envious at how quickly he appeared to have mastered it.

His heart sank when Major Kokliakous sent for him in early March. It could only mean that the Germans had solved the code and once again were able to ascertain whatever the resistance workers were planning in the way of disruption and sabotage.

To his surprise General Michaelaous was once again in attendance. 'We have decided,' began the General without preamble, 'that you should learn the German language. When you have mastered it sufficiently you will be moved to the department where the men are trying to de-code the German and Italian messages. They have had little success so far and we hope you may be able to find a repetitive pattern.'

'Yes, sir.' Stelios felt far from confident that he would be capable of deciphering the code.

'Each morning you will go to this address,' he handed Stelios a slip of paper, 'and the professor will coach you in the German language for two hours. You will then come here at mid-day and continue with your usual work.'

'Yes, sir. Thank you, sir.' Stelios saluted and turned to leave, but the Major cleared his throat.

'There is one more thing, Christoforakis.'

'Should your German friend meet up with you make sure you tell him you are learning his language. We would like him to think that you will be happy to work for Germany in the future.'

Stelios shook his head. 'There is no way I would consider working for the Germans.'

The General smiled. 'I am pleased to hear that, but we do not wish him to realise that you are learning German to try to break the code they use in their messages; far better that he should believe his doctrines have convinced you that life under a Nazi regime would be to your advantage.'

'Yes, sir.'

'It will be up to you to think of a plausible reason why you would want to work with them.'

Stelios swallowed. 'Are you asking me to be a collaborator?'

'That would be asking far too much of you. Just let this German believe you are a friendly young man and he may confide some useful information to you. You would then repeat that information back to us.'

Stelios frowned. 'I suppose I could tell him I wanted to be involved in the building programme he has mentioned.'

'Exactly.' General Michaelaous smiled approval. 'Another thing, Christoforakis.'

'Yes, sir?'

'You have been promoted to the rank of Captain.'

'Yes, sir. Thank you very much, sir.'

With a delighted smile on his face Stelios returned to his table. He wished he was able to wear his uniform to enable him to show off his new rank proudly. Promotion should mean a little more money was given to him at the end of each week. Although he was not expected to pay Despina for the lodgings the cost of the meals at the taverna had increased steadily and he was often removing drachmas from his cash box at the end of the week to subsidise his meals and cigarettes.

The Major and General exchanged glances. 'He seems keen enough.'

'Sarefis wants it set up. Steiner is on his list of 'removals'. He was supervising the deportation of the Jews in Thessaloniki. It could be an ideal opportunity to get him.'

The situation in Athens for the ordinary people had hardly improved despite the arrival of a ship from Turkey carrying grain that was distributed by the International Red Cross. For a few weeks there was a little more food available for the populace; then the situation became desperate again. If a shop opened its doors the word spread rapidly and long queues were formed by people hoping to buy a few ounces of rice, some beans or a couple of onions.

People could be seen scavenging on rubbish heaps, digging up any patch of greenery they found and every dog or cat was promptly captured and became a meal. The donkeys that had been used originally for transporting goods were left with nothing to feed on and their meat, often sold as beef in the butchers, became an important source of nourishment. The butcher paid highly for the carcass but then made twice as much again when he sold the meat to the desperate, starving Athenians.

The supplies that arrived at the train station from Bulgaria for the use of the occupying army were pilfered regularly by those who were ordered to unload the sacks. A small split was made close to the neck and a handful of wheat discreetly transferred to a pocket. If a cargo ship managed to arrive unscathed in Piraeus harbour the crew would sneak ashore at night and sell whatever goods they had managed to secrete to the men who had the monopoly of the black market.

The winter had been cold for everyone. There was no fuel

available and any wood that could be found was used to heat a meagre meal. Both Stelios and Tomas found their bedrooms cold and began to spend more time in the living room with Despina, often with a blanket wrapped around them to keep reasonably warm, but had to wash in cold water and a hot bath was no more than a memory.

Tomas found he was no longer recording army uniform and equipment to be sent to the storage depot, but genuinely engaged on listing the names of the dead, many of them civilians who had starved to death. He was depressed, worried about his family in Piraeus, and unhappy now to be working in the morgue. It had become so overcrowded that the smell of decay was permeating into every corner. The customary funeral rites of the Greeks were having to be ignored and the grave diggers were now digging large pits where a number of bodies could be interred at one time, but so many people were dying from starvation that their efforts were not solving the problem.

The size of the meals provided at the taverna had dwindled and both Stelios and Tomas were hungry most of the time. Despina no longer left them half a dozen rusks each for breakfast, beside one cup of weak coffee would be one rusk. Neither Stelios nor Tomas were able to make a cup of coffee at work as there was no coffee to be bought anywhere in Athens and they had to resort to drinking water unless they were prepared to go to a taverna and pay the high price asked for a glass of wine.

'I suppose you couldn't speak to Major Kokliakous on my behalf and ask if I could transfer to communications with you?' asked Tomas as they ate a thin soup with a few grains of rice floating around. 'I really don't think I can bear to be in the morgue much longer. When it was natural deaths from old age and illness it was no different from working in any other office. I had nothing to do with those people; they were just a cover for storing uniforms and munitions. Now it's awful. The people who are being brought in are much younger, children sometimes. There's insufficient storage space and yesterday I had five coffins in the corner of the office and two dead bodies beside them.'

'I can, but I don't hold out much hope. We appear to be fully staffed.' Stelios felt genuinely sorry for his friend.

'I thought they might have a space as you aren't there during the morning.'

Stelios frowned. 'I suppose that might be a possibility. There's never anyone at my desk even if I arrive early.'

'I'd be terribly grateful. I'd work anywhere else the Major or General wanted provided I can get away from the morgue. I have to walk past the laundry every other night to make sure Miriam and her family are still alive. Imagine what it would be like if I had to record her name?'

Stelios nodded. 'I'll speak to the Major, but I can't promise anything.' He was thankful that he was not working in such unpleasant conditions. He had to admit that he hardly ever thought of Daphne.

Stelios requested permission to speak to Major Kokliakous when he next had to take a message through to him.

'My friend, Tomas, the one who works in the morgue.'

The Major looked up sharply. 'What about him?'

'He's desperately unhappy there. He says the air is polluted with the smell of death and he feels physically ill all day. There are so many bodies being brought in that they are often placed in his office. Is there any chance he could have a move here to take my place in communications? I could spend more time concentrating on learning German. He's equally as proficient as me in Morse and typing.'

'I'll consider the request. Back to work, Captain.'

Tomas did begin to look ill and Stelios was concerned. 'Why don't you take a few days off?'

'If I don't work I don't get paid. If I don't get paid I can't afford even that miserable meal we have in the evening; besides, if Major Kokliakous is considering a move for me he won't take kindly to the knowledge that I've had time off.' Tomas shook his head. 'I just have to hope the situation improves.'

Stelios walked towards the house where he would have his morning lesson in the German language wondering if he dared to approach the Major again. He might be a Captain in the army now, but the Major still out-ranked him and could just as easily demote him back to a Second Lieutenant if he felt inclined.

'So where are you going?' A hand fell heavily on his shoulder and Stelios immediately recognised Herman's voice.

Stelios stopped and saluted. 'Heil Hitler. Pleased to meet you, my friend,' he said in heavily accented German.'

Herman looked at him in surprise. 'You speak German?'

'I am learning.' Stelios could feel his heart beating rapidly as he remembered his instructions from the General. He reverted to Greek. 'I have not seen you for some time. I thought you may have returned to Germany.'

'I have been busy in Thessaloniki. There was a problem up there with a group of people and I was asked to help to rectify the situation. Why are you learning German?'

'I thought about all you told me and I decided it would be to my advantage. I want to be a part of this improved country you have spoken about and I cannot expect to work for you if I only speak Greek.'

Herman's eyes narrowed. 'You want to work for us?'

'Eventually. When you begin the building you have spoken about you will need men who understand mathematics to calculate the stresses and strains and also the dimensions. I understand mathematics and I remember telling you that I wished I had studied to become a draughtsman. It would be the job of my dreams.'

Herman raised his eyebrows. 'You are an ambitious man.'

Stelios nodded. 'I think speaking and understanding the German language can help me to fulfil those ambitions.'

'You no longer wish to be a teacher or a book keeper?'

Stelios shook his head. 'I found teaching boring, continually trying to explain the same simple mathematical calculations day after day. Book keeping is little better.'

'You are still working as a book keeper?'

'In the afternoon only. In the morning I learn German. I am finding it a difficult language. I know many words now, but the grammar I do not always understand. My professor tries to explain to me, but he is an old man and has not taught the language for many years. I suppose you would not have the time to help me?'

'Me? I am not a teacher.'

'It would be a question of talking together and you telling me when I had made a mistake. I know my grammar and pronunciation is not always correct.'

'He does not correct you? That is his duty as a teacher.'

'He tries, but he tends to become confused when he tries to explain my mistakes.'

'Who is this teacher?'

'Professor von Schutz.'

Herman raised his eyebrows. 'That name is familiar to me. I would like to meet him.'

'I am sure he would be delighted to make your acquaintance.'

'How are you paying this man for the lessons he gives you?'

'Paying? I can hardly call it that. Herr von Schutz lives in a small room in a tenement. He is no longer able to go out. He is lonely and likes to have my company and the opportunity to find out what is happening in the city. If I am able to find some food I take it to him and he accepts that as his payment.'

'And what are you taking him today?'

'I have been unable to find anything.' Stelios led the way up the stone stairs to the first floor of the tenement building and knocked on the door. He opened it and called out, 'Herr von Schutz. It is Stelios.'

'Enter.'

Stelios smiled at the white haired old man who sat with a rug over his knees and a shawl around his shoulders. 'Good morning, Herr von Schutz. I hope you do not mind me bringing a visitor for you.'

'He is welcome.' The professor raised his eyes and looked at Herman. There was distaste written on his features as he saw the German uniform.

Herman looked around the cluttered room. There was a rumpled truckle bed in the corner, with a small table beside it and between the legs sat a bucket covered with a cloth that obviously served as his toilet. A tap was set into the wall with an open drain beneath it. On the other wall was a dresser, mostly full of books and photographs, along with a few plates, cups and glasses.

'I understand you are teaching German to this young man?'

'I am doing my best, but I have not taught for many years now. I know how to say the words, but I do not remember the rules for grammar construction so well and become confused.'

'Where did you teach?'

'At the University in Cologne.'

Herman looked at von Schutz thoughtfully. 'But you are not a German?'

'No, I am Austrian. My wife wished to return to her homeland and be close to her parents.'

'And where is your wife now?'

'Sadly she died some years ago.'

'And she was Greek?'

'From Athens. She had come to study music in Vienna and that was how we met. I was offered an opportunity to work in Cologne so we moved to the city.'

'And when did you decide to leave Germany?'

'We left in nineteen thirteen.'

'Really? Just as the war was starting. That was not the act of a loyal German citizen, Professor von Schutz.'

'I would have stayed had it not been my wife's wish to return to Greece.'

'It is a shame that you allowed your wife to persuade you in such folly. You, my young Greek friend, would do well to tell those foolish men who think they can fight us from the hills to return to their homes.'

Stelios spread his hands. 'I have no contact with them, nor do they have my sympathy.'

Herman snapped his heels together and saluted. 'Professor von Schutz, I am sure we will meet again.' he said as he left the room and descended the stone stairs noisily.

Stelios drew a breath of relief. He had been able to understand most of the conversation but the professor seemed unconcerned with the questioning.

'I am sorry, Herr von Schutz. That man is not a friend of mine. He is in the German army and interprets when people are interrogated. To be honest, I am frightened of him.'

Herr von Schutz nodded slowly. 'I understand your fear.'

'Have I put you in danger?'

The professor shook his head. 'It was only a matter of time. Tell your Major I have had a visitor. I am sure he will make other arrangements for your German lessons.'

'What will happen to you?'

Herr von Schutz shrugged. 'You do not have to worry about me. Go now, beware of that German and look to your own safety.'

Worried and confused Stelios hurried down to the shipping office. He called a brief good morning to Mr Argyrious before he ran up the stairs two at a time, arriving at the top completely breathless. Manos and Dimitris looked up in alarm.

'Don't do that, Stelios. We thought it was a raid and we hadn't been warned,' complained Dimitris.

'I'm sorry,' panted Stelios. 'I need to speak to the Major urgently. Is he in his office?'

'He was ten minutes ago.'

Stelios knocked and opened the door. 'Excuse me, sir. I have just come from Professor von Schutz. That German whom I know insisted on visiting him with me. I think the Professor may be in danger.'

Major Kokliakous looked at the concerned young man. 'I do not think you need to worry about the professor. He is well able to look after himself.'

Stelios shook his head. 'He does not go out and can hardly move out of his chair. How can he look after himself?'

'That is not your concern. Tomorrow you will go to his house for a lesson as usual.'

'Yes, sir.' Stelios saluted and turned to leave.

'By the way, I have decided to give your young friend a chance to work here.'

'My friend Tomas?'

'If that is his name. You said he was unhappy working in the morgue and we will need someone to take your place when you move on.'

'Thank you, sir. He will be very grateful.'

'Tell him to be here at ten.'

'Yes, sir. Thank you, sir.'

Stelios returned to his desk, but found it difficult to concentrate on his work. He should have asked the Major where he was destined to move on to. He wished that he had not agreed to learn German, although now he had learnt the basic rules of grammar he was finding the language relatively easy.

Professor von Schutz threw off the rug from his knees and the shawl from around his shoulders. He pulled off his cap with the white hair attached and tugged off the drooping white moustache, wincing as the adhesive pulled at his skin. He stuffed the cap and moustache into his trouser pocket. From behind the books on the dresser he took a revolver and ammunition, slipping both into his other trouser pocket. From the rumpled bed he withdrew his coat and a white stick, donned a pair of dark glasses and clapped his hat on his head. He opened the door to the room quietly and locked it behind him. On reaching the street he walked along slowly, tapping the ground on either side with his stick as a blind man would whenever he ventured out.

Tomas was delighted when Stelios told him he was to report to the shipping office the following morning.

'I hope that German officer won't decide to pay a visit to the shipping office on my first day.'

'I think it more likely he'll go to see the professor and terrorise him. I wish I wasn't going there for a lesson tomorrow. I'm wondering if it would be a good idea for me to take my revolver and give it to him.'

'Do you still have your revolver?'

Stelios nodded. 'What about you?'

'I took mine down to the morgue and added it to their collection.'

'I should have thought of that,' sighed Stelios. 'You don't think they'll raid our lodgings, do you?'

'Why?'

'I have my gun hidden in my room.'

Tomas looked shocked. 'If you are picked up and found to have a gun in your possession, even in your room, you're a dead man. Don't be a fool. Take my advice and hide your revolver somewhere outside. To take it to the professor's house tomorrow could be a mistake. If it was found in his possession he would probably be shot out of hand.'

'I suppose you're right. If they did decide to come to our lodgings and find that gun I'm certain to be arrested and interrogated at the very least.' Stelios slipped his arms into his coat. 'I'll be as quick as possible.'

It was over an hour before Stelios returned, sporting a large bump on his head and his glasses awry.

'Am I glad to see you! I was convinced you had been arrested. What's happened to your head?' asked Tomas.

Stelios sank down in his chair and placed a new packet of cigarettes on the table. 'I thought I was going to be. I had the revolver in my boot and I had just arrived at that piece of waste ground down by the foot of Lycabettus when a patrol appeared. I pushed the gun into some undergrowth. They shouted at me and began to come towards me. I took a chance and relieved myself, hoping they would believe that was why I had stopped.'

'And did they?'

'The proof was there,' Stelios attempted a weak grin. 'They told me I was a filthy Greek, one hit me on the head with his revolver and I was told to get on my way.'

'You were lucky.'

'I know. I didn't dare return here straight away so I wandered through the back streets and actually found a shop with some cigarettes. I could see by the way they looked at me that they wanted me out of their shop as quickly as possible. Do you think my glasses can be straightened out?' Stelios finished anxiously.

Tomas took the wire frames in his hands and began to bend them carefully. 'I don't want to snap them. They really need to be heated so they can be bent back into shape.'

'Shall I light a match?'

'No, you'd need more heat than you get from a match. I'll tell Despina that you dropped them and trod on them accidently. I'll ask her if I can have a piece of wood from the scullery fire see if the heat from that is sufficient.'

Stelios accompanied Tomas to the scullery and watched as his friend heated the metal and bent it carefully until it was straightened. Although he only needed them to correct the sight in one eye he had become used to seeing clearly and had no wish to have a recurrence of the headaches that had plagued him when at University.

Despina insisted on applying a cold cloth to the bump on Stelios's head. She parted his hair gently and clucked her tongue when she saw the skin had actually been broken.

'That is going to be sore for some time,' she announced. 'How did it happen?'

'Picked up a paper from beneath my desk and misjudged the distance,' smiled Stelios ruefully. 'That was when I knocked my glasses off and trod on them.'

Stelios continually looked behind as he walked along the road to the tenement building where he had been having his German lessons feeling distinctly uneasy. He climbed the stairs and knocked on the door as usual, but received no reply. His heart beating wildly and expecting the worst he tried the door handle, but the door was locked. He knocked again more loudly and a door at the end of the hallway opened.

'What do you want?'

'I came to call on the professor.'

'Who?'

'Professor von Schutz. He lives here.'

The man shook his head. 'No one lives there. The place has been empty since the old man died.'

'That can't be right. I've been coming here every morning to visit him.'

'You've got the wrong building. Try the next house.' The man shut his door and Stelios stood there in bewilderment. He was certain this was the tenement building where he had been coming every morning. He turned to retrace his steps down the stairs feeling miserable. Had something already happened to the old man or had he really entered the wrong building?

The door on the ground floor opened and Stelios saw a revolver pointed at him. He automatically raised his hands.

'Get inside,' the man ordered. 'Keep quiet and stay out of sight. Hurry. Over there.' A man spoke quietly whilst he waved his revolver at Stelios. 'Stay here until I tell you it's clear to come out.'

Stelios opened his mouth to ask what was happening, but the man frowned and placed his finger on his lips, closed and locked the door. Feet could be heard pounding up the stairs and Stelios shrank back as far as he could into the corner. He heard the professor's door being smashed open and then shots were fired.

He was trembling violently, listening to shouts and fire being exchanged, intermingled with an occasional scream and finally silence. The man who had told him to remain in the room returned; a grim smile on his face and his revolver still held in his hand.

'A few vermin exterminated. Out now and clear the area as soon as possible. One got away and he'll soon send twice as many to hunt us down.'

Stelios needed no second bidding. He scuttled out of the building as fast as he could, pushing his way through the group of armed men. On reaching the street he hurried to the corner and to his relief he was not met by a German patrol. Walking as quickly as possible, Stelios made his way to the shipping office. He needed to inform Major Kokliakous that the professor's building had been the scene of an attack. He felt sick; what had happened to the old man?

On entering Tomas looked up with a broad smile on his face which was immediately replaced with a look of concern when Stelios shook his head at him. Without greeting his other companions he knocked immediately on the Major's door and entered.

Major Kokliakous looked up. 'Pleased to see you are safe and sound. I heard there was a little bit of trouble at the professor's lodgings.'

Without asking permission Stelios sank down in the chair. 'His door was locked and a man further down the hall said no one lived there. The next thing I knew there were men with guns everywhere. What happened to the professor?'

'He's quite safe. How many Germans were shot?'

Stelios shook his head. 'I don't know. I saw two lying there in the hallway and I was told that one had got away.'

'Is that how you got the bump on your head?'

Stelios was not prepared to admit the truth. 'No, sir. Hit my head on the desk when I bent down for a paper.'

'It was a good morning's work, none the less. You did well.'

'Am I permitted to ask what happened?'

Major Kokliakous considered Stelios's request for a moment. 'This is confidential, of course. If your German friend asks you ran away when you heard the shooting. The authentic Professor von Schutz was an engineer. He was working in the department that was developing submarines when the First World War broke out. His conscience would not allow him to continue and he gave details and plans of the proposed submersibles to the British. In German eyes he was a traitor. The British gave him asylum and he has lived there quietly for many years.

'The man you visited for German lessons is an Austrian Jew, hence his knowledge of the language. He was willing to impersonate the professor. All across Greece there are loyal citizens willing to risk their lives by drawing the German troops into an ambush. We knew that your German friend was watching you and sooner or later he would want to know where and with whom you were spending each morning. It was an ideal opportunity. He would think he was going to arrest a German traitor and no doubt receive promotion and accolades from that man Hitler. When you arrived there today our men were waiting for him. He was obviously suspicious that it could be a trap and sent his soldiers in ahead of him. As he sent them in first he was able to escape.'

Stelios licked his dry lips. He was not happy to know that Herman had been watching him. 'I wish I had known. I was truly concerned about the old man.'

The Major gave a rare smile. 'I believe you. Make sure that German officer continues to regard you as a friend. Here,' the Major passed Stelios a screw of paper. 'Make yourself a coffee to bring the colour back to your face.'

Stelios took it and then hesitated. 'Is there enough for each of us? They'll think it strange if I am the only one who has any coffee.'

'There should be sufficient, then back to work, please.'

'Yes, sir. Thank you, sir.'

Tomas was longing to ask Stelios what had happened that had caused him to arrive early for work, walk straight into the Major's room and then produce a cup of coffee for each of them.

'Is the professor alright?' he asked quietly.

'Fine. No problem.' Stelios continued to concentrate on the message he was decoding. Despite being told by Major Kokliakous that the information he had been given regarding the professor was confidential he would certainly discuss it with Tomas that evening.

Having returned from their evening meal at the taverna Stelios related the events that had taken place when he arrived at the tenement building and also Major Kokliakous's explanation about the professor.

Tomas had shaken his head. 'You were lucky you weren't shot when those German troops arrived.'

'I was hiding in a room on the ground floor. I was safe enough,' declared Stelios, feeling brave now the event was over.

'Yes, but suppose the outcome had been the other way around and our soldiers had been killed? The Germans would have searched the building and probably shot anyone they found.'

Stelios shrugged. 'It's more likely they would have hauled me off for questioning. I think I would rather have been shot judging from some of the rumours I've heard.'

'Then we would none of us have had that cup of coffee you produced.'

'Courtesy of Major Kokliakous. I can't guarantee that he'll give you another tomorrow.'

A bell rang twice in the attic rooms where the men were working.

Immediately they packed their Morse code machines into their respective cases and placed them in a drawstring bag. Dimitris unlocked the door and signalled that they should leave, whilst Manos tuned in the radio to the station that broadcast German propaganda continually.

Stelios shook his head. 'I was told one man should always stay. You take my bag.'

'I'll stay as well,' volunteered Tomas and handed his bag to Manos.

The two men did not argue and disappeared swiftly into the lavatory unlocking the far door and locking it again behind them. Stelios and Tomas exchanged glances, opened folders and bent their heads over them. Within minutes feet could be heard running up the stairs and the door was flung open.

Six Germans entered, their guns drawn, followed by Herman whose arm was in a sling. Stelios and Tomas raised their hands. Herman looked around the room quickly and turned off the radio.

'Where are the other men who work here?'

Stelios shrugged. 'I've no idea. They haven't come in today.'

The soldiers opened the door to the lavatory and then the one to Major Kokliakous's room. To Stelios's relief both places were empty.

'Why are you not at your German lesson?'

'The professor said he was scared after you had visited him and he did not feel he could continue with my lessons.'

'He is not at his apartment. Where do you think he has gone?'

'I have no idea,' answered Stelios honestly.

Herman studied Stelios for a moment then appeared to believe him. 'You two may put your hands down, but stay standing beside your desks. Turn out your pockets.'

Stelios and Tomas hurried to comply, placing their cigarettes, matches and drachmas on the tables in front of them, along with the key to Despina's house. Herman glanced at the innocuous items and picked up the keys.

'Which doors do these unlock?'

'Our lodgings.'

Herman nodded and compared them, noting they were both the same. 'You will only need one. It will save us from breaking down another door. Tell me your address.'

Stelios did so, knowing if he gave a false address it was likely that the men would return and the correct information beaten out of him. It was also probable that Herman knew exactly where they lived anyway.

'Remove your boots.'

Both men pulled off their boots and a soldier lifted and inspected each one, finding nothing hidden inside.

'Search them.'

Stelios and Tomas allowed themselves to be ignominiously patted down and their empty pockets inspected.

'You may replace your boots.' Herman kicked their boots towards them and turned back to his troops. 'Turn out that cupboard,' he ordered.

Whilst two soldiers kept Stelios and Tomas covered with their revolvers the other troops set to with a will, throwing the miscellaneous collection of broken chairs, boxes, china, damaged light fittings and burnt saucepans in a heap on the floor. The cupboard finally emptied Herman glanced at the mess of rubbish.

'You will remove all of that to another room on the ground floor.'

'Yes, sir.'

'Now.'

Stelios and Tomas had no choice but obey. They picked up a broken chair each and escorted by the soldiers began to descend to the ground floor, accompanied by Herman. Mr Argyrious looked at them in feigned surprise as they entered the vestibule.

'You will unlock a door to one of the ground floor rooms and this rubbish can be placed inside,' ordered Herman.

'Which room?' asked Mr Argyrious. 'I will need to find the right key.'

'I suggest you find it swiftly or my men will break down one of the doors.'

Mr Argyrious scrabbled around inside a drawer and finally produced a key. 'I believe this is the key to the first door at the bottom of the stairs. If I am wrong it should open the door next to it, or maybe the one opposite.'

'I hope you are correct. If not I will ask my men to break open all the doors.'

Mr Argyrious shrugged to indicate his indifference to Herman's threat.

'Where are the other men who work for you?'

'I have dismissed them. There is insufficient work now for four men to be employed.'

'You two men,' Herman pointed to Stelios and Tomas. 'You will return up to your workroom and bring down the rubbish. Two of my men will escort you.'

Stelios and Tomas obeyed and without a word climbed the stairs back up to their workroom to spend the next half an hour tramping up and down until the useless artefacts had been moved into a ground floor room to Herman's satisfaction.

'You may return to your work,' he waved his revolver towards Stelios and Tomas and gave a command to the German soldiers who had accompanied him.

Stelios and Tomas climbed wearily back up the stairs and once in their workroom both men lit a cigarette.

'I thought he was supposed to be a friend of yours,' complained Tomas.

Stelios shrugged. 'He says he's my friend. As far as I am concerned he is another German soldier. I neither like nor trust him.'

'I would love to know why he's wearing a sling. Do you think he took a bullet in his arm yesterday when the Professor was raided?'

'Pity it only hit his arm,' remarked Stelios sourly. 'It could have prevented us from being raided. Where are going to hide our machines in future?'

'We'll no doubt be told of a safe place. I certainly don't want to have to carry all that rubbish back up here.'

'What do you think they were looking for?'

'Guns and ammunition probably.' Tomas winked. 'They'll not find any here.'

'Do you think they will have searched our lodgings?' asked Stelios with a worried frown.

'Bound to have done. Good job you got rid of that revolver. You haven't got a second one hidden away anywhere have you?'

Stelios shook his head. His only concern was the tin box in which he kept his money.

'What do you think we should do?' asked Stelios.

Tomas shrugged. 'I think we stay here until the end of our usual working hours unless Major Kokliakous or Mr Argyrious says otherwise. If by any chance they're watching the building they'll be suspicious if we leave early instead of continuing with our work.'

'And tomorrow?'

'Come to work as usual, until we receive any other orders.'

'I wonder if Manos and Dimitris managed to get somewhere safe?' Stelios frowned. 'If they were picked up carrying the Morse machines that could really mean trouble for them and us. Herman would be bound to remember them as the other men who worked here. He claims he has a good memory for faces.'

'I'm sure they're well able to look after themselves.' Tomas tried to reassure himself as much as Stelios.

The two men spent the remainder of the afternoon speculating on the fate of Dimitris and Manos and certainly did not open the folders that sat on their desk. Mr Argyrious spoke to them both as they were leaving.

'Come to work as usual tomorrow. If we are raided again there will be nothing in your room except the folders dealing with the finance. I told the German Captain that I had insufficient work to employ four men.'

'Are Manos and Dimitris safe?'

'I'm sure they are, along with the equipment. The Major asked me to tell you that he will be contacting you.'

Stelios and Tomas returned to their lodging and Despina met them with an apologetic smile. 'I'm sorry; I had to let the Germans in to inspect your rooms. I hope they haven't damaged anything.'

'Did they return the key of the front door to you?'

Despina shook her head. 'They hammered on the door and demanded to be let in. I opened it for them. They certainly didn't use a key.'

'That means they could come again at any time and let themselves in,' said Stelios morosely.

'They didn't hurt you?' asked Tomas anxiously.

'They had no reason to touch me. One kept me at gunpoint whilst the others searched. They couldn't find anything incriminating and after an hour they gave up. I've spent the remainder of the day clearing up. Why they had to knock furniture over and plates off the dresser I do not know.'

'I'm very sorry that you have had trouble due to us,' apologised Tomas.

Despina shrugged. 'It has to be expected. Check your rooms for anything they may have taken. I haven't touched them. I thought it better that you sorted them out for yourselves.'

Stelios hurried down the passageway. His bedding lay on the floor, with the mattress propped up against the wall, the chair and table overturned. The lid to his chest was open and his clothes scattered around. Lying open and empty was his cash box. Seething with anger he righted the table and chair, replaced the mattress on his bed and collected up his clothes. He should have found a more secure hiding place for his savings.

The two men treated themselves to a glass of wine at the taverna to drink with their meal; a small amount of meat that had been grilled on a skewer and looked like chicken with a handful of cooked rice.

Stelios looked at the meat suspiciously. 'Do you think this is really chicken or a piece of cat?'

Tomas almost choked. 'Fancy saying that when I was eating a piece!' He poked at the remaining three small pieces that still sat on his plate. 'It looks like chicken and it tasted alright.'

Stelios cut off a small piece, sniffed and then placed it in his mouth. It did not smell bad and it did taste like chicken. 'If I die from food poisoning it will be your fault.'

'If you have food poisoning I will probably have it also. You won't be able to blame me. You'll have to blame the taverna owner.' Tomas lowered his voice. 'Thank goodness you disposed of that 'you know what' or you wouldn't be sitting here speculating about food poisoning.'

'They took all my savings.'

'Savings? You actually had some savings? How did you manage that?'

'I lived well within my means before the war. I was saving up ready for when Daphne and I were married. I wanted to find somewhere decent for her to live.'

Tomas sighed deeply. 'I haven't anything saved and I'm no nearer to marrying Miriam than I was a year ago.' He lowered his voice. 'I can't go to the synagogue for instruction. They are only allowed to hold a service in there once a week and soldiers are everywhere. Abraham says they stop and search both the men and women for no good reason or say the synagogue is full and won't let any more people in.'

'That's just petty.'

'I think they are trying to intimidate them. Abraham says the Jewish population in Thessaloniki have been made to wear the yellow stars on their clothes and their newspapers have been closed down. They've all had to register for labour duty. I imagine that means building roads and railways. The Greeks are encouraged to shun them and avoid doing any form of business with them.'

'Are they hoping they will leave the area?'

Tomas shrugged. 'I don't know, but where would they go? Many of them have already been turned out of their homes so the Germans can live in them. They've been taken in by friends or relatives, but there's a limit to how many people can fit into a house.'

The next two days Stelios and Tomas spent at the premises of Mr Argyrious dragged. Stelios did make a serious attempt at adding the figures in the folders, but Tomas continually interrupted him when he was half way down a column of figures with either a question or a comment. If he did manage to complete the lines of addition he invariably found that when he turned the page the sum had already been done and a note written beside it of how much was owed and the percentage of the debt that would have to be written off.

Herman, accompanied by twenty soldiers, paid a further visit to the offices and demanded that every door was opened so they could check that the rooms were truly empty. Mr Argyrious complied, puffing and panting his way up from one floor to another, fumbling with the keys, until they finally reached the top floor.

Stelios and Tomas had their heads bent industriously over their work when they entered.

'Stand,' ordered Herman and both men pushed their chairs back and complied.

'Heil Hitler,' said Herman and saluted.

Stelios gave Tomas a nod and lifted his own arm. 'Heil Hitler,' both men mumbled.

Herman instructed his men once again to inspect the rooms and this time the door at the back of the lavatory was unlocked. Herman glared at them.

'My men tell me that the lavatory leads to rooms on the lower floors.'

'I did not know that,' declared Stelios honestly, although he had been certain Manos and Dimitris had disappeared that way. 'I thought it was a cupboard.'

'Why would anyone wish to lock a cupboard in a lavatory?'

'I have no idea.'

Mr Argyrious stepped forwards. 'I can answer that question. We had a young man working here some years ago as a cleaner. He was a good worker, but not exactly bright. He was continually getting lost by using the wrong doors. I decided there was no necessity to have them all unlocked. After he left I never bothered to unlock them.'

Herman looked at Mr Argyrious dubiously. 'I wonder if you would be so ready with your excuses and explanations after a beating from my men?'

'I can only tell you the truth. You could beat me to a pulp and I would be unable to tell you anything differently.'

'Do not tempt me,' remarked Herman. 'I am confiscating all the keys to this building. You are closed down with immediate effect. You two, collect any belongings you have and leave now.'

Stelios and Tomas lifted their coats from the back of their chairs.

Mr Argyrious looked at them sadly. 'I'm sorry to see you go. You have worked conscientiously and efficiently for me.'

'Thank you, Mr Argyrious,' said Stelios. 'I have enjoyed working here.'

'Me too,' agreed Tomas. 'If you reopen please consider me for a position on your staff.'

'Escort these men off the premises,' ordered Herman and Stelios and Tomas found themselves hustled down the stairs and out of the door.

'What do you think will happen to Mr Argyrious?' asked Tomas as they hurried away from the building.

Stelios shrugged. 'Who knows? If they believe him he'll be sent off home, but it's equally likely that he'll be taken in for questioning.'

'I do hope they believe him,' said Tomas fervently. 'If they torture him he'll probably confess to the real use of the building and then they'll be after us as well.'

Despina was surprised to see them arriving back at the lodgings in the middle of the afternoon.

'That German came to the offices again and he has closed them down. We were told to leave immediately,' explained Stelios.

Despina nodded. 'I was just about to go out and see if I could find a food shop open.' She placed her headscarf over her straggly grey hair and picked up her basket.

Tomas looked at Stelios and sighed. 'I wish we were moving. Now your friend knows where we live and also has a key to the door I don't feel particularly safe.'

'No German is a friend of mine. I do hope he doesn't plan to visit us during the night.'

'Should we take it in turns to sit up, just in case that is his plan?'

Stelios shook his head. 'What would be the point? There's nowhere we could go except out of the main door. Once his troops were in the building we would be trapped, even if one of us was sitting waiting for them.'

'Do you think we should take a chance and leave now?' asked Tomas.

'He could have someone watching the house and the moment we try to leave we'll be arrested,' remarked Stelios despondently.

'Why should we be arrested?' asked Tomas reasonably. 'When they raided Mr Argyrious they found nothing incriminating and there was nothing in our rooms. I'm sure if they were going to arrest us they would have done so earlier.'

Stelios shrugged and lit a cigarette. 'They don't need a reason to arrest you. It's probably best if we just stay here.'

'Suppose they did pick up Dimitris or Manos and they have

talked by now? They're not likely to believe that we were innocent book keepers if they had the Morse machines on them. It would be obvious they were receiving and sending messages. I think we should leave now whilst we have the chance.'

'Where would we go? I vote we stay here and take our chance.'

The two men continued to argue over the merits of staying or leaving. Stelios was adamant that they should stay and finally Tomas agreed. When the front door opened both men looked up expecting to see Despina, instead Major Colonomous slipped inside and closed the door firmly behind him. He looked unkempt and his clothes were decidedly shabby.

The Major placed a key on the table. 'Tomorrow you will report for work at the premises of Leoforakous in Soutsou Street. That is the key to the door. If you are stopped you are looking for any food shops that are open. You enter the taverna next to Leoforakous and ask the owner if you can inspect his kitchen. He will let you out into the back yard and you will open the door on your left and lock it behind you. There is a light switch behind the door. Climb to the top floor and switch off the light. All the doors are locked except the one on the top floor where you will find your equipment. Return here by a different route at the end of the day and keep to your usual routine during the evenings. Understood?'

Stelios and Tomas nodded and before they had time to ask any questions the Major opened the door and was gone. The two men looked at each other.

'I imagine that means we continue to live here,' said Tomas.

'If we are being watched it would look suspicious if we did move. By staying here we are proving to Herman that we are a couple of innocent young men who were working for Mr Argyrious as book keepers. If I meet up with him again I will be resentful about losing my job.'

'Be careful,' warned Tomas. 'He could find some very unpleasant work for you to do and there would be no way you could refuse.'

Stelios sighed deeply. 'I just wish this war had never started. I was happy working in the finance department for the army and receiving my pay at the end of the week.'

'We have to be grateful that we still have our money from the army. We'd be begging on the streets otherwise or dead from starvation.'

'If we don't go out soon and find a taverna with something for us to eat I shall be dead from starvation anyway,' remarked Stelios.

The two men looked at the Leoforakous building dubiously. The windows and door were boarded up and the building looked totally derelict.

'Do you think we're in the right place?' asked Tomas.

Stelios shrugged. 'There's a taverna next door. Let's ask to have a look at their kitchen.'

At Stelios's request they were led through to a small area where there were two sinks, a pile of plates and a hot plate. Everywhere needed to be thoroughly cleaned and Stelios was pleased they had not been expected to ask for a meal. The back door was opened and the men ushered out, the owner not having spoken a word to them.

'Friendly type,' Tomas murmured under his breath and took the key to the door from his pocket. It turned easily in the lock and Stelios groped for the light switch. A flight of stone steps led up between concrete walls and he led the way, treading carefully and using the dim light that filtered down to them to ensure they were not going to encounter an obstruction or that the steps did not end abruptly so they would fall into a dark abyss below.

At the top of the flight a door barred their way and Stelios felt for a handle. Tomas inserted the key that had unlocked the door in the yard. It turned easily and they entered a large room that was full of light from the windows at the back of the building and in the roof.

Stelios drew a breath of relief as he entered, then tried to struggle and call a warning to Tomas as his arms were seized and a hand clamped over his mouth. He was released almost immediately and Manos grinned at him.

'Sorry. Can't be too careful. There's no lookout or warning signal here.'

'How do you get out if there is a raid?' asked Stelios.

'Our only option is back down those stairs. It's the fire escape for the building. This was a paper warehouse originally. We just have to hope that we hear the Germans breaking down the main door. Your only other option is to climb through a window and hide out on the roof. I suggest you go and have a look. It isn't as dangerous as it sounds. There's a low parapet and once you are round the corner you can get onto the other roofs.'

'Suppose a German follows you?'

Dimitris clasped his hands together. 'That is when you start to pray.'

Tomas and Stelios took it in turns to climb out of the window and make their way gingerly along the parapet to the corner of the roof. Provided they ignored the drop below the short journey was not too hazardous.

'Is it possible to reach the ground floor through one of the other the buildings?' asked Stelios.

Dimitris shrugged. 'I've no idea. They most of them appear to be derelict.'

'Why don't we take some roof tiles off and see if we can get in?'

Tomas looked up at the ceiling of the room they were in. 'If the ceiling of their top room is as high as this we'd probably end up breaking a leg as we jumped down,'

'It might be possible to fix a rope.'

'It's worth considering, but it would mean quite a bit of work. I, for one have no real head for heights and we don't know how the tiles are fixed. We might need some special tools,' said Manos. 'I think we're pretty safe here.'

'We thought we were safe at Mr Argyrious's premises.'

'We probably would have still been there if you hadn't brought your German friend to pay us a visit.' glared Dimitris. 'If we remove some tiles from the roof of one of the buildings the next thing we'll know is that we're raided and as we try to escape there will be Germans waiting in that building for us.'

'I had no choice,' apologised Stelios. 'Had I refused he would have arranged a raid thinking I had something to hide. I hoped that having made an inspection he would be content and leave us alone.'

Dimitris eyed Stelios speculatively. 'If he comes again ...' He left the sentence unfinished but drew his finger across his throat as an obvious threat.

For the following three months the men worked undisturbed, their desks and chairs were wooden boxes that would give no reason for suspicion should they have to vacate the premises in a hurry. Their Morse code machines could be placed in a small case at the end of the day and concealed in their trouser or jacket pocket and the radio left in full view. There were no typewriters here and all the messages had to be written out by hand before being taken through to the Major.

Stelios was relieved that there had had been no sign of Herman and no Germans had come to raid the building where they were working. Despite having a reasonable working knowledge of the German language he was no closer to deciphering the code the Germans used for their messages when Major Kokliakous passed them through to him.

'I am very sorry, sir. I have tried any number of combinations, both mathematical and alphabetical and I cannot make any sense out of them. Sometimes I think I have identified a vowel only to find that it does not occur again in the message. I have tried to make words with the letters I have and then inserting vowels, but that doesn't work either. I'm convinced it is mathematically based, but I can't discover the formula. Is there anyone else working on the project? If we consulted together we might manage to crack it between us.'

Major Kokliakous sighed. 'There are others who are trying to fathom it out. So far everyone has failed.'

'I'm prepared to keep working on it unless you order me to do otherwise, sir.'

'Keep at it for the time being. The original code you devised is still working well as we change the combination every two weeks, but you will have noticed that from the messages we receive and transmit. It's a consolation to know that even if we are unable to break their code we are at least giving them a few headaches with ours. Have you seen anything of your German friend?'

Stelios shook his head. 'No, sir. I hope he has moved on elsewhere.'

'Unfortunately he may well be returning. General Sarefis and his men have inflicted great losses on the Bulgarians due to ambushes and sabotage. The Bulgarians have called on the Italians to assist them in finding the perpetrators, but they have not been successful. It is possible the Italians will ask the Germans to come to their assistance as they did before. If he does return we may well move you to alternative accommodation.'

Stelios grimaced. He thought they were settled and he had grown to like Despina. They had become used to varying their routes and times to the Leoforakous building, visiting one of the tavernas in the vicinity of their lodging during the evening and hoping they would be able to find enough food to satisfy their immediate hunger.

The German soldiers patrolled the streets in the centre of Athens continually. They would stop innocent citizens, search them and terrorize them, but few arrests were made. Occasionally a raid would take place on a private house in the hope of finding some incriminating evidence of subversion by the occupants. After a few days held in the prison and a beating they usually returned to find their property had been ransacked, their possessions removed or their house had been taken over by a contingent of German soldiers and was being used as a barracks. If more Germans returned to Athens more atrocities were likely to take place.

The Athenians were unable to resist the harsh treatment that was handed out to them. They were underfed to the point of starvation, many living in crowded unsanitary conditions and suffering from the cold during the winter months. The youngest and oldest being the most vulnerable.

'I hope the General is able to keep them busy up on the border, particularly Major Herman Steiner.'

'There are many others who are far more merciless and depraved than him,' replied the Major sadly.

'I'm sure there are,' agreed Stelios, 'but at least they would not know me. I know Dimitris blames me for the raid on Mr Argyrious's premises.'

'That was unfortunate, but we have to take responsibility for the incident. We should not have used you when we tried to set up the assassination of Steiner and then expected you to return to your workplace. Steiner was bound to pay you a visit.'

'Had you succeeded I would have been proud of my part in the operation. If I can assist in any way in the future I will be only too willing to volunteer.'

Major Kokliakous shook his head. 'At present do nothing to arouse Steiner's suspicions or come to the attention of any of the other troops. I'll remember your name if there is an opportunity to make use of you in the future.'

'Yes, sir. Thank you, sir.'

The news that the Gorgopotamus Bridge had been destroyed by the guerrillas with the assistance of a unit of British saboteurs was greeted with mixed feelings in Athens. Both the Germans and Italians would be cut off from their usual source of supplies, but that could mean there was even less food available for the Athenians. The Greeks were convinced that the Germans planned to starve them out of existence. The loss of the Turkish ship "S.S. Kurtulus" when it foundered on rocks close to Marmara did not help the situation. It was frustrating and depressing for the population to know that there was food in the countryside, but no transport to bring it into the city.

Stelios repeated his conversation with Major Kokliakous to Tomas. 'I think the Major believes Herman will be returning to Athens.'

'We can't avoid him forever.'

'I know,' sighed Stelios. 'I just hope he is 'removed' before we are.'

1943

Christmas and the New Year had passed with barely a celebration. The citizens of Athens attended church, under the watchful eye of German troops, praying they would not be molested on their way home or during the night. Families and neighbours had pooled their meagre rations and did their best to enjoy a little extra food; many of them suffering later as their stomachs were unaccustomed to digesting more than a couple of rusks smeared with a tomato paste and accompanied by some grass or dandelion leaves.

Everyone prayed fervently, either for the return of a son or husband, some for food to feed their families or for the Germans and Italians to leave their soil for good and never return. Stelios was reminded of the Christmas he had spent with Tomas's family and his thoughts turned to Daphne. He was not consumed by longing for her, but he certainly did not want any harm to come to her. She was the most suitable young woman he had met whom he felt he could marry.

In February the heartening news came that the German army in Russia had surrendered. Surely that would mean Hitler would start to withdraw his troops and free the countries he had occupied. The citizens of Athens waited hopefully, but the Germans showed no sign of leaving.

A week later the famous poet Kostis Palamas died. The Athenians mourned him and after a speech at his funeral calling for a national awakening the people rose to the occasion. Ignoring the presence of the German soldiers the crowd begin to sing the Greek National Anthem and chant “long live Greece, long live freedom”.

The blockade on the food supplies that had been imposed by the Allies had been lifted and once again a little more food was available to the people, encouraging their spirits and hopes to rise. Demonstrations against the German occupation took place and those who had been forced to work for the Germans went on strike.

The Germans reacted by issuing orders that any man found carrying a gun was to be shot and for every German soldier that was killed a hundred civilians were to be shot. The non-communist resistance group led by Napoleon Zervas found they were no longer welcome in the villages that had been supporting them, due to fear of the reprisals, and asked for a truce. The other main resistance groups disagreed with him and continued to fight on, claiming the Greek people had become more unified in their objective of ridding their country of the unwelcome invaders.

Tomas continued to pay surreptitious visits to Miriam and would return with mixed feelings. Delighted that she and her parents were still safe and well, but depressed that they could not make any wedding plans. The news that had filtered through from Thessaloniki worried him. The Jews were being forced to demolish their cemetery and use the stones on building projects. How much longer would it be before the same fate befell the Jews and their cemeteries in Athens?

He was even more disconcerted when news came through that the Jews of Thessaloniki had been sent to a labour camp in Poland.

‘I imagine this is one of the building projects Herman told me about; where the women look after the men who are out working on construction.’

Tomas shook his head. ‘Why would they take just the Jewish people? Why not take the able bodied locals?’

'Maybe the Jews volunteered to go. Life had become pretty unpleasant for them.'

'Life isn't easy here and I for one would not volunteer to go and work for the Germans. I can't believe that it will be any easier in a camp in Auschwitz. What kind of accommodation will they have whilst they are building apartments? I would have thought that there would have been enough rebuilding necessary in Thessaloniki to keep them fully occupied.'

'They must have apartments ready built for them. They wouldn't take them otherwise,' replied Stelios naively.

'I'll ask Abraham if he knows any details when I go down to see Miriam.'

Abraham shook his head sadly. 'All I have heard are rumours. Some say the local Greeks turned against them and requested them to be deported; others say it is because they were actively working against the Germans and the camp is actually a prison.'

'It doesn't make sense. I know Stelios told me that German he knows considered Jewish people to be undesirable.'

'That is the problem, Tomas. In German eyes we are undesirable. Because we have a different religion and customs that they do not understand they consider we are a threat to them.'

'Most of you are just decent, hard working people. I do wish you had taken your family away from Athens where they would be safe.'

'I don't think there is anywhere safe now. Many of us came here originally to escape persecution from the Spanish. Now we are being persecuted again. We are no more of a threat to them than those of you who practise the Greek Orthodox religion.'

'Have many Jewish men joined the resistance workers?' asked Tomas.

Abraham gave Tomas a sly look. 'How would I know? Some men have left town, but they didn't tell me where they were going. Now if you want a few minutes with Miriam you'd better go into the back room. You've already been here long enough to collect your laundry.'

Tomas was only too delighted to be able to go into the back room, but he also realised that it was Abraham's way of terminating their conversation. Abraham probably knew exactly which men had joined the resistance, but he was not prepared to pass that information on, even to Tomas.

Over the next few months the Jews from the zones that the Bulgarians and Germans controlled were also sent away from the area. Their homes were distributed amongst those in favour with the Germans; the collaborators and their friends or relatives. Within days the houses had been dismantled as the new occupants looked for hidden gold and jewellery that they were convinced the Jews had concealed. The synagogues in Thessaloniki were blown up, whole areas where the Jews had lived were demolished and the Jewish cemeteries were bulldozed to resemble a ploughed field.

The Italians in the zones they occupied and administered were less willing to persecute the Jews. They made life uncomfortable and uncertain for them, but they did not single them out for reprisals. In September, when Mussolini's government fell, negotiations were undertaken with the Americans that allowed the Allies to enter Italy. The Italians were ordered to surrender. Those who surrendered to German troops were declared traitors and shot; other Italian battalions who were stationed in Egypt surrendered to the Allies and were considered to be prisoners of war.

The Germans took over the territories previously occupied by the Italians and immediately singled out the Jewish community for deportation. Many Jews fled to Athens, believing they would be safe in the city which had been primarily under the control of the Italians. The Germans turned their attention to the mountain areas where their forces attempted to dislodge the centres of resistance that had been set up in remote villages. Whole villages were destroyed and their occupants shot as reprisals for harbouring or assisting resistance workers.

Attention turned to the Jewish population living in Athens and an attempt to turn the Athenians against their neighbours by radio propaganda was unsuccessful. The Grand Rabbi was summoned and ordered to submit the names and addresses of members of the Jewish community. The Grand Rabbi destroyed the records and advised the Jews to leave Athens or go into hiding, before he was safely removed from Athens and joined the resistance movement.

Tomas was seriously concerned about Miriam and her family and once again tried to persuade Abraham to leave.

'I wish I had taken your warning seriously when the Germans first arrived,' said Abraham sadly. 'It is too late now. I thought it was my duty to stay here and help care for my elderly relatives, but it was a mistake. They have died over the years, mercifully from old age, although I am sure malnutrition and the cold they suffered during the winter months played a part. Now there is nowhere to go.'

'I could ask Despina if you could come to our lodgings. I'm sure Stelios would put up with sharing a room and Naomi and Miriam could have my room,' suggested Tomas.

Abraham shook his head. 'I appreciate your offer, but I feel sure we would soon be found and then your lives would be in jeopardy. I cannot expect this unknown woman and your friend to place themselves in danger to save us. We will have to rely on our prayers for our salvation.'

Tomas walked away from Abraham's laundry, noticing that a number of the houses were already abandoned. He felt annoyed and frustrated. These people must have gone somewhere, so why couldn't Abraham?

Stelios commiserated with him. 'I think they will be safe enough. The police are disobeying orders and not arresting them on trumped up charges.'

'I thought about asking Despina,' confessed Tomas, 'but Abraham said I could be putting her in danger along with us.'

'He's probably right. I wonder if Major Kokliakous would know of a safe place where they could live? We've had no problem here. He must be living somewhere locally and also Manos and Dimitris.'

'Do you think I could ask him?'

Stelios shrugged. 'There's no harm in asking.'

Major Kokliakous regarded Tomas sympathetically. 'These people are not employed by the army in any way?'

'They have a laundry and they have always dealt with the cleaning of the army uniforms,' replied Tomas hopefully.

The Major smiled thinly. 'That is hardly being employed by the army. Why are you concerned about this family?'

Tomas blushed. 'I wish to marry their daughter.'

Major Kokliakous raised his eyebrows. 'Isn't that a rather unwise liaison?'

'I have to follow my heart, sir.'

'Then I hope for your sake they stay safe.'

Despite Abraham saying that Despina should not be approached Tomas asked her if she would be willing to take in the Jewish family.

Despina shook her head vehemently. 'I have nothing against the Jewish community, but this apartment is not suitable. Your room would not have enough space for three beds.'

'I could sleep on the floor,' volunteered Tomas.

'That would be a solution to the space, but I dare not take the risk. We were raided once by that German and have not been troubled since. If he decided to come back and found I was sheltering a Jewish family we would all be arrested. I'm sorry, Tomas. If I can think of a solution I'll let you know.'

Major Colonomous listened to Despina. 'I'll have a word, but I can't promise anything.' If General Michaelaous agreed it could be time to make use of the young man who could speak German.

Major Kokliakous sent for Stelios during the early afternoon. 'I have received some orders for you.'

'Yes, sir.' Stelios hoped he was not going to be sent into an area where there was fighting.

'Are you still willing to assist in any way?'

'Yes, sir.'

The Major nodded in approval. 'You are to return to your lodgings and shave. Cut your hair as short as possible and then report to this address.' He handed Stelios a slip of paper. 'Once there you will dress as a German soldier and accompany another similarly attired. Remove your spectacles. I trust you can see well enough without them to find your way around?'

'I only need them for close work,' Stelios assured him.

'You will march openly through the streets to an area at his direction,' continued the Major. 'Once there you will escort the occupants of the building to a place of safety. You do not speak to these people, but if you are stopped by a German patrol we are relying on you to convince them that the family are under arrest. I need not remind you that you do not mention these proceedings to anyone. If your companions ask where you are going you say you have been asked to deliver a message.'

'Yes, sir.' Stelios felt tremendously important to be entrusted with the mission, but also full of trepidation. If he had to converse with the German soldiers would his knowledge of their language be sufficient for them to think he was actually German?

Abraham looked up in alarm as the German soldier levelled his revolver at him. He raised his hands and the officer smiled.

'Put your hands down, Abraham. We're not Germans. We are friends. We've been asked to move your family to a place of safety. Pack whatever you can carry as quickly as possible and come with us.'

Abraham glanced at the men dubiously. They were wearing the uniform of German soldiers. Could he trust them or was he taking his wife and daughter into a trap?

'Where are you taking us?'

'To a safe house; provided you move yourself. We have to leave as quickly as possible.'

'Suppose I want to stay here?'

'The choice is yours. If you decide to stay we'll leave now.' The man replaced his revolver into the holster. 'There are others who need our help.'

Abraham licked his lips. 'Give us a few minutes.'

The officer nodded, turned the "open" sign to read "closed" and locked the door.

Abraham removed the drachmas that were in the box under the counter and pushed them into his pocket. Whether these men were German or Greek his money would be safer with him.

Looking pale and frightened Naomi entered the laundry room carrying a sack with Miriam behind her. Miriam looked at the soldiers defiantly and her eyes opened wide. She was about to speak when one placed his fingers to his lips and shook his head. She leaned towards her mother and spoke quietly in her ear.

'It is Tomas's friend.'

Abraham followed them in, a sack in each hand.

'Can you manage two sacks?'

Abraham nodded. 'I can carry them. They're not heavy.'

'Very well. We can't help you or it would look suspicious. We will escort you as if we are arresting you. Walk with your heads down. We are collecting two other families. If we are seen by a patrol we will shout out that we are arresting Jews. They may spit at you or use abusive language but hopefully they will let us pass on without question.'

'Suppose they do stop us?' asked Abraham.

'My companion can speak German. Provided they do not look too closely at our insignia we should be able to talk our way out of trouble by pulling rank if nothing else.'

Tomas went to pay his customary visit to Miriam and returned distraught. 'The laundry is locked up. Everywhere down there is deserted. Do you think they have been deported?'

Stelios shook his head. 'I'm sure if that had happened we would have heard.'

'Not if they moved them at night,' replied Tomas miserably. 'I just want to know they are safe.'

'Ask the Major tomorrow. He may have some news. He did say if he could think of anywhere they could go he would tell you.'

'He can't have found somewhere safe for all the Jewish people from the area.'

'You said that some of the houses were abandoned when you visited last week. I expect most of them have gone to stay elsewhere in the city. They won't be so noticeable if they are spread amongst everyone else.'

Tomas gave Stelios a sceptical look. 'They have to wear a yellow star on their clothes so everyone knows they are Jewish.'

'Then I hope they've had the sense to cut it off. Provided they don't do anything that draws attention to them they should be safe enough. Abraham told you he had relatives in Athens. They may have gone to stay with them.'

'He told me they had died.'

Stelios shrugged. Whatever he said was not going to allay Tomas's fears and he had been forbidden to tell him the truth. When questioned about the shortness of his hair he declared it had been irritating him and he thought he might have lice.

Tomas approached Major Kokliakous diffidently. 'I'm sorry to bother you, sir, but do you have any news of the Jewish family who run the laundry? There's no sign of them and many of the houses in the area appear to be abandoned.'

'I believe their Rabbi advised them to leave and go elsewhere. I can assure you they have not been taken by the Germans.'

Tomas let out a sigh of relief. 'Thank you, sir, but where are they?'

Major Kokliakous shook his head. 'I am not at liberty to disclose their address. I could be putting the lives of their hosts in danger. You are expressly forbidden to go around asking after them.'

Tomas hung his head. 'Yes, sir.'

'We can but hope that the situation does not last for too much longer. Once the Allies have pushed the Germans out of Italy they will no doubt come to our aid.'

Relieved that Miriam and her parents had not been arrested and transported Tomas returned to his work and relayed the news to Stelios.

'I'm pleased to hear it,' commented Stelios and turned back to deciphering the message he had received a short while earlier.

It became routine for the next few weeks for Stelios to be sent out of the office at various times to take a message to an address on the Major's orders.

'Why are you always the one chosen to go out?' asked Dimitris. 'Why can't one of us go?'

'You'd have to ask the Major,' replied Stelios. 'I just do as I'm told.'

Although Stelios enjoyed accompanying Christos to various addresses and "arresting" the Jewish citizens he was petrified that one day he would bump into Herman. There was no way he would be able to deceive him into thinking he was a German. Dressed as officers with the equivalent rank of a Major on their collars and epaulets the troops they did encounter saluted them hurriedly and made no attempt to detain or question them.

The families they escorted were taken to various different houses in the Pagrati area and once the door had been opened to them Stelios and Christos left to return by a devious route to the safe house where both men changed into their own clothes and returned to work.

There had been one occasion when Stelios almost bumped into Dimitris. He was sure Dimitris was suspicious by the way he narrowed his eyes as he looked at him. Stelios immediately turned to Christos and began to speak in rapid German, not thinking about his grammar. He placed a hand on Christos's shoulder and turned him back the way they had come. Stelios gesticulated wildly, still speaking loudly in German and hurried back down the road and around the corner.

Stelios shrank into a doorway. 'Is anyone following us?' he asked. 'I'm sure that man recognised me. That was why I began to speak German and insisted we came back down here.'

Christos looked around the corner, but the road appeared deserted.

'I can't see anyone.'

'We need to get away from this area as quickly as possible. If that man did recognise me he could tell a German patrol. I'm not sure my German would be good enough for me to talk us out of trouble if they began to question us.'

Swiftly they walked through the back streets, Stelios watching for any sign that Dimitris might be following them.

Dimitris eyed Stelios suspiciously when he entered their makeshift office the following day. 'Did I see you in the Pagrati district yesterday?'

Stelios frowned. 'It's possible. Whereabouts is it?'

'The other side of the railway line.'

'I may have been there. I never know where these areas start and finish. I was wandering around looking for some soap. You don't know where there is any available, I suppose?'

Stelios spoke to Major Kokliakous and told him he thought Dimitris may have recognised him and the evasion proceedings he had taken.

'I know he blames me for the raid on Mr Agyrious's premises and I believe he thinks I am collaborating with the Germans.'

The Major looked at Stelios sympathetically. 'I will avoid using you for "removal" duties for a while, but send you out with innocuous messages. If he brings his concerns to me I can offer him the position of messenger. That should allay his suspicions.'

The Allies were making inroads into Italy and the Germans were gradually being pushed back into Albania. At the same time the Russians were moving towards Romania and the Germans were gradually being isolated from their homeland. This news made the resistance even bolder with their acts of sabotage and ambush. The reprisals against the Greeks were savage. Men from the villages were rounded up, taken to an open area and mown down with machine gun fire, whilst their families watched in horror. Before leaving the area the Germans would burn the village to the ground, leaving the surviving residents homeless.

Stelios was relieved that he was no longer asked to meet Christos and masquerade as a German. The Jewish community had disappeared completely from the area they had once inhabited. Rumours were spread that they had escaped to Turkey or Romania and Tomas spent many anguished hours contemplating the fate of Miriam and her parents.

To Stelios's horror he saw that Herman had returned to Athens and sent up a fervent prayer that the man would not seek him out or decide to pay a surprise visit to their lodging. He warned Despina that the German was back in Athens but she appeared unconcerned.

'He found nothing when he raided before. He has no reason to come again.'

Despite Despina's reassuring attitude Stelios felt most uneasy.

Despina heard the familiar coded knock on her door. 'Go to your rooms,' she said to Stelios and Tomas and they obeyed fearfully.

The key turned and Despina greeted her visitor with a smile. 'What brings you here, Alexandros?'

General Michaelaous pulled his wife to him and gave her a brief kiss. 'Is all well here?'

'The men are no trouble.'

'I need you to speak to them. They are not to leave the house this evening. Tell them to pack their belongings and wait for instructions.' He placed a small packet in Despina's hands. 'Give them only a small amount of food and then the coffee afterwards. Don't drink it yourself. You understand what you have to do once they have left?'

Despina nodded. 'I remember my instructions. Stay safe, Alexandros, you know where you will be able to find me.'

As soon as Alexandros Michaelaous had left Despina locked the door and went down to the rooms occupied by Tomas and Stelios and knocked on their doors.

'It is quite safe to come out.'

Both men opened their doors with a look of relief on their faces.

'I have a message for you,' she said immediately. 'Pack your belongings and be ready to move out this evening. I can only provide you with a couple of rusks with tomato paste by way of a meal. I'm sure you will be given something more substantial when you reach your destination.'

'We can go to a taverna as usual,' offered Tomas.

Despina shook he head. 'You are not to leave the house. You must not be missing when your escort arrives.'

Stelios was surprised to hear they were moving so soon. He had only spoken to Despina a few days ago and she had advised them to continue to stay with her.

'Suppose Herman comes looking for us again?'

'If he should come here again I will tell him that after being raided by his men I no longer wished to have you lodging here and I will have no idea where you are living now.'

'Suppose they try to force the information from you?' Stelios hesitated to use the word "torture".

'If I don't know I can't tell, whatever they do to me. I have a few household jobs to complete. Help yourselves to a rusk in the meantime.'

It took neither man more than a few minutes to place their clothes into their sacks, along with their razor, comb, toothbrush and any other personal possessions that were in their room. Stelios considered taking his empty cash box with him and decided to leave it behind. He had no surplus money to store in there.

Despina was still in her bedroom when the men returned to the living room and Stelios produced a pack of cards.

'No point in just sitting here. We might as well do something to pass the time.'

'I wish Despina would hurry up with that food. My stomach is empty. Do you think we could help ourselves to another rusk?'

Stelios shook his head. 'There are only four in there unless Despina has some hidden away. How I would love to have moussaka.'

'Stop it; you're making my mouth water. I can hardly remember what proper food tasted like.'

'I can't remember what it felt like to have a full stomach,' complained Stelios. 'We've been better off than many even so.'

When Despina emerged from her bedroom they looked at her hopefully.

'Bring your sacks along here,' she ordered. 'He won't want to be delayed.'

They obeyed, returning to the living room and placing their sacks in a corner, both delighted to smell the aroma of coffee.

'I've only a couple of rusks , I'm afraid,' apologised Despina as she poured a cup of coffee for each of them. 'I hope this will make up for such meagre fare.'

'Much appreciated,' said Stelios. 'Are you having some?' he asked, seeing there was some left in the jug.

Despina shook her head. 'It is for you, not me.'

'That's very kind of you,' said Tomas as she refilled his cup and he drank deeply. 'How did you manage to get hold of some real coffee?' His tongue felt thick in his mouth and his words were slurred.

'It was given to me.'

Tomas wanted to say something else, but he could not remember what it was. Despina's face was going in and out of focus as he looked at her and he tried to blink as he felt his eyes closing. Despina placed his arms on the table and pushed his head down to rest on them and then did the same to Stelios. She opened the door to the apartment and beckoned two burly men inside.

'They're ready. Their sacks are in the corner.'

Without a word each man lifted an inert body and slung him over their shoulders, holding his legs with one hand and a sack in the other. Despina closed the door behind them, removed the coffee and cups from the table, flushed the remains of the coffee down the lavatory, rinsed the cups and jugs in the clean water and flushed the lavatory a second time before replacing the china in the kitchen.

She went into her bedroom tied a second scarf over her head, pushing her grey hair out of sight beneath it. She placed three blouses and two skirts over the clothes she was already wearing, a shawl around her shoulders and then her coat on top.

From the corner she picked up a shopping basket covered by a cloth, checked quickly around the room to ensure she had not left anything she wanted behind and exited the building. Keeping to the back streets and shuffling along she made her way to Plaka.

Tatiane opened the door to her and raised her eyebrows. Despina nodded and followed her sister into the living room.

'Help me off with my coat, please. I can hardly move my arms.'

Tatiane obliged and Despina flexed her arms thankfully. 'I didn't want to be seen carrying a sack so I wore all my clothes. I didn't realise how tight my coat would be.'

'Go down to your room and make yourself comfortable. I hope you'll be able to stay here with us now.'

'I'll have to wait until I've heard from Alexandros.'

Tatiane tutted. 'I always said you should not have married an army man. He's taking advantage of you.'

'It's the least I can do to help, and be thankful; it's due to him that you have food on your table.'

Despina lifted her basket and walked down to the spare bedroom. She knew her sister disapproved of her being involved with the resistance, but she really had no choice as she was married to General Michaelaous. She took her comb from the basket and dragged it through her hair. She hoped her sister might have some soap so she could give it a wash. She could pin her hair up again now, the way she was accustomed to wearing it. She had hated leaving it down, making her look so unkempt and slovenly.

Stelios opened his eyes and groaned. He was lying on the ground in complete darkness and there was a disgusting smell that made him want to retch. He groped around with his hands, relieved that he was not tied up, and felt a body beside him. He stiffened. Where was he and who was he lying next to? He flexed his legs and they were not tied either. It was little consolation to him. He was obviously a prisoner in a dungeon somewhere and there had been no need to restrain him as there was no way of escape. Panic welled up inside him, his breath coming in rapid gasps.

He tried to think, all he could remember was drinking coffee with Despina. He wished he could have a drink now, his throat felt so dry. He moved his head to one side, hoping a change of direction would alleviate the smell, and realised his head was resting on something relatively soft. He put up his hand and could feel sacking beneath his fingers. He stretched his hand out again and touched the body lying beside him. It was warm.

'Tomas,' he whispered. 'Tomas, is that you?'

A grunt answered him and the body shifted slightly and Stelios tried again. 'Tomas. It's me, Stelios. Are you awake?'

This time a groan answered him and the man put his hand up to his head. 'Let me sleep. I've a hell of a hangover.'

'No, Tomas, you can't sleep. Wake up.'

'My head.'

'Never mind your head. We've got to find a way out of here.'

'The door.'

Stelios shook his head in despair. Even if there was a door how would they find it in the darkness and where would it lead? Gingerly he sat up, exploring the area around him with his hands. If there was a door the only way to find it would be to walk around the walls and judging by the nauseous smell he would be continually treading into something very unpleasant.

His fingers came into contact with something hard and cold and he withdrew them quickly. Whatever it was did not move and he risked touching it a second time, realising by the shape that it was a bottle and there was liquid inside. Cautiously he lifted it up and fumbled to remove the cork. He sniffed, but could smell nothing except the stench that surrounded him. He placed his finger on the opening and tipped the bottle until he could feel that his finger was wet. He licked it gingerly. It appeared to be water; there was certainly no other discernible taste. Taking a chance he placed the bottle to his lips and took a sip. He waited, his body did not go into a spasm and the tasteless liquid was definitely water. He took a mouthful and allowed it to dribble down his parched throat.

He replaced the cork and held the bottle safely between his knees. This time he shook Tomas vigorously. If he could get Tomas to wake up sufficiently to drink some water he would begin to feel better. He desperately wanted to speak to his friend.

'Tomas, wake up. I've got some water. I'll give you some if you sit up.'

Tomas stirred again. 'Water?'

'Yes, water, but you have to sit up to drink it.'

'Can't.'

'Yes you can. I'll help you.' Stelios removed the bottle from between his knees and settled it carefully in the indentation made by his head on the sack. He stood up, his legs feeling weak, and stretched out his hand hoping he would be able to steady himself on the wall. He could feel wood beneath his fingers and ran his hand along, hoping he had found the door. There seemed no end to it and certainly no door frame.

Feeling steadier on his feet he felt his way carefully behind Tomas and placed his hands beneath his armpits. 'I'm going to lift you now. Try to help yourself by pushing up with your hands.'

Tomas was very little help, but with a struggle Stelios managed to get him into a sitting position. 'Sit absolutely still,' he ordered. 'Don't try to move and I'll give you some water.'

Once Stelios had managed to locate Tomas's mouth the man drank greedily until Stelios removed the bottle. He wanted some more for himself.

Tomas let out a sigh and Stelios took it as a sign that his friend was now fully awake.

'Tomas, are you listening to me?'

'Yes.'

'I don't know what's happened, but I think we're in a prison somewhere. We have to find a way out if we can.'

'If we are in a prison cell,' Tomas answered slowly, 'then everyone else is dead.'

'What do you mean?'

'The smell. It's dead bodies that are decaying.'

Stelios gasped, revolted by the idea and could feel his panic returning. 'You mean there are dead bodies around us?'

'Has to be. Once you've smelled them you always recognise the smell again.'

'So we've been put here to die and decay like them?'

'Probably.'

'Why would they leave us a bottle of water?' mused Stelios.

'Just to make our suffering more prolonged I expect.'

'I wish I could see something, anything, just to have some idea of where we are.'

'Light a match.'

Stelios cursed himself for not thinking of that earlier. He felt in his pockets and his cigarettes and matches were there, along with a few drachma notes. He struck a match, shielding the flame with his hand and tried to take in his surroundings by the flickering light.

There was an open space in front of him, but darkness beyond. Knowing that he was not going to tread in excrement he took a few steps forward and struck another match.

This time he could make out the shapes of coffins stacked against the far wall, but before he could see any more the match died on him.

'Tomas, there are coffins everywhere.'

'I told you it was the smell of death.'

'If they just put prisoners down here to die why would they bother to have coffins for them?'

'It would smell worse otherwise. I told you, it wasn't too bad at the morgue until it became overcrowded with bodies and the smell began to permeate everywhere.'

'What happened to them?'

'Once a day they were allowed to remove some coffins and take the bodies for burial. The problem was there were never enough graves dug and more people seemed to die than be removed.'

'Get up on your feet, Tomas, and reach out for my hand. There's nothing in the way and if we walk out a few steps we'll be able to see more.'

'We need more than the light of a match.'

'Alright, I've a few drachmas in my pocket. I'll make a spill with one of them. That should burn longer.' Stelios begrudged burning the note, but he felt it was essential they found out exactly where they were being held.

The lit drachma note gave considerably more light and Tomas looked around. 'We're in the morgue. I'm sure we are. The door should be that way, I think. Come on.'

'What about these sacks? Are they ours?'

'Have you looked inside?'

'How can I?' asked Stelios exasperated.

'Well feel inside. If you can feel clothing they are probably our sacks. We ought to take those with us when we leave.'

Stelios untied the neck of the sack and felt inside. There

definitely were clothes inside. He groped in the darkness for the sack that Tomas's head had rested on. Slowly he moved a few steps forward and leaned the sacks against his legs.

'When I light a match come and take a sack. I can't manage both of them and keep striking matches.'

Without warning light flooded the room and both men closed their eyes involuntarily.

'At least you're awake and we don't have to carry you again,' said a rough voice. 'Time to move on. Bring your sacks.'

Stelios drew a deep breath of relief then regretted his action as the smell caught in his throat and made him choke. Whatever their fate was to be at least they were not going to be left in the morgue to add to the number of corpses. Stumbling, still half blinded by the light, Stelios and Tomas followed the man out through the door and into another room, stacked floor to ceiling with coffins. Two coffins, open and empty, stood on the floor and Stelios felt his knees trembling.

'Put a sack in each one and then climb in and make yourself as comfortable as possible.'

Stelios opened his mouth to protest and the man held up his hand. 'Don't argue. We haven't got long. We'll only put one nail at each end so you'll have plenty of air. You'll go on the cart first and have some others stacked on top of you. We don't want to be told our time is up before we have you out of here.'

'Where are we going?' Stelios could hardly utter the words he was so gripped with terror.

'To a safe place. Nothing to be alarmed about. Hurry up or I'll be giving both of you a knock on the head.'

Tomas and Stelios exchanged fearful glances and placed the sacks into the coffins, stepping in after them and lying down.

'It won't be for very long,' the man assured them as he hammered a nail into each end of the coffin lid.

Stelios felt himself lifted off the ground and then pushed roughly onto somewhere flat. Within minutes he heard something being placed on top of him which he surmised was a coffin and then another. He hoped the lid would not be pushed down so tightly that no air was able to penetrate. Even with only one nail at each end he would be unable to free himself with the weight of the other coffins above him. He tried to take shallow breaths to make the air last as long as possible and curb the panic that was taking hold of him.

The journey through the streets of Athens seemed to take forever until the cart finally stopped and the coffins were removed. Stelios pushed at the lid, relieved when a nail popped and it raised enough for him to take a deep breath of air. Once again he felt himself lifted and carried, then deposited on the ground.

The lid was wrenched off and he looked up at the man he had seen earlier in the morgue.

'Into the church. Don't sit with your companion. Leave your sack.'

Hastily Stelios climbed out of the coffin, his legs stiff from lying in the one position, and hobbled over to the church. He could see there were a number of mourners inside and guessed they were the relatives of those who had arrived on the cart. He slipped onto a chair beside an old man who was wiping his eyes on his coat sleeve and said a heartfelt prayer of thanks for being away from the morgue and released from the confinements of the coffin. He looked around surreptitiously for any sign of Tomas.

The priest conducted the service and after a final blessing of the sad congregation he led the way outside where the coffins were being lowered into a communal grave under the watchful eyes of German soldiers. A final prayer was said, and the grave diggers began to shovel earth into the large hole. Supporting each other and with bowed heads the men and women filed past the priest who blessed each one of them. When Stelios reached him he clasped his hand and passed him a slip of paper.

'Do not wait for your friend. Follow the family ahead of you. Go safely, my son. May God be with you.'

'Thank you, Father.' replied Stelios automatically and hurried out of the churchyard in the wake of the couple who were walking in front of him.

Stelios was relieved to leave the churchyard without being challenged by the soldiers. Once safely away he looked at the slip of paper in his hand, thankful that he knew the area where the address was situated. It was an effort to place one foot in front of the other as he walked cautiously along the side streets. His head felt heavy and he could still smell the decay from the morgue, making him nauseous. He sniffed cautiously at the sleeve of his jacket, and thought it could be his clothes that smelt. He would have liked to lie down and sleep until he felt better, but did not dare.

When he finally reached a small house which was half hidden by thick bushes growing in front of it he felt overwhelmed with relief. The door opened swiftly at his knock and he was beckoned inside. Tomas was sitting at the table eating a bowl of something that smelt extraordinarily good to Stelios and his stomach rumbled.

'I expected you to arrive before me,' Tomas smiled in relief. 'I was getting concerned that something had happened to you.'

'I couldn't see you at the church. I made a detour around the other side of the hill.'

The man who had opened the door to Stelios placed a second bowl on the table and indicated that Stelios should sit and eat before he once again retired to the back room.

Stelios removed his jacket, noticing that Tomas wrinkled his nose in distaste as he hung it on the back of the chair.

'You stink,' he remarked.

'I doubt if you smell any better. I'd like to have a thorough wash and some clean clothes.'

'I haven't seen our sacks,' said Tomas miserably. 'We may not have any clean clothes.'

Stelios shrugged, he could no longer resist from eating the tempting bowl of food.

'Who is he?' asked Stelios quietly when he had mopped his plate clean with a piece of stale bread.

Tomas shrugged. 'No idea. Hasn't spoken a word since I arrived.'

'Do you think he's a mute?'

'Could be, or he resents having us here and isn't prepared to be friendly.'

'He can't be deaf or he wouldn't have heard us knock on his door.'

'I think he was watching from the window.'

Stelios rose and walked over to the window, lifting the edge of the curtain. 'You can't see the front door from here. There's a bush in the way.'

The man entered from the back room. 'I am not deaf and nor am I dumb. I decided to wait until you had both arrived before speaking to either of you. I am Phoebus. First names only.'

'I'm Tomas.'

'And I am Stelios.'

Phoebus placed a bottle of wine and three glasses on the table. 'Enjoy this whilst you can. My cellar will not last forever.' He pulled a chair out from the table, poured the wine and sat down, leaning towards them and speaking quietly.

'You are not to leave this house until you have had a visitor. In the meantime you can have a wash. I have some water heating. Your sacks are in the back room so you can change your clothes. Leave those you are wearing now on the floor and they will be dealt with. I will show you to your rooms, but you are not to open the shutters. It would be advisable to sleep for a while until the full effects of the sleeping draught finally wears off. If necessary I will wake you when your visitor arrives.'

Stelios felt considerably better once he had eaten, washed and changed into fresh clothes. He had expected to have to share a room with Tomas and was delighted to be able to shut the door and pull off his boots. Swiftly he placed his clothes in the chest; his books he placed on a small table along with his comb, razor, tooth brush and a pack of cards. He opened the door to the cupboard on the far wall and was surprised to see the key was in the lock on the inside.

His Morse code machine was missing, but he felt too weary to spend time speculating on its loss and decided Phoebus's suggestion of a rest would be a good idea. It was possible they might be expected to move on somewhere else during the evening.

It seemed he had no sooner closed his eyes than Phoebus was tapping on the door and saying he was to go down to the living room. He pulled on his boots, ran his comb through his hair and descended the stairs. To his surprise General Michaelaous was sitting at the table with Phoebus, a glass of wine in front of both of them. Automatically Stelios saluted.

'Sit down, Stelios. As soon as Tomas arrives I will apprise you of the situation.'

His words sounded ominous to Stelios and he waited impatiently for Tomas to join them.

Phoebus produced two more glasses of wine and Stelios hesitated. Did this contain another sleeping draught?

'Could I have a glass of water, please? My mouth is so dry.'

Phoebus went to the back room and returned with a two mugs of water placing one before Stelios. 'No doubt your friend will have a dry mouth also.'

Tomas entered, he sat at the table and placed his head in his hands. 'I've a terrible headache. I thought a sleep would have cleared it, but it seems even worse now.'

'Drink the water. You're probably dehydrated,' commented Phoebus.

'Are you capable of listening and understanding me?' asked General Michaelaous.

Tomas nodded and immediately regretted his action. 'Yes, sir. I'll do my best.'

'Unfortunately Dimitris was arrested and he had his equipment in his pocket. No doubt he has been interrogated and due to the unsavoury methods used he has talked. Fortunately Major Kokliakous witnessed his arrest and was able to contact Manos and tell him not to report for work the following day. Although Manos insists he has never disclosed his address to Dimitris we thought it wise to move him elsewhere. Your lodgings were known so we decided we must move you immediately.'

'What about Despina?'

'Despina is safe. If they decide to raid her house they will find no sign of her or either of you. This is a safe house and I am relying on both of you to ensure it stays that way. For the next week you are not to go out and do not shave. Once you each have a beard you will not be so recognisable.'

'Herman told me he had a very good memory for faces.'

'If you are not around then Herman will be unable to recognise you. I repeat, under no circumstances are you to leave this house until I have visited again and given you permission. Phoebus will show you the safety procedures we have in place. It is to be hoped you will not need to use them. Any questions?'

'Yes, sir. Why were we drugged and taken to the morgue for the night? I thought we had been placed there to die a lingering death. It was a terrifying experience.'

General Michaelaous looked at Stelios sympathetically. 'It was the safest way to move you. The Germans do not examine the bodies that are taken in, nor do they open up the coffins to inspect the occupants.'

'I just wish we had been warned,' grumbled Stelios.

'There was no time. Once I knew Dimitris had been arrested I had to make arrangements swiftly.'

'What happened to my Morse equipment?'

'That was removed from your sacks for your own protection. Anything else?'

Stelios shook his head. 'I can't think of anything, sir.'

'In that case I will leave and visit you again when I consider it safe. Obey Phoebus's instructions and you should come to no harm.'

To Stelios's surprise General Michaelaous left the house through the back room.

Phoebus looked sternly at both men. 'You heard what the General said. You are to follow my instructions implicitly. You will always leave and enter here by the front door. I will show you the back entrance later. The back door is never locked. Locked doors tend to get broken open. Make sure when you do go out you have nothing on your person that discloses this address. If you are stopped and asked you will give an address on the other side of the city. If you are escorted there you will go to an empty house and say you have been sleeping there – understand?'

'Yes, sir,' replied Tomas and Stelios nodded.

'If I am not around you can help yourselves to the food I will have left prepared, but make sure you share it fairly and wash your dishes. You do not help yourself to my wine.' Phoebus smiled at them. 'I'm sure you will both be very conscientious. Now, if you follow me I will show you the back entrance that you will be expected to use in an emergency.'

He opened the door in the back room which led out to a small yard with high walls. At one side there were a flight of narrow stone steps which he mounted, beckoning to Stelios and Tomas to follow him. At the top of the flight was a narrow door and Phoebus pushed it open. They found themselves in a small dark area littered with cases and broken furniture.

'Close the door,' ordered Phoebus and switched on a small flashlight that gave them just enough light to see their way across the room without bumping into the obstacles. On the far side was another door and when Phoebus opened it they saw a similar flight of steps leading downwards. He descended them confidently and Tomas and Stelios followed more cautiously. On reaching the ground he led them to a door set into the wall and almost hidden by foliage. Once on the other side they were again in a walled yard, but this time there was a door in the far wall.

The door led out to a path with walls on one side and overgrown bushes and weeds on the other. At regular intervals there were doors set into the wall and at the last one Phoebus stopped.

'This is the last house in the road. It is boarded up and looks deserted. This is where you will hide should it become necessary.'

Phoebus pushed open the wooden gate and led the way into a paved yard. 'Be careful to step on the paving slabs and not trample the weeds. You do not wish to disclose that anyone has been this way.'

He walked to the back door of the house which opened smoothly at his touch. It was dark inside, only a small amount of light filtered through the windows which were haphazardly boarded up. He led the way into the front room where the only furniture was a large, solid looking table with a piece of thick string beneath it.

'This is where you will hide should a patrol come searching for you.' Phoebus bent down, picked up the string and pulled. A whole section of the floor began to lift up. 'You go down into this hole, it is not deep, and once there you pull the string down after you and shoot the bolts home. You will find a flashlight down there, but you use it fleetingly, just to get your bearings. The passage way is low and you make your way to the far end where you will be beneath the garden. There is food and water down there along with a couple of blankets. You will stay there until I come to say it is safe to emerge.'

Stelios looked at the dark hole in horror. To be down there for any length of time would remind him of the time spent in the morgue. 'Suppose for some reason you were unable to come back? How long are we expected to stay down there?'

'If I am unable to return there is a friend who will come in my stead. If no one comes it would be advisable for you to stay hidden until your water has run out. It would mean we had been arrested and our houses under scrutiny.'

Phoebus lowered the false floor back into place and both Stelios and Tomas had to admit that apart from the hole where the string was currently inserted it was impossible to tell where the trap door and the floor met.

Phoebus ushered them back out into the yard. 'Remember to walk on the paving stones.'

Phoebus pulled the garden gate closed behind them and continued to walk down the path, both sides now having trees and bushes, for some distance before it suddenly opened up onto the road and the Hill of Philopappos was before them.

'If you need to leave the house where you have hidden in a hurry this is the exit you will use, but try not to damage the foliage. We do not want to draw attention to the fact that the path has been used. There are various routes available from here to all parts of the city. Familiarise yourselves with them so that you are able to move swiftly.'

'What about your neighbours? Suppose they see us in the gardens and using this path?'

Phoebus shook his head. 'The neighbours are under instructions not to open their shutters or windows except during the hours of darkness. They will be too busy going about their own business to take any notice of you. Should they see soldiers arrive they'll be either hiding or making an exit. Did you count the number of doors we passed?'

Tomas shook his head.

'Seven, I think,' said Stelios.

Phoebus nodded. 'If for any reason you should need to return by this route count the doors and enter at the seventh gate. Go through the gate and into the next door garden. Climb the steps to the storage room, exit the other side into my yard and enter my house by the back door. Is that clear?'

'That room was awfully dark. It's full of furniture and rubbish for us to bump into,' observed Stelios.

'There is a small flashlight up there. It will give you enough light to see across the room. Make sure you leave it there. You will find that the objects stored up there are moved frequently as I sweep the room. We do not want a trail of footprints in the dust.'

They followed Phoebus back towards his house, both men counting the doors as they walked along the path. To Stelios's surprise when they entered the garden of the seventh house he told them to wait.

Stelios and Tomas exchanged glances. Had their new lodgings already been discovered? Stelios shuddered. He had no wish to go down into the hole beneath the floor.

Phoebus returned swiftly and beckoned to them to mount the steps leading to the room that would lead them back into Phoebus's yard.

Once back in the living room Phoebus turned to them. 'If anyone should come looking for you that is the way you will leave the premises. Of course, if you are in your rooms at the time that will not be possible. Did you open the cupboard?'

Stelios nodded. 'I did. The key was on the inside and I replaced it outside.'

Phoebus shook his head. 'The key is on the inside deliberately. Come with me and I will show you your other escape route.'

Dutifully they followed him back up to their rooms. He went first to Tomas's and opened the door to the cupboard. He took the key from the lock and walked to the back of the narrow cupboard where he pulled another door open to expose a small landing with a flight of stairs leading downwards.

'You will wait there, Tomas. Now to your room, Stelios.'

Phoebus repeated the procedure and when he pulled open the door at the back of the cupboard Stelios saw Tomas standing there.

'That's clever,' said Tomas admiringly.

'If you should need to leave by this route you lock the inside of the cupboard and when you have passed through the second door you lock that behind you also. It will give you a few extra minutes to make good your escape. We will now meet Fotias, my next door neighbour.'

Stelios and Tomas followed Phoebus down the stairs and into the living room. Fotias looked up from his newspaper and nodded to them.

'My new lodgers,' explained Phoebus. 'I was just showing them another exit.'

'Pleased to meet you,' said Fotias. 'I hope I'll not have occasion to meet you again as that would mean you were in trouble. Should you need to come through my house I shall deny all knowledge of you. I understand Phoebus has shown you the garden route so you will know where to go.'

'I'll take them back home now and leave you in peace until our game on Wednesday.'

Fotias nodded and smiled. 'You'll need to be on your mettle. I'm on a winning streak at the moment.'

Phoebus led the way back into his own house, entering through Stelios's cupboard and placing the key in the lock on the inside. He handed Tomas his key. 'Inside the cupboard, remember.'

'Do all the houses lead through to each other?' asked Stelios.

Phoebus shook his head. 'Only this pair has communal access. Originally these two houses were owned by one of the wealthier inhabitants of the city. The parents bought the house next door when it was for sale ready for when their oldest child married. It was practical to have a shared storeroom and to be able to enter each other's house without needing to go outside in all weathers. It was particularly useful when the parents needed nursing in their old age.'

'And you and Fotias decided to make use of the arrangement.'

'Under the present circumstances it seemed practical. We do not visit each other using that route which is why I told him I was bringing you both to meet him. I would not want to frighten the wits out of him by suddenly walking into his living room.'

'Surely we'll frighten him if we have to use that route?' frowned Stelios.

'If you need to pass through his house I hope you will be

moving so fast that he hardly sees you. You do not stop to apologise or ask his permission.'

'What are we supposed to do with ourselves if we are not allowed out?' asked Tomas.

'You may spend the day as you wish. Play cards, back gammon, read, talk, sleep; whatever you please. During the hours of daylight you do not open your shutters or window. Once it is dark you may open them, but you must not use a light until you have closed them again. Anyone out on the hill would be able to see a light and could become curious.'

The days seemed endless to both Stelios and Tomas whilst they were confined to Phoebus's house. It had been a relief when General Michaelaous finally called. He declared himself satisfied with their beard growth, but looked at Stelios carefully.

'When you go out you do not wear your spectacles. Few people wear them and it makes you noticeable.'

'If we are going back to work may I take them with me?'

'Certainly. You can carry them in the pocket of your cassock.'

'My cassock?'

General Michaelaous smiled at Stelios's incredulity. 'When you go out you will be wearing a priest's robes and hat. Each day you will make your way to the Church of Agios Emmanuel. It will be safe for you to continue with your work there. You can choose your names that the other men will know you by. I suggest you become used to calling each other by those names. If you have any suspicion that you are being watched when you return here you must part at the corner and go separate ways. Enter the first church you see and stay there for at least an hour.'

'Will Manos be working with us?' asked Tomas.

The General shook his head. 'We have moved him elsewhere. Too many priests working together could give rise to suspicion.'

'And Dimitris? Is he in prison?'

'I'm afraid Dimitris succumbed to the treatment that was meted out to him. He met his death at the hands of his interrogators. As we expected your lodgings were searched and, of course, they found nothing.'

Stelios shuddered. 'Thank you, sir, for ensuring we were safe.'

General Michaelaous let out a sigh. 'We try, but it is not always possible. We believed that after the German surrender in Russia and the Italians joining the Allies we might be nearing the end of our trials. The surrender of the island of Leros means we are as vulnerable as ever. All we can do is send equipment to the resistance and support the Allied cause by sending out false messages to mislead the Germans.'

Stelios felt self conscious when he left the house dressed as a priest, a large wooden cross hanging round his neck. He tried to resist gathering the skirt of his cassock tightly around him and holding it up from the ground to prevent soiling the hem as he walked down the street with Tomas. He hoped no one would ask either of them for a blessing as they made their way to the church.

Father Constantinus greeted them gravely. 'Welcome Father Aristo, Father Elias, I understand you are joining our community whilst you undertake some work. You will be in the room at the rear of the church and should be undisturbed. I have been told that you will be leaving your equipment here each evening and I am still trying to think of the safest place to store it. Maybe you could find somewhere you think would be suitable. At the end of each day one of you will deliver any communications you have received to the blind beggar who will be sitting outside the main door. One of you will bend down as if to bless him and place the messages into his begging bowl. Do not stop and talk to him.'

Stelios and Tomas nodded. After the fate that had befallen Dimitris they would certainly obey implicitly any instructions given to them. They were sure Herman would be looking for them as two of the other men who had worked at the Argyrious building.

'If anyone came looking for us would we be able to have any warning?' asked Stelios.

'I would protest loudly and bang my staff on the ground. I'm sure you would hear me. Make sure you are engaged on an innocuous occupation with the radio broadcasting their Nazi propaganda. Should that event occur I would not be able to prevent them from searching everywhere.'

The room they were shown into held three tables and half a dozen chairs, a sink with some cups stacked at the side and a row of hooks where spare robes for the priests were hung. On the centre table was a large Bible and beside it a radio and their Morse code equipment.

'There's nowhere here to hide as much as a pin,' declared Tomas.

'Then we'll have to look inside the church. There should be plenty of nooks and crannies there where we can put our machines safely out of sight.'

'Shall we go and look now or wait until the end of the day?'

'I think we should find somewhere now. If we have an unwanted visitor we want to be able to dispose of them quickly.'

Tomas looked at Stelios sceptically. 'No doubt the visitors you're thinking of would come into the church. There'd be no opportunity to hide them in there. We'd be seen.'

'I was thinking of overnight storage,' replied Stelios airily, feeling stupid that he had not realised how impractical it would be to rely on a hiding place in the church.

Tomas moved the black robes to one side exposing the stone wall, he felt beneath the tables and chairs, tipping them up to see if there would be a practical place to hide their Morse code machines. His eyes roamed around the bare walls, the only adornment being a large crucifix.

'Hopeless,' he announced. 'If we could reach the crucifix easily we might be able to wedge them behind the cross pieces.'

'They'd probably fall down even if we could reach it. They would need to be fixed and we certainly wouldn't have time to do that.' Stelios was feeling pessimistic. There wasn't a rubbish cupboard here where their equipment could be stuffed into a cushion cover and hidden.

'Got it,' said Tomas finally. 'Help me to unscrew the waste pipe under the sink. We'll disconnect it at the joint and force it apart. We can tie our drawstring bags together and wedge them inside one on top of the other. There should be just about sufficient space.'

'Suppose someone uses the sink?'

'We put a notice on there saying "out of order". If anyone does turn the tap on the water will spill out onto the floor.'

'What if we want a drink?'

'Then make sure you hold the cup under the tap,' replied Tomas impatiently. 'Unless you have a better idea, help me to undo the waste pipe.'

Together they struggled and finally the collar holding the two pipes together bent sufficiently for them to ease one pipe out from the other.

'Perfect,' announced Tomas as he straightened out the collar as best he could. 'We'll tell Father Constantinus and leave our equipment there overnight and also use it as a quick hiding place if necessary.'

Stelios looked at his friend admiringly. 'I would never have thought of that.'

'I remember when we had a blockage at home and my father took the pipe apart to remove it.'

Stelios nodded as if conversant with plumbing. When he had lived at the farm in Plaka they had used the pump outside in the yard; when he lived in Aghios Nikolaos there was a cold water tap in the kitchen area and the sink drained into a bucket beneath. Whilst he lodged in Heraklion hot water had been brought to him each morning and whilst at University in Athens Tatiane had allowed him to heat water over the fire in the kitchen as he needed it. He had never had to consider blocked waste pipes as the dirty water was usually just thrown outside into the yard.

'Well,' grinned Tomas, 'Now we've sorted that little problem out we ought to get down to some work I suppose.'

The days passed uneventfully and they were not challenged by the German patrols. Stelios often found he woke in the night, sweating with fear and gasping for breath where he had dreamt he was still in the morgue or shut in the coffin. At such times he would have to rise and walk around, opening the shutters and window to place his head outside and take deep breaths of air.

Messages arrived frequently and it was good to be able to discuss the information they contained together. They smiled happily when a message came to say that the resistance had captured seventy eight Germans and executed them, but were thrown into anger and despair when a message came to say that retaliation had been swift and merciless.

The Germans had marched on Kalavryta, shooting anyone they met on the road. The men had been taken and shot whilst the women and children had been imprisoned in a building and it was then set on fire. The Germans had systematically fired all the houses in the village, leaving nothing but blackened ruins. Both men had spent some time on their knees that evening, along with many local people who had come to mourn on behalf of their countrymen.

1944 - 1946

News filtered through that the Russian army was making headway towards Romania. The German High Command was becoming increasingly concerned. If the Russians managed to enter the Balkan States their troops would be cut off from the rest of Europe and virtually surrounded. The resistance became bolder and declared a National Liberation Party, drawing even more destitute villagers into their ranks. People who had lost their families and homes now had nothing more to lose.

Tomas was concerned about Miriam and also about his own family. He had tentatively suggested to Stelios that they walked down to Piraeus to see them, but Stelios shook his head.

'I am anxious to know that they are safe as much as you are. If Herman is watching out for us and spotted us leaving here we would be putting Phoebus and the safe house in danger.'

'If we left by the back path no one would see us,' protested Tomas.

'If we were seen at your parents a neighbour could say they were sheltering resistance workers and they would probably be shot. I don't think we could walk down there wearing our robes. They are just to disguise us at work and what excuse would your parents have for a visit from two priests? We just have to be patient, Tomas.'

Tomas paled visibly. 'I hadn't thought of endangering my parents. I do wish I knew if Miriam and her family were safe.'

Stelios hesitated. 'The Major assured you they had not been deported by the Germans.'

'That was then. Anything could have happened in the meantime.'

'I'm sure we would have heard. As far as I know there haven't been any Jews deported from Athens. The Rabbi destroyed all the details he held.'

'They could still have been arrested. If I knew their address I could at least walk past occasionally and check they were still there.'

Stelios shook his head. 'That could put them in danger. Sooner or later someone would realise that you were a frequent visitor to the area and want to know why.'

Tomas sighed deeply.

'Don't be too despondent. Now the National Liberation Party has been set up our ineffective puppet government will have to listen to their demands. If they say we should drive the Germans out of Athens I will certainly ask for a gun so I can take part. I often wish I hadn't thrown mine away. I had one or two opportunities when I could have shot Herman.' Stelios spoke boastfully with a conviction that he did not feel. He had no desire to take part in any fighting that ensued and would never have had the courage to shoot Herman.

The Greek government, in exile in Egypt, had attracted the soldiers who had been evacuated from the mainland and formed the Royal Hellenic Army along with and under the guidance of the British troops who were stationed in the Middle East. Joining the Allies in the Nile Delta they took part in the Second Battle of El Alamein suffering casualties.

In April there was a widespread mutiny in the Greek Brigades in favour of the non-communist party. This was against the British interests at that time and both units were disbanded and their personnel interned or used in non-combat duties. The mutiny had spread to the Greek navy, but Greek naval officers, loyal to the government in exile, recaptured the ships and the crews were interned.

A further unit was formed in Egypt by three thousand five hundred politically reliable officers and became the III Greek Mountain Brigade and fought valiantly in the Battle of Rimini. Despite the Greeks' fervent wish to be rid of the Germans there were divided loyalties between the non-communist and pro-communist supporters.

Stelios tried to talk to Tomas about the opposing political parties, but Tomas shook his head. 'I don't know anything about politics. I'm not educated like you.'

'You don't have to be educated to have an opinion.'

'I feel I should listen to both arguments and have enough political knowledge to be able to make a judgement. I'd like to see our king back on the throne and have our lives back to normal.'

Stelios did not pursue the matter. He could not envisage their lives ever being normal again, even if they did succeed in driving the Germans out of their country.

The more military success the Allies had the more desperate and atrocious the German reprisals became. Sickening reports came of a massacre that had taken place at Distomo, close to Delphi, where the troops had gone from house to house, stabbing babies and women, shooting the men and beheading the priest before setting the village on fire.

Stelios and Tomas continued to obey their instructions, walking sedately to the church each day, receiving and sending messages to the outlying army units. Stelios no longer felt safe in his disguise as a priest; if the priest in Distomo had been beheaded what was to stop the Germans from doing the same to him?

Each night he was wracked with nightmares, sometimes he was back in the morgue, other times imprisoned in a coffin with the lid firmly nailed down, and more recently he had seen Herman's face as he was told to kneel and wait to feel cold steel hit his neck. When he awoke, sweating with fear, he would lie awake, staring into the dark room, not daring to close his eyes should a horrendous dream return. He dreaded having to hide in the hole beneath the floor of the empty house.

The Allies continued to make inroads into the occupied territories, driving the Germans out or taking them captive. The Athenian citizens began to feel hopeful that their ordeal would shortly be over.

The communist party had taken over swathes of territory in the north of the country as soon as the Germans had been dislodged from the areas, but they were as violent in their retribution as the Germans had been. In September members of a security battalion at Meligalas that had been assisting the Germans, were declared collaborators and traitors and executed.

Finally, in October the Allies marched into Athens, the Germans hurrying to vacate the city before their arrival. The puppet government, that had been placed in the Athenian parliament by the Germans and had no power whatsoever, was becoming concerned. Would the people believe that they had been under orders that could not be disobeyed or would they think they had collaborated willingly? If the Germans did leave, they would be powerless to prevent the Athenians from taking their revenge against them.

Once again the Greek flag flew from the Parthenon and the exiled government decided it was safe to return to Greece. Papandreou formed a National Unity Party and began to assess the damage that had been done to their country, their people and the infrastructure. In Macedonia a group of young men had formed an alliance and were busily building roads, bridges, schools and hospitals, but they were also searching out any who had collaborated with the Germans and executing them. The situation was volatile and the group was growing larger and more powerful daily.

Stelios and Tomas were told to continue to masquerade as priests and live with Phoebus until further notice. In due course they were told they would receive a message with a date to report to the army headquarters They were still cautious about moving around the city as occasionally gunfire could be heard where a small number of Germans had been hiding out and discovery by the Allies ensued in a short gun battle.

The troops that had been evacuated to Egypt began to return, along with those who had fought with the resistance on Crete having been unable to reach the coast in time to leave the island. Families celebrated or mourned when a loved one did not return and would remain hopeful that he would arrive in due course.

Tomas walked down to the Jewish quarter in the vain hope of seeing Miriam and her family at the laundry, but their house was still deserted. He enquired from the neighbours who had returned if they had any news of the family and at last he was rewarded. A woman felt sure she had seen Abraham not far from where she had been hidden by a Christian household, but could not tell Tomas the exact address.

'I'm sure they will return when they are convinced it is safe to do so,' Stelios tried to reassure his friend. 'Why don't you walk down to Piraeus in the meantime and check on your family?'

'Don't you want to come to see Daphne?'

'We can't both be missing. If you're delayed for any reason I'll cover for you and say you're feeling unwell. Just make sure you are back when we have to attend the meeting at the offices.' Stelios had given very little thought to Tomas's sister over the past few years. 'Tell Daphne I'll be down to visit her as soon as possible,' he added.

Tomas returned the following day to report that his family were safe and well. 'They're all thin, and Pappa looks really old and tired. He was made to go and work down at the docks. He's never done that kind of manual work before. Daphne says she's longing to see you and Mamma says you're welcome to visit at any time.'

Stelios nodded. He would probably wait until there was some transport running again between Athens and Piraeus before he bothered to make the journey.

'Have there been any further messages about reporting at the army offices?' asked Tomas and Stelios shook his head.

'Only the first message, the same as the one you received.'

Tomas pulled a face. 'I really do not fancy going back there after our previous experience. Are you sure it's a genuine message?'

Stelios shrugged. 'Why shouldn't it be? They probably want to give us new instructions now the war is over.'

'Do you plan to stay in the army?'

Stelios hesitated, then nodded. Due to the dire state of the economy and the political unrest throughout the country he no longer had any ambition to work in the government as the Minister of Finance.

'It's a safe job, so I'll stay until something better comes along. What about you?'

'That depends upon Miriam. If she wants to stay close to her family in Athens then I'll continue in the army. If she's happy to move down to Piraeus I'll join my father in his business. Many people chopped up their furniture to use as firewood during the winter. They're going to need new tables and chairs so there should be plenty of business.'

Stelios raised his eyebrows. Inflation was rocketing and the drachma had been devalued. It was unlikely that anyone would be able to afford to buy new furniture.

Throughout the city were soldiers, but this time in the remnants of their uniform, tattered jackets, torn trousers and stained shirts. Some were on makeshift crutches, having lost a leg, others had the sleeve of their jacket pinned down where their arm was missing, but the ones Stelios found the most disturbing were those who were sitting in doorways, shaking and twitching uncontrollably.

Stelios and Tomas walked to the army office, ensuring they arrived in time for the designated meeting.

'I keep expecting Herman to come up behind me,' said Stelios as they crossed the road.

'Do you think we should use the main entrance or sneak in around the back?' asked Tomas.

'The front,' said Stelios firmly. 'There's no reason why it should be locked now.'

They were pleased they had arrived well before the appointed time as more men began to crowd into the room. They clustered together in small groups looking around warily and greeting those they knew.

'There's Manos,' said Tomas in delight. 'Let's go and ask him what happened after Dimitris was arrested.'

Stelios began to follow Tomas across the room and then saw Christos enter.

'You go and talk to Manos. I'll catch up with you in a moment. There's someone here I need to speak to.' Stelios threaded his way through the waiting men until he reached Christos.

'Hello, Christos. Remember me?'

Christos nodded, and Stelios continued.

'My friend has a problem. He's trying to trace the family that we moved from the laundry. They've not returned yet and I wondered if you knew the address where they are living.'

'I've no idea where any of them went after we delivered them to the safe house in Pagrati.'

'Is there any way you would be able to find out or get a message to them to say it is safe to return?'

'Maybe.'

'I'd be terribly grateful. My friend is going frantic with worry. I was not allowed to tell him we had moved them to a safe area so he has no idea what has happened to them.'

'What's his interest?'

'The daughter,' grinned Stelios. 'He has plans to marry her.'

Christos raised his eyebrows. 'What's wrong with a Greek girl?'

'Nothing in my eyes, but he's only interested in her.'

Christos nodded and began to walk away. 'I'll see what I can do,' he called over his shoulder.

Finally General Michaelaous, and the Majors Kokliakous and Colonomous entered, along with other men of the same rank, whom Stelios did not recognise. They were smartly dressed in their army uniforms and Stelios noted that the General now displayed the insignia of a Colonel and the Majors were now Generals. Stelios felt scruffy and unkempt in his civilian clothes.

Colonel Michaelaous clapped his hands and called for silence, although the level of talking had dropped to no more than a murmur.

'Fellow soldiers,' he began, 'I am both thankful and honoured to see that so many of you have been able to join us. The government would like me to extend their thanks to all of you who risked your lives to stay in Athens and work under cover. Gather round so you can all hear. If you have a question ask me before I move on. Understood?'

The men nodded and muttered 'Yes, sir.'

'I am sure you all realise the sad state that Athens has been left in by the German soldiers. Buildings and roads need to be repaired. We have to get the hospitals re-equipped and the schools open. Transport is needed to bring food supplies and raw materials to the city and the vehicles need attention to ensure they are serviceable. The buildings need to be inspected for stability before we can ask men to go in and make repairs. At the very least they will need to be repainted to get rid of the swastikas that have been daubed on the walls.'

The Colonel looked at the men who stood before him. 'Another concern is the unrest spreading from the north of Greece. Rebuilding progress has been made there by a group who support the communist ideals. A detachment of soldiers will be sent to the area to monitor and if necessary deal with the situation if it becomes out of hand. Now we have rid ourselves of the Germans and have our own government again we do not want internal strife hindering progress.

'As I said, there is much to be done in Athens before we can be proud of our city again. The manual labour, the roads and buildings, will be worked on by the men who were employed in these activities before the war with the help of the army. Most of you standing before me held the rank of Captain and worked in essential office jobs. We would like you to continue to do so.'

Stelios smiled happily. He had no desire to be sent to northern Greece or asked to work repairing roads.

The Colonel looked at the men assembled before him. He found it difficult to put a name to many of the faces. 'One thing that we did learn from the Germans is the need to be able to identify people. The Ministry of Public Order is responsible for compiling this information. The government has asked for our help in setting up offices in local public buildings where people will be required by law to come and register their name, date of birth, place of birth and their current address. If they have any visible distinguishing marks those will also be recorded and they must sign to say the details are correct.'

A hand shot up. 'Not everyone will know the date they were born, sir.'

'Not everyone can write,' added another voice.

'Quite so. Among the older generation it is very unlikely they will know exactly when they were born. A sibling or a parent who is still alive might be able to help. If they are unable to sign their name their mark must be witnessed by a member of their family and an officiating officer, but they must not be maligned for their ignorance. As time passes the system will become more efficient. Currently we need a way to enable us to distinguish one man or woman from another.

'Reliable, efficient, office workers are needed to help with the compilation of the lists. The government proposes to broadcast to the people that they will have to go to the registration centre nearest to their home and have their personal details recorded. They will also have posters printed with this information and they will be placed on walls throughout all areas of the city.'

'What happens if people don't go and register?'

'The government is passing a law to make registration compulsory for everyone. Each man and woman will be given a card that they should carry with them at all times. If they are asked by the police to produce it failure to do so would result in arrest and they would be taken to the nearest registration centre. Once the people realise that this is a very simple and logical requirement of them I am sure they will comply.'

Another hand shot up. 'I understand my details were registered when I joined the army. Do I have to register again?'

'Yes, you will be required to register the same as every other citizen. All service men will have to carry an identity card along with civilians.'

'What about the Jewish population?' asked Tomas.

'Everyone who is a citizen of Greece, regardless of their ethnic origins or religion will be expected to register their details the same as everyone else,' replied the Colonel and Tomas could not suppress a smile. If Abraham had to register his family he would be able to find out where they were living.

'What about children?'

'They will be included on their parent's card until they reach twelve years and after that they will have to register and have a card in their own name. Once the system is up and running efficiently new born infants will be required to have a card within the first six months of their life and when someone dies the family must hand in the card to the authorities. Some of you will be required to assist with this work.'

'What about the people who do not live in Athens? Will they have to come here to be registered?'

'Whilst the work in Athens is being completed the outlying areas will be visited. As soon as our army transport system is up and running again we will take employees of the Ministry to the outlying areas and set up an office. The soldiers who accompany them will visit the villages and impress upon the villagers the necessity of registration, taking them to a centre if necessary. The Ministry aims to have the project virtually completed within a year and after that it will the responsibility of the villagers to go to their nearest large town to register their children or a death in the family.'

'Where do we get these registration cards from?'

'Printers are being employed around the clock to have sufficient number at each centre when they open. More will be delivered as they are needed.'

Stelios smiled. Listing people's names and addresses seemed simple enough.

'Many young men entered the army expecting to be a soldier for life. Now many of them will have lost members of their families and ed back home to assist in the family business. If any of those men wish to leave the army now they are free to do so, but they will need to have an official discharge paper. There will also be veterans who wish to leave the service. An office will be set up in this building specifically to deal with those requests. Any man who cannot produce his discharge paper when requested will be considered to be a deserter and dealt with accordingly, whatever his rank,' continued the Colonel.

'The soldiers who have returned from Egypt will be given the same information regarding discharge or continuing their career in the army. There are a number of men who have been shipped back from Egypt who come from Crete or other islands. They will obviously wish to go back home and will also need official reassignment papers or discharge papers. Whether you are working on discharge or registration you will have a soldier working with you who has been maimed. A missing arm or leg does not stop a man from being a useful member of the community, although he will no longer be an army employee. The government will be making arrangements for these men to be suitably employed elsewhere or if employment is impossible due to their injuries they will receive a pension to enable them to live decently. We do not want more beggars roaming the streets. Any more questions?'

'Yes, sir. When do we start?'

'Tomorrow you will go and collect uniforms from the storage depot.'

Stelios gave an audible groan. He did not wish to visit the morgue again and if the uniforms had been stored there they would probably smell.

The Colonel looked around to ascertain the source of the noise. 'The depot is in a disused building close to Omonia Square. There will be a sign outside. As you leave here you will be given a chit that you will present to the officer in charge. It entitles you to two pairs of trousers, two shirts, a jacket, overcoat, a pair of boots, belt, cap and the insignia of your rank. You will dress in this uniform whenever you are on duty collecting information. You will each be given the address where you will report in a week's time. Initially we will be using the schools and any other public buildings that are declared structurally sound for the registration process. Anything else?'

The men shook their heads. It sounded easy, pleasant work, without the constant fear of being arrested or shot hanging over them.

'I will call out the names of those who will be in charge of the registration details and the building where they will report for duty next week. I will also call out the name and rank of the officer who will be in charge of each detail. The list will be posted in the main hallway of this building so you can check your assignment. Once your name has been called you may leave unless you have any further questions. Those of you who are living in private accommodation, not with your families, will remain there until further notice. Once the various army accommodation units have been repaired you will move back into them.'

The Colonel began to call out the names of the men and Stelios listened carefully, he expected to be near the beginning of the list as his surname began with "C". Men began to leave the room and finally the Colonel placed the list on the table. Tomas's name had not been called and Stelios hoped that meant they would still be working together.

'The following men will be in charge of issuing discharge papers. This will be done from this building and will begin at the same time as the registration of citizens. Request forms will have been printed by then and official discharge papers will be delivered shortly. It will be a more time consuming process than registration. The soldier will fill in his request and hand it to an officer who will check that it is complete. The man will be asked to return a week later to collect his discharge papers if all is in order. The records of all enlisted men will be available for checking and should you have any suspicion that the man is not entitled to be discharged or reassigned you will refer his name to Major Christoforakis who will be in charge.'

Tomas nudged him. 'Major, well done.'

Stelios shook his head. 'There must be someone else with the same surname.'

'It is essential that filing is strictly alphabetical and kept up to date. When the soldier returns he does not want to spend his day here whilst you search for his papers. He will be given enough money to cover his travelling expenses to return to his home and enough to buy a meal. The amount of travelling expenses will depend upon his final destination and must be signed for.'

Stelios raised his hand. 'How will the money be paid, sir? Will the man go to the bank or will we hold funds here?'

'That will be your main job, Major. You worked in finance before. Each Friday you will check the number of men who have requested discharge and calculate the total amount that will have to be paid out. You will send that figure to the bank and on Monday the correct amount will be delivered to you. Devaluation will be taken into account, but not inflation. When the men return for their final release papers they will have to be content with the sum they are given. Obviously the amount given to the recipients and the amount drawn from the bank must agree at the end of the week.'

Stelios hardly heard the answer. He had been upgraded to the position of Major.

Tomas grinned delightedly. 'Are we able to apply for leave, sir?'

'You may apply, but the decision will depend upon your commanding officer. There can certainly be no leave granted for the next six weeks. Once most of the initial work has been completed it is hoped that you will all be able to have a short break over the Christmas period. Any more questions?'

Stelios left the room feeling dazed. 'Why have I been promoted and not you?' he asked Tomas.

'Probably due to you developing the code and your little episode with Professor von Schutz. Daphne will be pleased. She can boast to the neighbours that she is going to be married to a Major.'

Stelios wore his new insignia of Major on his uniform with pride.

'Will I have to salute you and call you "sir" now?' asked Tomas.

Stelios grinned. 'You should have been calling me "sir" a long time ago. I was promoted to Captain, remember, when we were working for Mr Argyrious.'

'Hard to distinguish a soldier's rank when he isn't wearing uniform,' replied Tomas. 'What do you have to do now you're a Major?'

'Keep you other men up to the mark. No slovenly dress or careless work.'

'Anyone could do that. I mean, what other duties will you have?'

Stelios shrugged. 'At the moment I have no idea. I'm sure I'll be told in due course. I just hope the unrest between the political parties doesn't escalate. I have no desire to go to war against my fellow Greeks.'

'I wondered,' began Tomas tentatively, 'whether you would be able to find out anything about Miriam now you're a Major.'

'I have asked someone who might be able to help.'

'Really? Thank you, Stelios. Who is it? Anyone I know?'

'I don't think so.'

'How do you know him then?'

'I met him when I was taking messages for the Major.' Stelios was still unsure whether he should mention meeting Christos and masquerading as a German. 'He said he'd let me know if he found out anything. He's working in one of the registration departments so can ask around at the other venues.'

Stelios was delighted to be working with finance again. At the end of the first week he made sure that a figure three looked like an eight and waited to see if the bank cashier noticed. When he checked the money that was delivered on the Monday the amount agreed with his falsified total and he smiled in delight. Despite having a pay increase now he had been promoted to the rank of Major a little extra would not come amiss, particularly now the drachma had been devalued.

Christos entered his office and signalled that he would like to have a private word with him outside. Stelios turned to the officer sitting closest to him.

'I have to take a short break. Take your time with the forms. I don't want to find too many waiting for me when I get back.'

Christos was waiting for him and the two men leaned against the wall and lit their cigarettes.

'I've found that family you were asking about,' said Christos immediately.

'Thanks, that's good news.'

'Not exactly. There was an accident and the man is dead.'

'What happened?'

'A building collapsed. A chunk of masonry hit the man and killed him outright.'

'What about the women?'

'His wife suffered cuts and bruises to her legs, but his daughter was hit in the face by debris and glass. She's still in the hospital.'

Stelios paled. 'She's going to recover?'

Christos shrugged. 'I can't tell you any more than I was told.'

Stelios drew deeply on his cigarette. 'My friend will have to go to the hospital and see how she is for himself. I appreciate the trouble you took.'

'I just asked the Jewish families who came in to register. If I hear any more I'll let you know.' Christos ground out his cigarette and walked away.

Stelios returned inside to his desk. He would wait until they took a break and then tell Tomas and give him the afternoon off to visit the hospital and find out the seriousness of the situation for himself.

Tomas walked into the hospital full of misgivings. How badly injured was Miriam? He had plied Stelios with questions about the accident, but Stelios had no further information to give him. He searched up and down the corridors, going in and out of long rooms filled with rows of beds, until he finally asked for directions and was sent down a long passage to the far end of the hospital building. At the doorway he stood and looked for Miriam.

Naomi hobbled painfully towards him. 'Tomas, it's good of you to come.'

'I only heard this morning. How is Miriam? What happened? I've been told that Abraham was killed – I'm so sorry.'

A tear crept down Naomi's cheek. 'We went to the Synagogue to give thanks that the Germans had left and we were safe. We planned to return to the laundry on Monday. As we walked back to the family who had sheltered us we heard some shooting and people were running around waving guns. We took cover in the doorway of a building, not realising it was unsafe. A bullet ricocheted and hit the wall. We moved a little further inside and then the whole building began to collapse. We managed to run back outside but a piece of masonry hit Abraham on the head.' Another tear ran down Naomi's cheek. 'Some of the debris hit my legs and gave me a few cuts and bruises, but poor Miriam has suffered badly.'

Tomas swallowed, his eyes swivelling around the ward, trying to see Miriam amongst the occupants. 'What happened to her?'

'A window came down at the same time and the flying glass cut her face. She is going to be badly scarred. They said they would wait until the bandages came off to see if she has lost the sight in one eye. They haven't mentioned that to her.' Naomi shook her head. 'Just as we thought we were safe and our troubles were over.'

'Oh, Naomi, how awful for you.' Tomas placed his arms around her. 'Is there anything I can do?'

'I'm sure Miriam would like you to visit and talk to her. I'm staying here with her as much as possible. Yiorgo and Lisa have been very good. They have said I can continue to stay with them for as long as necessary. Yiorgo took me to Abraham's funeral. I had to go in a wheelchair as my legs were too painful for me to walk very far. Lisa comes in every day with some food for Miriam and to give me a little time to myself.'

'Show me which bed Miriam is in and I'll stay with her whilst you go and have something to eat and drink. Take as long as you like. My commanding officer gave me the afternoon off.'

'You're a good boy, Tomas.' Naomi progressed slowly to the third bed down in the ward and touched Miriams's arm. 'You have a visitor, Miriam. Can you guess who it is?'

Tomas looked down at the still figure and caught his breath. Her head was swathed in bandages, covering one eye and there were cuts on her cheeks, two looking red and ugly where they had been stitched.

Miriam opened her eye and tried to smile. 'Tomas.'

Tomas took her hand, trying hard to compose himself and not let Miriam see how devastated he was by the extent of her facial injuries.

'I would have visited you earlier, but I was only told today that you were here. Are you very sore?'

'My face hurts, but they say it will heal up in time. The window glass cut me.'

'Your mother told me you were avoiding a gun battle and a building collapsed.'

'We didn't notice any groups of men as we walked to the Synagogue. It just happened so quickly. They appeared from nowhere as we walked back. We just wanted to take shelter from the bullets. Poor Pappa. If he hadn't pushed me I could have been hit on the head and killed like him. Is my face very bad, Tomas? They won't let me have a mirror.'

'You have a couple of scars, but they will fade,' lied Tomas. The two lines of stitched cuts looked so wide and ugly that he thought Miriam would have to learn to accept her disfigurement. 'You are even more beautiful than I remembered.'

'Stay with me Tomas.'

'I'll stay until your mother returns, then I will need to get back to work.'

'You look very smart in your uniform.'

'Stelios looks even smarter. He's a Major now.'

'He deserves his promotion. He and another soldier took us and some of the other families to a safe house.'

'Did he?' said Tomas in surprise. 'I didn't know about that.'

'He didn't tell you?'

Tomas shook his head. 'I'll ask him when I get back to the office. We're still working together. He's in control of the discharge department for the soldiers who want to leave the army and return to their families.'

'Will you go to Piraeus to be with your family?'

'Not without you, Miriam. I'm not going anywhere without you. As soon as you're well enough to leave the hospital we'll make arrangements to be married.'

'You are willing to convert to the Jewish faith?'

Tomas looked at Miriam sadly. 'No, I can't do that. I was hoping you would be willing to become Orthodox now you have experienced living with Christians.'

'They are good people, Tomas, but I cannot accept their beliefs.'

'Could I just say I was of the Jewish faith?'

'The Rabbi would never just take your word for it. Had the war not intervened and you had continued going to the synagogue for instruction you would understand that.'

Tomas hung his head. He had never had any intention of converting sincerely to Miriam's faith and had hoped that by attending the synagogue and receiving instruction from the Rabbi that it would be sufficient acknowledgement for him to marry her.

'I'm sure we'll find a solution. I don't want you lying there worrying about it. You concentrate on healing and we'll face any other obstacles when you're completely well again.' Tomas patted her hand reassuringly. 'Is there anything you would like me to bring in for you when I visit tomorrow?'

'I can't think of anything. It's painful to eat at the moment because moving my jaw hurts my face. Lisa brings in some soup each evening and that's easy to swallow.'

'Have they doctors said how long will you be here?'

'They plan to remove my bandages next week. If everything has healed as they hope I will be allowed home then.'

'You'll go back to the laundry?' Tomas could not believe the two women would be able to run the business alone.

'We have nowhere else to go. We cannot stay with Yiorgo and Lisa forever.'

Tomas returned to the army offices and made straight for Stelios's desk. 'Why didn't you tell me?' he demanded.

'Tell you what?'

'That you knew where Miriam was living.'

Stelios shrugged. 'I was forbidden. Besides, I didn't actually know where she was living. Christos and I took them and the others to a safe address in Pagrati. I had no idea where they went from there. I tried to assure you that she was safe.'

Tomas looked suitably abashed. 'Thank you, Stelios.'

Stelios shrugged. 'I was only used as I could speak a bit of German. They hoped it would be sufficient if we were stopped and questioned.'

'That was brave of you. I reckon that was why you were promoted to Major.'

'How is Miriam?'

'Her face will probably be badly scarred and her mother said she may have lost the sight in one eye.'

Stelios raised his eyebrows. 'As bad as that. I'm sorry, Tomas.'

'It's not your fault. Her scars don't worry me, but she says she can't marry me unless I convert to the Jewish faith. She refuses to become Greek Orthodox. What can I do?'

'Conversion sounds like the only answer. Why don't you wait until you see how she looks when she comes out of hospital? You might decide you don't want to marry her after all.'

Tomas gave Stelios a scathing look. 'I love Miriam. I don't care if her face is so hideous that she has to keep it covered when she goes out. She's still Miriam.'

'Are you two going to be gossiping for the rest of the afternoon?' A man, waving his completed papers, pushed his way between them.

Stelios held out his hand to receive them and Tomas moved away to his own desk. He handed out papers and explained how they should be completed to each man in turn, but his thoughts continually returned to the dilemma he faced over marriage to Miriam.

'When are you and Daphne getting married?' he asked Stelios abruptly as they walked back to Phoebus's house.

'I haven't really had time to give it much thought,' replied

Stelios, not admitting that he had given his proposed marriage no thought at all. 'I really need to find some suitable accommodation where we can live. All of Athens is a mess at the moment, so many of the buildings are uninhabitable and with the fighting that is taking place I can't expect her to come here. Why?'

'Miriam said she and her mother are going to return to the laundry. They can't possibly run that between them without any help. If you and Daphne were married that would free up her room at home. Naomi could have her bedroom.'

Stelios stopped and looked at his friend. 'What exactly do you have in mind?'

'I could leave the army and go to work with my father. We could live with them until I can afford a house of our own.'

'Have you spoken to your parents? They might not be willing to have Naomi and Miriam move in with them.'

'Would you come down with me on Saturday? You could arrange a date with Daphne and then I could speak to my father and mother.'

Stelios looked at Tomas dubiously. 'Is that a good idea?'

'You've got to make a date at some time with Daphne – unless you're calling off your betrothal of course.'

Stelios shook his head. 'That isn't what I meant. Maybe you should broach the subject with your parents first, before I speak to Daphne.'

Tomas shrugged. 'Whatever. Will you come down with me?'

'I suppose so,' sighed Stelios. 'I hope there will be a bus running so we don't have to walk all the way there and back. My feet are still sore from where we had to parade through Athens after the Germans were kicked out.'

Olga and Nikos were pleased to see Tomas visiting them again so soon and Daphne greeted Stelios shyly.

Olga looked apologetically at Stelios. 'I'm sorry our house is in such a poor state. Did Tomas tell you that we had to use most of our furniture for firewood? Nikos is gradually making a replacement table and some chairs. In the meantime we are managing as best we can.'

'At least you were able to save a Poseidon. I'm happy to sit on a stool with a bowl of food in my lap. I don't need a table and chair,' Stelios assured her.

'You've come to talk about wedding arrangements, I expect. Daphne has been waiting anxiously for you.'

Stelios nodded. 'All in due course. I believe Tomas wants to talk to you first. Would it be alright if Daphne and I went for a walk into town? I promise I will take good care of her and not behave inappropriately.'

'If her father agrees I have no objection.'

Tomas scowled as Stelios gave him a bright smile and left the house with Daphne. He had hoped Stelios would be there to support him in his idea.

'So, Tomas, what is it you want to talk about? Have you decided to leave the army and come and join me in the carpentry business?'

Tomas shifted uncomfortably on the cushion where he sat on the floor. 'That depends, Pappa. It depends upon you and Mamma agreeing.'

Olga and Nikos listened quietly whilst Tomas explained the accident that had befallen the Jewish family and the plans the women had to return to the laundry and try to manage it between them. 'I was wondering,' he said hesitantly, 'if you would consider having them come to live here. Naomi could have Daphne's room when she and Stelios are married.'

'Daphne's room is hardly big enough for two people,' demurred Olga.

Tomas blushed. 'Miriam would share my room.'

Nikos raised his eyebrows. 'Does that mean she has converted and become Orthodox?'

Tomas shook his head. 'She says she cannot and I'm not

prepared to follow the Jewish faith.'

Olga sucked in her breath. 'That would mean you were living a sinful life together.'

'No, Mamma. It would mean we each followed our own religions, but in our eyes we would be man and wife and promised to each other. It would only be until I had enough money saved to rent or buy somewhere of our own.'

Nikos regarded his son sternly. 'Have you really thought about this? They have different religious observances from us. We could find each other's customs offensive.'

'I'm sure we wouldn't,' replied Tomas earnestly. 'During the war they were hiding in a Christian household. Here they could go to the synagogue on a Saturday and any other days that were special to them, just as we would go to church on a Sunday or Saints' Days. If there are any other observances they have to make they would have to take place either at the synagogue or privately in Naomi's room.'

'And if we refuse to contemplate the idea?'

'I will leave the army and move into the laundry to help them with the work.'

Nikos sighed. 'You're obviously determined to be with this young woman. Your mother and I will have to discuss it. It's not a decision to be taken lightly.'

Stelios returned with Daphne, who looked decidedly miserable. Her mother looked at her anxiously. Had this eligible young man, so recently promoted to being a Major, decided not to marry their daughter?

Tomas looked at Stelios eagerly. 'Have you two decided on a wedding date?' he asked.

Stelios shook his head. 'I've explained to Daphne that accommodation in Athens at the moment is virtually impossible to find. I will continue to look, of course, but we cannot get married until I know I have somewhere that would be suitable for her to live. You may have no tables and chairs here, but many families in Athens are having to shelter in derelict buildings if they cannot stay with relatives. Everything possible is being done to ensure that properties are safe. Others are being pulled down and it is proposed to rebuild on the site.'

Nikos frowned. 'How long do you think this will take?'

'I have no idea. There is fighting between the two political parties in Athens, many atrocities are taking place. People are still being arrested and tortured; men and women being killed.'

'So how long do you intend to postpone your marriage? A year?'

Stelios shrugged. 'I cannot say. I sincerely hope it will not be as long as that, but until the political situation has been resolved I cannot subject Daphne to such a dangerous and uncertain future.'

'I am not sure she is any safer in Piraeus. There is continual fighting here.'

'At least she is in an area that she knows and has friends and neighbours. She would be a stranger in Athens and I would have to leave her alone whilst I went to work. If the situation deteriorates further the army may be called upon to support the government. As a Major I would be expected to bear arms and participate with the other soldiers. I could be condemning Daphne to widowhood.'

Tomas left Piraeus unhappily. His parents had accepted that Daphne and Stelios could not be married yet with equanimity. It was evidently a relief to them that they did not have to consider having their son and Miriam living under their roof without being married. He was thankful he had not suggested the idea to Naomi, but that now left him with no option but to offer to move to the laundry with them.

Stelios left Piraeus with a feeling of relief. He felt no overwhelming passion for Daphne, although he was fond of her and thought she would make him a suitable wife. The longer he could postpone their marriage the happier he would be, but he had no desire to take part in any fighting that might occur.

The unrest in Athens continued, and families often found themselves fighting each other for supremacy between the pro and anti-communist supporters whilst the government tried ineffectually to mediate.

Tomas moved into the laundry with Naomi and Miriam, but continued to serve in the army. He explained to Stelios that it was difficult for the two women to complete the washing and ironing required. Naomi attended to the customers, whilst Miriam stayed hidden in the back area dealing with the washing and as much of the ironing as she could. Naomi found it painful to stand for any length of time and Tomas would often spend his evening ironing shirts for the army whilst Miriam prepared a meal and Naomi rested.

'Without my army salary it would be difficult for them to manage at all. Once Athens is peaceful again the business will probably pick up and I'll be asking you to sanction my discharge so I can work there throughout the day.'

'You haven't mentioned to your parents again about moving down to Piraeus?' asked Stelios.

Tomas shook his head. 'Until you and Daphne are married they haven't a spare room and I know they're not happy that Miriam and I are not officially married.'

'Why don't you apply for a Civil Wedding? It's allowed now between people of different faiths. Would your parents find that acceptable?'

Tomas wrinkled his brow. 'I don't know. They still won't be happy that Miriam is Jewish and would probably consider that we were living in sin. I know I wouldn't be allowed to receive any sacraments as the church does not approve mixed faith marriage.'

Stelios shrugged. 'You'll just have to decide. Does Miriam mean more to you than the approval of your parents and the church?'

'That's the problem. I can accept that the church will refuse me the sacraments, but my parents will be devastated. Not only will I be living in sin with Miriam I will also be condemned to hell when I die,' answered Tomas sadly.

Apart from the centre of Athens the whole area was controlled by the communist supporters. An attack on the village of Velvendos in December only inflamed the situation and Papandreou demanded that all guerrillas should be disarmed. The rebels ignored the edict and responded by demanding the removal of Papandreou, whom they considered to be collaborating with the Allies and preventing Greece from becoming an independent nation. Papandreou took refuge in the Grand Bretagne Hotel and resigned as Prime Minister. His position was filled by Plastiras, a retired General and in February the government signed a peace treaty with the rebel movement that had tried to usurp them, but it did little to calm the situation.

Plastiras resigned in April and was replaced by Voulgaris. Still trying to take control, the movement that had started in the north of the country, he applied to the District Court in Athens for a new statute of rights in June. The situation was further fuelled when Velouchiotis, the leader of the resistance, was killed shortly afterwards.

Fighting continued between the opposing political parties and Voulgaris was unable to bring an end to the volatile situation and resigned, his place being taken by Archbishop Damaskinos. He was no more successful in bringing peace and stability to the country.

Tomas and Miriam decided they would have a Civil Wedding. His parents did not approve of his decision, but grudgingly agreed that the couple would at least be officially married in the eyes of the law, although they refused to attend the ceremony.

Naomi did not approve either, wishing Tomas would convert to their religion, but she kept her feelings to herself. There was no way Miriam would ever find another man willing to marry her. Two livid scars ran across the left side of her face and the doctors had been unable to save the sight in her left eye. Rather than leave her with an empty socket they had stitched her eyelids together. The left side of her face was hideous, but the right remained as flawless as before. Whenever she had to leave the house she wore a thick veil to hide her disfigurement.

Although Tomas had described the damage to her face, Stelios recoiled in horror the first time he visited and she removed her veil.

'I'm sorry I reacted badly,' apologised Stelios later. 'Although you had told me I was not prepared for how awful she looked.'

'I don't notice her scars now,' replied Tomas cheerfully. 'I'll ask her to keep her veil on the next time you visit.'

'There's no need,' Stelios assured him. 'I'm prepared now. It was just rather a shock.' He did not add that he would not visit the house again as the sight of Miriam's face made him feel physically sick. Even wearing her veil he would know exactly what she was hiding beneath it.

At first a steady stream of soldiers approached Stelios applying for discharge from the army service. Some were disillusioned veterans who wanted to spend their remaining years with their families and others were young men who disagreed with the government and wished to join with the rebels in their fight for supremacy.

Now he only had three men, including Tomas, working in the department with him and he had discovered that some men had applied a second time for discharge, hoping to get a further payment. He had to spend time checking the army records for each applicant.

If, after checking the records, he was doubtful about their entitlement to a discharge payment he had to ask for their registration card and approach the registration offices for authentication of the details. Some men did not return, realising that their scheme had been unsuccessful, whilst others tried to brazen it out and insist that he must have made an error.

Stelios was surprised one morning when the man standing before him greeted him by name and spoke in German. ‘Good morning, Stelios. Do you remember me?’

He looked up in alarm, expecting to see Herman standing at his desk.

‘Professor von Schutz!’ he exclaimed in relief. ‘What brings you here?’

‘I’m applying for my discharge.’

‘I didn’t realise you were in the army. I thought you were a retired professor.’

‘That was exactly what you were supposed to think. I heard you were quite concerned about my welfare when that little skirmish took place at the apartment.’

Stelios nodded. ‘You are – were – an old man. I was convinced they would hurt you, particularly after you admitted to Herman that you were an Austrian Jew and had left Germany at the outbreak of the first war.’

‘I told him part of the truth. I am an Austrian Jew and I did meet my wife in Vienna. We decided to make our home in Greece and I joined the army. Immediately after your German friend’s visit I left the apartment. My job on that occasion was done. I know you wear spectacles, but you are certainly not the most observant young man.’

Stelios flushed. ‘What do you mean?’

‘I saw you daily when I sat outside the church as a blind beggar.’

‘You!’

‘I kept waiting for you to recognise me. It is quite useful to pretend to be blind. People often think you are deaf as well. You made some rather derogatory remarks about my appearance, I recall.’

‘I apologise. I had no idea it was you.’

‘Well, at least that shows I was efficient in my role. I spent time in other places throughout the day and many others were less than complimentary about me.' The man smiled. 'I feel I have done enough now and would like to return to being an ordinary citizen again.'

'What work are you planning to do when you leave the army?'

'Nothing. I will have a good pension after spending almost forty years of my life as a soldier. I just hope the banks stay solvent so it is paid to me regularly.'

Stelios looked at the discharge papers that he held, stood and saluted rapidly. 'I will personally see they are processed as rapidly as possible, Brigadier.'

The man nodded and pointed to Stelios's insignia denoting he was a Major. 'I see you have also received promotion.'

'I believe that may have been due to taking German lessons from you. I have to admit that I remember very little of the language now, sir.'

'Shame. You were becoming quite proficient. I understand I have to call back in a week's time to collect my final discharge papers.'

'I could complete them for you immediately, sir. I don't think there is any necessity to check the authenticity of your application.'

The Brigadier shook his head. 'How do you know I am not masquerading as a Brigadier? You should not be too trusting, young man. I will return next week. I am not in a rush to go anywhere.'

Stelios returned the Brigadier's salute as he walked away. He had been well and truly taken in by the man pretending to be a professor and then as a beggar. Maybe he should check the authenticity of the application and even refer it to Colonel Michaelaous.

Stelios had bought a new cash box and was gradually adding to his savings. He was in a dilemma. Tomas was continually urging him to visit Daphne in Piraeus and finally make a date for when they could be married and he knew he would not be able to delay very much longer. The unrest in the country could last for years and Athens was no more unsafe than Piraeus. Once again he began his search for an apartment that he felt would be acceptable to Daphne, concentrating on the suburbs.

He invested in a motor bike, realising that if he was to live that far away from the army offices he would need a reliable form of transport each day. Tomas was delighted when he told him and immediately suggested a visit to his family that weekend. Unable to think of a suitable excuse, Stelios agreed to drive them both down to Piraeus.

Daphne was overjoyed to see him and hoped his unexpected visit would mean they could set a date for their wedding. Stelios shook his head.

'I am looking for somewhere we can live. The centre of Athens is far too expensive, even a room in a tenement building is beyond my army salary. I am hoping I can find somewhere reasonable on the outskirts.'

Daphne looked at him doubtfully. 'Stelios, we have been betrothed for a number of years and you continually make excuses to delay our wedding. If we are not man and wife by this time next year I will expect to be released from our arrangement. I do not want to end up an old woman who has never experienced the pleasure of marrying and having a family of her own. If there is someone else in your heart please be honest and tell me. I will be hurt, but I will also understand.'

'There is no one else, Daphne. I swear I have been faithful to you from the first day we met. If the war had not intervened we would have been married for some years by now. I promise, as soon as the situation calms and there is no more fighting, we will be married.'

Daphne shook her head. 'The fighting could last for years. I want a definite date, Stelios, and I will expect to become your wife on that day.'

Stelios regarded his future wife with a certain amount of

misgiving. He had expected her to be accepting of his concerns for her safety and prepared to wait until he was ready to make a commitment. She was now showing him a determined side to her nature that was a surprise to him.

'Now you have a motor bike there is no reason why you could not live down here with us. You would be able to ride up to Athens each day and you would know I was safe with my family.'

'I do not want to be beholden to your family for giving me a roof over my head. It is my duty to provide for you. I have no objection to living in this area, but I insist we have an apartment of our own. We will be newly married and will want to spend time together without others around us.'

Daphne blushed. She understood what Stelios was implying, but she was unwilling to back down from her ultimatum.

'Tomas is quite happy to live with Miriam's mother. I will ask my father if he knows of anywhere suitable in the area, but I still want a firm date from you, Stelios, and no further excuses.'

Stelios sighed. 'Provided I am not sent anywhere to fight we will agree on a date in May. It is possible that we will have a stable government by then and our troubles will be over.'

Despite Stelios's optimism Kanellopolous, who had become Prime Minister after the Archbishop, resigned from his position less than two weeks later, with Soufoulis succeeding him. By the end of 1945 Greece was no nearer to internal peace, despite having had six different men attempt to bring the situation under control.

By March of 1946 fierce fighting had once again broken out between the Government and the rebel communist advocates. In an attempt to settle the conflict Prime Minister Soufoulis declared there would be elections held at the end of the month and he would expect everyone to abide by the outcome.

Stelios felt apprehensive. If the resulting elections were not to the Government's satisfaction would the conflict continue or even escalate? He was also becoming concerned about his own position in the army. Far fewer men were coming forward and asking for discharge papers and he knew it would not be very long before he was redundant. The registration programme had proceeded reasonably smoothly in Athens, despite the unrest, but many of the outlying districts had ignored the instruction. He considered approaching the General and offering to undertake visiting the villages and insisting they complied. It could be a better option to volunteer now rather than wait to be sent to some miserable village in Thessaloniki or Macedonia.

He had visited Daphne every other week, taking Tomas with him, since her ultimatum. She chattered happily to him about the arrangements her mother was making at their local church.

'What about your relatives and friends, Stelios? You know you can invite as many as you wish, but Mamma does need to know how many she should cater for.'

Stelios shook his head. 'Your mother needs to do nothing extra on my behalf. I have no relatives and although I know many men in the army I can only describe Tomas as my friend. I very rarely socialise with the others. As Major I am only supposed to associate with others of the same rank.'

'Aren't you lonely if you don't join friends during the evenings?'

'Not a bit. I usually meet up with Tomas one evening each week, and we still work together. I am quite happy to spend my free time alone, besides, I go out most evenings looking for an apartment where we can live.'

'Have you had any luck?'

'I've seen two that I think might be suitable. One is quite small, but close to a shopping area. The other is a larger apartment, but it is quite a long walk to the nearest shops. That would not be very pleasant for you during the winter.'

'You are very considerate, Stelios. Not many men would have thought about the discomfort of shopping when it is cold or wet. I will happily have a smaller apartment with the shops close by.'

Stelios smiled. He thought if he pointed out the inconveniences attached to the larger apartment Daphne would happily accept the smaller. In truth they were both within easy walking distance of general stores, but the rent was considerably less for the smaller one.

'If you're quite sure I'll visit them tomorrow evening and make an agreement with the landlord.'

'I am sure, besides if I find it too small when we start to live there we can always look for somewhere larger.'

'Of course,' Stelios promised rashly. Now his wedding to Daphne was imminent she allowed him to hold her and kiss her. She had even placed his hands on her breasts on one occasions and sighed with pleasure as he squeezed them gently. He was beginning to experience physical sensations that had never troubled him before. He no longer had nightmares about the morgue, but would wake up in the night groaning in discomfort, wishing he had Daphne by his side for relief.

The election results went against Soufoulis and his Liberal party and he handed over his duties to Poulitsas. The people were still dissatisfied and after a fortnight the government was in the hands of Tsaldis. This appeared to pacify the people and to Stelios's relief Athens had a feeling of normality that had been absent since the Germans first invaded.

Stelios realised he had no excuse now not to marry Daphne and he was actually looking forward to holding her naked body in his arms. He had signed an agreement with the owner of the sparsely furnished apartment on the outskirts of Athens and no longer lived in the army building. Tomas had visited and voiced his approval, although commenting on the cheap and shabby furnishings.

'I decided to leave it as it is so that Daphne can choose some new items herself.' In Stelios's eyes the furnishings were quite adequate for their needs. 'I'm sure she will know exactly what she wants to live with.'

'You're probably sensible to wait a while. I'm sure my father would make any new furniture Daphne wanted. I've asked him to make us a new bed. I've been trying to encourage Miriam to come out with me to look for a new mattress. We have her parents' old one and it is decidedly lumpy. Will you be getting a new one?'

Stelios shrugged. 'Maybe. It will depend upon Daphne.'

'Miriam is so looking forward to your wedding.'

'She's coming?'

Tomas nodded. 'I insisted. She's my wife. She will be Daphne's sister-in-law. Of course she will come.'

'I thought she might decide to stay home.' Stelios was not sure if he wanted Miriam to attend his wedding. She could be an embarrassment due to her injuries.

'I hope they will become friends. When they first met they seemed to like each other. Miriam is so self-conscious about her disfigurement, although it hardly shows beneath her veil, that she avoids going anywhere except the local shops. It might give her more confidence if Daphne was willing to go out with her.'

Stelios had arranged for a taxi to take him, Tomas and Miriam down to Piraeus and collect them the following evening. It had been arranged that he would stay the night with family friends who lived in the next road and Olga and Nikos had grudgingly agreed that Tomas and Miriam could stay with them.

'Just the one night,' said Nikos. 'We still don't approve of your decisions.'

'Miriam and I are very happy together.' Tomas smiled to himself. He hoped his parents would accept his wife more readily when he told them Miriam was pregnant and they would look forward to becoming grandparents. He would wait until after the wedding celebrations to tell them the good news.

Stelios ensured that his boots were polished to a high shine and brushed his uniform carefully before Tomas arrived to escort him to Daphne's house. To Stelios's embarrassment Tomas had a tambourine with him that he struck continually, causing the neighbours to look out and many began to follow them along the road.

Reaching his home Tomas banged on the door and waited for his father to appear.

'Everyone ready?' he asked and Nikos nodded.

The small procession walked through the streets to the church, dividing into two groups when they arrived, the women sitting on one side and the men at the other. Miriam went to take a seat at the back of the church, but Olga shook her head.

'Come and sit with me. You are Tomas's wife so you should sit at the front.'

For a moment Miriam hesitated, then followed Olga to the two chairs that were set out in front of the other rows. Tomas smiled with pleasure as he escorted Stelios down the aisle to wait before the altar for Daphne to arrive with her father. He hoped this meant his mother was finally accepting Miriam.

Stelios felt incredibly nervous and hoped it was not noticeable as he stood before the priest. He was surprised at the number of neighbours who had filled the small church, no doubt because they were looking forward to attending the wedding feast that would follow, he thought sourly.

Daphne smiled adoringly up at him as she took her place beside him and he managed to smile back. At least she had not been maimed during the war and was an attractive young woman whom he would not be ashamed to call his wife.

Stelios lay on the thin mattress feeling decidedly pleased with himself. He and Daphne had fumbled their way through their first intimacy, excusing their ignorance on tiredness. Their second experience, a short while ago, had been far more satisfactory for both of them.

'We should get up,' said Stelios as he stroked Daphne's hair.

'Why?' she asked. 'I'm happy lying here.'

Stelios bent and kissed her. 'So am I, but I need to take you out to show you where the shops are. Tomorrow I have to go in to work and I don't want you wandering around and getting lost. We'll go to a taverna later and have a meal. I don't expect you to cook for me tonight.'

'I'm not sure I could eat anything. Mamma and the neighbours made so much food. We should have brought some back with us. I wouldn't have needed to think about cooking for a week.'

'If you didn't need to cook what would you do whilst I am at work?'

'Well,' Daphne's eyes roamed around the small room. 'Some cleaning wouldn't come amiss. There's a cobweb up in the corner.'

'I don't want you to spend all your time cleaning. I haven't married you to gain a housekeeper.'

'So why have you married me?'

'Because I wanted you as my wife. I don't want to arrive home and find you exhausted from cooking and cleaning each day.'

'If I was tired we could go to bed.'

'And you would want to go to sleep. I can think of more interesting things to do.'

'Such as?' Daphne looked up at him whilst her hand strayed beneath his night shirt.

'You want me to show you?'

'Yes, I think you should.' She ran her hand down his hardened member and with the other hand she pulled up her own nightwear.

Stelios reluctantly rode into work the following day. He and Daphne had finally left their apartment and he had walked with her for a brief visit to the local shops before he suggested they returned for a siesta. It was quite late when they left the apartment a second time and ate at the local taverna and he wished each day could follow the same pattern. He had been foolish to delay marriage for so long.

To his annoyance those soldiers who wanted to leave the army no longer formed queues at his door and he was unable to add to his income by more than a few drachmas at a time. A recruitment drive was in process and he spent most of his time handing out papers and answering questions to those who wanted to enlist. The last man who had requested discharge papers was from Crete and that had been a week earlier.

'I tried to settle in Athens,' he explained. 'It seemed like a good opportunity for promotion but it didn't happen. There's little point in staying here when I'm not happy. I'm a country man. I didn't realise how much I would miss the fields and mountain slopes so I want to return and work on my father's farm.'

Stelios listened to him in disbelief. How could anyone want to return to a farm after living in the city? He signed the discharge application and instructed the man to return the following week to collect his travelling expenses and final release papers.

Added to his frustration was the knowledge that Daphne was no longer content with their small apartment and was urging him to find somewhere larger. She had pointed out, quite reasonably, that as she was now expecting their first child they needed more space. He was not sure how he felt about becoming a father, although Tomas seemed to revel in the novelty, never tiring of telling Stelios how baby Abraham was progressing.

He attended a meeting with the Majors and Generals and tentatively suggested that his services could be better employed in charge of the Finance Department, repaying the expenses incurred by the various battalions that were stationed around the country. To his surprise they had agreed and a week later he moved to his new office.

Once again, being in charge of vast sums of money, he felt happier. The drachma had been devalued and he was certain that if any discrepancy should come to light he would be able to excuse his error by blaming it on the cashier at the bank along with the calculations of the new drachma rate. After increasing his income by three hundred drachmas in the first month he felt more confident about looking for a larger apartment and keeping Daphne happy.

Stelios was surprised when he found a letter addressed to him waiting on his desk. Upon opening it and reading the contents he crumpled it up and threw it to one side in disgust. He did not consider the unfortunate death of the Cretan for whom he had signed the discharge papers was any concern of his. It was even more unfortunate that it should have been his cousin Andreas who had been in attendance. He drew a sheet of paper towards him and wrote a curt reply, confirming his identity. That should be the end of the matter.

To Stelios's horror, having decided on the apartment they had viewed, Daphne had insisted they also needed some additional furniture. Her father had made them a table and chairs which they would take with them and he was also in the process of making a cradle ready for the baby, although Tomas had offered Stelios the one his father had made for baby Abraham. Daphne had refused the offer.

'A new baby deserves to have a new cradle. We can always keep it for the ones that follow. Besides, suppose Miriam and I were both expecting at the same time; we couldn't share a cradle. Once Pappa has finished making the cradle I will ask him to make us a dresser and a small chest for the baby's clothes.'

Reluctantly Stelios had agreed. He thought it a waste of money. They could easily have borrowed the cradle and the child's clothes could have been stored along with their own. He had to remind himself that although Daphne's father was a carpenter, she had lived in a house far superior to the farmhouse where he had been brought up. It was only natural that she should expect the same degree of comfort now she was married.

He was planning to sell his motor bike and surprise Daphne by purchasing a small car. It could be no more difficult to drive than a motorbike and he knew she would expect to visit her parents each weekend with their baby. At present he hired a taxi once a fortnight and they visited for the day. He could not afford to hire taxis each weekend.

A further letter arrived from Andreas, breaking the news to him that his father had died whilst working at the salt pans and urging him to visit his mother. Stelios was cross with himself. He should have ignored the first letter when it arrived. Finally he answered it, saying he saw little point in visiting Crete after so long away and explaining that he had recently married and had no leave due to him for a considerable amount of time. As an afterthought he added his good wishes to them all and Andreas.

As he had dreaded, his letter brought a reply, full of news and saying how delighted everyone was to know he was fit and well; congratulating him on his marriage and yet again urging him to visit his mother before it was too late. Finding he had a cheque for almost fifteen hundred drachmas enclosed delighted him. It was his share of the money that his father had hidden in his cupboard and Yiorgo had shared it out equally amongst them. That would certainly help with the expenses of moving to the new larger apartment and leave a considerable amount over. He was now pleased he had bothered to reply to Andreas's first letter. He deposited the cheque in the bank, pushed the letter into his jacket pocket and conveniently forgot about it.

Daphne was excited. They were to move to their new apartment the following weekend. Once her first flush of enthusiasm for the small apartment had worn off she realised how shabby it was. Her parents had visited her and she had noticed the look of concern on her mother's face and her father's frown.

'It is only temporary,' she had explained. 'Stelios had to find somewhere for us to live when we were first married. Now we have time to look around for a more suitable apartment.'

She was longing to be in their new home. The rooms were more spacious and there was a balcony where she would be able to put the baby to sleep during the mornings. She packed the clothes she had been making ready for their baby carefully into the chest her father had made. She wanted to ask him to make them another where they could store their own clothes and Stelios would need a cupboard where he could hang his uniform.

Daphne lifted Stelios's jacket from the back of the chair where he had left it the previous night for her to take to the laundry to ask Miriam to sponge and press it. As she folded it over her arm a letter fell from the pocket and she picked it up curiously. It did not have the army crest on it, but had a postmark to say it had been posted in Crete. Who was writing to Stelios from Crete? He had no family over there. She placed the envelope on the table and went to get her shawl and headscarf. Although it was a beautiful day there was a brisk wind blowing and she did not want to risk catching a chill and subsequently harming their baby.

She returned to the living room for Stelios's jacket and her eyes were drawn to the letter again. She would just have a quick look and see who had signed it. Andreas's signature meant nothing to her, but the line above it made her gasp – "I can only urge you, once again, to visit your mother before it is too late."

Daphne frowned. Maybe the letter did not belong to Stelios, but why should he have it in his possession? She unfolded it further and began to read, her incredulity growing.

My dear cousin Stelios,
After receiving your letter I made a journey down to Plaka to tell your mother myself that you were alive and well. You cannot imagine how overjoyed she was. Not having heard from you for so long she was convinced you had perished during the war. She has taken the death of your father with fortitude; many of the other women in the village were also widowed and do not have any family to comfort them.

After the death of your father a considerable amount of money was found hidden in his cupboard. Yiorgo shared the amount out and put aside a share for you. He gave your share to me to deal with when we knew you were still alive. I asked the bank for a cheque and have enclosed this for you.

Anna is still caring for your mother devotedly, along with Maria's two children. Sadly they are now orphans as their father joined the resistance movement along with Yiorgo. Babbis lost his life whilst leading an attack on a German battalion that had killed every man, woman and child in a village after accusing them of sheltering resistance workers. Yiorgo said his action was heroic and little Yannis is very proud of him.

Yiorgo returned, physically unharmed, but he has been badly affected emotionally. He appears to have very little energy or inclination to work on the farm, despite the urging of his nephew. Little Yannis worked manfully to keep his father's farm in good repair, but now Babbis is not returning they have decided to pull down the buildings and invest in more sheep and goats. It is hoped that Yiorgo will soon recover from his melancholy.

Marisa has grown into a beautiful young woman, despite a determined nature. She insists she will marry Victor, the Italian soldier who was billeted on them, as soon as she is of age to do so without her family's consent. Anna is against the idea as it will mean Marisa goes to Italy to live.

Now I have the most distressing news of Spinalonga. The inhabitants of the island were denied food and water supplies during the war. They had made such strides and improved their lives over the previous years. Yannis had insisted on a building programme and finally convinced the government to pay them a pension and allow them visitors. They were able to trade between themselves and live a normal life despite their affliction and being prisoners on the island. By the time liberation came so many had died of starvation, Yannis's wife amongst them.

Father Minos is still living with them and he has written to the government asking for help. More sufferers have been sent there and two blocks of apartments have been built to house them, but repairs are needed once again on the old houses, but Yannis and his companions are not strong enough to undertake the work again. I am planning a visit to the island again as soon as my duties permit.

I am very relieved that my parents decided to follow Annita to New Orleans. They are safe and well and Annita and Elias now have four children three girls and a boy. I hope one day they will come back to Crete for a visit. I cannot contemplate being absent from my parish to visit them, as the sea journey can take a number of weeks.

Once again, I urge you to visit your mother before it is too late.

Your cousin, Andreas.

Daphne read the letter through a second time. Why had Stelios always denied having a family? She would have to find a way to discover the truth. She copied the address written on the letter into a notebook and placed the envelope into her apron pocket. Stelios had seemed troubled over the past few weeks; maybe it was the letter that was the cause.

Stelios returned home and Daphne looked at him with concern. 'You look so tired, darling. I think you should apply for some leave.'

'I haven't any due to me.'

'Surely you could think up some excuse.'

'Excuses have to be backed up by reasons. I can't ask for more leave because I'm tired. I'm tired because I have had to catch up from when I had my last leave.' Stelios did not admit that he disliked taking extended leave, worried that his pilfering might come to light whilst he was out of the office.

'You could explain to them that we are moving to a larger apartment and you need some time to pack your belongings,' argued Daphne.

'They would ask why I had married a woman who was incapable of packing my clothes.'

'Then your papers,' persisted Daphne.

'I've only personal papers at home. I should be able to cope with those.'

'I could do them for you. I usually tidy up when you've left them all over the table. In fact this one fell from your jacket pocket when I went to take it to the laundry.' Daphne withdrew the envelope from her apron pocket and held it up.

Stelios made a grab for it. 'I need that.'

Daphne held it just out of his reach. 'What's so important about it?'

'I need the address. Give it to me.' He snatched it from her hand and Daphne bit her lip. Should she confess that she had read it and now knew he had a family in Crete?

'I'll get the supper.' She felt hurt by the failure of her husband to confide in her.

Daphne decided not to mention the letter again and Stelios concluded that she had not read it. If she had, surely she would have asked him for an explanation of the contents?

1947 - 1957

A National Referendum had been conducted in September of 1946 and by an overwhelming majority the people had decided they wanted the monarchy restored and King George II returned to Athens. This did not bring about the hoped for peace in the country.

King George II died on 1st April 1947 and was succeeded by his brother, Paul. The unrest and uncertainty this caused allowed the communist based Democratic Army to gain even more territory. The Government National Army began to move against them, trying to regain control of the areas, but it was a slow process.

Stelios was given promotion to Lieutenant Colonel and he accepted reluctantly. The higher his rank the more likely it was that he would be expected to take command in an area where fighting was taking place. He explained that he wished to continue to live in Athens with his wife and baby son. He insisted he was more than happy to remain in charge of the Finance Department.

His previous efficiency in the department stood him in good stead and after deliberation it was decided to leave him in charge of finance although this would mean he could not be promoted above the rank of Lieutenant Colonel if he wished to stay in the department for the remainder of his service years.

Although Stelios had no desire to leave Daphne alone in Athens he wished that baby Nicolas had never arrived. The child always seemed to cry during the night and disturb his sleep. He complained bitterly to Daphne.

'How am I supposed to get a nights rest with him waking me up? Can't you keep him quiet?'

'I do my best. He only wakes and cries because he is hungry. Once he is a little older he will sleep through and I will be as grateful as you for a night's sleep.'

'Until that time I will sleep in the living room,' stated Stelios.

Daphne shook her head. 'You cannot be expected to give up your bed. I'll sleep in Nicolas's room with him until he no longer needs a feed during the night.'

Stelios did not argue. He hated the sound of the child crying. It reminded him with unpleasant clarity of his nephew, Yannis, crying when Anna cared for him after their sister's death.

To Stelios's surprise, once baby Nicolas stopped demanding food in the early hours and slept through the night, he found he loved the child dearly. It became a pleasure to return home after work and have Daphne tell him how they had spent their day. When Nicolas began to show an interest in the world by looking around him and reaching out his arms to be picked up he was delighted. Every Saturday they would drive down to Piraeus and show him off to Olga and Nikos, often taking Tomas, Miriam and their little boy Abraham with them. Stelios still felt a shudder go through him when Miriam removed her veil, but Daphne appeared to take no notice of her disfiguration.

It was a relief to Stelios when Miriam said she was unable to accompany them as she needed to stay at home to be in attendance on her mother. Naomi's legs were worse, often ulcerated, and even standing a short while was painful for her.

Olga and Nikos fussed over both their grandsons, but Stelios was convinced that Nicolas was their favourite. He was a good

Greek boy, attending the church with his parents each week, whilst Abraham went to the Synagogue with his mother one week and to the Greek Orthodox Church with his father the next.

Abraham was walking now and was fascinated by the remaining wooden statue of Poseidon that stood in the corner of the living room. He would place his arm around it and stroke the smooth wood.

'I think he will be a carpenter like his grandfather,' said Nikos hopefully.

'If that is what he wants to do I'll not stop him,' smiled Tomas. 'When he is a little older you will have to show him how to use your tools safely.'

Stelios listened, hoping Nicolas would have more ambition than to become a carpenter. He had no intention of leaving the army and he would be able to ensure his son's rapid progression up the ranks if he decided to join him. He would certainly oppose any inclination Nicolas had to become a fighting man and insist he worked in a clerical capacity if the country was still in a state of unrest when the boy had finished his schooling.

In August Marshal Papagos decided the time had come to remove the insurgent National Party and began a full scale offensive against them. Stelios waited, dreading that he might be sent to join the fighting forces. He was overwhelming relieved when a ceasefire was declared in October of 1949. At last the country was at peace.

Although the country was no longer physically engaged in fighting political rivals there was no stability within the government and during the year there were a succession of Prime Ministers, Venizelos holding office for just over a year until the return of Plastiras representing the National progressive party.

Stelios received another letter from Andreas with the news that his mother had finally suffered another stroke and died peacefully. He added that Yannis had managed to be with her at the end having floated over from Spinalonga in a bath tub. Stelios felt this was a veiled criticism of him as he had not bothered to make the journey from Athens to visit her. He sent a brief reply, offering his sympathy to Anna and Yiorgo and thanking Anna for looking after her.

Stelios continued with his work in the finance department, firmly resisting any proposals of further promotion and taking only a few days' leave at a time. He was disconcerted when Daphne announced he was to be a father again. Nicolas was a delightful small boy and Stelios had no desire to suffer a succession of sleepless nights again or share his affection with another child.

'How have you stopped Miriam from having any more children?' he asked of Tomas.

'Self-control,' grinned Tomas. 'We certainly can't afford another at the moment; maybe later. We've virtually closed the laundry since Naomi died. It was too much for Miriam to cope with alone and there wasn't enough money coming in for me to leave the army. We're actually thinking of selling the business.'

'Selling?' Stelios looked at his friend in surprise. 'What will you do then? Ask for promotion?'

Tomas shook his head. 'We're making arrangements to go to Australia.'

'Australia!' Stelios gasped.

'Don't mention it to my parents. We haven't told them yet. We may not be accepted as immigrants so there's no point in distressing them unnecessarily.'

'Why are you going to Australia?'

'We've discussed it, Miriam and I. If we're going to make the break with Greece we should do it now. Abraham has only just started school so it's better to go now rather than in a few years' time. Besides, there's no stigma attached to mixed marriages over there provided we don't live in the Greek or Jewish communities. We considered going to America, but a couple who attend the Synagogue said Australia held out more opportunity. Their son is doing really well over there.'

'But you won't be able to be in the army,' protested Stelios.

'Miriam could start up a laundry and I'm sure I'll find something that will bring us in an income. I want Abraham to be brought up in a country where he feels free, not always in fear of fighting breaking out again or where Jewish people are persecuted for their faith.'

Stelios mulled over Tomas's words. It was a big step for anyone to consider taking, going to a country so far away where they spoke a different language.

'Suppose you hate living there?'

'Then we'll have to save up enough money to return. We'll speak Greek at home so Abraham won't lose his mother tongue. You should think about it, Stelios.'

Stelios shook his head. 'Daphne would never consider leaving her parents and now she's pregnant again I couldn't subject her to spending weeks at sea.'

Tomas shrugged. 'If we are able to go I'll write and tell you about the life. You might well change your mind when you hear I'm making a fortune and you are still a Lieutenant Colonel in the army.'

Tomas, Miriam and Abraham sailed for Australia from Piraeus the following April. Olga had cried copiously when they told her and did her best to persuade them to stay in Greece. She even begged them to leave Abraham behind with her and Nikos, but neither Tomas not Miriam were willing to contemplate the idea.

'I know he's your grandson, but he's our son. His place is with us. As soon as I have enough money we'll come back on a visit or I'll pay for you to come out and stay with us.'

Olga's only consolation was that Daphne and Stelios would be giving her another grandchild, but Abraham was such a delightful little character with a ready smile that she was uncertain if another could ever take his place. By contrast Nicolas was such a serious little boy, a replica of his father.

Daphne's second pregnancy was as trouble free as her first and she and Stelios were delighted when she gave birth to a little girl in the early hours. When Stelios went to visit her in the hospital she was lying back in the bed with a contented smile on her face.

'She's a beautiful baby. I should be home by the weekend and I wondered if you'd be willing to drive down to Piraeus and bring my parents up to see her. I know it means you'll have to take them back down again in the evening, but if you went on the Saturday you could sleep in on Sunday and go to church later in the day.'

'Of course I'll collect them.' Stelios thought it extremely unlikely he would be able to sleep in on the Sunday morning. If the baby was not crying for a feed Nicolas would be demanding his attention.

'I thought I'd ask Mamma if she would be willing to look after Nicolas for a week; just until I'm feeling a bit stronger. You wouldn't mind, would you, Stelios?'

'Of course not. I know she'll look after him well and it will give you a chance to work out a routine with the baby.'

'She'll be pleased it is a little girl so she can be called after her.'

Stelios shook his head. 'Couldn't you think of another name? I really do not like Olga. It sounds hard, like a big Russian peasant.'

'Mamma's not a bit like a Russian peasant,' smiled Daphne, 'but if you really dislike the name we can call her something else.'

'We could call her Elena, after my aunt who cared for me.'

Daphne looked at Stelios in surprise and was about to say that his mother's or sister's name would be more appropriate when she remembered she was not supposed to know he had relatives on Crete.

'If that is what you'd like to call her I have no objection. I'm sure my Mamma will understand.'

Stelios suffered the sleepless nights whilst Elena was a baby, but he was determined they would have no more children. Two were enough for anyone. Daphne was already saying that the apartment was too small and they needed to find another so the children could each have a room to themselves. He would want Nicolas to go to University when he was older and Elena would wish to be married at sometime. Both events would cost him money. As it was he had a very healthy savings account. His army salary had increased, but so had the cost of living, and without his continual falsification of the figures he dealt with they would have had little left over each week for luxuries.

When he received another letter from Andreas he opened it eagerly in hope that there might be another cheque enclosed. There were only sheets of writing paper covered in Andrea's neat handwriting.

My dear cousin, Stelios,
I only write to you when I have important news to impart as I understand that you do not have the time to write long replies back to me.

I promised Anna that I would write and tell you about Marisa's wedding. Victor returned to Crete. Anna's only objection to them being married was that Victor is Italian and was an enemy of our country during the war. She said he always behaved well whilst living with them and helped her on the farm and in various other ways that she did not disclose.

Victor visited Spinalonga with Marisa. She wanted Victor to meet her uncle of whom she has grown very fond. Marisa wanted Yannis at her wedding, but he is not allowed legally to leave the island. She decided that she would have two weddings, one in the local church and another on the island with the service conducted by Father Minos. Arrangements were made for her to have her wedding party on the island and I understand it was a very joyous affair, enjoyed by both the villagers who attended and the islanders.

Anna is heartbroken that Marisa has left Plaka and is now living in Italy, but Victor has promised that Anna will be able to visit them once they are settled and he will also bring Marisa back to Plaka to visit as often as possible.

I am sure you will want to wish them every happiness.

Your cousin, Andreas.

Stelios read the letter through a second time. It was unbelievable that visitors were allowed to go to Spinalonga and mix freely with the lepers. To have a wedding party on the island was the height of foolishness. Leprosy germs would be everywhere. What were Anna and Yiorgo thinking of to allow such a thing? Victor may have been in the Italian army, but he was obviously a very foolish man to ignore the risk of contracting the disease to please his new wife. There was no way he would have allowed Daphne to place him in such a dangerous position.

A further letter from Andreas arrived over a year later giving Stelios the news that Marisa had given birth to a boy without any problems. He added that Yannis had been petitioning the government to allow a new treatment for leprosy to be available to them on Spinalonga and all the occupants were being given vigorous medical tests.

Stelios sniffed in derision. The government were obviously wasting money and the valuable resources of doctors by examining the occupants of Spinalonga. Everyone knew there was no cure for the disease.

Stelios read the next letter he received from Andreas with a feeling of incredulity and disbelief. After the medical tests had been carried out on the inhabitants of Spinalonga it had been discovered that most of them were "burnt out". This was wonderful news as it meant their disease had halted and their suffering and deformities would become no worse.

Many of them, including Yannis, had already been transferred back to the hospital in Athens. Stelios paled and felt himself go cold at this news. At least if they were confined in the hospital there they would not be wandering around the city infecting the inhabitants. They should have been left to live out their days on Spinalonga.

Andreas also included news that little Yannis, who was now a young man, had requested the money left to him by his grandfather. He had seen him in Heraklion but Yannis had been very reticent, simply saying he was there on business, but would not disclose the nature of that business.

Stelios shook his head. The business the boy was engaged in was probably visiting prostitutes and drinking himself into oblivion. The money would not last him very long and then he would find himself back in Plaka, asking his uncle to take him back to work on the farm. Someone should have advised young Yannis on a profitable way in which to invest his money. His own savings account grew steadily, but he was careful to only deposit small amounts into it at a time. He did not want any questions asked about his income.

Six months later Stelios receive another letter from his cousin. The decision had been taken to close Spinalonga permanently. Those who were free from infection could return to their families or stay living at the hospital. Anna and Yiorgo had urged Yannis to make his home with them, but he had declined the offer.

Letters arrived with monotonous regularity from Andreas, informing Stelios that little Yannis had married and that Marisa was a mother again and she and Victor were planning to visit Plaka just as soon as she was strong enough and they felt their baby boy was able to cope with the flight. He would grit his teeth as he read them, often not bothering to send even a cursory reply, but his silence did not stop Andreas from trying to draw him back into the family.

Little Yannis had bought a shop in Aghios Nikolaos and he and Ourania had moved to the town. 'About time,' thought Stelios.

How could anyone bear to live in Plaka? There was nothing there. Yannis was also a partner in a hotel. He had bought land outside Heraklion that was useless for farming and had now sold it to a firm who wanted to build a hotel there. He had retained an interest in the hotel in exchange for dropping his selling price and provided the hotel was a success he would have an income for life without having to do anything to earn it.

'Some people seemed to have everything given to them in life,' thought Stelios grudgingly. 'If my father had given me the money I asked him for I could have gone back to University and studied to become a draughtsman or architect.'

Now Elena was no longer a baby she was as delightful to Stelios as Nicolas, but entirely different from her brother. Whereas Nicolas was studious, always asking questions and reading a book, Elena was full of fun and mischief. Daphne had cajoled him into purchasing a camera and the photographs he took of both of them he would send to over to Tomas and Miriam in Australia.

Stelios hated writing letters. Daphne wrote frequently to her brother and his wife and he would add a little at the end. He missed Tomas; he had no close friend in Athens now, but found he had little to say to him in a letter. Tomas would write at length about the delicatessen shops he had opened. The first shop had sold primarily Greek food and became so popular that he had decided to invest in a second one and then a third. He was making far more money that he would have done had he stayed in Athens.

Stelios was genuinely pleased when Tomas wrote to say he and Miriam, along with their son, Abraham were planning a visit to Athens.

It's about time we came back and saw my parents. They're not getting any younger. I've been saving hard for the last eighteen months so we can afford the fare. We are going to fly. We're all a bit nervous about that, but it will be far quicker than taking a ship and when you work it out no more expensive as we would need two cabins. Abraham is far too old to share with us for more than an occasional night.

We're looking forward to seeing you and Daphne and also Nicolas and Elena. We are both quite envious of you having a little girl, but we had to make a big decision a few years ago that cost a good deal of money, but I'm sure you will agree it was worth it.

Stelios wondered if Tomas's parents thought the opening of another delicatessen was more important than visiting them.

We are planning to hire a car at the airport to drive to Piraeus. I hope you, Daphne and the children will be able to come down to see us there. We would also like to drive up to Athens to visit you so we can spend time together catching up on our years apart and Abraham is keen to meet Nicolas as he says he cannot remember him at all.

This time Stelios did bother to write a reply, saying how pleased he was to know they would be visiting and asking how long they planned to stay. He took the letter to the post office and held the door open as an old man shuffled out slowly. As he exited the man looked up to thank Stelios for being patient and their eyes met.

Stelios recoiled in horror. It was Yannis. He was certain it was Yannis. He let go of the door he had been holding open and hurried down the road. He could hear Yannis shouting hoarsely after him and increased his pace, turning into the first side road he came to and entering a shop. He stood inside, breathing heavily, hoping he had evaded Yannis successfully.

'Can I help you?' The assistant behind the counter looked at him curiously.

'I – I would like a bottle of water, please.'

A half smile on her face the assistant shook her head. 'We

don't sell water, sir. We are haberdashers. There is a shop a little further down that would be able to help you.'

Stelios ran a trembling hand across his forehead.

'Are you feeling ill, sir?'

'I've had a shock.'

'Maybe you would care to sit down for a short while.' The assistant indicated the chair that was in front of the counter for a customer's use. 'I can get you a glass of water.'

Stelios sank onto the chair gratefully. His heart was pounding and he was concerned that he might be having a seizure. The owner of the shop returned with the assistant who handed him the water and he drank a few mouthfuls quickly.

'Would you like me to call a doctor for you, sir, or notify a relative to help you home?'

Stelios shook his head. He was making a ridiculous exhibition of himself, even more embarrassing was the fact that he was wearing his army uniform.

'No, thank you. Thank you for your concern. I am perfectly well now to continue on my way.'

Shakily Stelios rose to his feet and he knew the owner and the assistant were watching him as he walked down the road. Thank goodness Daphne had not been with him. What would she have thought of a strange old man calling after her husband?

Stelios asked Daphne to post the letter to Tomas, claiming to have forgotten his errand and for the next few weeks Stelios avoided the area where the post office was situated. If he spotted an old man approaching towards him he would cross the road or enter a shop. The encounter with Yannis had totally unnerved him.

Stelios drove down to Piraeus and looked for a space near to his in-law's house where he could park. He left it to Daphne to explain to their children that Miriam had to wear a veil because she had suffered an accident that had left her face badly scarred. Elena was curious and continually asked for more details; how had it happened, when, why, what did her face look like, and Daphne hoped Miriam would be wearing her veil to hide her disfigurement. She had tried to impress upon her daughter that she was not to mention it to Miriam or ask her any personal questions, but she knew her daughter well enough to know that her instructions would be ignored.

'This is close enough,' said Stelios as he reversed their car into a space a short distance down the road. 'I hope Tomas and I will still get on. It will be like meeting a stranger after all this time.'

'Of course you will,' replied Daphne scornfully. 'Out you get, you two, and remember all I've said to you about manners.'

Nicolas nodded, but Elena tossed her head. She certainly wanted to know more about this mysterious lady who wore a veil.

Tomas clasped Stelios to him. 'It's so good to see you again, my friend. Daphne, you look well. I hope that's a sign that Stelios is looking after you properly. Let me meet your children. Goodness, Nicolas is so big I would never have recognised him and Elena is a little beauty. The photographs you sent us certainly don't do them justice.'

'How is Miriam?' Stelios managed to ask.

'She's fine, never been better. She and Abraham are waiting outside in the garden for you. I was left inside to make sure there was someone here to greet you when you arrived. Pappa and Mamma are out there with them.' Tomas winked at Stelios. 'It was quite a relief to have five minutes to myself. Mamma keeps touching me to make sure I'm real.'

They followed him through the house and out into the small walled garden at the back. A tall, thin young man rose with his hand extended. 'Hello, Aunt Daphne, Uncle Stelios, I'm Abraham.'

'Abraham!' Stelios looked at the boy in disbelief. He was already taller than his father. 'You were a baby when I last saw you.'

'I had a bit of a growth spurt last year. I just have to hope it doesn't happen every year or I'll end up with my head in the clouds. Hello, you must be Nicolas. I have to admit I don't really remember you. And you are Elena? I'm very envious that you have a sister, Nicolas.'

Elena was looking around the tall frame of her cousin. 'Where's your mother?' she asked.

'Sitting over there waiting to say hello to you.'

Daphne followed where Nicolas indicated and was surprised that Miriam had her back to them. Was she not prepared to be friendly? They had been close friends when they lived in Athens and visited Piraeus each weekend.

'Come on, Mamma, come and say hello.'

Slowly Miriam rose from the garden chair and turned to face them with a broad smile.

'Miriam,' gasped Daphne. 'Your face!'

Miriam smiled even more widely. 'Isn't it wonderful?'

'Where's the lady with the bad face who wears a veil?' asked Elena in a loud voice and Daphne tried to hush her daughter.

Miriam held out her hand to Elena. 'I'm the lady who used to wear a veil because I had an ugly scar on my face.'

Tomas thrust glasses of wine into their hands. 'It's a marvel, worth every penny. Sit down and Miriam will tell you how it happened.'

'Did it get better and go away?' asked Elena.

'Not quite like that. I had to take Abraham to the doctor, he had an ear infection. I was trying to explain the problem to the nurse and she said she couldn't understand me. I thought it was because she was Chinese and my veil was muffling my words so I lifted it up. She nearly passed out. She thought I'd come to see the doctor for myself. I assured her I was completely well and it was Abraham who needed the doctor.'

'I'd kept Mamma up all night as I was crying with the pain,' grinned Abraham, 'but I think she's forgiven me now.'

'What did the doctor do?'

'He couldn't do anything, but he talked to me and said great strides had been made with skin grafts and scar tissue removal since the war. So many men had returned badly burnt. He recommended that I consulted a plastic surgeon and wrote me a letter of introduction. Tomas and I went along to see him and I have to admit I didn't have any great hopes. He explained that I would need to have the old scar tissue cut away and then new skin grafted onto my cheeks. It was going to be a slow and expensive process.' Miriam smiled at Tomas.

'He couldn't guarantee that the procedure would be a hundred percent successful, but he did say Miriam wouldn't feel she needed a veil whenever she left the house.'

'And your eye – can you see again?'

Miriam shook her head. 'No, I'll never get the sight back. It was the last thing he did. He opened up my eye lids. Where they had been stitched together originally they had actually healed over. He had to open them and remove the surplus skin. When they had healed sufficiently I was fitted with a false eye.'

'It's amazing. No one would ever know now. I even have a job remembering how you used to look,' said Daphne.

'How long did it take?' asked Stelios.

'Three years from start to finish, but it was all worth it.'

Elena looked intently into Miriam's face. 'Did it hurt when the doctor cut you?'

Miriam shook her head. 'He put me to sleep so I wouldn't feel any pain. It was a little bit sore when I woke up.' Miriam was not going to tell the girl that it had been excruciatingly painful for the first week, particularly the surgery on her eyelids.

'Which is your false eye?' asked Elena.

'This one.' Miriam touched it gently with her fingertip.

'Does it hurt when you touch it? It hurts to touch my eye.'

'It's made of glass so it doesn't hurt me.'

'Can you take it out?' asked Elena and Daphne looked at her daughter in horror.

'I'm sorry, Miriam.'

'There's no need to be. Abraham was just as curious,' smiled Miriam. 'No, it's specially fixed so that it won't fall out. Imagine if it fell out whenever I looked down at my shoes!'

Elena giggled. 'What would people say if they saw you looking for your eye on the floor?'

'They probably wouldn't believe me.'

Stelios stirred uncomfortably. He was pleased Miriam had not gone into more detail about her operations and he certainly did not want her to take her eye out.

'If we hadn't gone to Australia Miriam would still be wearing her veil,' said Tomas. 'I don't know how advanced surgery is over here now, but when her accident first happened no one suggested that there could be some surgery in the future to help her.'

'We had to make a decision,' continued Miriam. 'We were planning on having another baby, hoping we would have a little girl, but the plastic surgery was going to be very expensive. We couldn't afford both. We thought we might try for another child when I had recovered from the operations, but they had to be spaced out and by the time they were finished Abraham was twelve. I was also advised to wait a further year to ensure no complications arose from the surgery before starting another baby. I could have rejected the skin grafts or my replacement eye due to pregnancy and that would have meant more surgery. It was then going to be rather a large age gap between Abraham and a sibling.'

'Would that matter?' asked Daphne.

Tomas shrugged, 'Probably not, but we had to think about Abraham's future. He wants to go to University.'

Stelios looked at the boy who was leaning laconically against the garden wall. 'What subject are you planning to take?'

'I want to specialise in Nuclear Science. I have to make sure my physics and maths are good enough, of course.'

Stelios swallowed. Nicolas was not unintelligent, but he doubted he had the ability to become a scientist.

'Isn't that making bombs and things?' asked Nicolas.

Abraham smiled and shook his head. 'That's Nuclear Physics. I'm interested in the science; there's so much being developed in the way of space exploration. A monkey has been sent up and there's talk of sending a man into space next year.'

'Is that what you want to do? Explore space?'

'No, I'm interested in how you manage to lift a rocket off the ground with a fuel that is so powerful it shoots up through the atmosphere. There are other uses for nuclear science, of course, new ideas are coming along all the time. I find it a fascinating subject. What about you, Nicolas? Have you decided on a career?'

Nicolas looked helplessly at his father. He had not given a thought to any occupation.

'He's not really mentioned anything yet. He's not as old as Abraham, remember,' answered Stelios.

'Abraham has always been interested in science and experiments. That's another reason why we wanted to make our visit now. His tutors say he should be able to take his physics and maths examinations next year,' said Tomas proudly. 'Provided he passes he will be eligible to attend seminars and expected to write a dissertation that he can submit to the University the following year when he applies for his place. He is going to have to work hard and won't be able to take time out for extended holidays.'

'What about your shops? Have you closed those whilst you're away?'

Tomas shook his head. 'I've left the managers in charge. They are quite capable of running them without me standing over them all the time. They are able to contact me if necessary, but I doubt they will have the need.'

'Why didn't you tell us about your face earlier?' asked Daphne.

'I didn't want to mention it until it was over. The surgeons warned me that it might not be a hundred percent successful. I could even have ended up looking worse. Tomas kept my spirits up by convincing me everything would be a fine. Once it had been completed we decided to save up for a visit and keep my face a secret until we arrived.'

'I am absolutely delighted for you. It can't have been easy living with a veil over your face for years.' Daphne smiled at her sister-in-law. 'I don't think I could have been as brave as you.'

'I had Tomas. Without him I would have been tempted to do something rather drastic. Looking after my mother helped in a perverse way. She became dependent upon me and by the time she died I no longer thought about my face and I also had Nicolas to care for.'

'Haven't you become a Brigadier yet?' asked Tomas of Stelios.

'You know I haven't. I'm content to be a Lieutenant Colonel and work in the finance department. If I had promotion to a higher rank it would mean moving and I might be expected to train the new recruits. I hated those weeks of training and as I can't shoot straight I'd probably be put in charge of drilling and marching.'

Olga and Nikos listened to the two men talking. The years they had been apart seemed to have dropped away and they sounded like two young men again. It was difficult to imagine that both men were in their forties. They were proud of the success their son had made of his new life in Australia, thrilled that Miriam no longer needed to wear a veil, and pleased Abraham was such an intelligent youngster. Their only regret was that they lived so far away and Abraham had decided to embrace the Jewish faith rather than become Greek Orthodox.

1961 – 1979

When Tomas, Miriam and Abraham left Piraeus and returned to Australia they had urged Olga and Nikos to visit them.

'You can come at any time. We'd love to show you our adopted country.'

Both Olga and Nikos looked at their son in trepidation. He would expect them to fly in an aeroplane – such a thing was against nature. If man had been meant to fly he would have been given wings. There was no guarantee that a heavy machine like an aeroplane would manage to stay up in the air and there was an ocean to cross. Neither of them could swim, so what would happen if the plane landed in the water?

Tomas tried to assure them that flying was perfectly safe, but they were adamant. They were too old to undertake such a venture.

Stelios also refused Tomas's invitation. 'I'd not be able to get more than two week's leave. By the time we had arrived and recovered from the flight we would be boarding the plane again to come back. Elena is far too young to think of making such an arduous journey. We have a problem keeping her quiet and sitting down in the car just to drive down to Piraeus.'

'Surely you could apply for an extension to your leave allocation?'

Stelios shook his head. 'I don't like to be out of the office for too long. Even when I've only been away for a few days there is such a back log of work to catch up on. Someone else would have to be drafted in to take over my responsibilities and I would have to spend time training them up. I really do not have the time to do that and then return to find the whole department is in disarray and have to spend weeks sorting out the confusion. I plan to retire when I'm sixty and then we could come over. Nicolas and Elena will probably be married by then and it would just be Daphne and myself. Far less trouble for you than having to think of ways to keep our children amused.'

Despite Tomas's assurances that the children would be no trouble, Stelios would not change his mind much to Daphne's annoyance. She would have liked to visit Australia and see where her brother lived.

'The flight alone would be extortionate,' Stelios explained. 'We'll keep saving and when I retire I promise we will make the journey. Just be patient. When I've retired we'll be able to stay for a number of weeks, hire a car and travel around to see something of the country.'

With that promise Daphne had to be content.

Tomas wrote to say that Abraham had passed his examinations in physics and maths easily; there was even talk that he might be able to attend University a year earlier. Stelios read the letter enviously. How he wished he could claim that his son was capable of achieving so much. Nicolas seemed no closer to choosing a career than he had two years earlier. The only thing he was definite about was that he had no intention of joining the army and rising through the ranks due to his father's influence.

There was still political unrest throughout Greece. The Prime Minister changed with regular monotony, few lasting more than a few weeks in the office before being replaced. When King Paul died in 1964 the country genuinely mourned him. At his funeral all the armed services marched through the streets of Athens and Stelios joined with the other officers in the parade, watched admiringly by Daphne, Nicolas and Elena. He hated having to parade. It meant training for two weeks before the event to ensure that there was synchronisation in the marching and he would have preferred to be sitting in his office.

King Paul was succeeded by his son, King Constantine, and the current government eyed him warily. The young man had not been trained in statesmanship and seemed to have some wild ideas. They would have to be curbed. Once again, Prime Ministers were elected one week only to be dismissed the next, and it was rumoured that the King was instrumental in the continual conflict between the parliamentary parties. Various political scandals were blamed as emanating from him and his actions.

Stelios waited apprehensively. He did not want to experience another civil war, nor did he want his children subjected to the horrors that would accompany it. Adding to his troubles was Nicolas. The boy had left school and still not mentioned any ambition regarding a future career. Finally he had persuaded his son to go to University and qualify to be a teacher.

'I'm not sure I want to be a teacher,' protested Nicolas.

'Well what do you want to do?' asked Stelios impatiently.

Nicolas shrugged. 'I don't know.'

'Then you go to University to become a teacher,' announced Stelios firmly. 'At least you will have an occupation until you do decide what you would prefer to do. You can always follow another career at a later date, but if you don't have the additional education now you could regret it.'

Tomas had written again, boasting that Abraham had gained honours in his University examinations and had applied to go to the Kennedy Space Centre. If he was accepted and after a year decided to stay there he and Miriam would consider selling the shops and their house and joining him in Florida. Stelios read the news with mixed feelings. He had promised Daphne he would take her to Australia when he retired. There would be no reason to go there if Tomas and Miriam were in America.

Daphne began to nag her husband to move to a larger apartment in a more fashionable area of the city.

'There's nothing wrong with this apartment,' declared Stelios.

'This area has become run down,' explained Daphne. 'I'd like to live in a better neighbourhood. We could move closer to Piraeus and I would be able to catch a bus to visit my parents during the week. They're not getting any younger. If I make the journey now it takes me two hours by the time I have travelled up to the centre to take the metro and then the bus at the other end. It's the whole day gone.'

Daphne continually remarked about the shabbiness of the easy chairs they had bought some years earlier and that the tables and chairs were scratched and showed signs of wear, however much she polished them.

'It's foolish to buy anything new now,' she said brightly. 'It will be more practical to wait until we have moved.'

Reluctantly Stelios agreed to his wife's request. He knew that a move would mean the additional expense of new curtains, larger carpet squares for use during the winter months along with the new furniture she wanted.

In 1967 the government consisted of military men. Conflict between King Constantine and the government increased, and in December of 1967 the King flew to Kavala with the idea of making Thessaloniki his base and with the help of the army generals forcing the current government ministers to stand down. The generals did not support him and the coup failed, leaving King Constantine and his family to flee to Italy.

Once again Stelios was grateful that he had not entered the government before the war and had also refused promotion above the rank of Lieutenant Colonel in the army. Greece was under a military dictatorship.

His money making ruse had finally come to an end. The cashier with whom he had dealt with for years retired and his replacement had far sharper eyes. He picked up the discrepancy between a three and an eight immediately when Stelios submitted his weekly calculation of the amount to be paid to him to settle the army's bills.

Stelios did not dispute the calculation. To do so would have drawn attention to himself and the way in which he wrote his numbers. That could mean that previous records were examined and his years of bad figures scrutinized. Although Stelios would insist he had always received only the correct amount from the bank and would accuse the cashier of falsifying the figures to his own advantage it could still leave suspicion hanging over him. He decided it was in his own interest to accept the easy way of increasing his salary was no longer an option open to him.

Following the failed coup by King Constantine the government voted to abolish the monarchy in 1973 and proclaimed that Greece was a republic. Stelios was reminded of Herman Steiner's words that a country did not need a monarch. He sincerely hoped they would not emulate Hitler. In 1974 a New Constitution was drawn up and the army was no longer in control of the country and Stelios breathed a sigh of relief.

Nicolas was working as a teacher in a local school, and although not happy, he could not envisage any other work that would be more interesting. Every job became mundane when you were familiar with the routine. Elena was completely content. She had decided that she wanted to take a secretarial course and had obtained a position in the Bank of Piraeus. Being accomplished and accurate in her work she had become the private secretary to the manager. This also gave her preferential interest rates for loans and she had promptly taken a course of driving lessons and bought a car.

Abraham had accepted a junior technician's appointment at the Kennedy Centre, but Tomas and Miriam had not joined him. Tomas explained that after discussing the move with both Miriam and his son he had decided to stay in Australia until he was of retirement age and could claim his Greek army pension. The salary that Abraham earned was more than sufficient for him to return to Australia each year and visit his parents, and on each occasion he had broken his journey in Athens and visited his elderly grandparents.

Stelios and Daphne dutifully visited Olga and Nikos, who were now in their seventies, each weekend. Most times Nicolas accompanied them and was happy to see the latest carpentry work his grandfather was employed on. People were gradually turning to the mass produced furniture that was available in the shops and Nikos found there was less and less demand for his craftsmanship. His fingers were not as nimble as they had been and the work took him considerably longer to complete. Elena accompanied them less often as she was expected to work most Saturdays and usually spent the evening with friends.

Daphne was not sure she approved of the life the girl was living. Although she had gone out to work and had met friends at the weekend during the morning or afternoon she would not have been allowed to go out unaccompanied at night. Elena laughed at her worries.

'Times have changed, Mamma, since you were a girl.'

Daphne shook her head. 'Times may have changed, but the way people think has not. You will end up with a bad name and be classed as a loose woman.'

'I will not,' replied Elena furiously. 'I behave myself. We meet in a group and spend the evening together. I do not make assignations with any of the men I know and I am not interested in any of them as prospective husbands. If one of them did ask me to go out with him I would insist he came and met you and Pappa and asked your permission.'

Daphne asked Stelios to speak to his daughter, but he had taken very little notice of her concerns. Just because the girl drove a car and went out with friends in the evening did not mean she was immoral. Times had changed and women had far more freedom since the war. Neither of their children showed any inclination to get married. At least he would not have that expense eating into his savings for the time being.

Stelios had something else worrying him and had not confided his fears to his wife. He no longer ran up the stairs to his office, finding that if he tried to do so he was gasping for breath by the time he was half way. At first he had decided it was his age catching up with him, after all he was nearly sixty now. He could not expect to run around as he had previously. He began to cough, particularly first thing in the morning, and blamed it on the pollution that was in Athens. The morning that he coughed and his chest was painful for some time afterwards did not alarm him unduly, but he decided he should consult a doctor. He probably had a chest infection.

The doctor sounded his chest and took note of the wheezing and rasping breath. 'How many cigarettes do you smoke each day?'

Stelios shrugged. 'About forty.'

The doctor nodded. 'How long have you been smoking?'

'Since I was about fifteen.'

'Well, I will send you to the hospital for an X-ray. It's a little late now to tell you to stop smoking, I imagine, but it could help if you cut down.'

The X-ray had come back showing a shadow on Stelios's lung and it worried him. The more he worried the more cigarettes he smoked and the more he coughed until Daphne became concerned that he appeared to have so little energy and his skin was sallow.

'I think you should go to the doctor, Stelios. You are obviously not well.'

'There's nothing wrong with me,' he replied irritably. 'I'm working hard at the moment to get the office in order and train up my successor. Once I've retired I will be able to relax.'

Daphne smiled. 'We'll be able to start making arrangements to go to Australia then. I'm looking forward to our visit so much.'

Stelios was called for a further X-ray and then a follow-up visit to his doctor. After the prognosis he received he knew he could no longer keep his illness from Daphne. Once over the first shock at hearing Stelios's news Daphne urged him to visit the priest and confess his sins.

Stelios refused. He was certainly not going to confess he had falsified the army accounts for years, but he did have nagging feelings of guilt about his family, particularly Yannis. He should have stopped and spoken to him when they met at the post office. If his brother was allowed to wander freely around the city he could no longer be contagious.

His cancer developed rapidly over the next two months and he was no longer able to go to the army office, forcing him to resign due to ill health. Most days he sat in a chair at the apartment, morosely staring into space, whilst Daphne hurriedly complied with his every request. When he had a bout of coughing he became totally exhausted and would sit with his eyes closed, then he would begin to mutter to himself. Daphne always listened carefully; was Stelios just talking to himself or was he asking her for some attention?

Names and events that meant nothing to her were mumbled by him and then he would often sleep for a while. Daphne hesitated to wake him, but knew this would mean he would be awake in the night, disorientated and rambling. At the weekends Nicolas or Daphne would sit with him to allow their mother to have some much needed rest, but each week nursing him became more difficult.

After a particularly tiring and stressful week Daphne called the doctor. 'Is it possible for a nurse to come in? I just cannot manage alone anymore to get him out of bed.'

The doctor called and examined Stelios, concerned at the

deterioration that had taken place. He sat with Daphne and explained that her husband needed professional medical care and the only place he should be now was in a hospital.

'He could linger for another month or even two. You cannot be expected to cope with him. Although he has lost weight he is still a heavy man for a woman alone to assist. I will make arrangements immediately for his transfer. Provided you are able to be there with him for most of the day he may not even realise he is no longer at the apartment.'

Reluctantly, but also with a feeling of relief, Daphne had agreed to Stelios being admitted to the local hospital. In the evenings when she finished work Elena would drive over and collect her mother, insisting that she rested after spending the day sitting beside Stelios's bed and tending to him. Nicolas would always have arrived home first and would be in bed catching up on some sleep until Elena had prepared a meal. Having eaten with them he would allow Elena to drive him to the hospital to be with their father over night.

Daphne protested that they should not be expected to nurse their father, but both of them insisted that she could not bear the burden alone and they must help her as much as possible.

'You cannot be with him all the time,' declared Nicolas. 'You'll be so exhausted that you will collapse. Whilst Pappa is asleep I can sleep in the chair. It won't hurt me and I can always telephone you if necessary.'

Daphne gave in. She realised that it was only sensible and practical that her children spent time with their father so she was able to return home and sleep, but she felt guilty that the burden had been placed on them.

She was disconcerted when Nicolas arrived home and said that throughout the night Stelios had been demanding to see Yannis, rambling on about a farm, Anna and the children.

'What is he talking about, Mamma? Was Pappa married before he met you?'

Daphne shook her head. 'No, he was probably remembering something from his childhood.' She recalled the letter she had read many years earlier where Yannis and Anna were mentioned.

'The doctor said he wanted to speak to you when you are there today. Would you like me to take the day off from school and be there with you?'

'Thank you, Nicolas, but I don't think the doctor will be telling me anything I don't already know.' Daphne smiled sadly at her son.

To her surprise the doctor did not tell her that Stelios's demise was imminent. 'He seems very distressed about members of his family and wants to see them. Is there any way you could contact them?'

Daphne raised her eyebrows. 'I don't know. I can try. I have an address for a cousin who lived in Heraklion, but he may not be there now.'

'I think you should try. He's very troubled at the moment. A visit from them could help him to be more peaceful.'

Daphne scrabbled through her underwear drawer until she found the notebook with the address she had copied from the letter Stelios had received years ago from Andreas. She was not sure what she should say. She could not admit that she had read the original letter; but how would she know of him if Stelios had denied the existence of any relatives? She spent most of the day turning the problem over in her mind and when Elena arrived to take her home she thought she had the solution.

Immediately upon arriving back at the apartment she drew out a sheet of paper and wrote the address and telephone number of the hospital on it.

Dear Sir,

Forgive me for writing to you if this matter is not your concern. I believe you to be the cousin of my husband, Stelios Christoforakis, who is gravely ill and not expected to live very much longer. He is very troubled in his mind and keeps asking for Yannis, Anna and Yiorgo. If you know the whereabouts of these people please would you contact them on my behalf and ask if it is possible for one or all of them to visit him as quickly as possible.

Daphne sealed the letter and asked Nicolas to be certain to post it when he departed for the hospital that evening.

When Stelios began to ask for Yannis and Anna again Daphne assured him they were coming and the news seemed to console him. She had no idea if the letter would be received and her request acted upon. For all she knew the people Stelios was asking for could be dead.

Daphne turned as the door to Stelios's private room opened and an unknown man and woman walked in. Nicolas and Elena looked at them in surprise and Daphne drew in her breath.

'You must be his relatives from Crete.'

Yannis nodded, whilst Anna stepped forward and took Stelios's frail hand. 'He's conscious,' she said quietly to Yannis. 'Do you want to speak to him?'

Yannis stepped forward, taking in the shrunken body that was his younger brother. Who would have believed that the healthy boy he had searched for pottery with would succumb to death before him; a man who had been declared an incurable and spent most of his life on Spinalonga.

'Can you hear me, Stelios? Thank you for making Mamma and Pappa proud of you when I failed.'

Stelios's eyes opened and a look of shocked recognition was evident. 'Yannis!' he managed to utter and his eyes closed again.

'I think we should leave him to sleep again now. The doctor said we should only stay a short while.' Daphne bent and kissed her husband. 'We'll come again tomorrow.'

Once outside Daphne turned to Anna. 'You will come back to

our apartment, won't you? We should talk and get to know each other now we have finally met. Stelios never mentioned you. In fact,' Daphne blushed 'he told me he had no family. I did read a letter his cousin had sent to him after the war and he mentioned your names and some others that I don't remember.'

Anna left Daphne's apartment feeling utterly exhausted. Listening to Yannis recounting their early life as a family and his time on Spinalonga, with her adding details about the war and the children she had brought up as her own had taken its toll. Daphne, Elena and Nicolas had been fascinated by every detail.

Yannis was shocked and hurt. He could understand that Stelios had not wished to acknowledge him, but to have disowned the rest of the family and said they were dead was wicked of him. He was unable to sleep until nearly dawn when he fell into a deep slumber and was awakened by his wife shaking him.

'Daphne is on the telephone.'

Still half asleep he walked into their living room. 'Hello? Daphne?'

'Yannis, I'm at the hospital. Stelios is asking for you.'

'For me? You must be mistaken.'

'He's quite coherent and most insistent that he wants to speak to you.'

'Give me half an hour. I'll bring Anna with me.'

On reaching the hospital Yannis was still unconvinced that Stelios wished to see him again. He sent Anna into the room and waited outside until Elena appeared.

'Pappa wants to see you.'

Silently Yannis followed Elena into the room and stood where Stelios could see him.

'Not – too – bad,' gasped Stelios eventually, having looked his brother up and down through half closed eyes.

'I'm burnt out. I'm not infectious,' Yannis assured him as he moved closer.

'Doesn't – matter – now.'

'Why did you say everyone was dead, Stelios? I can understand that you didn't want to admit you had a brother suffering from leprosy, but why disown everyone else?'

'Education – career – Daphne. Might – have – found – out. Better – all — dead.' Making an effort Stelios raised his hand and touched Yannis's.

'Forgive – me – Yannis.'

Yannis closed his misshapen fingers around Stelios's thin hand. 'I understand. There's nothing to forgive.'

Stelios let out a sigh and closed his eyes. Daphne stepped forward and kissed him gently. 'You always made me very happy, Stelios.'

Stelios opened his eyes and smiled at her before his head fell back limply on the pillow.

If you have enjoyed reading Stelios, you will be pleased to know that the next book – Kyriakos –is planned for publication in December 2016.

Read on for a 'taster' of what is to come......

KYRIAKOS

September 2012

Kyriakos looked at Ronnie and took her hand. 'In that case Miss Ronnie will you marry me?'

Ronnie drew in her breath. She had realised how deeply she cared for Kyriakos when he had been injured. 'I'll have to think, Kyriakos.'

'What is there to think about? Either you love me or you do not. If you refuse me I'll not embarrass you by asking you again.'

'Oh, Kyriakos, it is not a question of loving you. I tried to show you my feelings at Owen and Laura's wedding, but you never made another approach to me. I thought it was drinking too much champagne that had made you kiss me.'

'So what is your problem?'

'I am an American and you are a Cretan. Will your mother accept you marrying a foreigner?'

Kyriakos shrugged. 'You are partly Cretan.'

'Only a very small part of me and remember my ancestry.'

'My mother does not have to know your family history.'

Ronnie shook her head. 'I'm not ashamed to admitting that my great grandparents had leprosy. There should be no stigma attached to the illness today. I would rather your mother knew now than heard it at a later date.'

'I will tell her. She will understand,' Kyriakos said confidently.

'There are other problems to consider.'

'You think your mother would not approve?'

Ronnie shrugged. 'My mother would say it was up to me who I live with or marry. There is the house and.....'

Kyriakos held up his hand. 'The house is no problem. You say it can be put right. I can help you if you need some extra money.'

'Forget the money. I am more worried about being sent to prison.'

'I would still want to marry you even if you had been imprisoned.'

Ronnie sighed in exasperation. 'Kyriakos, be serious. I could be deported back to America. I have not said that I will not marry you, but I just feel we should give it some very serious thought.'

'I have given the matter thought for over a year. Please, Miss Ronnie, will you marry me?'

Ronnie placed her hands over her face. 'I cannot give you an answer now. I have to get my life back in order first. It would not be fair to say yes and then find I was going to be imprisoned and deported back to America at the end of my sentence. Even without that threat hanging over me there are so many problems that we would need to discuss and agree over.'

Kyriakos raised his eyebrows and pulled Ronnie's hands gently away from her face. 'So what are these other problems?'

'First of all I have to get permission from the Greek government to live here permanently. At the moment I am here on a visitors' work permit.'

Kyriakos shrugged. 'That is no problem. It would be changed to a permanent visa once we were married.'

Ronnie shook her head. 'I understand they look into your background quite carefully. I would probably have to declare that my father is serving a gaol sentence.'

'Your father? He is in prison? You told me he was dead.'

'My step-father is dead. I always think of him as my father. My natural father was sent to prison when I was a small child.'

'What did he do?' Kyriakos was feeling concerned now. Had Ronnie's father committed murder?

'He was a very talented artist. Far cleverer than me. So clever in fact that he was able to forge paintings done by some of the old masters and claim they were originals. For a long time no one questioned their authenticity, then he made a mistake. He sold a copy to a man whose friend had the original. They had both paintings examined and tested by experts and, of course, the one my father had sold was proved to be the forgery. I'm not sure how much longer he has to serve, but you realise that if I have to declare that on an application form the Greek authorities would have every right to refuse me a permanent visa.'

'That is not right,' Kyriakos spoke vehemently. 'Your father's crime is not your fault.'

'I know, but try telling that to immigration authorities. If Babbis does press charges against me for blackmail it could give them an added reason to deport me.'

'But you are going to charge Babbis with arson. He set fire to your house.'

Ronnie shook her head. 'I can't prove that. Old Kassie told Giovanni that she saw the man who lit the fire, but when Giovanni mentioned being interviewed by the fire service and the police for a statement she said she didn't want to be involved with the law. She was obviously hoping to be paid for her information, but Giovanni refused to give her anything. He said there could be a reward after an arrest had been made. Even if she does tell the authorities will they take any notice of her? They'll probably say she couldn't see clearly as it was at night or that she is too old to be a reliable witness.'

'You believe she is telling the truth?'

'Yes, I do. I think Babbis did it because I humiliated him before his colleagues.' Ronnie shrugged. 'It was probably foolish of me. I should have gone to the police and lodged a complaint against him, but I was so convinced they would say I was a stupid woman who had misinterpreted his actions.'

Kyriakos placed his hand on Ronnie's. 'I believe you. Giovanni believes you. That is important. He will confirm that you were very distressed and spent the night at their house as you were frightened Babbis would go to your apartment. These problems can be sorted out. The Pirenzi family has far more influence in this area than Babbis Skourlatakis.'

'More influence or more money?'

Kyriakos shrugged. 'Both; now what are these other problems that are worrying you?'

'Where would we live?'

'Here, in Elounda, of course.'

'You have no accommodation at the taverna and you live with your mother.'

'You can live there also. That will be no problem.'

Ronnie shook her head. 'That will become a big problem, no, listen Kyriakos.' Ronnie held up her hand as he was about to interrupt her. 'I do not speak Greek and your mother does not speak English. We will not be able to communicate with each other. Two women in one kitchen doesn't work at the best of times. Your mother would complain about me and I would complain about her. You would be trying to keep the peace between us.'

'So we find somewhere to live on our own. Maybe Giovanni would let us live in one of the self catering units or Vasi allow us to have a room in his hotel.'

'Neither of those ideas are practical, Kyriakos. Giovanni closes the apartments down in the winter as they have no heating and Vasi closes his hotel for maintenance and decoration at the end of the season. I wouldn't want to live in a hotel all the time anyway.'

'So, we arrange for your house to be repaired and then we live there.'

'That is not convenient for either of us. You do not close the taverna until midnight, sometimes later. I like to be up and painting early as the sun rises. If we lived in Kastelli you would not be home until at least one in the morning and I would be leaving the house at about three. We would never see each other. You would be leaving the house to come here as I returned for a siesta. That is not having a married life.'

'You come up to my taverna most days,' replied Kyriakos truculently.

'Of course. I like to come to see you and it is easy. A short walk up the road, but if we lived in Kastelli and it meant I had to drive to Elounda to see you it would not be so easy. I might want to stay at home and finish some painting.'

Kyriakos shook his head sadly. 'You are making excuses. You do not want to marry me.'

'No, I'm not making excuses, but I am trying to explain to you the problems. We need to have them settled before we make any decisions. I do not want to move in with your mother and a month later tell you I am leaving because I cannot live in the same house with her. I do not want us to live in Kastelli. You would start to complain about driving home at night when you are tired and that when I left in the early hours of the morning I was disturbing you. We would soon start to argue. I would say you should close the taverna earlier and you would say I should go to paint later.'

'I could not close the taverna earlier. I cannot ask customers to leave.'

Ronnie sighed. 'I understand that. I cannot ask the sun to rise later in the morning. I am just using these as an example of how difficult it would be to actually spend any time together if we lived in Kastelli.'

'So what do you want?'

'First I have to get the problem with the house sorted out. Then I can find out about the paperwork I need that would allow me to marry you. There is no point in us trying to make plans further ahead until we know the answer to those two questions.'

'You can ask Nicola and John.'

'What do you mean?'

'Nicola had to apply to the Greek Embassy before she was given permission to marry John. She could tell you what was needed.'

Ronnie smiled. 'That's a good idea. If I asked Nicola before my mother arrives I would know if there was anything I needed to ask her to bring out for me. It could still depend upon the outcome of the enquiry into the arson at my house.'

Will Ronnie be able to marry Kyriakos?

Will the police be able to prove that Babbis started the fire in Kastelli?

What will happen when Ourania's senility increases?

What will Yannis do with his shop in Plaka?

How will John react when he learns that the decomposed bodies in the tower on Spinalonga are to be moved and given a Greek Orthodox burial?

So many questions to be answered in Kyriakos.

Beryl Darby
ANNA
The second book in a continuing saga

For up-to-date information about the titles in this continuing saga of a Cretan family, see the website:

www. beryldarbybooks. com

Beryl Darby
GIOVANNI
The third book in a continuing saga of a Cretan family

Beryl Darby
JOSEPH
The fourth book in a continuing saga of a Cretan family

Beryl Darby
CHRISTABELLE
The fifth book in a continuing saga of a Cretan family

For up-to-date information about the titles in this continuing saga of a Cretan family, see the website:

www.beryldarbybooks.com

For up-to-date information about the titles in this continuing saga of a Cretan family, see the website:

www.beryldarbybooks.com

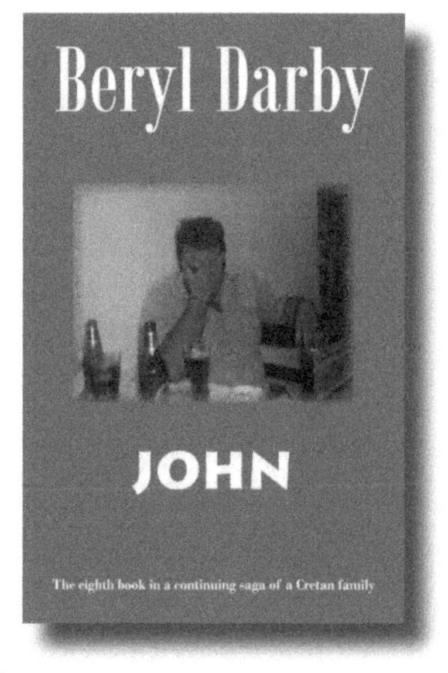

For up-to-date information about the titles in this continuing saga of a Cretan family, see the website:

www. beryldarbybooks. com

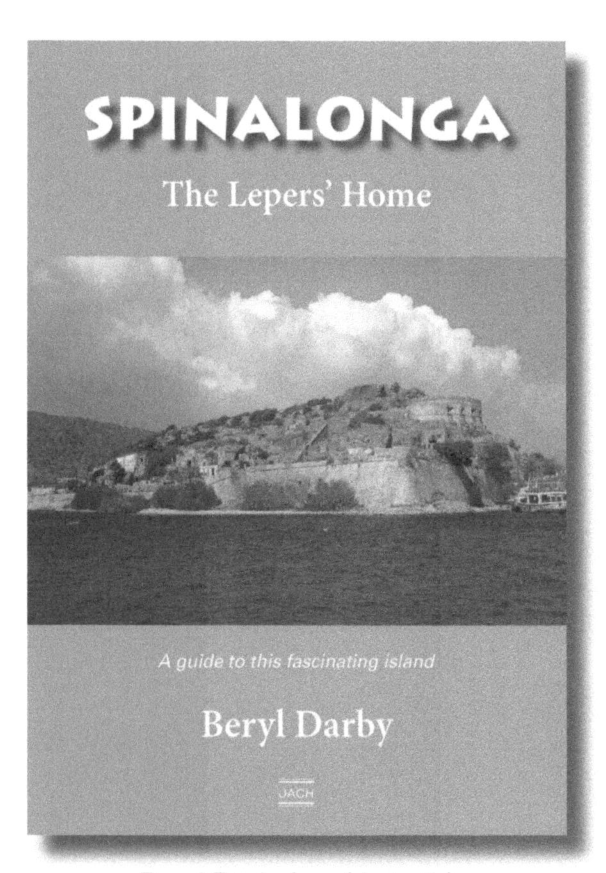

Beryl Darby's guide to this fascinating island

www.beryldarbybooks.com